Praise for the Joe Pickett Series

"Joe Pickett, the conscientious game warden in these rugged novels . . . shows the tough-and-tender qualities that make him such a great guy to have on your side."

—*The New York Times*

"Picking up a new C. J. Box thriller is like spending quality time with family you love and have missed. . . . It's a rare thriller series that has characters grow and change. An exciting reading experience for both loyal fans as well as newcomers."

—Associated Press

"Box is a master."

—*The Denver Post*

"Wyoming game warden Joe Pickett strides in big boots over the ruggedly gorgeous landscape of C. J. Box's outdoor mysteries."

—*The New York Times Book Review*

"Look up tried and true in the literary dictionary and you'll find a picture of C. J. Box, thanks to his superb Joe Pickett series. . . . A thriller of rare depth and emotion, featuring pitch perfect plotting and characterizations every bit the equal of Cormac McCarthy and Larry McMurtry."

—*The Providence Journal*

"Box gets everything right: believably real characters, a vivid setting, clear prose, and ratcheting tension."

—*The Plain Dealer*

"Pickett is one of the most appealing men in popular fiction."

—*Chicago Tribune*

Titles by C. J. Box

The Joe Pickett Novels

Three-Inch Teeth
Storm Watch
Shadows Reel
Dark Sky
Long Range
Wolf Pack
The Disappeared
Vicious Circle
Off the Grid
Endangered
Stone Cold
Breaking Point

Force of Nature
Cold Wind
Nowhere to Run
Below Zero
Blood Trail
Free Fire
In Plain Sight
Out of Range
Trophy Hunt
Winterkill
Savage Run
Open Season

The Hoyt/Dewell Novels

Treasure State
The Bitterroots
Paradise Valley
Badlands
The Highway
Back of Beyond

The Stand-Alone Novels and Other Works

Shots Fired: Stories from Joe Pickett Country
Three Weeks to Say Goodbye
Blue Heaven

Out
of
Range

C. J. BOX

G. P. PUTNAM'S SONS
NEW YORK

PUTNAM
— EST. 1838 —
G. P. PUTNAM'S SONS
Publishers Since 1838
An imprint of Penguin Random House LLC
penguinrandomhouse.com

First G. P. Putnam's Sons hardcover edition / May 2005
First Berkley Prime Crime mass-market edition / May 2006
First G. P. Putnam's Sons premium edition / July 2016
First G. P. Putnam's Sons special value edition / May 2024
G. P. Putnam's Sons special value edition ISBN: 9780593716427

Printed in the United States of America
1st Printing

To the game wardens of Wyoming . . .
and Laurie, always.

PART ONE

Our distance from the source of our food enables us to be superficially more comfortable, and distinctly more ignorant.

GARY SNYDER,
THE PRACTICE OF THE WILD: ESSAYS

Moving the keelboat and pirogues upriver required a tremendous effort from each man; consequently they ate prodigiously. In comparison with beef, the venison and elk were lean, even at this season. Each soldier consumed up to nine pounds of meat per day, along with whatever fruit the area afforded and some cornmeal, and still felt hungry.

STEPHEN E. AMBROSE,
UNDAUNTED COURAGE: MERIWETHER LEWIS,
THOMAS JEFFERSON, AND THE OPENING
OF THE AMERICAN WEST

BEFORE GOING OUTSIDE TO HIS PICKUP FOR HIS GUN, the Wyoming game warden cooked and ate four and a half pounds of meat.

He'd begun his meal with pronghorn antelope steaks, butterflied, floured, and browned in olive oil. Then an elk chop, pan-fried with salt and pepper, adding minced garlic to the cast-iron skillet. His first drink, sipped while he was cooking the antelope, was a glass of Yukon Jack and water on the rocks. By the time he broiled a half dozen mourning dove breasts, he no longer bothered with the ice or the water. As he sat down late in the evening with an elk tenderloin so rare that blood pooled around it on his plate, he no longer used the glass, but drank straight from the bottle.

He ate no vegetables; unless one counted the sautéed onions he had slathered on a grass-fed Hereford beef T-bone, or the minced garlic. Just meat.

He needed air, and stood up.

His mind swam, the room rotated, his heavy boots clunked across the floor. He paused at the jamb, using it to brace himself upright. He stared at a flyspeck on the wall, tried to will the quadruple images he was seeing down to a more manageable two.

Finally, he opened the door. It was dark except for a blue streetlight on the northern corner of the block. A full moon lit up the crags of the mountains, casting them in dim blue-gray. The chill of the fall was already a guest. He stumbled down the broken sidewalk toward his truck. As he approached, his pickup seemed to swell and deflate, as if it were breathing.

"Something smells good inside," a voice said. It startled the game warden, and he squinted toward it, trying to concentrate, to hear it over the mild roar in his ears. A neighbor wearing a tam on his head was walking a poodle down the middle of the street.

"Meat," Will Jensen said abruptly, almost shouting. It was sometimes hard these days to hear his own voice above the roar.

"See you," the neighbor called as he walked down the street. "*Bon appétit!*"

These people here, Will thought. *A goddamned poodle and a tam.*

HIS .44 MAGNUM, HIS BEAR GUN, was on the truck's bench seat where he had left it. Will drew it out of the holster. Holding it loosely in his right hand, he turned back for the house, tripped over his own boots, and fell in the gravel. A red finger of alarm probed into his brain, concern about accidentally discharging the weapon in his fall. Then he snorted a laugh, thinking, *Who cares?*

HE DIDN'T KNOW HOW MUCH LATER it was when he stirred awake. He was still sitting at the table, but had passed out face forward into his plate. Crisp grouse skin stuck to his cheek, and he pawed at it clumsily until it fluttered to the floor.

Angry, he swept the table clear with his arm. Grease smeared across the Formica. The dirty plate cracked in half when it hit the wall.

Where was his .44?

He found it on his bed, where he had tossed it earlier. Along with the weapon, he grabbed a framed photo of his family from the bedside table. He took them both back into the kitchen.

Forlorn was a word he had come to like in recent months. It was a word that sounded like what it described. "*Forlorn,*" he said aloud to himself, "*I feel forlorn. I am a forlorn man.*" Something about the word soothed him, because it defined him, made him admit what he was.

What in the hell was wrong with him? Why did he feel this way, after so many years of balancing on the beam?

The roar in his ears was now so faint that it reminded him of a soft breeze in the treetops. His eyes filled with unexpected, stinging tears, and he drank a long pull from the bottle. He cocked the .44, watched the cylinder rotate. He opened his mouth and pressed the muzzle against the top of his palate. There was a burning, acrid taste. When was the last time he cleaned it?

Why did that matter now?

He stared at the photo he'd propped up on the table. It swam. He closed his eyes so tightly that he saw orange fireworks on the inside of his eyelids. He tried to concentrate on the .44 in his fist and the muzzle in his mouth. His stomach was on fire; he tried to fight the urge to get violently sick. He tasted the bitter whiskey a second time.

Concentrate . . .

2

THE WEDDING OF BUD LONGBRAKE AND MISSY
Vankueren took place at noon, on a sun-filled Saturday
in September, on the front lawn of the Longbrake Ranch,
twenty miles from town. Everyone was there.

The governor and his wife, most of the state senate,
where Bud served as majority leader, the state's lone con-
gressman, and what seemed like half of Saddlestring
filled 250 metal folding chairs and spilled over into the
lawn. Both U.S. senators had sent their regrets. The crisp
blue shoulders of the Bighorn Mountains framed the
wedding party. The day smelled of just-cut grass and
wood smoke from the barbecue pit behind the house,
where a prime Longbrake steer and a 4-H pig were roast-
ing. It was a still, windless morning. A single cloud
grazed lazily along the peaks. The only sounds were from
car doors slamming as more guests arrived, pulling into
the shorn hay meadow that served as a parking lot in the
back, and occasional mewls from cattle in a distant holding corral.

Joe Pickett sat in the second row. He wore a jacket

and tie, dark slacks, and polished black cowboy boots. He was in his mid-thirties, lean, medium height. His thirteen-year-old daughter, Sheridan, sat next to him in a new blue dress. She shone brightly, he thought; long blond hair still streaked with summer highlights, a touch of pink lipstick, open, attractive face, eyes that took in everything. She watched intently as her mother, Marybeth, and eight-year-old sister, Lucy, took part in the ceremony. Lucy was the flower girl, wearing white taffeta. Marybeth, the matron of honor, stood on a riser next to Dale Longbrake and the rest of the wedding party. The men wore black western-cut tuxedos and black Stetsons.

Joe and his wife exchanged glances, and he could tell from her eyes that she was exasperated. Her mother, Missy Vankueren, was an experienced wedding planner, having been the featured bride in three previous ceremonies. Missy had been designing the event for over a year with the intensity and precision of a general implementing a major ground offensive, Joe thought, and she had enlisted a reluctant Marybeth as her second lieutenant. Endless discussions and phone calls had finally resulted in this day, which Marybeth had come to refer to as "Operation Massive Ranch Wedding."

Joe nodded toward the mountains and whispered to Sheridan, "See that cloud?"

Sheridan looked. "Yes."

"I would wager that by Wedding Five, Missy will have figured out how to get rid of it."

"*Dad!*" she whispered fiercely. But the corners of her mouth tugged with a conspiratorial grin. He winked at her, and she rolled her eyes, turning back to the wedding that was about to begin.

There was a growing murmur as the bride appeared, on cue, beneath an arch of pink and white flowers. Joe and Sheridan rose to their feet with the rest of the crowd.

Applause rippled from the front to the back as Missy appeared, glowing, wide-eyed, looking demurely at the throng she had turned out.

"I can't believe that's my grandmother," Sheridan said to Joe. "She looks . . ."

"Stunning," Joe said, finishing the sentence for her. Missy looked thirty, not sixty, he thought. She was a slim brunette, her face and hair perfect, her eyes glistening in a too-large head that always looked great in photos. She held a bouquet of pink and white flowers against her shimmering plum dress.

Joe heard Bud Longbrake say, in a reverent tone of appreciation he usually reserved for great cutting horses or seed bulls: "*There's* my girl."

THE RECEPTION WAS HELD BEHIND the huge log home, under hundred-year-old cottonwoods. A swing band from Billings played on a stage, and couples spun on a hardwood floor that had been moved to the ranch just for the occasion from a vacated mid-forties dance hall in Winchester. The floor was unique in that it was mounted on carriage springs and had been used for Saturday night dances when big bands used to stop over in Wyoming en route to real paying gigs on the east or west coasts.

Joe ushered Sheridan through the reception line, shaking hands. Bud Longbrake slapped him on the shoulder and said, "Welcome to the family."

I've got a family, Joe thought.

Missy reached for Joe, and pulled his head down next to hers. He felt the bouquet she still clutched crush into his hair. "Never thought I'd pull this one off, did you?" she whispered.

Surprised, he pulled away. She grinned slyly at him, and despite himself, he grinned back. She was a substantial adversary, he thought. He'd hate to meet her in a dark alley.

"Congratulations," he said. "Bud is a fine man."

"Oh, I think I got the best of the deal," Bud said, wrapping his arm around Missy's slim waist.

"You did," she said, flashing her wide smile.

And her name is already on the ranch deed, Joe thought. *She owns half of everything we see as far as we can see it. She pulled it off, all right.*

Marybeth was next, and had been carefully watching the exchange that took place a moment before.

"You look wonderful," he said.

Thank God it's over, she mouthed. He nodded back, agreeing with her.

"Welcome to the family," Bud was telling Sheridan.

Joe shot him a look.

"JOE, ARE YOU SURE SHE said *that?*" Marybeth asked later, as they sat at a table under the trees with their plates of appetizers. Joe had waited for Sheridan and Lucy to find their friends before he told Marybeth about her mother.

"I'm quoting."

Marybeth shook her head, looking hard at Joe to see if he was joking. She obviously determined he wasn't. "She's something else, isn't she?"

"Always has been," Joe said. "What I can't figure out is how you survived."

Marybeth smiled and patted his hand. "Neither can I, at times."

Joe sipped from a bottle of beer that had been offered to him from a stock tank full of ice.

"You two have a very strange relationship," Marybeth said, looking across the lawn at her mother.

"I didn't think we had one at all."

Missy had never made a secret of the fact that she felt Marybeth had married beneath herself. Instead of the doctor, real estate magnate, or U.S. senator Marybeth should have chosen, Missy thought, her most promising daughter wound up with Joe Pickett, a Wyoming game warden with a salary that capped out at $36,000 a year. Marybeth's career as a corporate lawyer or a politician's wife, in Missy's view, had been unfulfilled. Rather, Marybeth stayed with Joe as he moved from place to place in their early years together, before Joe was named game warden to the Saddlestring District. Then Sheridan came along, followed by Lucy, and in Missy's eyes it was all but over for her daughter. Because of incidents relating to Joe Pickett and his job, Marybeth had been injured and could have no more children. Then a foster daughter had been lost. It was frustrating for Missy, Joe thought. There she was, providing a living example of how to keep trading up—casting off husbands in exchange for newer, wealthier, and shinier models—and her daughter just didn't get it. Missy literally tried to show Marybeth how it could be done by marrying Bud Longbrake right in front of her, Joe thought.

Marybeth still had fire, intelligence, beauty, and ambition, Joe and Missy both knew. She also had a growing melancholy, which she tried hard to overcome.

"Look at Bud's kids," Marybeth said, nodding toward a table set as far away from the others as possible while still being in the shade. "They just don't look happy. Don't stare at them, though."

Joe shifted in his chair. Bud had a son and a daughter from his previous marriage. The son, Bud Jr., had flown in for the wedding from Missoula, where he was a street musician and a professional student at UM. Bud Jr. wore billowy cargo shorts, leather sandals, a T-shirt, and a sour expression. Missy had told Joe and Marybeth that although Bud Jr. had never wanted anything to do with the ranch while growing up, he was content to wait things out, wait for Bud to pass along or sell the ranch. Even after taxes, Bud Jr. stood to gain a huge inheritance. It was the same with Sally, Bud's daughter. Thrice married (like her new stepmother, who had just surpassed her in the race), Sally lived in Portland, Oregon, and was currently between husbands. Sally was attractive in a wounded, Bohemian way, Joe thought. He had heard she was an artist, specializing in wrought iron.

Joe turned back. "No, they don't look happy."

"They don't like it that Bud made Missy cosignatory on all of this," Marybeth said, waving her hand to indicate literally all they could see. "Bud Jr. got hammered at the dress rehearsal last night and shouted some things at his father before he passed out in the bushes. Sally was there last night for about a half an hour, before she disappeared with one of Bud's ranch hands."

"Welcome to the family," Joe said to his wife.

THE NEW TWELVE SLEEP COUNTY sheriff, Kyle McLanahan, stood in front of Joe and Marybeth in the food line. The piquant smell of barbecued pork and beef hung heavy in the light mountain air.

"Kyle," Joe said, nodding.

"Joe. Marybeth. Congratulations are in order, I guess."

"I guess," Joe said.

"Same to you," Marybeth said coolly. "I haven't seen you since the election."

McLanahan nodded, hitched up his pants. Looked toward the mountains. Squinted. "We've got a lot of work to do."

"Yup," Joe said.

Kyle McLanahan had been the longtime chief deputy for local legend O. R. "Bud" Barnum, who had been sheriff for twenty-eight years. Barnum had owned the county in a sense, having a hand in just about every aspect of it. His downfall came over the past five years, as his reputation eroded, then rotted and tumbled in on itself. That Barnum's decline coincided with Joe's arrival in Saddlestring was no coincidence. The Outfitter Murders, mishandled by Barnum, had begun the slide. Barnum's shadowy involvement with the Stockman's Trust continued it. The ex-sheriff's complicity with Melinda Strickland in her raid on the Sovereign compound started the local gossip that Barnum had lost his commitment to the community and was looking out only for himself. The sheriff's deception during the cattle mutilations had turned the weekly Saddlestring *Roundup* against him. Joe had been in the middle of everything, one way or another. Seeing the writing on the wall (and in the newspaper), Barnum withdrew from the running two weeks before the election. Instead, McLanahan had stepped into the race, as had Deputy Mike Reed. In Joe's opinion, Reed was an honest cop and McLanahan was McLanahan—volatile, thickheaded, a throwback to the Barnum style of politics and corruption. McLanahan won 80 percent of the vote.

"Have you been listening to your radio this morning?" Sheriff McLanahan asked Joe. "I saw your truck in the parking lot."

Joe shook his head. "I'm off duty."

Because Marybeth and Lucy were in the wedding, they had left the Picketts' small state-owned home early that morning in Marybeth's van. Joe had brought Sheridan in his green Ford Game and Fish pickup after breakfast, but he hadn't turned on his radio during the drive.

"Then you haven't heard that they found a game warden dead over in Jackson," McLanahan said.

Joe felt a shiver run through him. "*What?*"

SHERIDAN HAD QUICKLY BECOME BORED with Lucy and her friends in the play area that had been put up far enough away from the reception that the children wouldn't bother the adults. The placement had Missy's stamp all over it, Sheridan thought. A swing set had been erected, as well as smaller-sized tables and chairs complete with plastic tea sets.

She wandered away from the play area and the reception into the makeshift parking lot. It was tough being thirteen. Too old to play, too young to be considered one of the adults. Her parents were fine, she thought, they never treated her with disrespect, although her mother was starting to bug her in ways she couldn't yet say. In a situation like this, with adults all around, she was patronized. She climbed into her dad's pickup truck and looked at herself in the rearview mirror. At least she finally had contact lenses and didn't look so much like a geek, she thought.

Absently, she clicked on the radio. It was set to the channel reserved for game wardens and brand inspectors. She sometimes liked to listen to the interplay between the men and the dispatchers, usually women, at the headquarters in Cheyenne. There was a surprising amount of activity on the radio for a Saturday morning in early September.

"THE JACKSON GAME WARDEN," McLanahan said, following Joe and Marybeth to their table. "Found him dead this morning in his house."

"Murdered?" Joe asked. He felt Marybeth tense up.

"Naw. Ate his own gun."

Marybeth gasped.

"Forty-four Magnum," McLanahan said. "Not much left of his head, is what I hear."

Joe was out of his chair and three inches from McLanahan's face. He hissed, "That'll be enough with the details right now in front of my wife."

McLanahan feigned hurt and surprise. "Sorry, Joe. I thought you'd want to know."

The new sheriff turned and left, heading for his table on the other side of the yard.

"Joe, was he talking about Will Jensen?" Marybeth asked.

"No," Joe said, confused. "It couldn't have been. He must have his information about half-right, as usual."

Marybeth shook her head. "I remember when we met Will and Susan. Remember their kids? Sheridan and their son tore around their house while you and Will talked at their kitchen table."

It made no sense to Joe. Jensen was a rock, a larger-than-life man who was considered one of the best there ever was within the department. Will Jensen was what game wardens wanted to be, the kind of man Joe aspired to be.

"I remember thinking," Marybeth continued, looking up at Joe, "I remember thinking how much they were like *us*."

Joe sat back down, shaken. "Let's hold off on this until we find out what the situation really is. Remember, all the information we've got at this point is from Deputy McLanahan."

"*Sheriff* McLanahan," Marybeth corrected gently.

Joe looked up, saw Sheridan running toward them from the cars, her blue dress flapping.

"All I know is that Will Jensen did not commit suicide," Joe said bluntly. "That's not possible."

"Joe . . ."

"Dad!" Sheridan gushed, stopping in front of them, breathing hard from her run. "Guess what I just heard on the radio?"

3

THE DRIVE BACK TO THEIR HOME FROM THE WEDDING took place in the soft light of pre-dusk that deepened the greens of the meadows and blazed the muffin-shaped haystacks with bronze, as if they were lit from within. The ranch country rolled toward the mountains like swells in the ocean, shadows darkening in the folds of the terrain. Joe had noticed the soft bite of approaching fall, and now he could see that a few cottonwoods in the river valley were beginning to turn.

Sheridan was silent and sleepy in the passenger seat. Marybeth followed Joe in her van, giving him plenty of distance on the dirt road so that the dust his pickup kicked up would settle back down.

"It's pretty," Sheridan said. "This *should* be my favorite time of year."

"It's the best time, I think."

"Maybe someday I'll agree with you," she said. "But I've got the blues."

Joe knew what Sheridan meant. His daughter had begun junior high the week before, which meant a new school, a new schedule, and many more students. Her load of homework had tripled from the year before. And she was trying out for the volleyball team. Because Lucy and Sheridan now had different school schedules, Marybeth spent much more time driving them from place to place, delivering them or picking them up after school or activities. Joe had been taking Sheridan to school, and she put on a brave face for him, but he knew she was nervous and emotional about the change.

Joe loved the fall, even though it meant that big-game hunting seasons would soon be under way and he'd be in the field checking licenses and hunters from before sunrise until well after dark for nearly two and a half months. It was his busiest time as a game warden, and often exhausting. But, as always, he would throw himself into it, establish his rhythm. And, as always, he would find himself a little disappointed when it was over and fall surrendered to winter. He loved working hard, being outside, feeling his senses tingle as he approached a hunting camp not knowing who or what to expect. For two months, nearly every single human he encountered would be armed. These were men who lived their lives solely for the reward in the fall of their one-week or two-week hunt. They wanted to drink hard, eat like soldiers after a year-long march, hunt a pronghorn antelope, mule deer, elk, or moose, and burn out all of the primal energy and desire that they'd stored up during the previous year of humiliation and frustration. Sometimes, he encountered men in the field who didn't want to meet a game warden that day. That's when things got interesting.

Now, though, Joe was tired; he had eaten and drunk too much, even danced a few dances with Marybeth, Sheridan, and Lucy. Missy, flushed with wine, had dragged him from their table to the springy dance floor. As it turned out, it was her next-to-last dance before she joined Bud in his black Suburban and headed for the tiny Saddlestring airport. The newlyweds would take the seventeen-passenger commuter plane to Denver, then fly to Italy for their honeymoon. They would be gone for ten days. Bud would be back in time for the fall roundup when they moved their cattle from the mountain grass to the valley floor.

But as he drove, Joe could not stop thinking about Will Jensen, wondering what the circumstances could have been that made him kill himself. It didn't make sense to him. Will had been tough, levelheaded. Devoted to his family and his job. Or at least that's what Joe had thought.

THE PICKETTS LIVED IN A small two-story house eight miles from Saddlestring on the Bighorn Road. The house was owned by the state, and had been their home for six years. It sat back from the road behind a recently painted white fence. There was a detached garage that housed Joe's snowmobile and the family van, and a loafing shed and corral in back for their two horses. The Saddlestring District was considered a "two-horse" district, meaning that the department budgeted for at least two horses, tack, and feed. From the front yard, the southern face of Wolf Mountain dominated the view. Between the house and the mountain, the East Fork of the Twelve Sleep River serpentined through a willow-choked meadow toward the main river and town.

As Joe entered the house, he glanced through the open door of his tiny office near the mudroom and saw that the message light was blinking on his answering machine. At this time of the year, Joe got a lot of calls. Hunters, fishers, ranchers, outfitters, and citizens called any time of the day or night. Most assumed Joe worked out of an office in some kind of Game and Fish Department building. The reality was that his office was a tiny room in his own house. Marybeth and Sheridan served as unpaid receptionists and assistants, and even Lucy answered the phone or the door at times. In a state and community where men greeted each other on the street during the fall by asking, "Got your elk yet?" the game warden played a prominent role.

He sat down at his desk and loosened his tie, watching as Marybeth and Lucy passed by his open door. Both were carrying huge bouquets of flowers from the wedding that Missy had insisted they take with them. Joe's office filled with the scent of flowers.

There were three messages. The first one was from Herman Klein, a rancher on the other side of Wolf Mountain. Klein reported that the elk were already moving down out of the timber and eating his hay. Since he had requested more elk fence be constructed around his stacks the previous year, he was hoping that contract crews would be out soon, before winter. Joe cursed and made a note on his pad to call his fence contractor in the morning and follow up with Herman Klein. One of the few responsibilities that had become easier for Joe since he started was that he no longer had to construct elk fence himself, but could contract locally for it. Unfortunately, the local contractor was unreliable.

The second call was strange. Joe could hear a man's labored breathing and faint, tinny music in the background, but no words were spoken. It went on like that until the time allotted for the message ran out. Joe looked at the telephone handset with puzzlement, then erased the message. It was the third such call in the past month. That was too many calls to assume a mistake or a misdial. But there was nothing he could do about it.

The last message was from Trey Crump, Joe's supervisor in Cody.

"Joe, it's Trey. I assume you've heard by now that Will Jensen took his own life over in Jackson."

Joe sat up in his chair. Now it was absolutely confirmed.

"We still don't know all of the details yet," Trey continued, sounding weary and sad, "but the ME in Teton County ruled out any foul play. The method of death was obvious, I guess."

There was a long pause. Then: "The Teton District isn't a district we can allow to be vacant for even a few days. The elk season opens up at the end of next week, two weeks before yours does. There's way too much action over there, and too much crap going on to leave it go."

Joe's heart jumped. The year before, he had put in a request to be considered for a new district. Twelve Sleep County seemed like a slowly closing vise. Too much had happened there. Although Joe still loved the Bighorns, and his district, he knew that in order to advance within the department he might have to move. If nothing else, he and Marybeth had discussed relocating to a place with more opportunities.

"The director called me this morning and asked me for a recommendation for a temporary game warden. I recommended you," Trey said, laughing tiredly. "I thought he was going to shit right there. But I told him there are only two men I could recommend for an area as hot as Teton. One of them is you. The other, God bless him, was Will."

Joe looked up. Marybeth leaned against the doorjamb, trying to read his expression.

Trey said, "I already talked to Phil Kiner in Laramie. He's got a trainee with him so he can break loose and come up to Twelve Sleep in a couple of weeks for the deer and elk openers. He trained up there when he first started out, so he knows the country in a general way. He's not you, but he'll get along okay. But I'd like to ask you to get over to Jackson as soon as you can. Can you do it? Call me as soon as possible, let me know."

Joe cradled the phone.

"Was that Trey?" Marybeth asked.

"Yup."

"Is it true about Will Jensen?"

"It's true."

She shook her head. "I just can't understand it."

Joe shrugged at her in a "what can I say?" gesture.

"Did he ask you to transfer?"

Joe tried to read her face. It was impassive, but her eyes sparkled and gave her away. She was intrigued.

"Temporarily."

"Are you going to do it?"

"What do *you* think about that?"

"When would you start?"

"I'd leave Monday. The elk opener is next week."

"In *two days*?"

She folded her arms, eyes locked with Joe.

SHERIDAN HAD CHANGED into a sweatshirt and jeans and brought her world history assignment into the living room so she could spread it out on the coffee table. She noticed that her mother's back filled the office door, and by her posture Sheridan could tell that her parents were having a serious discussion. Sheridan had assigned levels to her parents' discussions, and shared them with Lucy.

Level One was simply banter, but sometimes with an edge. During Level One, her parents moved freely around the house, talking as if Sheridan and Lucy couldn't hear them or didn't exist. Level Two was when her father was in his office and her mother blocked the door. They could still be overheard, but they didn't necessarily want to be.

Sheridan watched as her mother stepped into the office and shut the door behind her. As she did, Lucy came down the hall still wearing her flower girl's dress. That was a difference between Sheridan and Lucy: Sheridan couldn't wait to change when she got home.

"We're at Level Three," Sheridan whispered to Lucy.

"What about?"

"Something about Jackson," Sheridan said, still whispering. "I didn't get it all."

"I'D BE MORE EXCITED IF I could go with you," Marybeth said. "But with school just starting, and all of the shuttling I need to do with the girls, I can't." Not to mention Marybeth's still-fledgling office management business, Joe thought. Marybeth did the accounting and inventory management for the local pharmacy, a new art gallery, and Wolf Mountain Taxidermy.

"Maybe I can call Trey and pass on it," Joe said.

"Don't you dare," she said quickly. "This could be an opportunity. And obviously, Trey thinks highly enough of you to offer you this."

"I don't know how long it will last, or if it'll lead to anything."

"And we don't know that it won't," she said. "Jackson Hole is about as high profile as you can get in this state."

Joe knew that Will Jensen had shunned a high profile, but it came with the territory. The department sometimes sent press clippings out when game wardens made the news or were featured in local press. There were twice as many stories about Will Jensen than any other employee.

"Jackson is different," Joe said lamely. "It's a whole different animal than Saddlestring."

Marybeth walked over and sat on his desk. "Are you saying you don't want to do it?"

"No, I'm not saying that. But now isn't a very good time to leave you and the girls, even if it's for a couple of weeks."

She laughed. There was an edge of bitterness in the laugh that bothered him. "Joe, once hunting season starts, we don't even see you anyway. It's not like you're around to . . ."

"Do my share?" he finished for her, feeling his face get hot.

"That's not what I was going to say."

Joe was stung. "For the last two years, I made just about every one of Sheridan's games," he said. "I went to Lucy's Christmas play last year."

Marybeth smiled, showing she didn't want to argue. "And you missed everything else," she said gently. "Teacher conferences, Lucy's choir, back-to-school night, Sheridan's play, the school carnival . . ."

"Only in September and October," he said defensively.

"And November," Marybeth said. "But Joe, my point is that you'll be gone anyway. So if you're gone here or you're gone there, it won't burden us very much. We're three strong women, you know."

His neck still burned. Being a good father and husband meant everything to him. He sincerely tried to make up for his absences in the other months, and had started taking Sheridan on patrol with him when he could to make up for the time he was away. He planned to do the same with Lucy as she got older.

"Trey said Phil Kiner can come up in a couple of

weeks to fill in," Joe said grumpily. "So you won't need to worry about that."

"We'll still get the phone calls, though," she said. "And the drunken hunters who stop by. And a mad rancher every once in a while. That's just the way it is."

"Man . . ."

She leaned over and kissed him on the forehead. "There's no doubt that we're best when we're working as partners, Joe. No doubt. Things are still a little . . . fragile around here."

He turned his head away, but stroked her thigh, listening.

"But if we're ever going to provide better for our girls, we've got to be willing to take some risks. If this leads to a better job or a better salary for you, it's something we need to do."

"You'll be okay, then?"

She smiled down at him. "For a while, sure. I just hope it doesn't drag on too long. If it does, you'll have to come get us and take us with you."

"You think you'd like Jackson?"

Marybeth shrugged. "I don't know. It's got better restaurants. There's definitely more to do. But I'm not sure I'd want to raise our kids there."

"I'm not sure either," he said.

"But you can scout it out for us while you're there. You can check out the schools, the atmosphere. Then let me know what you think."

He shook his head. "That's a decision we'd make together, like every thing else."

"That's what I mean about being better as partners," she said.

"I'll call Trey and tell him I'm in," Joe said.

*   *   *

OUTSIDE THE DOOR, SHERIDAN AND Lucy exchanged glances.

"The kids from Jackson are the snottiest kids in the state," Sheridan whispered. "When we play them we try to destroy them, but we never do. You should see their bus. It's the best bus there is."

"But don't they have skiing?" Lucy asked, wide-eyed. "And a Ripley's Believe-It-or-Not museum?"

The door opened suddenly, filled with their dad.

"Show's over, girls," he said. "Don't you have homework?"

HE WENT OUT TO FEED the horses. A single pole lamp threw ghostly blue-white light across the corral. The horses, the paint Toby and young sorrel Doc, nickered when they saw him coming, knowing it was time to eat. Joe tossed them hay and watched them eat, a foot on the rail. The profile of Wolf Mountain was black against a dark sky smeared with stars.

He would miss Wolf Mountain, he thought. And Crazy Woman Creek. And the view he got from his favorite breaklands perch, where he could see the curvature of the earth.

He rubbed his eyes. He was getting ahead of himself here, he thought. It was much too soon to start thinking about things like that. There was plenty to do before he left for Jackson.

As he walked back to the house, he thought about the second call. The one where a man simply breathed until the message ran out. It was likely a crank, or a mistake. But since Joe identified himself on the voice mail, the man had to know whom he was calling. Joe's number was in the slim Twelve Sleep County telephone book. The caller could be anyone: a hunter Joe had cited, a rancher he had tangled with, even a state or federal employee Joe had been on the opposite side of a land use issue with. Whomever, it was likely someone harmless.

But if he was going to be out of town for a couple of weeks, Joe didn't want to chance anything when it came to Marybeth and his daughters. He'd need to ask for some help.

4

AFTER CHURCH ON SUNDAY, JOE AND MARYBETH planned to spend the rest of the afternoon getting him packed so he could leave early Monday. For some reason, both assumed that it would take much longer than it actually did. Joe found himself feeling oddly disappointed that they had completed their task within an hour. He had a duffel bag of red uniform shirts and blue Wranglers, underwear, his Filson vest, coats, heavy parka, and boots. All of the gear he would need was already in his pickup, the place he spent most of his day anyway. Joe roamed the house and the barn, trying to find things he couldn't do without while he was in Jackson. There was little. He topped off the duffel with a few books he'd not yet read, and a small framed family photo from his desktop that he wished was more recent.

ABSENTLY LISTENING TO A BROADCAST of the first week of NFL football on the radio, Joe drove down the two-lane highway that paralleled the river en route to Nate

Romanowski's place and did a mental inventory of items in his truck.

His standard-issue weaponry consisted of the .308 carbine secured under the bench seat, a .270 Winchester rifle in the gun rack behind his head, and his 12-gauge Remington Wingmaster shotgun that was wedged into the coil springs behind his seat. He also had a .22 pistol with cracker shells that was used for spooking elk out of hay meadows.

In a locked metal box in the bed of his pickup were tire chains, tow ropes, tools, an evidence kit, a necropsy kit, emergency food and blankets, blood-spatter and bullet-caliber guides and charts, flares, and a rucksack for foot patrolling. Taped to the lid of the box was a new addition: Joe's Last Will and Testament. He had written it out the night before. Not even Marybeth knew about it yet. He wondered idly if Will Jensen had thought to draw one up.

NATE ROMANOWSKI LIVED IN A small stone house on the banks of the Twelve Sleep River, six miles off the highway. Romanowski was a falconer with three birds—a peregrine, a red tail, and a fledgling prairie falcon—in his mews. But when Joe drove onto his property, Nate was saddling a buffalo. Joe noticed that Nate was sporting two black eyes, and that his nose was swollen like a bulb.

A few months before, Nate had told Joe about his newfound fascination with bison. It had sprung from reading an article in an old newspaper he had dug out of a crack in the walls of his home. The article was a first-person account from a correspondent who had just returned from the Cheyenne Frontier Days rodeo after witnessing an event called "Women's Buffalo Riding." Apparently, women contestants mounted wild bison and were turned loose in an arena to see who could stay on the longest. There was a grainy photo of a cowgirl in a dress and baggy pantaloons astride a massive bull. In the photo, though, the bull looked docile. This account fascinated Nate, he said, because he had never thought a human could ride a buffalo around. Then he asked himself, *Why not me?* The idea quickly became an obsession. Sheridan, who received falconry lessons from Nate on Friday afternoons, had mentioned to Joe that Nate had bought a buffalo from a rancher near Clearmont. And here it was.

Joe parked his pickup beside Nate's battered Jeep and got out. The afternoon was clear and warm, and Joe could hear the hushed liquid flow of the river.

"I couldn't use a regular saddle," Nate said by way of a greeting. "The cinches were two to three feet too short. So I had to make my own cinches in order to make this work."

Romanowski had appeared in Saddlestring three years before. He was tall, rangy, and rawboned, with long blond hair tied back in a ponytail. He had a hawk's beak nose and piercing, stone-cold blue eyes. Most of the people in the county feared him, and several had seriously questioned the basis of Joe's friendship with a man who openly carried a .454 Casull, an extremely powerful handgun. Nate had come from Montana, leaving a set of suspicious circumstances involving the deaths of two federal agents, and Joe had almost inadvertently proved Nate's innocence for another murder. Upon his release from prison, Nate had pledged his loyalty to Joe and the Pickett family, and had not wavered in his blind commitment. There were rumors involving Nate's background that included years in covert operations for a secret branch of the defense department. While he didn't know the specifics, Joe knew this to be true. He also knew that Nate was capable of precision violence, and well connected to questionable people and groups throughout the country and the world. Joe had no clear explanation as to Nate's means of support. All he knew was that he sometimes vanished for weeks (always calling ahead to cancel Sheridan's falconry lesson) and that he sometimes cautioned Joe about coming out to his place at certain times when, Joe guessed, certain visitors were there. It was something they never talked about, although a few times Nate had offered tidbits. Joe didn't want to hear them.

The buffalo stood in the center of a newly constructed four-rail corral. The corral was built solidly, but the east side of it was pitched out a little, most likely from the buffalo leaning against it or trying to push his head through. Joe wondered if the corral would contain the animal if it really wanted out.

Joe draped his arms over the top post and set a boot on the bottom rail. He was impressed, as always, by the sheer size and presence of a buffalo. The bison was a giant brown-black wedge, front-loaded with heavily muscled shoulders and a woolly, blunt head. Bison, he knew, were pure front-wheel-drive creatures, with the ability to accelerate to forty miles per hour from a standing start. Conical pointed horns curled back from its skull. Marble-black eyes glowed from beneath thick, dirty curls.

Nate tightened the cinch and the buffalo flinched. Joe prepared for a violent explosion, and he found himself stepping back involuntarily. The buffalo turned his head and stared at Nate.

"This is as far as I got last week," Nate said, looking over.

"What happened to you?"

Nate touched his eye. "He didn't like the saddle at first."

"But he does now?"

Nate shrugged. "Not really. But he finally understands what I'm up to, and he seems resigned to the fact. I've tried to persuade him it will be fun."

Joe nodded. Nate communicated with animals on a base level, in a wholly mysterious way. He didn't train them, or break them, but using cues and gestures he somehow connected with them. It was a methodology learned from working with falcons, who, after all, had the option (rarely acted upon) to simply fly away anytime they were released to the sky.

"Your saddle in the back of your truck," Nate said, sliding a halter ever so slowly over the head of the buffalo. "Are you going somewhere?"

"Jackson," Joe said. "The game warden there committed suicide. They've assigned me there, temporarily."

Nate looked up, obviously trying to read Joe's face.

"What?" Joe asked.

Nate said, "Things are different in Jackson. I've got some acquaintances over there. I've spent some time there myself."

Joe waited for the rest, but it didn't come.

"Do you have a point?" Joe asked.

He shrugged. "My point is things are different in Jackson."

"Thanks for that," Joe said, leaning on the fence.

For the next few minutes, Nate soothed the big bull, running his hands over him, speaking nonsense soothingly. Joe could see the buffalo relax, which was confirmed by a long sigh. He could smell the bison's grassy, hot breath. Nate gracefully launched himself up on the saddle.

"This is the first time he's let me on," Nate said quietly.

"He seems to be okay with it," Joe said, although they could both see the buffalo's ears twitch nervously. "Does he buck?"

"See my face?" Nate said. "Yes, he can buck."

Joe waited for something to happen. Nothing did. Nate just sat there.

"Now I've got to get him to move and turn," Nate said. "It'll take some time."

Joe had a vision of Nate Romanowski, wearing his shoulder holster, riding the buffalo through the streets of Saddlestring in the anemic Fourth of July parade. The thought made him snort.

"HOW MANY OF THESE CALLS have you received?" Nate asked later, over coffee in his stone house. The buffalo had been unsaddled and turned out to pasture.

"Three in the last month."

"Could it just be a misdial?"

Joe nodded. "Sure. But how likely is that?"

"Can't you get somebody to trace the call? Or get Caller ID?"

"I ordered it this morning. The next time there's a call, we should be able to figure out who it is. Then maybe we'll know why."

"I'll check in with Marybeth while you're gone," Nate said.

"I'd appreciate that. Things get a little wild at times during hunting season. She's more than capable of handling anything, as you know, but it makes me feel better to know you'll keep an eye out."

"A deal is a deal," Nate said.

Joe wanted to say more. To remind Nate that the "deal" about protecting Joe and his family was one Nate had come up with, something Joe never proposed or really accepted. Being allies with a man like Nate made Joe uncomfortable at times because it went against his instincts. Nate was a strange man, a frightening man. But at times like these, he needed a guy like Nate, who was always a man of his word and didn't care about appearances, constraints, or even the law.

"Thanks for the coffee," Joe said, standing.

"Don't go crazy over in Jackson," Nate cautioned.

"This from a man who is trying to ride a buffalo around." Joe smiled.

"If you need help, call me."

Joe stopped at the door and looked back. "And vice versa."

THAT NIGHT, JOE SAT AT HIS DESK and made a list of ongoing projects and the status of each to e-mail to Phil Kiner in Laramie. Maxine sat curled at his feet, knowing, like dogs always knew, that she would be abandoned soon and making him feel as guilty as possible for it by staring at him with her big brown eyes. The whole evening had been that way.

It had started at dinner with a melancholy pot roast and vegetables Sheridan complained were undercooked. Joe recognized her attitude for what it was: She was at an age where if she was angry with her father or mad at the world in general she took it out on her mother, who was the disciplinarian in the family. Lucy's way of showing her disapproval for his leaving was to ignore him and pretend he wasn't there, which to Joe was even worse.

He looked over his long e-mail message. He knew he would forget things, and there was no way he could provide the background necessary on specific hunters Phil may have a problem with, or the idiosyncrasies of individual landowners. It was strange, Joe thought, not knowing for sure if he was coming back to his district.

5

A TRAVELER GOING FROM EAST TO WEST OVER THE BIG-
horn Mountains has three choices of routes: U.S. 16
through Ten Sleep Canyon and Worland, U.S. 14 de-
scending through Shell Canyon and Greybull, and U.S.
14-A, via the Medicine Wheel Passage and on to Lovell.
Joe chose 14-A not only for the challenge of its switch-
backs but for the view he would get when he broke over
the top of the range and saw the vista of the Bighorn
Basin laid out flat, brown, and endless. He chewed gum
to help his ears pop as they clouded with elevation, and
looked over frequently to check on Maxine, his Labrador, who he'd left at home until he could scope out his
new district. Fine, gritty snow peppered his windshield at
the ten-thousand-foot summit, the snow appearing from
a virtually cloudless light blue sky.

His feelings were decidedly mixed. The memory of
the morning with his young family stayed with him.
Sheridan and Lucy had been dressed for school and
scrambling along the countertop in the kitchen, assem-

bling their lunches. Marybeth was preparing for a day of bookkeeping at the pharmacy. She wore khaki slacks and a sweater, her blond hair cut shorter than she had ever worn it. He liked it but still wasn't used to it. Joe had stood stupidly near the mudroom entrance, watching them. Their good-byes had been a little frantic because they could all hear the school bus lumbering down Bighorn Road. After the girls were on the bus and the doors were shut, Joe and Marybeth walked to his pickup, which was fully packed and ready to go.

"Call me often," she had said.

"As often as I can," he said, kissing her.

"In fact, call me when you get there. So I know you made it all right."

The scene was less than dramatic. So why did he feel that something seminal had happened? Why did he feel both guilty *and* elated?

AS HE DESCENDED THE WESTERN SLOPE, the snow vanished as suddenly as it had appeared and the temperature began to rise quickly. By the time he hit the flats, heat was shimmering on the old asphalt highway and roses were growing in boxes in downtown Lovell, which he left in his rearview mirror.

A squawk from his radio interrupted Joe's thoughts. He picked up the handset. It was dispatch calling with a message from Trey. The meeting place that morning would need to be changed. There was a bear problem.

TREY CRUMP WAS WAITING FOR JOE in his pickup, which was parked in the trees at the culmination of a rugged two-track road, four miles from Dead Indian Pass. After

Joe pulled up next to Trey's pickup, his supervisor got out of his truck and climbed in with Joe. Joe grasped the big man's hand.

Trey looked larger than he really was, with a squarish block of a head, a thick mustache going gray, and heavy jowls. A big belly strained against his uniform shirt. He was a terse man in aura and appearance, but his deep-set, compassionate eyes gave him away as the romantic he really was. Joe liked and admired Trey, but he rarely saw him in person. Trey wore badge number 4, meaning he had the fourth highest seniority within the division. Joe had recently received his new badge, moving from 52 to 44. Since there were only fifty-five full-fledged game wardens—and thirty-five trainees not yet assigned a district—Joe was proud of his new badge number. With Will Jensen's death, Joe would now be badge number 43. He felt more than a pang of guilt for even thinking about that.

Trey apologized for not meeting Joe for breakfast at the Irma Hotel in Cody, but said he had received a 5 A.M. call-out for a problem grizzly bear that had been breaking into cabins in the Sunlight Basin. The suspect bear was named Number 304, and he was well known in the area. That morning, the 450-pound grizzly had pushed down a steel-reinforced door, entered a cabin and dismantled it, ripping the cabinets from the wall and tossing a cast-iron stove from the kitchen into a bedroom.

"This is a bad situation," Trey said, his voice deep and filled with gravel. "I could use your help."

Joe could see the roofs of some of the cabins below in the heavy timber, and a culvert bear trap set up in a sun-drenched meadow. The trap was designed on wheels so it could be pulled behind a vehicle to the problem area and baited with a road-killed deer or antelope. When the bear entered the metal opening and tugged on the bait, a heavy steel door crashed down and locked. The trap, with the angry bear in it, could then be hitched to a pickup and driven away to a remote location, where the bear would be released. Either that, or euthanized on the spot if the Interagency Grizzly Bear Management Team pronounced a death sentence on the animal.

Joe grimaced. He had had enough of grizzly bears the year before, when a runaway from Yellowstone had bee-lined for the Bighorns. He'd seen firsthand what an animal like that could do to a man.

"We're overwhelmed with bears right now," Trey said with a heavy sigh. "Three different call-ins came in just this morning. That's why I'm alone here—my bear guys are off on the other calls. They wanted to stay here to help me with 304 because we all kind of like the guy, and we hate to see him go."

For the first time, Joe noticed that Trey's scoped rifle was out and lying across the hood of his supervisor's truck on a pair of old coveralls.

"You've got to kill him, then?" Joe asked.

"That was our recommendation to the Feds," Trey said with resignation. "This is the fourth time 304's damaged property in the basin. No matter how far we take him away, he finds his way back. He's got no fear of humans anymore."

From a scanner in Trey's pickup, Joe could hear a low and steady pulsing tone. He knew from experience that the radio collar was transmitting the tone on 304. The bear was still in the area. They would sit and wait for it.

Joe scanned the ridges and slopes of the mountain basin, looking for movement. He saw none.

Trey said, "The sad thing is that 304 lived in these mountains for six or seven years without incident. One of the cabin owners left dog food out on his porch. 304

learned that he liked dog food and kept coming back. Pretty soon, the bear figured out that if he busted *into* the cabin he could find all kinds of things to eat. But it started with the dog food, and you know what they say."

"A fed bear is a dead bear," Joe said.

"Yes, goddamnit."

NIGHT CAME. THE SLIVER OF MOON was a surgical white slice in the sky. Joe and Trey sat silently in the cab of the pickup, listening to each other's breathing.

"Sorry to start out your trip like this," Trey said. "I bet you want to get over there."

"Not a problem."

"Joe, I've got to ask you something."

Joe grunted.

"After that incident last year, are you okay to work with me to get this bear?"

Joe turned to Trey and found his supervisor studying him. "I'm fine with it."

"Are you sure? Because if you aren't . . ."

"I said I'm *fine* with it, Trey."

Trey eventually moved from Joe's pickup to his own so he could sleep. Joe looked at his cell phone to see if he had a signal so he could call Marybeth and tell her about the change in plans. There was no signal. Instead, he checked in with dispatch and asked the dispatcher to advise Marybeth and the station in Jackson that he would be late arriving.

He tried to sleep. Cold crept into the cab from the doors and windows. The pulsing tone of the bear's collar served as a heartbeat for the stakeout.

At 2:30 there was a metallic *clang* from the dark meadow below. Joe sat up with a start, banging his head against the steering wheel. He looked over and saw that

Trey had heard it too, and had turned on his dome light and unrolled his window.

As Joe opened his door, there was a roar from below that not only ripped through the silence but also seemed to roll through the earth itself.

"Sounds like we got him," Trey said. There was no joy in his voice.

Joe felt a shiver that raised the hair on his forearms and the back of his neck.

6

EVEN BEFORE THE HEADLIGHTS PAINTED THE INSIDE OF the culvert trap, Joe could smell the grizzly. The odor was heavy and musky, what a wet dog might smell like if it was twice the size of an NFL linebacker.

"Jesus Christ," Trey said when they could see the bear huddled at the back of the trap, his eyes blinking against the artificial light. "He's even bigger than the last time I saw him."

"Is it 304?" Joe's voice was weak, as if the presence of the bear had sucked something out of him. The bear filled the back of the trap; his huge head hung low, his nose moist and black. A stream of pink-colored saliva hung like a beaded ruby necklace from his mouth to the half-devoured roadkill on the floor of the trap. The bear was frightened, and breathing hard, which made the trap rock slightly back and forth.

"Yup, it's him."

On the seat between them was a tranquilizer gun loaded with a dart filled with Telazol. Once the bear was down, Trey had told Joe, they would need to confirm

304's ear tag and inject the animal with a lethal dose of euthanol to kill it.

Joe drove close to the steel gate on the trap and turned the wheels slightly, giving Trey a good shot at the bear.

"I hate this," Trey said, cocking the tranquilizer gun and aiming it out the window. "I hate this with all of my heart."

The gun popped and Joe saw a flash of the dart through his headlights as it flew into the back of the trap. Joe couldn't see where the dart hit within the thick fur of the grizzly, but he heard the bear grunt.

"Hit it?" Joe asked.

"I'm pretty sure I did."

"How long before he's down for the count?"

"Five minutes."

They waited ten. Joe couldn't tell if the bear was sleeping or not. He could still see eyes reflecting the light, still see the stream of saliva.

Trey said, "I think we're okay now," and slid out of the truck with his shotgun loaded with slugs and a kit containing the lethal dose of euthanol. Joe exited the driver's side with his weapon, and the two game wardens approached the front of the trap. Joe could hear the bear breathing, and the odor was very strong and mixed with the smell of blood from the roadkill. They snapped on their flashlights. Trey shone his on the locking mechanism of the trapdoor, while Joe trained his on the bear.

What Joe saw scared him to death. The grizzly not only blinked at the light, but turned his head to avoid it.

"Trey . . ." Joe whispered urgently.

"*Shit!*" Trey hollered, wheeling around. "*The gate didn't lock!*"

The grizzly bear roared and charged the front of the trap with such speed and force that the unlocked gate blew wide open, the steel grate clanging up and over the top of the culvert. Joe had never seen an animal so big move so fast, and he knew that if the bear chose him as a target there was nothing he could do about it. He found himself backing up toward the truck while raising his shotgun and he felt more than saw Trey blindly fire toward the huge brown blur as the bear ran toward the dark timber.

304 crow-hopped the instant Trey's shotgun went off as if kicked from behind, then kept going. Joe aimed at the streaking form, saw it, lost it, and didn't pull the trigger.

For a moment, they both stood and listened to the bear crash through the timber with the sound and subtlety of a meteorite. Joe was surprised he could hear anything over the sound of his own whumping heartbeat.

IT TOOK NEARLY TWENTY MINUTES for Trey and Joe to calm down and assess the situation. Joe was glad it was dark so that Trey wouldn't see his hands shaking.

He held the shotgun close to him, listening for the possible warning sounds of the bear doubling back on them, while Trey examined the trapdoor to try to figure out why it didn't work.

"I don't know what went wrong," Trey said morosely, pulling himself clumsily back to his feet and snatching his shotgun from where he had leaned it against the trap, "but it looks like I might have hit that bear. There's a splash of blood out here on the grass."

They followed the bear's churned-up trail through the meadow to where it entered the trees. There were flecks of blood on blades of grass and fallen leaves. Joe felt his heart sink.

"We've got a wounded grizzly and there's nothing

more dangerous than that," Trey said, his voice heavy. "We've got to hunt him down."

Trey called dispatch and gave the dispatcher their co-ordinates. "We'll stay out here until we find him. Please call my wife and Marybeth Pickett in Saddlestring and tell 'em what the situation is. Oh—and call Jackson Hole. Tell 'em Joe Pickett is going to be a little late for his new job."

FOR THE NEXT THREE DAYS they drove the primitive back roads, pulling Trey's horses in a trailer, tracking the wounded bear. They found where he had fed on a rot-ting moose carcass, and picked up his track where he had crossed a stream. The bear had tried to break into an-other cabin—they could see deep gouges on the front door and the shutters as well as a gout of blood on the porch. Joe found it remarkable and sickening how much blood this bear had lost, and both he and Trey kept ex-pecting to find the bear's body any minute. Joe admired the big bear nearly as much as he feared it. He would have liked to simply let it go and die in peace, if there was a guarantee that the bear would die.

The tension in the situation, and between Joe and Trey, thickened. Trey admonished himself for taking a wild shot that wounded the bear, and Joe felt that Trey was blaming *him* for not firing. Joe blamed himself as well, and replayed the bear escape over and over in his mind as he rode. He wasn't convinced that he had fro-zen, but he sure hadn't shot the bear. Things had hap-pened so quickly that he hadn't had a sure shot. Had he?

ON THE SECOND AFTERNOON, they lost the signal. They drove to the highest hill they could get to and parked.

The only thing they could do, Trey said, was hope the bear wandered back into range of the receiver.

"We might as well get right to it while we're waiting," Trey said, his tone even more rock bottom than usual. "We've got a hell of a mess in Jackson, Joe. I want you to know what you're getting yourself into."

Joe nodded.

Trey made a pained face. "I'm getting more than a little concerned that some of my game wardens are letting the pressure get to them. I wish I knew how I could help them deal with it. But I don't."

Joe asked, "What do you mean?" But he knew. In the past year, a game warden at a game check station in the Wind River mountains had gotten into an argument with his son, shot him, then turned the pistol on himself. No one knew what the argument was about. Another game warden in southern Wyoming, assigned to a huge, virtually uninhabited district, simply vanished from the state. He was later found in New Mexico at the end of a three-week bender. He would tell anyone who would listen to him that the locals had been out to get him, that he had run for his own life. A departmental investigation could find no evidence of his charges, and he was dismissed.

Unlike any other law enforcement personnel Joe was aware of, game wardens were literally autonomous. They ran their own districts in their own way. Monthly reports to district supervisors like Trey were required, but because supervisors had districts of their own to contend with, they rarely micromanaged game wardens in the field. This was one of the many aspects of his job that Joe valued. It was about trust, and competence, and doing the right thing. But this kind of autonomy brought a secret lonely hell to some men, and ravaged them.

"It's not like there never was any pressure, back in the

old days when I started," Trey said. "We had poaching rings, hardheaded landowners, plenty of violent knuckle-heads to deal with. But we didn't have the political stuff as much."

"Is that what you think happened with Will?" Joe asked. "He let it get to him?"

Trey nodded. "I'm not sure, of course. He never really said that, except for the occasional bitching that we all do. But Jackson is such a hot spot for that kind of thing. The most extreme are there, it seems. Hunters versus animal-rights types. Developers versus environmentalists. Rich versus poor. Out-of-state landowners versus local rubes. Bear-baiting poachers versus happy hikers. Shit, and it's not just local, either. It's national and international. I'm afraid he thought that just about everyone wanted a piece of him, or had a gripe with how he did his job. He never told me that, but all you have to do is read the papers to see what he was in the middle of.

"Jackson is unique, Joe," Trey continued. "Everything there is ramped up. All of the different issues are hotter. Jackson is Wyoming's very own California, for better and worse. Things that happen there will eventually influence the rest of the state and beyond. Everybody knows that. It's why the big wars start there. Whoever wins those wars knows that no one else will fight as hard anywhere else. It's the front line."

Joe let Trey go on, knowing how rarely the man went on. Joe had been chosen as Trey's confidant, and he accepted his role with little comment.

Trey looked up and locked eyes with Joe. "Will Jensen, in the end, must have been a very troubled soul. I ache for the guy."

Joe said, "I've got to say that the last man I would have guessed to do this was Will."

Trey nodded. "Me too. He was a goddamned rock for

years. But something happened to him over the last six months. I don't know what it was."

Trey slumped forward for a moment, silent, then got out of the truck for a while and scoped the trees and meadow for a sign of the grizzly. The late afternoon sun cast shadows in the timber. Joe watched him, turning over in his mind what Trey had just told him.

"I wish 304 would come out where we can see him," Trey said, getting back in.

"About Will," Joe prompted. "The last six months."

Trey slumped against his seat. "Like I said, something happened to him. He didn't send in most of his reports, for one thing. The one or two I got were sloppy as hell. He got arrested for DWUI, twice at least. I think there may have been other incidents where the local cops let him off. I even heard something about him getting physically removed from some big-shot party when he tried to start a fight."

"*Will?*" Joe asked, shocked.

"Will. And I just found out his wife and kids moved out on him."

"Susan left him?"

Divorce was rampant within the families of game wardens, Joe knew, worse than for police officers. It went back to the nature of the job, the remote, state-owned homes, the single-mindedness most game wardens brought to their jobs (Joe included), and growing outside pressure. Plus, when he first became a game warden, Joe had quickly learned that some women liked men in a uniform. He had always resisted them. But he knew he wasn't perfect. Will Jensen, though, had been *close* to perfect. That's why he'd been assigned to Jackson.

Trey said, "I kick myself now, because I should have seen it coming. I should have gotten my fat ass over the mountains and talked with him. Maybe I could have helped him."

"Don't beat yourself up," Joe said. "Will obviously didn't ask you for any help."

"Would you?" Trey shot back.

Joe didn't think very long on the question. "Probably not."

Trey nodded triumphantly. "Of course you wouldn't. None of my guys would. Nobody talks about what's going on in their heads."

Joe noted that Trey, even in his concern, couldn't say the word *feelings*.

"But something happened to Will during the last six months," Joe said. "That's pretty fast, when you consider it."

Trey agreed. "I think so too. Unless he just bottled every thing up and then it blew."

AS THE SUN NOTCHED BETWEEN two peaks, Trey unfolded a map on the seat between them. There was still no signal from the bear.

"There are two districts out of Jackson," Trey said, pointing with a stubby finger. "South Jackson, which extends down through the Hoback Mountains and curls up like an 'L.' The North Jackson District, Will's old district, the one you'll be covering, extends from town all the way up to Yellowstone Park and over to the Continental Divide."

Trey stopped his finger on the staccato line indicating the Divide. "Right here, at Two Ocean Pass."

Joe did the math. The North Jackson district was 1,885 square miles, most of it spectacular, roadless mountain wilderness.

"The biggest area in the district is accessible only by horseback," Trey said. "It's considered the most remote area in the continental U.S. This is where the elk come down out of Yellowstone on their natural migration routes, and also where the outfitters have established camps. There's a state cabin up there owned by the department that you can base out of. You'll have thirty-seven outfitters to look after, and some of them are the crustiest guys you'll ever meet. Some of them are the most honorable men you'll ever run across. We have problems there with bear and elk baiting, salting mainly. I'm sure Will kept some files on them. You've heard of Smoke Van Horn?"

"Sure," Joe said. Van Horn was the loudest, most cantankerous outfitter in Wyoming. Newspapers sometimes referred to him as the Lion of the Tetons. Van Horn had theories about game management, trophy hunting, and how the state and federal government were screwing up his wilderness through wrong-headed policies thought up and administered by incompetent bureaucrats. He loved to show up at public meetings and take over, accusing the department or any other authority present of mismanagement and gross neglect. He had even self-published a tome called *How the Pricks Deny Me a Living*. He also claimed to be the most successful outfitter in the state, with a success ratio exceeding 98 percent.

"This is Smoke's country," Trey said ominously. "As well as the headquarters for animal-rights activists, wolf lovers, big-shot developers, politicians, movie stars, all kinds of riffraff."

Joe listened and nodded.

"The thing about the district is how big everything is," Trey said. "The elk herds are larger than anything you've ever run across in the Bighorns. There are four-teen thousand elk between Yellowstone and Jackson. Instead of the herds of forty or fifty that you're used to, you may get in the middle of herds up to three hundred. So you're going to encounter more hunters concentrated along the migration routes than you've probably ever seen before. There are also more grizzly bears, wolves, and mountain lions than anywhere else."

Joe nodded. He could feel his excitement building, as well as his trepidation.

"Remember one thing," Trey said. "Before you ride into those outfitter camps, stop and retie your packs on your horses. Make sure the hitches are perfect. You know how to tie a diamond hitch?"

Joe said he did.

"That's one way they measure you right off. If you've got good animals, and if the horses are packed tight with beautiful hitches, they'll think you know what the hell you're doing, even if you don't. You've got to gain their respect early on."

Joe was inwardly pleased that he had brought a well-worn copy of Joe Back's *Horses, Hitches and Rocky Trails*, the Bible of horse packing.

Trey said, "There's some new thing going on there too, something called 'the Good Meat Movement.' Will laughed about it at first. He thought it was just another Jackson thing."

"The Good Meat Movement?" Joe asked.

Trey waved his hand to dismiss the notion. "Something about rich people wanting to get back to basics, to be there when their food is raised, killed, and packaged."

"Really?" Joe said. "That sounds like hunting."

Trey chuckled. "It's not hunting, Joe. The way Will described it to me, it's more like personally getting to know the animal you're about to slaughter and have ground up into burger. So you can feel his pain, or something. Shit, I don't know."

*   *   *

"I TOLD YOU THERE WAS an objection to you going over there to fill in," Trey said almost casually, while Joe dug into packs in the back of his truck for jerky and granola— their dinner that night.

"From who? The governor?"

Trey smiled. Joe had once arrested the governor for fishing without a license. The governor had never forgotten it, and had been vindictive.

"Two more months," Trey said, grinning. "Two more months and that guy is out of there."

Governor Budd was term-limited. He had all but left the state, lobbying for a new job in Washington with the administration. So far, he hadn't received one. His unpopularity, even within his own party, had apparently preceded him.

"Some people are even predicting that the Democrat will win," Trey said. "So prepare for hell to freeze over."

"I'd be lying if I didn't say I'll be glad he's gone," Joe said. "Or that I didn't appreciate how you've stood by me all these years."

Trey waved Joe off and leaned against the grille of his green truck, gnawing on a piece of jerky. After he had washed it down with water, he had more to say. "Joe, I want you to find out what happened to Will. Now, you can't do a full-fledged investigation. The sheriff and the police department are already doing that, or have completed it by now."

Joe had assumed this was coming. He had hoped it would be.

"But I need to know what happened. What drove him to kill himself."

"Do you think it was murder?"

Trey shook his head. "Nothing I've heard indicates it

was anything other than suicide. What I want to know is what was so damned bad that Will felt the only way he could handle it was to shove a gun in his mouth."

"I'll find out what I can."

"Report back to me. Even if you can't figure anything out. We may never know what was in that man's head." Trey sighed. "If we can find out something, maybe I can help the next guy. I don't know. But when you've got a man who seems perfectly suited for the job, with a beautiful wife and great kids, and something like this happens, well . . ."

"It doesn't make sense," Joe said.

Joe felt Trey's eyes on him. He could tell what Trey was thinking. The description of Will Jensen that Trey had laid out could also be used to describe Joe Pickett.

THE RECEIVER CHIRPED. Joe and Trey looked at each other. The bear had come back. Trey said they should saddle up his horses and go after it.

The signal was strong as night came, and they camped near a stream. It was strong throughout the night and in the morning. Bear number 304 was working his way back to the cabins. Trey predicted they would be on him by noon. They weren't.

IT WAS LATE AFTERNOON WHEN the signal strength on Trey's portable scanner went "all-bars" and both horses began to snort and dance, smelling the bear. The sun had just dropped behind the mountains. The fall colors were muted in shadow, and it had gotten colder.

Joe looked up and could see the ridge where they had originally parked, and thought it remarkable that the bear had led them back where the chase had begun. He had heard that bears often did that when injured, choosing familiar terrain over unfamiliar. Or maybe 304 was hungry again.

When he got a now-recognizable whiff of the bear, he found himself clutching up, and could feel his limbs stiffen. He dismounted and led his horse to a tree where he could tie him up. Trey did the same.

Trey walked over to Joe and whispered, "We need to stay within sight and range of each other. If he goes for one of us, the other one has to shoot. If it's up to you, Joe, aim in back of his front shoulder for a heart or lung shot. Don't shoot him in the head. I've heard of slugs bouncing right off."

Joe nodded, didn't meet Trey's eyes.

"You okay, Joe?"

"Fine."

Trey lifted the receiver, slowly sweeping it in front of him until he found where the signal was strongest. Joe looked up, following Trey's arm. A dense pocket of aspen stood alone on a saddle slope of low gray sagebrush. The bear was too big to hide in the brush, so it had to be in the aspen grove. As if reading his thoughts, Trey gestured toward the trees.

Joe jacked a shell into the chamber of his shotgun and quickly loaded a replacement into the magazine. He put his thumb on the safety as he walked, ready to flip it off and shoot.

They approached the pocket of aspen. Joe could hear a slight cold wind ripple through the crown of branches, sending a few yellow leaves skittering down. He could also hear the signal from the receiver. Before plunging into the grove, he looked over at Trey. Trey mouthed, "Ready?" and Joe tipped his hat brim.

* * *

THE SMELL OF THE BEAR was strong in the grove, hanging like smoke about three feet above the ground. It was dusk. Joe wished they had entered the aspen at least a half hour before, when there was more light. He promised himself that if they didn't find the bear within ten minutes he would call to Trey and they would pull out and wait for morning.

Even though Trey had been twenty yards away when they entered the aspen, Joe couldn't see or hear him now in the dense trees.

Joe noticed a nuance in the smell of the bear—the metallic odor of blood. He walked slowly, breathed deeply and as quietly as possible. He didn't want the sound of his own exertion to fill his ears and make him miss something.

He felt it before he saw it, and spun to his left, his boot heel digging into the soft black ground beneath the fallen leaves.

The grizzly sat on his haunches, looking at him from ten feet away. Joe saw the silver-tipped brown fur, some of it matted with black blood, saw the bear's chest heave painfully as he breathed. Joe stared into the eyes of the bear, and the bear didn't blink. The bear's eyes were black and hard, without malice.

Joe raised the shotgun and thumbed off the safety. He put the front bead of the muzzle on 304's chest, right on his heart. And he didn't fire.

Even when the bear false-charged and popped his teeth together in warning, Joe didn't pull the trigger.

But Trey Crump did, the explosion sounding like the whole aspen grove went up. 304 flinched as if stung by a bee, and roared, his mouth fully open so Joe could see the inch-long teeth and pink tongue. Trey fired again and the bear toppled forward, dead before he hit the ground.

As they rode toward their vehicles in the dark, dragging the carcass of the grizzly behind them, Trey asked, "Why didn't you shoot, Joe?"

Joe didn't want to answer, and didn't.

Because he was looking me straight in the eye, that's why. Because I found out I can't kill a bear when he is looking me straight in the eye.

THAT NIGHT, THEY ATE BIG STEAKS and drank beer after beer at a guest lodge in the foothills of the mountains. Old-timers at the bar had heard the story and sent over rounds of drinks for the game wardens. They, like Trey, admired old 304. But the bear had to go. A fed bear was a dead bear.

Joe left Trey at the bar and found a pay phone outside. It was cold as he shoved quarters in, and he could see his breath as he said, "Hello, darling," to Marybeth.

"Where are you?" she asked. Even colder.

He leaned back and looked at the sign out near the highway. "Someplace called the T Bar."

"In Jackson?"

"No," he said. "By Cody."

"*Cody.* Joe, why are you there? Why aren't you in Jackson? Why didn't you call like you said you would?"

Joe said, "Didn't you get the second message from dispatch?"

"What message?"

He told her the whole story, but he could tell by her tone she was still furious with him. As he told her how scared he had been when he walked up on the grizzly, she said, "Sheridan has been an absolute beast. I can't even talk to that girl anymore."

Joe paused. "Marybeth, are you listening?"

"For three days I've been worried about you. Do you know what that's like?"

"No," Joe said, looking out at the highway. "I guess I don't."

He didn't know if he was angry, guilt-stricken, or both.

"I'll give you a call tomorrow," he said, and hung up the phone.

Trey was watching him as he reclaimed his stool at the bar. "Everything okay?"

"Marybeth didn't get the second dispatch message. She didn't know where I've been."

"Uh-oh." Trey shook his head. "I wonder if my missus got it?"

"You better call her," Joe said.

"So I can look as miserable as you?" Trey said. "I think I'll have another beer."

THE NEXT MORNING, AS HE CROSSED the Shoshone River out of Cody, Joe felt ashamed of himself. He had not slept well in his motel room, despite a few too many beers. He tried to reassess where he was in time and place in regard to his new assignment. He was four days behind schedule, and he had not yet had a chance to really talk everything over with Marybeth, without distractions. He had frozen when he should have fired. He convinced himself that if the bear had gone after Trey, he would have reacted well and started blasting. Of course he would have, he thought. He had pulled his weapon and fired in anger before. Once, he had hit a man from a long distance, but he hadn't known it at the time. But he had never faced someone, or something like a bear, looking him straight in the eye.

LATER, HE FELT THE SHROUD lifting. The guilt he had felt earlier about leaving Marybeth and the girls was still there, but the challenge of what he was about to face surged hot and steady. He already missed his family, but the residue of the telephone call with Marybeth remained. It had not been a good conversation.

Sure, she had a right to be worried and angry. But he had wanted to talk with her, tell her how tough it had been to go face-to-face with that bear, and what he had done. Instead, it had all been about her. She made him feel guilty. She always made him feel guilty. He knew the last five years had been tough on her. She'd gone through more than anyone deserved. But would there ever be a time when he didn't have to walk around on eggshells? When she didn't seem to blame him for what their life had become?

He was being unfair. Despite everything, he loved her. Without her he would spin off the planet. He needed her to ground him.

But he looked forward to the change. He looked forward to his new district.

Had the pressures in Saddlestring, and in the house, really gotten to him to this degree, he wondered, that the prospect of riding up alone on armed men in a hunting camp seemed like a boy's holiday? He tried to shake that thought out of his head. He tried to make an argument that it was good to have a mission, good to have a tough assignment. It was good to be trusted by Trey, to have been chosen out of the other fifty-five game wardens for the hottest, most high-profile district.

As he drove up the canyon, he watched the signal on his cell phone recede to nothing, followed by a digital NO SERVICE prompt.

Here we go, he thought. *Here we go.*

7

EVEN THOUGH HE SHOULD HAVE BEEN PREPARED FOR them, even though he had seen them dozens of times in photos, paintings, movies, on postage stamps, and in person, Joe still felt his heart skip a beat when the timber opened up on the road south of Yellowstone Park and the Tetons filled up the late afternoon vista. Mount Moran in particular, with its comma-shaped glacier of snow, burned bright in the cloudless sky. The dark, rounded shoulders of the Bighorns, *his* mountains, had been replaced by the glittering silver-white Tetons, which thrust upward like razor-edged sabers trying to slice open the sky. He felt like he was switching his comfortable horizon with a new, dazzling, high-tech model.

He wondered if he would ever get used to seeing those mountains without feeling a flutter in his stomach each time he looked. It was hard, Joe thought, not to be intimidated by the Tetons. There were no other mountains like them in the world; so new, sharp, and lethal that foothills hadn't yet had the courage to approach them. He wondered if Will Jensen had ever gotten used to them. How could something that dramatic ever really provide the comfort of familiar scenery?

TRAFFIC SOUTH TO JACKSON through Grand Teton National Park was heavy, and Joe became part of a long parade of vehicles. The highway was choked with huge recreational vehicles helmed by older drivers who apparently thought the fifty-five-mile-per-hour speed limit was a challenge they wouldn't dare confront. He settled in, unable to pass because the exodus of tourist traffic in the oncoming lane was just as dense. Driving cautiously, he knew that the sighting of a moose, elk, or bear from the highway would instantly cause visitors to hit their brakes and, without pulling over to the shoulder, pour out of their vehicles with cameras and camcorders. On his left the ground rose in a gentle swell toward the Gros Ventre Mountains. On the raised flats, barely visible from the road, were old dude ranches. The movie *Shane* had been filmed on one of them, Joe remembered. It was the only movie he and his father had ever agreed on, maybe the only *thing* they had ever agreed on. Then he realized something that both scared and exhilarated him: *This was his new district.* As far as he could see in every direction, from the Tetons to the west, Gros Ventres to the east, Yellowstone Park to the north, to the town of Jackson ahead of him to the south, was his new responsibility.

Jackson was just a couple of hundred miles from Saddlestring, Joe thought, but it was a world apart.

THE BIG NEW TWO-STORY STATE BUILDING had a parking lot in front for visitors and a private lot in back for employees of various agencies. Joe cruised through the staff lot, looking for a parking space, but they all appeared to be designated. The only open one he saw was marked for W. JENSEN. Even though there wasn't anywhere else available behind the building, he chose not to use it. Not yet. Instead, he wheeled around the front, parked between two RVs, and entered the building through the double doors.

In the lobby, tourists stood and rifled through a rack of brochures offering horseback rides, an aerial tram ride to the top of the Tetons, chuck wagon cookouts, whitewater rafting, and other excursions, as well as accommodations.

A dark-skinned, wizened woman with coal-black hair peered over her gold-framed glasses at him as he approached her counter carrying his battered briefcase and day-pack. He nodded his hat brim to her, and she nodded back.

"Joe Pickett," he said.

She stood. She was not much taller standing than she had been sitting down. "Mary Seels. We expected you five days ago."

"Hello, Mary. I was helping my supervisor with a bear. You should have gotten word from dispatch that I'd be late."

She assessed him. He thought he saw a slight smile on her mouth, as if she were hiding her amusement. "I've heard about you."

He nodded again, not taking the bait, not saying, *What have you heard?* But he thought he already had her figured out, simply by the way she looked at him, with the same dispassionate sharpness of one of Nate's falcons, and by the way she projected her innate territoriality. Mary was the one who ran the place, he thought. She appraised him as if he had walked into the building hat in hand looking for the last bed in town, and she had the power to give it to him or turn him away.

"Will said you were a good guy," she said.

"I'm glad to hear that. I thought quite a bit of Will."

"If Will says you're a good guy, you're a good guy," she said, more to herself than to Joe. "I suppose you want to use his office?"

Inwardly, Joe cringed. He had not parked in Will's space because he felt he was encroaching.

"How many offices are in this building?" he asked.

She ticked her head from side to side like a metronome as she silently counted. "Twenty-some. We've got biologists, habitat specialists, fisheries guys, and communications people. Plus a library and a conference room. There's a corral out back. Will's four horses are kept there."

"Twenty offices," Joe repeated. "In my district I work out of my house. In a space about as big as your counter here."

"That's interesting," she said, her tone dismissive. "I hope you don't get lost here."

"Me too," he said.

There were a few beats of silence as Joe and Mary looked at each other.

"Are you going to move in or not?" she asked finally.

"Any empty rooms?"

"A couple. But they have the lousiest furniture, if they have furniture at all. People raid the empty offices for what they want all the time. You'll need a desk, won't you? A computer that works?" She was still testing him. "You know you want Will's office, so just take it."

He started to protest, but thought better of it. "Okay, ma'am."

"You can call me Mary," she said, again with that ghost of a smile, "but if you call me ma'am you'll get a hell of a lot better service around here."

He smiled at her.

"The office is upstairs," she said, and sat down to answer a ringing phone. "All of his files and records are up there. I'm sure you'll want to look at them."

"Yup."

Joe gathered his briefcase and pack from her counter and began to climb the wide stairs to the second floor. Mounted elk, deer, and big horn sheep heads watched his progress with glass-eyed indifference, as if they'd seen the likes of *him* before.

"Hey, Joe Pickett," Mary called out from her desk.

He stopped on the top step and turned to her.

She lowered the phone and cupped her hand over the receiver. "You might have a call here in a minute. Someone is saying there are some people pitching a tent out in the middle of the elk refuge. You might have to go check that out and kick them off."

He hesitated. "Okay . . ."

"And you have several messages from your wife. She didn't sound very happy." Mary smiled for the first time. It was a smile of pity.

"She didn't get the dispatch message either," he said.

"Welcome to Jackson Hole," she said.

WILL JENSEN'S NAMEPLATE WAS STILL in a fake brass slider next to the third door on the left. Joe hesitated, looking up and down the hallway, then cautiously opened the unlocked door and let it swing slowly inward. The mini-blinds covering the window were closed but bled laddered light. He waited a few beats before stepping inside. He couldn't help feeling voyeuristic, and a little ghoulish. Joe didn't want to be seen entering, didn't want anyone saying later that he had just barged into Will's old office like he owned the place. He reached inside the doorway, found the switch, and turned on the lights.

Joe's first impression was that Will had left the office planning to return to it. Papers fanned across the desk. An open can of Mountain Dew was on a coaster. A ballpoint pen, cap off and to the side, sat on the top of a large, thin spiral notebook. The fan on Will's computer hummed, indicating that it was sleeping and not turned off.

Joe stepped inside, leaving the door open, and dumped his briefcase and day-pack in the chair opposite the desk.

Overall, the room was spartan, the office of someone who rarely used it or couldn't get away from it fast enough. That fit with what Joe knew of Will and most of the other game wardens. Their actual workplace was outside, not inside. They used their desks with hesitation and profound regret, spending only as much time there as absolutely necessary between bouts in the field.

A cheap bookcase was a quarter filled with departmental memo binders and statute books. A retro Winchester Ammunition calendar was pushpinned into the wall. There were no personal photos, no drawings from his children. The only adornment was a framed, faded photo hanging on the wall, cocked slightly to the left, of the elk refuge in winter. Joe instinctively knew that Mary, or maybe Will's wife—but not Will—had put it there.

The left wall was dominated by a large-scale Forest Service map of the North Jackson district. Pins with tiny paper flags numbered 1 through 37 indicated where the licensed outfitter camps were located. The camps followed river drainages in a march toward Yellowstone.

Joe sat in Will's chair, still reluctant to settle in. The chair was uncomfortable, and was much older than the building itself. Joe wondered if one of the other employees had swapped out a chair at the news of Will's demise. He brushed the pen aside and looked at the spiral notebook. The red cover had a large "#10" written on the outside in black marker. Inside were entries scribbled in a tiny, cribbed block print.

> **10/02—0600. Rosie's / Box Creek / front country.**
> **MI 567B Blk GMC / Rosie's / Call / Okay per Disp.**
> **PA 983 Silver Ford 3/4 / HT / Rosie's / Call / Okay per Disp.**
> **WY 2-4BX Green Yukon / Rosie's / Call / Antlerless. Citation issued.**
> **1700—Turpin. 6b, 2s, 2 Wtbucks. Okay . . .**

Joe quickly figured out Will's shorthand code. It was similar to the notes he kept in his own field notebooks. In translation, the notes said that on October 2 at 6 A.M., Will was patrolling Rosie's Ridge and the Box Creek front country in his pickup, checking on elk hunters. While he didn't see the hunters themselves, who had most likely left their vehicles and set up somewhere in the vast country to look for elk, Will noted their parked vehicles—a black GMC from Michigan, a silver Ford three-quarter-ton pickup with Pennsylvania plates, and a green Yukon with Wyoming plates. Will had called in each of the plates to dispatch and requested a cross-reference computer check to determine the name of the hunter and whether or not that hunter had obtained a permit from the department to hunt elk in the area. While the out-of-state hunters checked out ("Okay per Dispatch"), the Wyoming hunter had a license that only allowed him to hunt antlerless elk, which meant his particular season didn't open up for two more weeks. Will had located the Wyoming hunter, confirmed that he had violated regulations, and issued a citation.

Later in the afternoon, at 5 P.M., Will had patrolled

through the Turpin Meadow campground at about the time that the first backcountry hunters were returning to their camps. The hunters had harvested six bull elk, two spike elk (yearling bulls), and two whitetail buck deer. All the kills had been clean and legal by properly licensed hunters, because no warnings or citations were noted.

Joe closed the notebook and sat back. The notes, once deciphered, presented a detailed account of his movements and actions. Using the notebook, citation book, and call-in record, a determined investigator could easily document what he did all day. Joe found that reassuring in his circumstances, since nearly everyone he encountered in the field was armed. The only game wardens who did mind, Joe knew, were the few with extracurricular activities like drinking while on duty or visiting lonely wives.

He reopened notebook #10 and scanned it. Since it was not yet October 2, it was from a previous year. On the last page with writing on it, in tiny script, he found where Will had written down the date of the year before. There were twenty or so fresh pages at the end of the notebook with no notes on them. Joe flipped back to page one, saw that the first entry was 01/02. So Will used a single spiral notebook for a given year.

He pushed back his chair and opened the desk drawers. They were remarkably empty, again the sign of a man who rarely used his office. But in the bottom left drawer he found a stack of new and used spirals exactly like the one on the desktop. Joe pulled them out and fanned them across the desk. The used notebooks were numbered 1 through 9, and were ragged and swollen with wear. The tenth he had already looked at. There were four unused notebooks, all clean and tightly bound. In the bottom of the drawer was a balled-up sheet of thin plastic, the original wrapper for the sheaf. Joe unwrapped the plastic and unfolded the paper band that had held the notebooks together. On the band it said there were fifteen to the package.

Which meant that the spiral for the current year was missing. Or in Will's pickup (where Joe kept his) or in Will's home. Joe opened his briefcase and slid all the notebooks into it. He would read them when he had the time, probably in the evening. What else would he have to do? He was determined to find #11.

JOE NEEDED TO CALL MARYBETH and smooth things over. But as he reached for the phone, he felt more than heard the presence of someone in the doorway, and he looked up with a start.

"Are you here for the funeral tomorrow?" a man asked in place of a greeting.

Joe pushed back awkwardly from the desk because one of the rollers on the chair was damaged, and stumbled when he stood up. The man in the doorway was tall and thin with light blue eyes, sandy hair, and a pallor that came from working indoors in an office. He wore a tweed jacket over a turtleneck, and Wrangler jeans so new they were still stiff. The trendy hiking boots that poked out from his jeans looked like they had been taken out of the box only a few hours before.

Joe introduced himself and held out his hand. The man shook it languidly, and pulled his hand away quickly.

"Should I know you?" Joe asked.

"I would think so," the man said. "I'm Assistant Director Randy Pope. From headquarters in Cheyenne. You were supposed to be here Monday night."

Joe certainly recognized the name, even though he had never met Pope personally. Randy Pope was in charge of fiscal matters for the agency. Most of the memos that crossed Joe's desk concerning procedure, the wage and salary freeze, the abuse of overtime and comp time, the unaccountability of game wardens in the field, had been issued by Randy Pope.

"Nice to meet you, Mr. Pope," Joe said, trying to sound friendly. "I'm late because I was helping Trey Crump out with a problem bear."

"The director is out of the state at a conference," Pope said, disregarding Joe's explanation. "He asked me to come to the funeral on behalf of the agency."

That explains your getup, Joe thought. *This is how you think people dress in Jackson.*

"You probably know I'm here to fill in," Joe said, feeling the need to explain why he was behind the desk in Will Jensen's old office.

Pope shifted his eyes from Joe to something over and to the right of Joe's head. "I heard about that," he said flatly. Clearly, Joe thought, Pope didn't approve of the arrangement. "We expected you earlier this week."

Joe patiently explained the hunt for the bear, saying he didn't know if the dispatcher forgot to forward the message or whoever got it didn't inform the office. Pope didn't seem to accept the excuse.

Joe had heard through Trey and others that Randy Pope desperately wanted to be named the next director. The current director was rumored to be short for the world, thanks to the pending gubernatorial election, and an opening would be likely. Directors were chosen at the discretion of the governor and the Game and Fish Commission, and historically had come from within the department, from the ranks of game wardens or biologists. To Joe's knowledge, there'd never been a director who came from the administrative side of the agency, the side that issued memos. Yet it was said that Pope had done his best to ingratiate himself with both gubernatorial candidates, as well as with the legislators who oversaw the department. He positioned himself as a man who was both within and without; a fiscally responsible insider who would curb rampant financial abuses as well as rein in the cowboys in the field. Joe had no doubt he was considered one of the cowboys.

Pope said, "Joe, do you realize what kind of trouble our agency is in these days?"

The question was out of left field, Joe thought. He shook his head.

"We're running deficits, bleeding red. We're being asked to take on more and more responsibilities by the state and the Feds, but our income streams are drying up."

This was no secret to Joe. Salaries had been capped and positions cut statewide.

"There are fewer hunters out there every year, Joe. It's no longer socially acceptable in many parts of the country to be a hunter. That means fewer hunting licenses are being purchased every year, which means less money for the agency to manage wildlife and everything else that has been thrown to us by the Feds—wolves, grizzly bears, endangered species . . . you name it. The only way to keep our division healthy is to practice sound fiscal management and good public relations. You never know when we'll have to go to the legislature for money."

"I'm aware of that," Joe said, not knowing where this was going.

"Are you?" Pope asked sharply.

"Yes."

Pope sighed. "I see everything, Joe. I'm the one who has to sign off on all of our expenses."

"Right."

"You don't know what I'm getting at, do you, Joe?"

"Nope," Joe said. But now he did.

"In the past six years, we've replaced two pickup

trucks, a horse, and a snowmobile for you. Total losses, all of them. That's the worst damage record in the state."

Joe felt anger start to rise.

Pope continued, the cadence of his words speeding up until he was literally biting them off. "You arrested the governor. You got in the middle of a vital endangered-species issue. You pissed off one of the governor's biggest contributors—who later got killed in your presence. Let's see . . . what else?" Pope pretended to be pondering, then answered his own question. "That Sovereign thing up in the mountains, that was next. We are *still* working on repairing our relationship with the Forest Service over that one."

Joe crossed his arms and waited for him to finish.

"Last year you *hit* a guy with your third pickup, right?" Pope said. "You smashed in the grille and bent the frame. What did that cost?"

"A few thousand," Joe said.

"The actual cost was six thousand, seven hundred," Pope spit out.

"I've also lost two service weapons," Joe said. "One got burned up in a fire, and the other got blown up by a cow. Don't forget those."

That stopped Pope for a minute, threw him off balance. He recovered quickly and went on. "Now we've got a game warden who got boozed up and blows his head off. He's not our first casualty lately. An outsider, or a legislator, might just think we're an agency out of control."

Joe's ears burned, and anger swelled in his chest. He tried to stay calm. Joe said, "You're out of line, Pope. I don't know what happened with Will Jensen yet, but you need to watch what you say. Will was never out of control. He devoted his life to the department, and maybe that's what finally got to him. Maybe the pressure you and your kind put on him finally made him break. He lost his family, Pope, but he kept working for you."

Pope started to argue but Joe raised his hand to silence him.

"That guy I hit with my truck deserved to be hit," Joe said. "He was in the act of mutilating someone, and that was the only way to stop him. Everything you mentioned was justified. It was all investigated, and I received no reprimands from my supervisor or anyone else who mattered."

Pope's eyes bulged. "But can't you see how it looks? I'm trying to keep our costs down and improve our image. I'm trying to help this agency *survive*. You are *not* helping me very much."

Bitter silence hung in the air between them. Joe fought the urge to spin Randy Pope around and kick him out of the office, right in the seat of his brand-new jeans.

Joe said, "I don't figure it's my job to make you look good, Assistant Director Pope. I think I've got a higher calling than that."

Pope glared at Joe. His face was flushed, and Joe could see little blue veins like earthworms pulse at his temples.

"So," Pope said, sarcastically, "*you have a higher calling*. But you're in Jackson Hole now, Joe. If you fuck up here, everybody will know it. You've got to be more respectful here. That starts with showing up on time."

"You know what?" Joe said. "I'm already getting tired of hearing that."

"And if you screw up, you're gone. Count on it," Pope said. "If we do another round of budget cuts, you'll be the first to go if I have any say in it."

Pope spun on his heels and was gone down the dark hallway.

"See you at the funeral," Joe called out to him. Then

he rubbed his eyes furiously. Will's funeral, yes. But maybe the beginning of his own career's funeral, he thought.

WHEN HIS TELEPHONE RANG IT took a few moments to figure out which button to push to answer it. Finally, he stabbed a lighted button and raised the receiver.

"Joe, this is Mary."

"Hi, Mary."

"That situation I told you about? With the people pitching a camp in the middle of the elk refuge?"

"Yes."

"It's been confirmed."

"I'll be right down."

AS HE PASSED THE COUNTER with his day-pack and brief-case, Mary called out after him. "Your dispatch code is 'Jackson GF60,' Joe."

He paused at the door. "Okay, ma'am."

She smiled at him, warmly this time. "That's good. I like that."

He strode into the parking lot to his truck, stopped, turned, and went back into the lobby. Mary looked up.

"How do I find the road to get into the refuge?" he asked.

She pointed due north and gave him directions to the access.

PART TWO

It must be admitted that the existence of carnivorous animals does pose one problem for the ethics of Animal Liberation, and that is whether we should do anything about it.

PETER SINGER,
ANIMAL LIBERATION

What we eat depends on where we live and how we have come to look at ourselves.

JIM HARRISON,
THE RAW AND THE COOKED

8

INSTEAD OF ELK ON THE NATIONAL ELK REFUGE, JOE could see a half dozen trumpeter swans near a marsh, looking like pure white flares against the rust-colored reeds on Flat Creek. In the distance in front of him on the sagebrush plateau, three mangy coyotes fed on something dead. Beyond the coyotes were two tiny dome tents strategically placed in view of the north-south highway into town. He approached the tents from the north, driving slowly over a worn two-track that wound through the flat of the 25,000-acre refuge. The coyotes scattered and loped away, then stopped and posed, waiting for him to pass so they could return to whatever it was they were eating. The late afternoon sun was an hour from dropping behind the Tetons, but already shadows from the peaks were creeping across the valley floor. In the winter, the area would be transformed, as the heavy snows in Yellowstone and Grand Teton national parks forced the herds south to the refuge, where they were fed alfalfa pellets to survive. The National Elk Refuge historically held between 7,500 and 11,000 elk, with thousands more fleeing to other refuges less well known.

As Joe drove across the field, he kept thinking about his confrontation with Randy Pope, and he knew there was unfinished business with him. Pope would be watching him like a hawk, waiting for him to screw up. Knowing his own personal history, he would. And there was something else troubling him, making him feel on edge, that he couldn't yet place. Something about Will Jensen's office. An impression that was beginning to form just before Pope walked in and blew it all away. What was it?

THERE WAS NO VEHICLE by the tents, but Joe could see a car parked about a mile and a half away on the other side of the eight-foot elk fence near the highway. The campers, for whatever reason, had obviously scaled the fence and walked in. With all of the campsites in the national forests and parks, Joe wondered why they had chosen the wide, treeless flat in sight of the highway and within earshot of the sizzling traffic. There was also some kind of construction project going on near the tents. Two people—men—were digging postholes in the ground. Near them was a long flat object, some kind of sign.

When a slim blond woman emerged from one of the tents and stood facing his pickup with her arms crossed in front of her and a defiant, determined look on her face, he realized why they were there. It wasn't a campsite—it was a statement.

Always cognizant of the risks of barging into the middle of someone's camp—even an illegal camp—Joe stopped his truck thirty yards away and shut off the motor. He swung out, clamped on his hat, and called, "Nice afternoon, isn't it?" Joe had long ago learned that the first words out of his mouth often set the tone for an encounter. Since he was nearly always outnumbered and generally outgunned, he preferred a friendly, conciliatory introduction. But he had a few other tricks as well. Never walk right up to someone as if squaring off. Always be a little to the side, so they have to turn a little to talk with you. Keep moving laterally without being obvious, so no one gets behind you. Maintain enough distance so that no one can reach out and grab you.

The two men digging the postholes stopped their work, which Joe sensed they didn't really mind doing. Both were in their twenties, one thin and wiry, the other soft and fat. The soft, fat man had dark circles of sweat under the arms of his sweatshirt and his forehead was beaded with moisture. The wiry man wore tiny round glasses and was pale from exertion. They both looked to the woman to speak for them after Joe's greeting.

"I've never seen you around here before," she said in a clear voice, "but I'm glad you like our weather."

"I'd guess that when the shadows from the mountains come over, it'll drop twenty degrees."

"Maybe thirty," she said.

"Hope you can stay warm," he said, looking at the tents. They were lightweight hiking models. He glimpsed a crumpled sleeping bag through one of the openings. He saw no sign of firearms.

He walked within a few feet of her and to the side and tilted his hat back on his head and stuffed his hands in his pockets; another deliberate, nonthreatening gesture. He could see her relax, almost instinctively. She was not unattractive, he thought, despite her complete lack of makeup and unkempt long straight hair, not so much parted as shoved out of the way of her face. She had delicate features and sharp cheekbones. She wore a fleece pullover, faded jeans, and hiking boots.

"You must be the new guy," she said, looking him over. "Are you here to replace Will Jensen?"

"At least for a while," Joe said, and introduced himself. He reached out to shake her hand, which meant that she had to uncross her arms.

"My name is Pi Stevenson," she said, almost demurely.

"Pleased to meet you," Joe said, and introduced himself to the posthole diggers. The slim man was named Ray and the fat man Birdy.

After meeting Birdy, Joe turned and looked at the sign that was lying flat on the ground, nailed to two long posts.

" 'Jackson Hole Meat Farm,' " he said aloud. Under the huge block letters was a smaller line that read animal liberation network. Then he looked up at Pi. "What does that mean?"

The defiance he had seen earlier returned to her eyes. "That's what this refuge is, a meat farm. It's a place where you feed and fatten wild creatures so that humans can slaughter them and eat their flesh in the name of *so-called sport*." She spit out the last two words.

As if hearing an unspoken command from Pi, Ray and Birdy lifted the sign and dropped the posts into the holes in the ground. The sign was now visible from the highway. Joe looked up and saw an RV slow, then pull off to the shoulder so the driver could read it.

"This Animal Liberation Network," Joe asked, "is that your outfit?"

"It's all of us," Pi said, indicating Ray and Birdy as well. "We're just a small part of a much bigger movement."

"Can Ray and Birdy talk?" Joe asked innocently.

Pi flared a little. "Of course they can. But I'm our spokesperson."

"I bet you get lonely in Wyoming," Joe said.

"*Yes*," she said, emphatically. "This may be the most

barbaric place there is. You can't even walk into a restaurant without being surrounded by the severed heads of beautiful animals."

"Then why are you here?" Joe asked.

She crossed her arms again. "Because the best place to make a statement about injustice is where the injustice is taking place, isn't it? Someone's got to be strong and brave."

Birdy interjected, "Pi's famous. She's the toughest, most compassionate person in the movement."

"I see that," Joe said.

"Thanks, Birdy," Pi said, rewarding him by sending him a sweet smile. Birdy flushed.

"So you're putting the sign here so that people coming into or out of Jackson will see it from the highway?" Joe asked, nodding at the line of cars that had now pulled to the shoulder to look at them. "To raise awareness of your issue?"

"That's correct," she said. "The two newspapers and the wire service guy interviewed me this afternoon, so we should get some play there."

"Hmmmm," Joe said, noncommittally.

"You're a flesh-eater, aren't you?" she asked Joe. "I bet you're convinced that humans are on one level of being and animals are beneath them. That animals are on this earth to serve us at our pleasure, to be our 'pets' when we want them to be and our food when we want to murder them and eat them."

Joe thought about it. "Yup, pretty much," he said. "I've heard it said that the definition of a Wyoming vegetarian is someone who eats meat only once a day."

He couldn't get her to warm up.

"You have so much to learn," she said. "But I don't hate you because you're ignorant. Have you ever heard the saying 'An insect is a cat is a dog is a boy'?"

"Nope," Joe said, a little disappointed that she hadn't even cracked a smile at his joke.

"It means we're all interconnected. We're *all* life. There aren't degrees of life, there is only life. Eating beef or elk is the same as eating a child. There's no difference. It's all just meat."

Joe winced.

"Americans, on average, eat fifty-one pounds of chicken every year, fifteen pounds of turkey, sixty-three pounds of beef, forty-five pounds of pork," she said. She was getting into it, stepping toward Joe, gesturing with her hands in chopping motions. "Then there's lamb—lamb!—and veal. Out here these people eat even more red meat than that, like deer and the elk that will be fed and fattened at the place we're standing. Wouldn't it be wonderful to see all of those creatures every day, instead of murdering them for their flesh?" She talked as if she were quoting, Joe thought.

He didn't want to get into the debate, but he had a question. "Isn't it different for a man to hunt his own food than to buy it wrapped in cellophane in a grocery store? And what about these elk? Would it be better if they starved to death in the winter? There isn't enough natural habitat for them anymore. They'd die by the thousands if we didn't feed them."

Pi had obviously heard this argument many times before and didn't hesitate. "As for your first question, meat is meat. As I said, an insect is a cat is a dog is a boy. As for your second, we never should have gotten to this stage in the first place. If we weren't raising the elk for slaughter, and feeding them, we wouldn't have this problem."

Joe nodded. "But we *do* have this problem. We can't solve it now by just saying we shouldn't have it, can we?"

"Touché," she said, smiling. "You have a point, if a weak one. But I've accomplished what I set out to do here."

"Which is?"

"To get you thinking."

Joe smiled back.

"So, are you going to arrest us?" she asked.

"Did Will arrest you?"

"Many times. Once he arrested me up on Rosie's Ridge, in the middle of an elk camp. I dressed up like an elk with these cute little fake antlers"—she raised her hands and wiggled her fingers over her head to simulate cute little antlers—"and walked around the hunters going, 'Who killed my beautiful wife? Who shot my son? Who shot my baby daughter in the guts?'"

"It was so cool," Birdy added. "She had those bastards up there howling."

Joe stifled a grin. The way she told the story was kind of funny. "Yup, I bet they were."

"I went a little too far with that one," Pi said. "It was too much too soon. The Wyoming legislature passed an anti–hunter harassment law after that, and Will was really angry with me. He said I wouldn't be accomplishing anything if I got myself shot, although I disagreed at the time. The movement *needs* a martyr. But I was too strident, I admit it. I even threatened Will, just so you know. I wrote letters to the editor about him, and put a picture of him on our website with a slash through it. I went a little overboard. He was just doing his job. So now we've scaled things back a bit. We need to work in incremental steps, to raise awareness."

"Which is what you're doing here," Joe said.

"Correct."

Joe shrugged. "Okay," he said, and started to walk to his pickup.

"Hey," Pi called out. "Aren't you going to arrest us?"

Joe stopped, looked over his shoulder, said, "No."

"But we're breaking the law," she said. Joe saw Birdy

exchange glances with Ray. As Joe had figured from seeing the light camping tents and the three-season sleeping
bags, the campers weren't really prepared or equipped to
stay long. They wanted to be arrested in order to get
more media attention. The shadow of the Tetons had
already crept over the refuge, and it would freeze during
the night.

Pi looked desperate. "You're not just going to leave us
out here, are you?"

"Yes."

"There are some real extreme hunter-types in town,"
Birdy offered. "You ever heard of Smoke Van Horn?
He's crazy. He's probably heard of our sign out here.
What if Smoke and his pals come after us tonight?"

"I'm sure Pi here can reason with them," Joe said with
a grin.

Birdy looked at Pi. Ray looked at Birdy. Pi glared at
Joe.

"You're a bastard," she said.

"That was harsh," Joe said, still smiling.

"Pi . . ." Birdy started to say.

"Why don't you throw the sign in the back of my
truck," Joe said, "and kick some dirt in those holes. I'll
help you pack up and I'll give you a ride to your car so
you don't have to hike."

Pi set her mouth, furious.

"Pi . . ." It was Birdy again.

"You *are* a bastard," she said again.

PI SAT IN THE CAB of the pickup, fuming, while Joe drove
across the refuge toward the highway. Birdy and Ray
were in the back, in the open, huddled near the rear window in light jackets. The sign and the camping gear were
piled into the bed of the pickup. It was dusk, and Joe

could smell the sweet, sharp smell of sagebrush that was crushed beneath his tires. He reached forward and turned on his headlights.

"It's an interesting subject, animal rights," Joe said.

"It's more than a *subject* for some of us," Pi answered.

Joe ignored her tone. "I'm around animals all day long. Sometimes I wonder what those animals are thinking, if they're capable of thinking."

"You do?" This surprised her.

"How could you not?" he asked.

She seemed to be trying to decide if she wanted to engage him, or be angry and refuse to talk to him.

"In the end, it's all about meat," she said.

"What?"

"It's about meat. What we eat is what defines us. People are starting to wake up to that, even here."

Joe said nothing.

"Have you heard of Beargrass Village?" she asked, the words dripping with venom.

"Nope."

She looked over at him. "It's a whole planned community, and I hate it. For a few million, people can live in what they call a planned environment where meat is raised and slaughtered for their pleasure. They call it the Good Meat Movement."

Joe remembered what Trey had said about it. "I heard something about it recently. Is it a serious thing?"

"No, it's just a veneer," she said. "It's a way for rich people to feel good about themselves. That's what this valley is about, you know—rich people feeling good about themselves, and dominating the land and creatures that they feel are beneath them."

"Bitter," Joe said.

Pi snorted. "Yeah. You fucking bet I'm bitter. I'm bitter about a lot of things."

Like factory farms, she said. She quoted verbatim from a book she was reading, *Dominion: The Power of Man, the Suffering of Animals, and the Call to Mercy,* by Matthew Scully:

" 'When a quarter million birds are stuffed into a single shed, unable even to flap their wings, when more than a million pigs inhabit a single farm, never once stepping into the light of day, when every year tens of millions of creatures go to their death without knowing the least measure of human kindness, it is time to question old assumptions, to ask what we are doing and what spirit drives us.' "

Then she asked, as they approached her car, "What spirit drives you, Joe?"

He was glad the ride was just about over and he didn't have to answer that question.

"We're here," he said.

HE HELPED THEM LOAD THEIR CAR. It was completely dark now, with a cold white moon. Their breaths billowed in the cold. Birdy started the motor in order to get the heater running. Ray sat in back, amid their packs and tents. Pi opened the passenger door to climb in.

Joe said, "Pi, can I ask you something?"

"What? It's cold, you know."

"You told me you really went after Will Jensen."

She nodded. "It wasn't just once either."

"But later, you realized that you needed to tone down your act, and you forgave him because you realized he was just doing his job, right? That in a way he was trying to protect you from yourself."

She looked at Joe suspiciously. "Yes."

"Did you ever tell him?"

Her eyes widened. She hesitated. Then: "No."

"I was just wondering about that," Joe said, "since his funeral is tomorrow."

"Pi, are you coming in or not?" It was Ray, finally speaking. "You're letting out all of the heat."

Pi shot him a withering look and closed the door.

"You think I should go to his funeral?"

"It's not my place to say that," Joe said.

"I'll give it some thought," she said.

JOE TOLD HER GOOD NIGHT and got in his truck and thought of Mary's "Welcome to Jackson Hole" greeting, seeing it for the double meaning she likely intended.

As he swung onto the highway, he was struck by the realization that he had no idea where he was going to sleep that night. It was too late to ask anyone at the office who had the keys to the statehouse, since they'd no doubt gone home for the weekend. Regardless, he wasn't sure he would be allowed to stay there yet anyway, since it was a crime scene. Which meant he'd have to try to find a cheap motel to stay in.

And he still needed to talk to Marybeth.

9

AS JOE DROVE BACK TOWARD JACKSON, A PORSCHE BOX-ster convertible passed him like a shot, the blond-haired woman driver slicing in front of him to avoid an oncoming RV as Joe tapped his brakes to let her in. She shot a "Ta-ta!" type wave in appreciation and passed the next car in line. The Porsche had Teton County plates, so she was a local. A local maniac, Joe thought, watching her weave through traffic ahead. As the lights of town appeared, his stomach grumbled. He hadn't eaten all day.

JOE SAT ALONE IN A raucous Mexican restaurant filled with tourists and locals out on Friday night. He blanched at the prices on the menu, knowing that the meal would exceed his state per diem. But because it was already late and he was starved, he didn't rise and leave. Instead, he ordered a Jim Beam and water from the helpful waiter who had introduced himself as "Adrian from Connecticut."

He smiled when he found himself contemplating bean burritos and rice.

"The vegetarian plate?" Adrian asked, swooping in from somewhere behind him.

Joe shook his head. "Nope. I'm a flesh-eater."

"Oh my," Adrian said, crumpling up his nose.

Joe ordered another drink during dinner while he cleaned his plate and jotted down details from the ALN call-out in his notebook.

As he finished and leaned back, full and feeling the effects of the bourbon on an empty stomach, Adrian arrived with another drink.

"I didn't order this," Joe said.

"Compliments of the Ennises," the waiter said with a flourish. "They're at the bar."

Joe leaned to the side so he could see between the tables. The bar was in an adjoining room, darker than the dining room, through a rounded, Spanish-style doorway. A couple sat on stools with their backs to the opening. As he looked at them, they swiveled around.

The man was short, compact, with a stern, wide-open face and short silver hair. He wore a jacket over well-tailored clothing. He looked like the kind of man who charged through a room, head bowed, shoulders hunched, expecting everyone to get the hell out of the way. The woman was ivory pale, with piercing dark eyes and full, dark-lipsticked lips. She was well dressed, in a thick turtleneck sweater with a black skirt, black hose, and black high-heeled shoes with straps over her ankles. Because she rested her feet on the bottom rail of the stool, he could see the pale orbs of her knees where the hose tightened against them in the darkness. Her thick hair was haloed from a neon beer sign. Joe raised the new drink and mouthed, "Thank you."

The man nodded back, businesslike. She smiled, slightly, and turned back to the bar. Then something happened that surprised Joe. She looked back over her shoulder at him, directly at him, full-on at him, and brushed aside a thick bolt of auburn hair, before turning away again. He felt a stirring inside.

"Who are they?" Joe asked Adrian from Connecticut the next time he came by.

Adrian made an exaggerated step back. "You don't know Don and Stella Ennis? My goodness."

"I'm new here."

"Then you need to meet them," Adrian said. "I don't even know where to begin."

AFTER PAYING THE TAB, which exceeded his per diem by eight dollars and made him feel guilty, Joe went into the bar. Don and Stella Ennis were no longer on their stools. He checked the booths at the side of the bar, wanting to thank them but reluctant to disturb their late dinner. He couldn't find them.

Joe asked the bartender, "Did the Ennises leave?"

The bartender, like Adrian, widened his eyes when he heard the name. "Are you the new game warden?"

"Yes."

"Mr. Ennis left you this." He pushed a fresh drink across the bar and handed Joe a business card. It read:

DON ENNIS
Developer, Beargrass Village

Joe flipped the card over and found a handwritten message.

"Welcome to town," it said. "I worked with Will. I'll be in touch."

Joe took a sip of the drink, then pocketed the card and went outside. The night air, crisp and sharp, washed over him as he walked to his truck. He couldn't stop thinking about what had just happened. Had she really been looking at him that way? Had he really been looking back?

Yes, he thought, on both counts.

He needed to call Marybeth, but wanted his head to clear first. And he couldn't bring himself to call her while the image of Stella still lingered so clearly in his mind.

BEFORE FINDING A MOTEL, JOE used a street map ripped from a telephone book to locate Will Jensen's home. It was on one of the old, narrow tree-lined streets near the base of Snow King Mountain, in a neighborhood created forty years before Jackson became the resort it was. Joe remembered the house vaguely from his single visit, and he parked his pickup on the street and looked at it in its dark stillness. Will's truck was still in the driveway. A massive old cottonwood, leaves already turned and crisp, obscured half the roof. The windows were black squares, dead like the eyes of the head mounts in the office building.

Joe reluctantly climbed out of his truck and crossed the street. He tried to open Will's truck door but found it locked. He peered inside, could see nothing in the darkness. The only light was a faint blue vapor light on the corner and the hard stars and scythe of the moon. The keys for the truck, he assumed, would be somewhere in the office building, or with the sheriff, and he would get them tomorrow. Joe walked up the cracked cement walk, crunching dead leaves that were curled together like fists. Three red strips of crime-scene tape sealed the door to the jamb. A letter from the Teton County sheriff was taped inside the screen door, warning visitors that the house was sealed pending the investigation.

What would it be like to live in a house where the

previous occupant had shot himself in the head? Joe shivered and tried to shake off the thought.

HE FOUND A CHEAP MOTEL that honored state rates and checked in. The bedspread was green and thin, there was a single thin plastic cup and a bar of soap on the sink, and the television was locked to a stand and mounted to the wall so no one could take it. The tiny desk was just big enough to hold his briefcase.

Sitting on the bed, he put the spiral notebooks in front of him. He would start with #1 tonight, maybe get through #2. Tomorrow, he would begin the search for #11, Will's last notebook.

But first he needed to call home. He looked at his watch. It was 11:30, an hour past when they usually went to bed. He debated whether to possibly wake her, simply to tell her he had made it. Then he pictured Marybeth up and awake, maybe reading, upset he hadn't called, possibly worried that something had happened.

He picked up the telephone. The line was dead. The receptionist, a sleepy woman with bloodshot eyes, must have forgotten to turn on his phone when he checked in. Should he rouse her? He decided not to. He pulled out his cell phone from his day-pack, then punched the speed dial button. Marybeth answered in four rings.

"Joe?" He could tell she wasn't happy. She sounded tired, and there was an icy edge to her voice. "You were supposed to call when you got there."

"I didn't get a chance," he said. His speech was slurred, as much from exhaustion as the bourbon. "I was too busy getting reamed by the assistant director and then I got called out."

"It's nearly midnight."

"I know," he said lamely.

"Why didn't you call this afternoon, then?"

"I told you. I hit the ground running over here."

"I just fell asleep. What are you doing up?"

"I just got in."

His cell phone chirped. It was about to run out of battery power, and he needed to recharge it, he told her.

"You sound like you've been drinking, Joe. And why are you calling me on your cell phone?"

"I tried to call from my motel, but the phone wouldn't work."

"Where are you staying?"

Joe looked up. What was the name of it? Jesus . . . One of those old western television series names.

"You don't *know*?"

"The Rifleman," he said finally, feeling stupid.

"Okay . . ." There was an edge of suspicion in her voice, and Joe didn't like it.

"Marybeth, I couldn't call earlier, all right? I'm sorry. There's a lot going on here and I got wrapped up in it. I'll call tomorrow and we can catch up, okay?"

"I'm wide awake now, Joe," her voice hostile.

His cell phone blinked off. He cursed and stared at it as if that would make it come back on. The charger was in his truck, and he started to get up, but stopped at the door. He wasn't exactly sure where he'd put it, and looking for it would take a while. He was tired, and resentful of her again. What was she accusing him of? Didn't she know he had a job to do? Why was it necessary to pile on the guilt? He got lonely, just like she did. All he wanted was for her to say she loved him, she missed him, and that everything was going to be fine.

He sighed. He'd call tomorrow, when he had some time, when he'd gathered his thoughts. Maybe before the funeral.

He picked up notebook #1 and began to read. Soon, the writing began to swim off the page.

JOE AWOKE TO THE SOUND of gunshots. He sat up quickly, disoriented for a moment. He glanced around, remembering where he was, surprised that he was still dressed and the bedside lamp was on. The opened notebook was on his lap.

No, it wasn't a gun. It was something on the other side of the motel room wall. Joe stood, rubbing his eyes. He looked at his watch: 4:45 A.M. He heard rustling in the next room, then another bang. The sound was coming through his closet. He opened the closet door, where he'd hung his uniform shirt and jacket on hangers that couldn't be removed from the rod.

He sighed, knowing now what had happened. Someone in the next room was packing up their clothing from the closet. Because the hangers couldn't be taken off the rod, as each piece was removed the rod swung back and banged into the wall.

Cheap motels, Joe thought. State-rate motels. Marybeth probably imagined him in someplace much finer. Maybe he should call her now and tell her how great it was.

He shook his head, ashamed at his thoughts, while he gathered up the notebooks and papers on the bed and stowed them neatly in his briefcase. He brushed his teeth, folded his clothes, turned off the light, and crawled into bed.

That's when something about Will's office hit him. Will Jensen was a meticulous man, from what Joe knew about him. His notes were precise, detailed, well reasoned. His office was spare and utilitarian, without a single frill or anything personal in it. Will was known for his even temper, his calmness. He was probably like Joe, who even when flustered or bad-tempered couldn't just forget about something and move on until everything was neat and in order. It didn't fit that Will, contemplating his own suicide, would rise from his desk in his office with papers scattered and a half-drunk can of Mountain Dew on his desk, his computer still on, and go home and end it all. Wouldn't Will have at least cleaned up a little, knowing what he was going to do?

10

ON FRIDAY MORNING, EX–TWELVE SLEEP COUNTY SHER-iff O. R. "Bud" Barnum was seated at his usual place in the Stockman's Bar when he saw the stranger. The tall man stepped inside, let the door wheeze shut behind him, and stood there without moving, letting his eyes adjust to the darkness inside. It was eleven in the morning. Barnum didn't know the man, which in itself meant something. Barnum knew everybody.

Rarely did someone simply happen by Saddlestring, Barnum knew. The town was too out-of-the-way. It wasn't conveniently en route to anywhere. The ex-sheriff had studied strangers coming into his town for over thirty years. He could usually size them up quickly. They tended to fall into categories: outdoorsmen, roughnecks, tourists, ranch hands looking for work, junior sales representatives stuck with a bad, far-flung territory. This man wasn't any of those. Something about him, the way he moved and the fact that he seemed supremely comfortable in his own skin, Barnum thought, was menacing.

The tall man was in his late fifties or early sixties, with a shock of gray hair and a chiseled face. He was slim with broad shoulders, and Barnum noted how the stranger's dark brown leather coat stretched across his back as he found a stool and sat down. The man had a flat belly, which to Barnum was a physical characteristic he mistrusted. Cop, Barnum thought, or military. He had that ramrod-straight, no-nonsense air about him. Barnum wondered if the tall man felt the same thing about *him* sitting there. Barnum knew *he* looked like a cop, and always had. His mother once told him he looked like a cop when he was born. She said that even as a baby he had those suspicious, penetrating eyes, and the jowly, hangdog face that seemed to say, in cynical resignation, "*Now what?*"

Barnum had been reading the Saddlestring *Roundup* and drinking coffee. He hated both the local newspaper and the bitter coffee, but this is what he did now that he was retired. It was part of his routine. He still began each morning at the Burg-O-Pardner, as he had when he was sheriff, drinking coffee, catching up on local news and gossip, and eating rolls with the other local "morning men." The morning men at the Burg-O-Pardner were the men who owned most of Saddlestring and much of the county. Most were retired now as well, but still had local business interests. Guy Allen owned the Burg-O-Pardner and had the majority share of the Stockman's. Just that morning, Guy had been talking about the weather in Arizona, how pleasant it was. He'd be leaving soon, going to his home in Arizona, as winter moved into Wyoming. So would half of the other morning men. Barnum, who still lived full-time in Saddlestring and probably always would, got quiet during discussions of Arizona weather. Any chance he'd had of buying a winter place somewhere warm had disappeared when a bad land investment the previous year had taken his pension, and the ensuing scandal had cost him his job and his reputation. All that was left of his career was a solid gold Parker pen his deputies had chipped in for. The pen was inscribed: TO SHERIFF BARNUM FOR 28 YEARS OF SVC. "svc" meant "service," McLanahan had explained, but the inscriber ran out of room on the pen.

He was acutely aware of how differently the morning conversations flowed since he was no longer sheriff. The men used to listen to him, to defer, to stop talking when he spoke. They would nod their heads sympathetically when he complained. Now he could see them glancing at one another while he spoke, waiting for him to finish. Sometimes, the mayor would cut him off and launch into a new topic. He was just another retired old bastard, taking up their time. The kind of old fart Barnum used to glare at until the interloper would pick up his coffee cup and go away.

When the morning men broke up around 9:30, Barnum walked down the main street and set up shop here, in the Stockman's, where he would remain most of the day and some of the night. If people needed to talk to him, they knew where he would be. If someone came into the place before he got there and took his seat, which was the farthest stool at the corner of the bar where the counter wrapped toward the wall, the bartender would shoo the customer away when Barnum walked in. *That's Sheriff Barnum's office,* the bartender would say.

Barnum didn't stare at the tall man who had come into the bar. Instead, he shot occasional glances at him over the top of the half-glasses he needed to wear to read the paper. The tall man ordered coffee, and as he sipped it he looked around the place, taking in the ancient knotty pine and mirrored back bar, the mounted big-game heads that stared blankly down at him, the black-and-white rodeo photos that covered the wall behind him. The Stockman's was a long, narrow chute of a room with the bar taking up over half of it and some booths and a pool table at the back near the restrooms. A juke-box played Johnny Cash's "Don't Take Your Gun to Town."

As the bartender refilled the stranger's mug, the man asked him something in a muted voice. Barnum couldn't hear the exchange over the song on the jukebox. Then the tall man stood and nodded at Barnum. Barnum nodded back.

"Cute little town you've got here," the tall man said, making his way toward the bathroom.

"It doesn't look like a place that can eat you up and spit you out, does it?" Barnum asked.

The tall man hesitated a step, looked curiously at Barnum, then continued.

As the restroom door shut, Barnum slid off his stool, walked the length of the bar, and stepped outside. The cold sunshine blinded him momentarily, and he raised his arm to block out the sun. The tall man's late-model SUV was parked diagonally in front of the bar. Barnum circled it quickly, noting the Virginia plates, the mud on the panels probably from back roads, the fact that the back seat was folded down to accommodate duffel bags, hard-sided equipment boxes, and a stainless steel rifle case as long as the SUV floor. He walked back into the bar and assumed his seat.

Barnum raised a finger to the bartender, a half-blind former rodeo team coach named Buck Timberman. Buck had been a big-time bullrider but had retired after a bull stepped on his head and crushed it, resulting in brain damage. He still wore his national finals belt buck-les, though, rotating them so he wore a different one each day of the week. Barnum liked Timberman because Buck was staunchly loyal, even stupidly loyal, and he still referred to Barnum as "Sheriff."

"Changeover time," Barnum said, thrusting his coffee cup forward.

"It's only eleven-thirty," Timberman said, looking at his wristwatch. "You've got a half hour before noon."

"So it's one-thirty Eastern," Barnum growled, "which means we've wasted an hour and a half of drinking time."

Timberman frowned while he drew a beer and poured a shot. "Why Eastern time?"

"Our new friend here is used to Eastern," Barnum said. "Didn't you notice how he said 'here'? He said *'here'* like JFK. He's from Boston or someplace, but he's got Virginia plates and a lot of outdoor gear in his rig. Judging by the dirt on that car, I'm guessing he didn't fly and rent, he drove out all the way."

"I ain't seen him in here before," Timberman said, taking the coffee cup and replacing it with the draft and the shot.

"Nope," Barnum said. "He was asking you something a minute ago. What was it?"

Timberman looked over Barnum's shoulder to make sure the tall man wasn't coming back yet. "He's got an interest in falconry. He asked me if I knew of anybody around here who might have birds available. He also asked me if we have a range where he can sight in his hunting rifle. And he wanted to know where the bathroom is."

WHEN THE TALL MAN RETURNED he found a shot of bourbon and a glass of beer next to his coffee cup. He looked toward Timberman, who pointed to the ex-sheriff.

"Cheers," Barnum said, raising his shot glass and sipping the top off.

"Thanks are in order," the man said to Barnum, tentatively raising his whiskey, "but it's pretty early in the day."

Barnum said, "It's never too early to treat a visitor to some cowboy hospitality."

The tall man sipped half of his shot, winced, and chased it with a long pull from the beer, never taking his piercing brown eyes off Barnum.

"Who says I'm visiting?" the tall man asked.

Barnum tipped his head toward Timberman. "Buck here said you were asking about falcons."

"So much for the famed confidentiality of the bartending profession," the tall man said evenly. In his peripheral vision, Barnum could see Timberman suddenly look down at his shoes and shuffle away.

"I asked him," Barnum said. "What he told me will be treated with confidence."

The tall man's eyes narrowed. "And who are you, exactly?"

"I used to be the sheriff here," Barnum said.

"To a lot of us," Timberman interjected, "he'll always be our sheriff."

Barnum humbly nodded his thanks to Timberman.

The tall man seemed to be thinking things over, Barnum observed, trying to decide if he was going to say more or take his leave.

"I might be able to help you out," Barnum said.

The tall man turned to Timberman, and the bartender said, "You ought to ask the sheriff."

While the tall man pondered, Barnum closed his newspaper, folded it, and put his reading glasses and gold pen in his shirt pocket.

"Let me ask you this," Barnum said. "Are you looking for a falcon, or are you looking for a particular falconer?"

The tall man's face revealed nothing. "I don't believe we've actually met."

"Bud Barnum. You?"

"Randan Bello."

"Welcome to Saddlestring, Mr. Bello."

Bello picked up his shot and beer, walked down the length of the bar and sat down on a stool next to Barnum. Timberman watched, then went to the far end of the bar to wash glasses that were already clean.

"I'm looking for a falconer," Bello said, speaking low and looking at his reflection in the back bar mirror and not directly at Barnum.

"I know of a guy," Barnum said to Bello's face in the mirror. "He's got a place by himself on the river. Carries a .454 Casull. Is that him?"

Bello sipped his beer. "Could be."

Barnum described Nate Romanowski, and let a half-smile form on his mouth. "If he's the one, he's been a thorn in my side since he showed up in my county. Romanowski and a game warden named Joe Pickett. I've got no use for either one of them."

Bello turned on his stool and Barnum felt the man's eyes bore into the side of his head.

"So you can help me," Bello said.

At the end of the bar, Timberman made a loud fuss over cleaning some ashtrays.

"I can't think of anything I'd rather do," Barnum said, surprised that his bitterness betrayed him.

"I see."

Barnum said, "I understand you're looking for a place to sight in. There's a nice range west of town with bench rests. I could make a call."

"Let me buy the next round," Bello said.

11

IN JACKSON, THE FUNERAL SERVICE FOR WILL JENSEN was being held in a log chapel built to look much older and more rustic than it actually was. Joe sat in the next to last row wearing the same jacket and tie he had worn for the wedding of Bud Longbrake and Missy Vankueren. His clothes were wrinkled from his suitcase. He had arrived a half hour early, to observe the mourners as they arrived, after calling home to find no one was there. There was a dull pain behind his eyes from the bourbon the night before and a practically sleepless night. It was cold in the chapel, and he welcomed the throaty rumble of a furnace from behind a closed door near the altar, indicating that someone had turned up the thermostat.

A brass urn sat squarely on a stand atop a red tapestry in front of the podium. Damn, Joe thought, there wasn't much left of Will, just his ashes in the urn and a framed photo of him in his red game warden uniform. In the photo, Will was saddling one of his horses and turning to the photographer with a loopy smile on his face. Who knew what was so funny at the time? Joe wondered. On

the other side of the urn was a framed photo of the Jensen family—Will, Susan, his two sons wearing ill-fitting
jackets and ties. The photo looked to be a few years old
to Joe because the boys appeared to be the same age they
had been when he saw them in the Jensen house for the
first and only time. In the photo, the family looked stiff
but happy. All those ties made Will, and the boys, uncomfortable, he guessed.

JOE HAD SPENT THE MORNING in the office, reading
through the first three spiral notebooks and halfway
through the fourth. Patterns were emerging. During the
deep winter, in January when the notebooks all began,
Will spent a good deal of time in the office, writing up
reports on often-controversial policy issues that he was
required to comment on, and visiting with local ranchers, outfitters, and the Feds. Spring was consumed with
more reports and comments, but also preparations for
the summer and fall, working with his horses, repairing
tack and equipment, signing off on outfitter camp locations, and making recommendations for season lengths
and harvests. During the summer months, he was out in
the field nearly every day, checking licenses of fishermen
on the rivers and lakes, doing trend counts of deer, elk,
and moose, or horse-packing into the backcountry to
check his remote cabin and repair winter damage. Fall, as
Joe suspected, was a whirlwind of activity once the hunting seasons started and opener after opener arrived. The
pattern in the fall was the lack of a pattern, and at first
Joe thought Will was flying by the seat of his pants, dash-
ing from place to place. Will patrolled the front country
and backcountry seemingly at random, covering his district in a way that seemed haphazard. One day he would
be in the southeastern quadrant in his pickup, the next

he would be on horseback in the northwestern corner—where he might be gone for days. But then Joe saw the logic in it, and admired the way Will worked.

The only way a single game warden could be effective in nearly nineteen hundred miles of rough country was to be as unpredictable as possible, to keep his movements erratic. If he patrolled in a systematic way, sweeping from north to south or methodically along the river bottoms, the poachers and violators could anticipate his location and change their plans to avoid him. But by moving from here to there, front country to backcountry, changing his itinerary and location, they would never know when and where he might show up. Joe had no doubt the hunters and fishers—and especially the professional outfitters—shared information about Will's whereabouts. If they didn't know when he'd be patrolling the outfitter camps, and from what direction, they'd have to be ready for him at all times, meaning proper licenses, good camp maintenance, and adherence to rules and regulations.

Joe had experienced the "familiarity" of hunters and fishers before, and had learned to be friendly but closed-mouthed about his intentions. Over a beer at the Stockman's Bar or with his family at a restaurant or function in Saddlestring, someone occasionally sidled up to him in all apparent innocence and asked him about his day—where he'd been, if he'd seen game, where he might be going tomorrow. Although the questions were often just conversation, sometimes they were more than that.

He'd learned not to say anything.

JOE TURNED IN HIS PEW when he heard the door open behind him and a murmur of voices. Susan Jensen arrived at the chapel with her two boys and three older people, two women and a man. The older man, no doubt their grandfather, ushered the two young boys ahead of him and down the aisle. Will's boys were small versions of their father, Joe thought. Stolid, serious, all-boy. The younger one took a swipe at the older one when the older boy crowded him, and the embarrassed grandfather leaned forward to gently chastise him.

Susan looked to be much older than Joe remembered; her face was pinched, pale, and drawn. She had short-cropped brown hair, blue eyes, and was well dressed in a professional-looking suit. Joe stood, and she looked up and saw him. A series of emotions passed over her face in that instant: recognition, gratitude, then something else. Revulsion, Joe thought.

"I'm real sorry, Susan," he said, moving down the aisle toward her.

"Thank you for coming, Joe," she said. Her eyes were blank, but her mouth twitched. Joe guessed she was cried out. "It's good of you to come."

He didn't want to admit he was there to take over Will's district. He wanted her to think he was in Jackson on his own accord.

"Are other game wardens here?" she asked, looking quickly around the empty chapel.

"The assistant director will be coming," Joe said, wishing it was the director, or someone other than Randy Pope.

"Okay," she said vacantly. He could tell she was disappointed, but resigned to it. There was a lot going on in her mind, he thought. If Will had been killed as the result of an accident or at the hands of another while on duty, the chapel would have been filled with red shirts. But that was not the case.

"Are you coming to the reception later?" she asked.

He hadn't thought about it. "Yes," he answered.

"Good." Then: "Is your wife here? Marybeth?"

"She couldn't make it," he said. "School, too many things going on."

"I know how that goes," Susan said, her eyes already wandering from Joe. "The single-parent household."

Joe tried not to cringe.

"Maybe I'll see you at the reception," she said, extending her hand. He took it. It was icy cold.

JOE HAD JUST SAT BACK DOWN, still reeling from the look of distaste that had passed over Susan Jensen's face, when the back door banged open and a rough man's voice said, "Damnit."

Joe turned to see a man closing the door with exaggerated gentleness. Then the man wheeled and entered the chapel, blinking at its darkness.

The man was big, barrel-chested, thick-legged, a wedge shape from his broad shoulders in a sheepskin coat to the points of his lace-up high-heeled cowboy boots. He wore a stained and battered gray felt hat, which he immediately removed to reveal a steel-gray shock of uncombed hair. His bronze eyes burned under wild toothbrush eyebrows, and he squinted into the room like a man who squints a lot, looking for distant movement on mountainsides and saddle slopes. He was a man of the outdoors, judging by his leathery face and hands and thick clothing.

"Didn't mean to throw the door open like that," he mumbled to no one in particular.

And Joe stood to say hello to Smoke Van Horn.

Smoke pumped Joe's hand once, hard, and let go.

"You're the new guy, huh?" Smoke said, too loudly for the occasion, Joe thought. He could sense Susan Jensen and her boys turning to see what the commotion was about.

"Yes, sir," Joe replied softly, attempting to provide an example to Smoke to lower his voice.

"Hope we get along," Smoke said, just as loudly as before. "Me and Will had some issues. But he learned to get along with me. For a while, at least." Smoke barked a laugh at that.

In the notebooks he had read that morning, Smoke Van Horn's name had come up several times. Smoke had been accused of salting by another outfitter as well as by a National Park ranger. Salting involved hiding salt blocks to draw elk to where his paying clients could kill them. Will had written that he'd asked Smoke about salting, and although Smoke hadn't really denied it, he hadn't admitted it either.

"Dared me to locate the salt station," Will had written in his notebook. "Couldn't find it. Suspect it's somewhere on Clear Creek."

"I'll be seeing you around, I'm sure," Joe said softly.

"No shit." Smoke laughed again. "You'll be sick of me, I'd guess. I have strong opinions."

But let's not hear them now, Joe thought.

Smoke looked to the front of the chapel, saw the urn and the photos.

"For Christ's sake," Smoke said, "they put him in a *jar.*"

"It's an urn," Joe said, glancing toward Will's boys, who were now watching Smoke and no doubt hearing him. "And Smoke, please keep your voice down."

Smoke eyed Joe intently, narrowing his eyes. "Already telling me what to do?" Smoke said menacingly, but at least his voice was lower.

"Will's family is up front."

Smoke began to speak. Then, in an action Joe guessed was unusual, the outfitter didn't say anything for a moment. He leaned forward, and Joe could smell horses on his coat.

"Will was too damned tough and determined to kill himself like that," Smoke said to Joe, his voice low. "I spent many an hour with him in the backcountry. We rarely agreed on anything, but I suspect he thought I was right more than he would let on. But he wasn't, you know, troubled. Except for the last few months, when the son of a bitch wanted to ruin me."

Joe leaned closer to the outfitter. He asked quietly, "You don't think he killed himself?"

"No fucking way," Smoke said, his voice loud again. "Sorry, boys," he said toward the front of the chapel.

"I'd like to talk with you later," Joe said. More people were starting to arrive, and Smoke was oblivious to them. He was blocking the aisle.

"That's why I come," Smoke told Joe. "When a man sets out to ruin me, I take a real personal interest in him. So I had to make sure he really was dead. I didn't expect to see him in a jar. Or an urn, or whatever the hell it is."

"Later," Joe said firmly, finding his seat.

Smoke Van Horn ambled down the aisle, somehow exuding a presence that was bigger than his huge physical self. Joe guessed that when Smoke picked an aisle, the rest of it would remain empty as the mourners arrived to find seats.

He guessed correctly.

JOE KNEW VERY FEW OF THE MOURNERS, and most looked like locals. The majority sought out Susan and her boys, and either hugged her, waved sadly to her, or, in some cases, simply stood and shook their heads, commiserating.

Randy Pope chose Joe's aisle, but sat three seats away. That was fine with Joe.

Pi Stevenson came in with Birdy. She had combed her

hair and looked almost businesslike in a casual suit. When she saw Joe she smiled at him, and he nodded back.

He looked over his shoulder to see the Teton County sheriff and two deputies, who sat in the last row, behind Joe. They wore their uniforms, hats on their laps. Even though the service had started, Joe twisted in his seat and shook their hands, introducing himself. Joe assumed they had been the investigating officers at the Jensen home, since the sheriff, not the town police, had placed the notice on the door there. The sheriff, named Tassell, according to his badge, did not greet Joe warmly. Tassell was handsome, in a distant, preppy kind of way, Joe thought. He had longish hair and a gunfighter's mustache that drooped over both corners of his mouth. He was young and fit, his shirt and trousers crisp. He probably looked very good in campaign posters. He was the antithesis of Sheriff Barnum in Twelve Sleep County the way Jackson was the antithesis of Saddlestring.

"Can I talk with you after the service?" Joe whispered.

Tassell stared at Joe for several beats, then said, "Sure, if you have to."

Joe turned back around. Because he seemed to be the opposite of either Barnum or the brand-new Sheriff McLanahan, Joe had assumed Tassell would be more approachable. A phrase he'd overheard Sheridan tell Lucy floated through his mind—"When you assume you make an ass out of 'u' and me." He smiled wryly.

The reverend took his place behind the altar and said, "We will sorely miss Will Jensen. . . . "

JOE HADN'T SEEN STELLA ENNIS come into the chapel, but when he glanced over during the service she was there. She had slipped in alone and now sat two rows ahead of Joe on the opposite side of the aisle. When he leaned forward, he could see her more clearly.

She was younger than he had thought the night before. She was also more beautiful, and he studied her profile—a strong jaw, pert nose, thick lips painted a darker color than the night before, smooth, firm cheeks, slightly almond-shaped eyes under thick auburn bangs. She looked straight ahead, at the altar. As Joe watched, her shoulders began to tremble. She bowed her head forward so that her hair obscured her face. She stayed like that for several moments, and when she looked over at him, her eyes were glistening with tears.

Their eyes locked for a moment Joe could only describe as electric. In her eyes he thought he saw sadness, confusion, and, strangely, pity. Then, as if she realized she was transmitting her feelings, she looked away from him quickly, breaking it off.

Why, Joe wondered, was Stella Ennis at the funeral? And why was she crying?

12

"DO YOU NOTICE THE SAME THING I NOTICE ABOUT THE food here?" Pi Stevenson asked Joe at the reception, which was held in a small meeting room at a chain hotel near the funeral home.

He hadn't realized she was behind him in line. "What?" Joe said.

"No meat," she said, raising her eyebrows with a sense of triumph.

Joe looked at the table and then at his small paper plate. Crackers, cheese cubes, celery, carrots, dip.

"I hadn't noticed."

"These are the things I pick up on," she said. "There's cheese, though. So this isn't a vegan spread."

Joe *hmmmm*'d, and took a small paper cup filled with red punch. He sipped it, disliked it, and looked for a place to put it aside.

"I heard a rumor that before Will killed himself, he gorged on meat," Pi whispered to Joe. "That's probably why they don't have it here. Did you hear that rumor?"

"No."

"That's what I heard," she said again.

"I heard it too," Birdy said, eavesdropping.

Joe had no idea how to respond, or if he even wanted to. Pi and Birdy seemed to be drawing some kind of connection between what Will ate and what he later did.

At the far end of the room, Susan Jensen was surrounded by well-wishers. Joe waited for the crowd to part in order to have a word with her. Her boys were with their grandparents, trying to stand in one place and behave properly. But they were boys, and they were fidgeting.

Joe noted that Smoke hadn't come to the reception, and neither had Stella Ennis. Sheriff Tassell was there, however, with his deputies, who were loading up their plates for the third time.

When he looked back, Birdy was offering him a business card: wildwater photography. His full name was Trenton "Birdy" Richards.

"I help him out at the shop," Pi said, pointing at the card.

"I appreciate how you treated us yesterday," Birdy said. "It was, like, civil. So if you're ever on the river, like, if your family is with you or something, and you want a nice shot of you in the whitewater, just let me know. I'll give you, like, a deal."

Joe pocketed the card. "You stand on the bank and take pictures of rafters?"

Birdy snorted. "I used to do that, like, when I first got started. Not anymore. I've got a full-auto setup now. Photocells on the rafts signal the camera, and I just download the digital images every afternoon. The pictures are ready when the rafters get off the water."

"Interesting," Joe said, making conversation.

"Pretty slick, is what it is," Birdy said, pleased with himself.

"Excuse me," Joe said, seeing the sheriff and taking leave of Pi and Birdy.

SHERIFF TASSELL LOOKED UP AS Joe approached, but continued to eat a cracker with a cheese cube. His animus was palpable. Joe assumed that Tassell was being territorial, like every county sheriff Joe had ever met, but he forged ahead anyway.

"I'd like to be able to get into the Game and Fish house later today if I could," Joe said. He pointedly did not say *Will Jensen's house.* "I couldn't find any keys at the office. I assume you're done inside."

Tassell didn't look directly at Joe, but continued to chew. "I don't know what you might hope to find in there that we haven't already looked at."

"I'm not sure you understand," Joe said, his voice patient. "That's where I'm expected to stay while I'm here. The department doesn't have the budget to put me up in a hotel while their house sits empty."

Hotel rooms in Jackson were by far the most expensive in the state, Joe knew. He was keenly aware that he had already overspent his per diem and the overage would need to come out of the family budget, stretched as it was.

Tassell met Joe's eyes for a moment, then looked away again. "I figured you were checking up on us."

Well, Joe thought, *that too.*

"I'll visit with my team and make sure they're through," Tassell said with no enthusiasm. "I need to run it by the ME also. I think he got the place all cleaned up, but I'm not sure about that. A .44 Magnum going through soft tissue makes a hell of mess on the ceiling and walls."

Joe said quietly, "I'll bet it does."

"I think his personal effects have been pretty much cleaned out and given to the wife." Tassell looked toward Susan Jensen. "Just a bunch of boxes. Clothes and stuff like that."

Joe wondered if he should ask to see them at some point.

"Do you know if there were any spiral notebooks in there?" Joe asked.

Tassell shrugged. "I don't remember any, but I didn't personally pack up everything or really look it over myself."

Yes, Joe would need to look inside the boxes. "Do you have his truck keys at your office? His truck's locked up."

"I believe we do," Tassell said woodenly.

"Can I—"

Tassell cut Joe off with a hard glare. "Look, I'm busy this afternoon. I can't just drop everything and cater to you. I've got a diversity training workshop scheduled for my officers that I've got to be at, and we need to meet with the Secret Service to set up the security for the vice president, who's coming in two weeks. I'll get to this stuff when I get to it."

Joe stepped close to Tassell, looked right at him. "Sheriff, we seem to have started off on the wrong foot, and I'm not sure why. But I'd rather work with you than against you. All I'm asking for is keys to the statehouse and truck."

Tassell didn't step back. "Bud Barnum was a legend among sheriffs in this state. He was old school, and I can't really call him a friend, but sheriffs tend to stick together."

Now Joe understood. "What happened with Barnum was his own doing," Joe said. "He can blame everyone else, but Barnum did himself in."

"That's not his version."

"I'm not surprised," Joe said.

"In his version, he doesn't blame everyone else. He blames *you*."

Barnum had cut a wide swath across northern Wyoming, Joe thought.

"I can't help that," Joe said.

"He says you get into the middle of things you should leave alone. That you press too damned hard into areas where things are best left to the professionals."

"Do you think that's why I'm here?" Joe asked.

"Aren't you?" Tassell asked back.

"I'm here to fill in during hunting season, and then I'm sure I'll be sent back home. I'm curious about Will, I admit that. It doesn't make sense to me that things were so bad that he took his own life."

That seemed to mollify Tassell slightly. He said, "Will may not have been all you seem to think he was, Joe."

Joe cocked his head. "What do you mean?"

"Will started losing it over the past six months or so. Even before the wife took the kids and moved out on him. He was becoming a public embarrassment, and we don't like embarrassments here in Jackson."

"What do you mean?" Joe felt a coldness growing inside.

"He was arrested twice for driving drunk. That was after a half dozen warnings. He spent a night in my jail when he was so blitzed he couldn't even get out of his own truck. He was arrested again just a couple of weeks ago for threatening one of our local business leaders."

"Will?" Joe asked, incredulous.

"Will. I arrested him myself out at the ski resort, where he was having the argument. Bet you didn't know *that*?"

"No," Joe said, "I didn't know that." He doubted that Trey did either, or he would have told Joe.

"Will just kept getting worse. I could see it coming." Tassell gestured toward the room. "And so could anybody who knew him. He was in a death spiral and it was only a matter of time.

"The ME concluded that Will's death was suicide," Tassell said. "There's no doubt about it at all, if that's what you were thinking. He got drunk, ate dinner, and shot himself at his table. Simple as that. There was a photo of his family on the table, which was probably the last thing he looked at. His fingerprints were the only prints on the gun."

"Is it true that all he ate was meat that night?"

Tassell looked at Joe quizzically. "Where did you hear *that*?"

"Just a rumor."

"Yeah, it's true. He cooked himself up quite a bunch of meat that night. All of the frying pans were dirty, and there was meat still on his plate when he died. It smelled pretty good in there, actually. But so what?"

"I'm not sure," Joe said.

"It's not that unusual, is it?" Tassell asked. "Hell, I do it myself. I ask the wife about once a month for what we call 'the Meat Bucket' dinner. Steak, pork, elk sausages. Maybe a piece of bread. She doesn't like it—she's a health-freak type—but she cooks it up."

"There wasn't an autopsy?"

Tassell shook his head. "No need. The cause of death was clear-cut. We don't do autopsies in Teton County when the cause of death is obvious. We have to watch our budget too."

Of course—so you can afford diversity training workshops, Joe thought but didn't say. He wondered how many murders there had been on Sheriff Tassell's watch. Joe couldn't recall hearing of any recently in Teton County.

As if reading Joe's mind, Tassell went on, "We lose a couple of people a year here, but not because of crime. A tourist or two may drown in the whitewater, or a skier might crash into a tree, or a ski bum will overdose on a slick new designer drug. But just because we don't have major crime doesn't mean we're not trained to handle it. This is a tight little community, and there are important people here with lots of money and influence. They don't like things happening that take place in bad country and western songs, you know? Those things should be left to the rest of the state. And they don't like bad news, either, because this is their special playground."

Joe watched Tassell carefully. What exactly was he getting at?

"This place is special," Tassell said. "We've got the highest per capita income than any county in the U.S., because of all the millionaires and billionaires. There are people here who don't think they need to play by the rules. And you know what," the sheriff said, arching his eyebrows, "they *don't*. They don't like a sloppy suicide happening in their town. Neither do I."

"I'm confused," Joe said.

Tassell looked away. "What's done is done. I don't want it dredged up again."

"You think I'm going to do that?"

"Maybe. That's what Barnum said you'd do."

Joe paused before responding. Tassell was obviously warning him off, but was it because there was something to hide or simply because a further inquiry would look bad and attract unwanted attention? Joe guessed the latter.

"Don't worry," Joe said. "It doesn't seem like you've got anything to fear from me."

"Let's hope not," Tassell said with finality. "Let's hope not."

Then he excused himself, saying, "I want another hit of that cheese."

"About those keys," Joe said.

"Come by the office around five," Tassell said. "We should be done with our workshop by then."

JOE WATCHED AS RANDY POPE gave Susan Jensen a long hug. Joe thought Pope held the clench three beats too long, moving it into the category of inappropriate behavior. Susan didn't appear to be hugging back.

Finally, Pope said something sincere to her and took his leave. As he passed Joe, Pope looked up.

"On behalf of the department, right?" Joe said.

"Don't you have work to do?" Pope snapped, his face flushing pink.

SUSAN JENSEN WORKED HER WAY through a group of well-wishers and walked purposefully up to Joe and said, "May I have a few minutes, please?"

"Of course," he said, following her through the room and into the hallway.

"I need a drink," she told him, as if apologizing.

Joe didn't need one, but didn't say so. The lounge was at the end of the hall, and Susan looked inside before going in.

"All clear," she said. She took a seat on a stool at the empty bar and ordered a glass of white wine. Joe liked her, and had from their first meeting. She was ebullient, smart, and a little caustic. Like Marybeth, Susan Jensen was a go-getter.

"Just tonic for me," Joe said to the bartender, who was young, fit, and sunburned—the Jackson look.

"You're not drinking, that's good," Susan said.

"Not today, anyway."

She waited for the explanation.

"I had a couple of extras last night," he said.

"Will used to be reasonable like that," she said. "He'd have a few drinks and then he'd go for weeks without one. It wouldn't even occur to him. But then he changed."

"Susan, I'm sorry," Joe said.

"Everybody is," she said, sipping, an edge creeping into her voice. "Everybody in that room is very sorry. We never had so many friends in Jackson who thought so well of us."

Joe didn't know how to respond.

"I'm sorry," she said. "I shouldn't have said that. It's catty. A few people have shown the boys and me real kindness. Some anonymous person even paid for the costs of cremation, which helped us out a lot. Will's life insurance policy won't pay because of what happened. I have a new job, but still, I've got to think about the boys, how I'm going to pay for them to go to college."

Joe hadn't thought of the fact that suicide was exempted in most life insurance policies. He felt a stab of anger, wondered how Will could have been so selfish.

"Joe, when you leave a man you want him to regret it. You want him to sit and stew and feel lousy for driving you away. Then maybe, you want him to get his act together and come crawling back on his knees. You don't want him to kill himself and leave you with *that*."

"I understand."

"I hope you do," she said. "If Marybeth ever leaves you, go crawling back to her like a whipped puppy. Don't internalize it, and brood about it, and think there's no way out."

He nodded. He wasn't sure why she was giving him this advice. She drained her glass, ordered another.

"I need fortification to go back into that room," she said.

He had so many questions for her. "Where will you go?"

"The kids and I live in Casper," she said. "We moved there four months ago. I've got a job at the newspaper, and we live with my parents. I started selling ads, and recently moved up to marketing director. It's a hard job, but I'm very good at it. We're making more income now than we ever did."

Joe thought of the parallels with his own family, Marybeth's new business, the obvious conclusion that it would likely prosper if either Joe took a different job or the family moved out of Saddlestring. He asked, "How are the boys handling the move, and now this?"

"Terribly," she said, matter-of-factly. "Will was a god to them. You can guess what it's like. You have girls, right?"

"Yes."

"Imagine if you had boys. If every day they watched you strap on your gun after breakfast and put on your hat and go out into the mountains to catch bad guys and protect the herds." She said "protect the herds" in a well-practiced way, and Joe guessed it had been some kind of joke between Susan and Will. "They worshipped him," she said. "They still do. They didn't see him like I did those last terrible months, when I'd come visit from Casper and we'd try to reconcile. Something definitely changed with him. A couple of times he would roar around the house, stumbling and cursing me. He never used to do that. His mood swings got absolutely crazy and unpredictable. He'd be manic one day and sullen the next. I didn't know him anymore, and he scared me. If the boys saw or heard him like that, I don't know what they'd think of him now."

Joe winced as she talked. He had thought about saying that it might not be all that different with his girls, but he refrained. He didn't want to have that kind of discussion.

"Susan, what happened to him?"

She shrugged. "That's the big question, isn't it?" Her eyebrows arched. "He said a few times that the pressure was building, that he was being squeezed alive. But that wasn't unusual. Things have always been like that here, you'll see. Will had a gift for dealing with it, though. At least he did at one time. He just went into his cave."

"His cave?"

She took a long drink. "That's what we used to call it. It was a mental cave he could sit in and depressurize after a bad day. He'd sit and stare at the television, or out the window. Sometimes he took the dog for a walk, or messed with his horses. It didn't matter what he did, because even though he was there, he really wasn't there, you know?"

"I do," he said. "When I feel like that, Marybeth and the girls say I've gone into Joe-Zone."

She smiled sympathetically. "He used to come back from backcountry patrols feeling pretty good, though," she said. "He said they cleared his mind and gave him his good perspective back."

Joe understood that.

"I took the job in Casper to give Will the option of getting out of this pressure cooker. I thought he'd follow me to be with the boys. I even found a couple of opportunities for him there, but he never took them. He stayed here and things got worse."

Joe shook his head, trying to think what he would do in the same situation, if Marybeth said she'd had it with his absences and threatened to move away. He'd follow her, wouldn't he? When he realized he was missing some of what she said, he apologized and asked her to repeat it.

Susan said, "I said he didn't give a lot of thought to the fact that while he was away for nights on end sleeping under the stars or whatever he did, he was completely out of contact with the outside world. He liked that, I guess. But he had a family here in town who never heard from him. I worried so much about him out there, Joe, that I would cry myself to sleep. Then I'd hate him. But I always got over it when he came back. When I saw you at the funeral, that was what I thought of."

"But things changed with Will?"

"Did they ever," she said, tapping the rim of her glass to signal the bartender for a refill. "Especially after we left. It was like his cave door closed shut and locked him out. He couldn't find any relief, so the pressure just kept building. Of course, he never said anything to me or asked for help. Not Will." Susan didn't even try to keep the anger out of her voice.

"What caused the biggest problems?"

"Are you asking me because you want to know about Will, or because you want to know what you're going to be dealing with here? Joe, I know you're here to replace him. I'm still in the loop."

He flushed, sorry he hadn't said it earlier. "Both, I guess."

She thought that over for a moment. "Will thought— and he was right—that it seemed like things were coming at him from all sides. The animal liberation people were after him. I was surprised to see that Pi woman here, considering that she literally put a contract out on him on her website. Then there was Smoke Van Horn and his bunch, the old-timers. They rode Will hard, tried to get him fired a few times. Smoke always showed up at the public hearings and ripped Will as well as the state and the Feds. Smoke was hard on Will, and I hate him for that. Oh," Susan said, smiling bitterly, "then there's the developers. They come from other places and they want to do here what they did wherever they made their millions. It drove them crazy that somebody like Will, who made less money than what their cars probably cost, could stall their projects by writing an opinion that would affect their plans."

Joe interrupted. "Are you talking about Don Ennis?" he asked, thinking about the business card in his pocket.

Susan's face tightened. "Don Ennis. Do you know him?"

"I sort of met him last night. He sent over a drink."

"Don and Stella Ennis," Susan said, more to herself than to Joe, as if recalling something unpleasant.

Joe recalled Tassell's comments about breaking up an argument at the ski resort. He would need to follow up with Tassell to see if the other party was Don Ennis.

Susan's eyes burned into Joe, and her voice dropped as if someone might overhear her. "Joe, all I can tell you is to watch out for that man. He gets what he wants, and he doesn't care who gets hurt."

Joe blinked at her sudden intensity.

"As for Stella," she said, "she's playing a game that only she understands. She might be the most dangerous of them all."

"What do you mean?" he asked.

Susan sat back, drained her glass. "I'm not sure what I mean. I just got this vibration from her. A dark kind of feeling. I think she's a predator. And Will," she said, drinking again although her glass was empty, "Will thought I was wrong about her. He thought I was jealous. And you know what? I probably was."

Joe felt that he needed to defend Stella. Did Susan see her crying during the funeral? Were those tears of a predator? But he didn't want to go there with Susan, not now. He changed the subject.

He asked, "What was he working on most recently?"

"I'm sorry, I can't help you with that," she said. "The boys and I had been gone for months. Even when we were together, he didn't talk about the specifics of his projects much. He tried to leave all of that at his office, or in his truck, or wherever. The only way I knew about the big things—like ALN, Smoke, or Ennis's Beargrass Village—was because sometimes he'd mention them in passing or I'd hear about it from someone or read about it in the newspaper."

"Susan, where did he keep his files? His notebooks?" He realized he sounded like he was grilling her. "Sorry for my tone."

"It's okay," she said, patting his hand. "I'm not sure about the files. I think at the office. He brought his notebook into the house some nights—he was always scribbling in those notebooks—but he never left papers or files around the house."

"Do you mind if I look through the boxes of what he left?"

"Feel free, Joe. I'm not sure what I'm going to do with them anyway. They probably belong to the state."

Suddenly, Susan turned her wrist and looked at her watch. If her glass hadn't been empty, Joe noticed, she would have spilled wine on her lap. "I need to get back to the boys and the, um, mourners."

"Thank you for your time, Susan. I really appreciate it."

Again, she patted his hand.

She slid down from the stool, a little shakily. Joe steadied her by holding her forearm until she was standing. She put the glass down and smoothed her skirt. She started to say good-bye and then stopped. "Joe, with all of your questions I nearly forgot why I needed to talk to you in the first place."

She said, "A year ago, just as Will was starting to lose

his bearings and six months before I left him, he took me out to dinner. It was a fairly nice evening, even though we couldn't afford it. Everything here just costs so much. Anyway, out of the blue, he said that when he died he wanted his remains scattered in a specific place. When I look back on that now, I think he knew something was going to happen."

She had her legs back and was walking out of the lounge, Joe following.

"Two Ocean Pass, that's the place," she said. "It's somewhere up in the wilderness area, where he patrolled. He described it pretty thoroughly, for Will."

She stopped in the hallway and turned to face Joe. He could hear the fog of conversation coming from the reception room, where no doubt mourners were waiting for the widow.

"He said a creek comes down from the mountains. I think he called it Two Ocean Creek. Anyway, the stream flows south through a big meadow and splits at a lone spruce tree. It's exactly on the Continental Divide. One part of the stream flows to the Atlantic and the other to the Pacific. He said it was the most beautiful meadow he had ever seen. He wants his ashes scattered there, by the tree."

Joe now grasped what she was asking.

"I'll never get up there," she said. "I don't even want to try. But it's in your new district, and you can probably find it."

"I'll do it," Joe said. "I'm honored." He knew vaguely of the location from the map on the office wall. "Do you want me to do anything else?"

She shook her head. "That's more than enough, Joe. I'll give you my number in Casper, if you don't mind calling me when it's done."

*   *   *

THE URN LOOKED LIKE AN extra large beer stein. Joe carried it to his pickup, thinking how light it was, wondering guiltily what the ashes looked like (brown, gray, or white?). On the street, a jacked-up Grand Am filled with teenagers slowed, and a window rolled down and an unformed simian face jutted out, asking, "Dude, where's the party?"

13

AT 4:45 P.M., JOE ENTERED THE OFFICE OF THE TETON County Sheriff's Department and told the receptionist he was there to meet with Sheriff Tassell. The reception-ist said the sheriff was in a meeting and couldn't be dis-turbed. Behind her he could see a hallway with several closed doors, and he could hear the hum of voices from behind one of them.

Joe was annoyed. "When will he be free?"

"He didn't say."

"Did he leave me a message? Or a set of keys?"

"And you are . . . ?" she asked archly.

He told her.

"No, there's nothing for you here."

Joe considered waiting, and looked around the small reception area. There were two chairs, and one of them was filled with a sinewy man wearing khakis, a polo shirt, a jacket, and light hiking boots. Not local, Joe thought, but buttoned-up and urban, attempting to appear casual and outdoorsy. The man looked straight back at Joe, as if daring him to take the seat next to him.

"Are you waiting for the sheriff too?" Joe asked.

"Could be," the man said. There was something coiled up about him, Joe thought. Then he noticed the earpiece, and the thin wire that curled from it into the man's collar.

"Are you Secret Service?" Joe asked, remembering Tassell's other meeting about the vice president's visit.

"Could be," the man said again. "I think the sheriff will be in there awhile."

Joe was being dismissed. He glanced at the receptionist, who was suddenly busy reading a magazine and wouldn't look back.

"When you see the sheriff," Joe told the receptionist, "please ask him to call me." He wrote down his cellphone number on a business card and handed it to her. "Tell him if he doesn't call me, I'll need to bother him at home later."

She took Joe's card without comment.

The Secret Service agent watched him coolly, but turned away as if to say, "You're dismissed."

HE DROVE OUT OF TOWN to the north and parked in a pullout overlooking the river. The urn with Will Jensen's ashes sat on the passenger seat where Maxine should have been, the seat belt securing it. The urn gave him a feeling of macabre unease.

The Tetons, backlit from the setting sun, were black sawteeth against the purpling sky. On the Snake River, through the gold aspen, Joe could see a blue rubber raft floating down the river filled with tourists bundled up in life vests. The guide who manned the oars pointed upriver for his guests, and Joe followed his gesture. A large bald eagle's nest, the size of a small car, it seemed, occupied an old-growth cottonwood treetop. With his binoculars, Joe could see two fledgling eagles in the nest. The mother duckwalked around the rim of the nest, looking down at her young ones. He could see their hooked beaks opening and closing, pink inside their mouths.

Which made Joe think of Nate's falcons. Which made him think of Saddlestring. Which made him think that he better call home. He plucked his phone from the cradle and hit the speed dial.

After five rings, Lucy answered.

"May I speak with your mom?" he asked, after Lucy had told him a long story about the substitute teacher she had that day, a man who said he really wanted to be friends with the kids in her class and asked them to call him "Mr. Kenny."

"She's not here," Lucy said.

"Well," Joe asked, after a beat, "where is she?"

"She had to take Sheridan to the hospital."

He suddenly sat up. "What?"

"Somebody poked her in the eye during volleyball practice."

So that's where she was when he called earlier—at Sheridan's practice. Jeez. "How badly is she hurt?"

"I don't know."

"Lucy," Joe said, trying to speak softly, "tell me what happened."

Joe could hear the television in the background. Lucy watched a string of cartoons every night before dinner, and he recognized the voice of SpongeBob SquarePants.

"I'm not sure," Lucy said, distracted. "Sherry called Mom a while ago and said she needed to come pick her up from practice."

"So it was Sheridan who called, not a coach or a doctor?" Joe felt mild relief, assuming Sheridan couldn't have been too badly injured if she had used the telephone.

"I think it was Sheridan."

"Lucy."

"Mom just told me they'd be back for dinner. That's all I know."

Joe shook his head. There was no reason to be angry with Lucy, or to admonish her. It had probably been a frantic call, and Marybeth had likely rushed out of the house. He would try her cell phone.

"Okay, sweetie," Joe said. "Tell your mother I'll call back soon."

"Dad," Lucy said, "I miss you."

Lucy liked to twist the knife, Joe thought.

"I miss you too. I love you."

"Love you . . ."

Joe speed-dialed Marybeth's cell phone, but was switched to her voice mail. In her haste, he assumed, Marybeth hadn't turned it on, or was out of range. There were several dead spots between their house and Saddlestring along Bighorn Road. He left a message, sat back, replaced his phone, and stared with frustration at the river. When he looked back at the phone he noticed that the LED display on his cell read: you have 1 message. Joe checked it; it was from Sheriff Tassell.

"The meeting's running late," he said wearily, "and then I've got a dinner. Meet me at the statehouse at ten tonight. I'll bring the keys."

Joe sighed.

The tourist boat passed in and out of view, obscured by trees and brush. The occupants of the boat were on vacation, Joe thought. They got to see an eagle's nest, and they'd go to a nice dinner after their trip and retire to their hotel rooms. Real life was suspended for them.

He looked at the Tetons, at the raft, at the urn, and thought, *They aren't the only ones.*

*   *   *

AS JOE DROVE TOWARD TOWN he rounded a blind corner and hit the brakes. The Boxster that had passed him the night before was stopped, blocking the right-hand lane, twin spoors of black rubber on the road where the car had braked and swerved. Instinctively, he reached out with his right hand to keep a dog or a child—neither of whom was there—from flying forward into the dash and windshield. His front bumper stopped inches from the back of the Boxster.

He swung out of the cab and walked around the Porsche with his flashlight, but he didn't need it. The headlights of the car illuminated the scene. It was ugly. A large doe mule deer lay in the road, blood pooling around her head. The Boxster's hood was buckled, the windshield a spider's web of cracks from the impact. A woman sat in the ditch, cradling a fawn in her arms. The fawn was small, spindly, its back covered with spots. Not more than six weeks old, Joe thought. It made him angry.

"Are you okay?" Joe asked, not really caring. He tried to keep his voice level.

The woman looked up. Her eyes reflected in the headlights. She had broad cheekbones and a drawn, skeletal quality to her face.

"I'm fine, but that poor deer and her fawn ran right out in front of me," the woman said. "I tried to stop but I couldn't."

Joe shone his flashlight on the crumpled hood of the car. "That's a lot of damage," Joe said. "How fast were you going?"

"I don't know," she said. "The speed limit, I think."

"No way," Joe said, looking at the damage, remembering how she tore around him the night before.

"Is the mother dead?" the woman asked.

Joe knelt down. There was shallow breathing from the doe, and her eyes stared into his. But he could tell from the unevenness of her fur over her rib cage that her ribs had been crushed. The blood that poured out of her mouth and nose was bright red and foamy, meaning her lungs were pierced by bone or cartilage.

"She's not dead yet," Joe said.

"Is she suffering?" the woman asked.

Joe looked up, squinted. "What do *you* think?"

The woman said nothing.

He heard an oncoming car slow in the other lane and pull over. A door opened and slammed. When he looked up, he could see the shapely silhouette of a woman in the headlights.

Joe stood and grasped the doe's front ankles below the joints and started to drag her off the road into the ditch. Her legs kicked involuntarily as he pulled, and she nearly kicked out of his hands. Stella Ennis, the other driver, appeared beside him and grasped the doe's rear feet. Joe looked over to see glistening tears in her eyes. But her face was determined. They got the deer off the pavement and into the grass in the ditch. Then he drew his Beretta.

"Don't kill her!" the Boxster woman pleaded. "Please don't . . ."

"Please turn away," Joe said softly. Stella turned, her hands to her face.

Joe shot the deer in the head. The shot cracked loud, and bounced back and forth against the wall of trees on either side of the road. The body gurgled, then sighed.

"My God," the woman with the fawn said. "That was horrible. What's wrong with you?"

Joe holstered his pistol and stepped back on the road. "Let me see the fawn."

"No!"

"Move your hands and let me see the fawn."

"Mr. Pickett . . ." It was Stella. Her tone was cautionary.

Slowly, the woman released the fawn, her face a mask of horror. The fawn reacted as if suddenly shot through with electricity, and it scrambled and kicked free of the woman. It stood on thin, stilt-like legs, obviously not knowing what to do. Then it collapsed in a heap.

"What did you do to it?" the woman cried. "Did you scare it to death?"

Joe wasn't sure what had happened to the fawn until he got down on his knees and looked at it. The other side of the fawn's head was crushed in from the impact of the car. When he shone his flashlight on the woman he could see dark blood on her shirt where she had cradled it.

Joe dragged the fawn to its mother. It weighed practically nothing.

Then he turned on the woman. "There are deer all over this road. Every single night. You should know that."

"It wasn't my fault," the woman protested, starting to rise. "The deer jumped out in front of me."

"No," Joe said, a hard edge in his voice. "You were going too goddamned fast. In all my years, I've never hit a deer, much less two of them."

"I *said* it wasn't my fault." The woman was angry now. Joe flashed back to Pope's admonition about being respectful, putting on a good face for the department. Then he looked again at the dead deer.

"These animals aren't here just to make scenery pretty for you. They're real and you killed them," Joe said. "Lady, you're a guest here."

The woman buried her face in her hands.

"Oh, *my*," Stella Ennis said with admiration, and he saw the white of her teeth.

"Thank you for your help," Joe said to Stella, starting to reach out with his hand but catching himself because of the blood on it. Despite that, she reached for him and squeezed his fingers. There was blood on her hands also.

"Call me Stella," she said.

Something inside him went *ZING*.

14

MARYBETH PICKETT HAD JUST FINISHED FEEDING THE horses when she heard the telephone ringing from inside the house. It was already cool and dark, and she was running two hours late for dinner because of their trip to the hospital. She ran from the corral toward the house and entered through the back door.

"I hope it's Dad," Sheridan said from where she was doing homework at the kitchen table. Lucy had told them he called and would call back. The kitchen smelled of onion, tomato, and garlic. A frozen pizza was warming in the oven, something Marybeth regretted. They were eating too much of that kind of stuff with Joe gone, she thought.

The sight of Sheridan's bandaged eye jarred Marybeth, even though she had seen the square of gauze applied by the doctor just hours before. It was likely not serious, the doctor had said. It wouldn't have been anything at all except that an opposing player's fingernail had scratched her cornea. The injury had occurred during a skirmish for a ball, Sheridan had told them. Nobody called it, players went for it, Sheridan got to it, and somebody reached around her from behind and raked her across the eyes. Officially, it was considered an accident.

"I hope it's him too," Marybeth said to Sheridan, snatching the receiver from the wall.

Silence.

"Joe?"

She could hear labored breathing and something else—muffled conversation?—in the background.

"Joe, are you on your cell? Can you hear me?"

"I want to talk with him," Sheridan said from the table.

Marybeth covered the telephone with her hand and shook her head at Sheridan, indicating, *It's not him.*

Then she remembered the Caller ID unit that had just been installed, that she had forgotten to look at before answering. The number had a 720 area code, which was unfamiliar.

"Who is this?"

An intake of breath, as if the caller was gathering his thoughts to speak. But he didn't.

"I'm hanging up," Marybeth said, and she did. *"Dam-nit."*

The caller's telephone number vanished from the screen. She retrieved it from the backup and wrote the number down on the first thing she could find, the margin of the front page of the Saddlestring *Roundup.*

"Who was that?" Sheridan asked.

"Wrong number."

"Then why did you write it down?"

Caught, Marybeth looked up. "In case he calls again."

"I heard you and Dad talking about someone calling us and not saying anything. Was that him?"

"I have no idea," Marybeth said, her voice more shrill than she would have chosen.

Sheridan glared at her mother. It didn't matter if one eye was obscured, the glare was the same. "You don't have to treat me like I'm an idiot, Mom. I'm thirteen. Do you realize how old that is?"

Marybeth braced for another argument. They were occurring with more frequency these days. "Sheridan," Marybeth said, already regretting her words, "do *you* realize how young that is?"

Sheridan slammed her pen down on her paper. "You treat me like I'm Lucy's age," she said. "I'm not. You forget how much I've gone through in my life."

"Oh, stop it."

"No," Sheridan said, her cheeks blooming red, "I won't stop it. If someone is calling our house and we might be in danger, I want to know about it. Don't keep me in the dark like a baby."

Marybeth took a breath, counted to three. "I don't know that to be a fact," she said. "We have no idea who is calling, or why. We don't know if it means anything at all."

Sheridan continued to glare. Lucy walked into the room, turning her head from her mother to her sister, as if watching a tennis volley.

"Was it so hard to tell me that?" Sheridan asked.

"Tell her what?" Lucy asked. "Was that Dad?"

Sheridan told Lucy, "Never mind."

"No," Marybeth said, "it wasn't your dad."

"When is he going to call?"

"I don't know," Marybeth said, an edge of frustration in her voice.

"He'll call," Sheridan said, picking up her pen and going back to her homework.

Don't be so smug, Marybeth thought, looking at her older daughter, for a moment resenting her and her absolute certainty, and just as quickly forgiving her.

Marybeth picked up the newspaper with the telephone number on it and headed for Joe's office. As she passed by the table, Marybeth mussed Sheridan's hair affectionately. Sheridan turned her head away sharply, as if her mother's touch offended her.

"Sheridan . . ."

"I'm trying to do my homework here, okay?" Sheridan snapped.

Let it go, Marybeth told herself. *Let it go.*

She put the newspaper on the stack of unopened mail for Joe. She intended to read him the return addresses on the envelopes when he called, to see if any of the letters were important and should be forwarded to him in Jackson. And she wanted to ask him if the phone number was familiar. That is, if and when he called.

15

SHERIFF TASSELL WAS LATE ARRIVING AT THE STATE-house. Joe had spent the time having an unsatisfying conversation with Marybeth, his cell signal fading and coming back, hearing snippets of sentences and asking her to repeat them.

"So Sheridan's okay?"

"Seems to be," Marybeth said. "It's her attitude that needs an adjustment. . . . "

There was more, but Joe didn't get it.

"So Sheridan's eye is fine?"

"Joe, I just told you . . ." Lost it again.

He got out of his truck and walked down the side-walk, pirouetting occasionally, trying to find a steady, strong signal.

". . . another call where the caller didn't say anything . . ."

"What?"

"It was from area code seven-two-oh. Do you . . ."

"Seven-two-oh?"

". . . she asked me about it, wondering if it was any-thing we needed to be concerned about . . ."

"Marybeth, stop," Joe said, frustrated. "Wait until I get into the house. I can use the phone inside. I'll call you from there and we can talk, okay?"

". . . they miss you, Joe . . ."

"Did you hear me?"

Suddenly the connection was good. "Hear what? Why are you snapping at me?"

"I'm not snapping," Joe said, looking up at the street-light. "My signal's going in and out. I'm only hearing parts of what you say."

". . . maybe you should call back tomorrow so you can talk with the girls . . ."

"I will. Now, Marybeth . . ."

The signal vanished.

Joe sighed, punched off the call as Tassell's Teton County Sheriff's Jeep Cherokee cruised down the street and pulled in behind Joe's truck.

"SORRY I'M LATE," TASSELL SAID, swinging out of the Cherokee. Before the interior lights shut off when the door closed, Joe saw a woman he assumed was Tassell's wife in the passenger seat, and at least two children in the back seat.

"You wouldn't believe how many social obligations there are here," Tassell said over his shoulder to Joe as he walked up the path to the front door, spinning a set of keys around his index finger. "Seems like we're obligated most nights."

Joe grunted.

Tassell said, "Tonight was the annual fund-raiser at the wildlife art museum. As sheriff, I have to go to these things. It's noticed when I'm not there."

"You could have left me the keys at your office."

Tassell stopped at the front door, fumbling in the dark

with the keys and the lock. "I wanted to check this place out first."

"Why?"

Tassell turned, but Joe couldn't see his face in the dark. "I want to make sure they cleaned up."

Joe hoped so too, but didn't say anything. He heard the zip of the key going in, and Tassell pushed open the door, the tape seals breaking open with a kissing sound. Tassell searched for a light switch, then both the porch light and the interior lights went on. Joe blinked and followed him in.

"It's clean enough, I think," Tassell said, surveying the room.

Joe stepped around Tassell. The home was no bigger than his own in Saddlestring. They stood in the dining room, with the kitchen appliances lining the wall near the door. The only nice thing, Joe noticed, was a fairly modern refrigerator with a water tap and icemaker on one of the doors. The table where Will shot himself was in the center of the room, with two chairs on either end of it. The cheap paneled walls were bare of adornments with the exception of a stopped clock. The ceiling was a dingy off-white and in need of paint. The overhead frosted light threw out mottled light due to at least one burned-out bulb and the shadowed remains of dead miller moths gathered in the frosted glass fixture. The room smelled of strong disinfectant.

Tassell walked to the head of the table, turned, and gestured to the ceiling. "That's where the bullet went," he said, pointing at a nickel-sized hole a few inches from where the paneling started. "I would have thought they'd plug that up, but I guess not."

Joe looked at the ceiling. He could see dried arcing wipe marks reflecting in the light, where the blood had been washed off. The paneling on the east wall also looked freshly scrubbed.

"This room was a mess," Tassell said. "A .44 Magnum does a lot of damage to flesh and bone. The damned gun kicked so hard it drove the front sight of the muzzle up into his palate." He demonstrated by jabbing his finger up into his mouth, pointing behind his front teeth.

He handed Joe the key ring. "His pickup keys are on that too."

"Thanks."

"What can I say? It's a shitty house but I guess it's your new home," Tassell said. "Well, I've got my kids in the car. I need to get them home."

"I'll probably be calling you with a few questions in regard to Will's suicide."

Tassell hesitated at the door. "That's not necessary."

FOR THE NEXT HOUR, JOE moved in. He stripped the bed and threw his sleeping bag on top of the mattress and hung his clothes in the closet, which was empty except for a pair of battered Sorel pac boots. Stacking Will's boxes along a bare wall in the living room, Joe thought the house had the same feel that Will's office did, as if he had no compulsion to make it his own. He guessed that when Susan left she took every thing, and that Will was fine with that.

Where to put the urn? No place seemed appropriate. Joe walked through the house, holding it in front of him with both hands. If there was protocol for this sort of dilemma, he didn't know it, so he left it on the table for the time being.

Joe was pleased to find that the telephone had a dial tone and the television worked. He found an all-sports channel and left it on, mainly to provide background noise in the empty house. Between the girls, Marybeth, and Maxine, there was always noise in his house, and the complete silence was uncomfortable to him.

It was after midnight when Joe went out to Will's truck and unlocked it to look for the notebook. The cab was a rat's nest of equipment, maps, clothing, and paperwork. It looked like Joe's own truck. Unlike the house or his office, this was where Will had really lived and worked. It felt as though he had just stepped out and locked up for the night; there was a sense of unfinished business inside, just like Will's desk at the building. Will hadn't even sealed up a bag of sunflower seeds that sat open on the console. Joe searched the cab thoroughly, even shoving his hand between the seats, where he found a half-empty pint of vodka. But no notebook.

As he searched the truck, his mind kept returning to his earlier encounter with Stella Ennis. He could still feel the *ZING* that had shot through him when he'd grasped her hand, although it had now receded into a warm, lingering buzz. That particular thing, that electric shock, had happened to him only twice before in his life. The first time was in the eighth grade, when Jo Ellen Meese whispered to him what time she changed into her nightgown and that her bedroom window was unlocked. The second time was when he saw Marybeth, in the middle of a group of girls, hurrying to class on a snowy day at the University of Wyoming. Marybeth had looked back, their eyes locked, and he knew she was the one.

Both experiences had resulted in something profound; his first time and, he thought, his true love.

Now it had happened with a married woman with blood on her hands on the side of a two-lane highway.

BACK INSIDE THE HOUSE, JOE walked through all the rooms. In addition to the master bedroom, there was a small bedroom with a set of box springs and no mattress. Despite the work of the cleaners, he could see crayon marks on the floor. This was the boys' room, he guessed. Across the hallway was a bathroom with a shower/tub, a stained toilet, and an empty medicine cabinet. They hadn't even left a towel. The utility room was empty and looked like it had been empty for months. Susan must have taken the washer and dryer, Joe assumed, and Will never got them replaced. The floor of the utility room was covered with dust and mouse droppings.

The refrigerator was empty except for an open box of baking soda in the back and a single can of beer. Joe popped the top of the beer and took a long drink. It was sour, and he gagged and spit it into the sink. He filled a lone plastic drinking glass from the cupboard with water from the refrigerator tap and tried to wash the taste out of his mouth.

The only real proof that Will Jensen had lived and died in the house, other than the old pair of boots and the hole in the ceiling, was in the freezer. The cleaners must have forgotten about it, Joe thought.

The freezer was still filled with packages of meat.

AT 3:30 A.M., JOE SUDDENLY AWOKE and wasn't sure where he was. His head spinning, he reached out for a lamp on his bedside table at home but, catching air, lost his balance, tumbled out of bed, taking his sleeping bag with him, and landed hard on the floor, crying, "*Jesus!*" The thump his knees made was loud, like a muffled shot, and it reverberated through the empty house, causing what he at first thought was the sound of a bird spooking and flushing somewhere in the dark.

He wasn't sure how long he remained motionless on the floor on his hands and knees, his head hanging, trying to focus his mind. Had he hit his head in the fall? he wondered. He didn't remember doing so. But he practi-

cally swooned as he sat back on the floor, dizziness returning. Slumping to the side, he slid out of the bag and
lay on the floor, his bare skin on cold wood, his eyes
open, until he finally started to get his bearings.

Joe stood up shakily, padded to the doorjamb and hit
the light switch beside it. The bedroom flooded with
harsh light. He stood there, naked, rubbing his eyes but
not able to clear the cobwebs from his vision.

Still not entirely lucid, he looked around the room
and remembered where he was. His sleeping bag was a
tangle on the floor, his pillow on the mattress but puckered with sweat. Had he dreamed about flushing a bird?
Where had *that* come from?

As he pulled on his Wranglers and a T-shirt, he recalled the sound. It had a rapid, thumping cadence, like a
pheasant breaking wildly from the brush. Or, he thought,
feeling the hair prick up on his arms, like the sound of
someone running away.

Joe looked around, trying to recall where he had put his
weapon before going to bed. He slipped his .40 Beretta out
of its holster and tiptoed down the hallway. Methodically,
he checked out each room, opening closet doors, peering
around corners, but the house was empty, the doors bolted,
the windows locked. His head was still feeling thick and
fuzzy, as if a terrific bout of the flu was coming on.

Assured that he was alone, Joe sat in a chair at the table and put his Beretta on the tabletop. He rubbed his
eyes and face, debating whether he should try to wake up
fully or go back to sleep. He felt somewhere in the middle of both.

Maybe it was simple exhaustion, he thought. He
hadn't slept well for almost a week. He was out of his
home territory, out of his routine. He missed Marybeth
and his daughters. He let his head flop back and found
himself staring at the bullet hole in the ceiling.

"This is where Will sat," Joe said aloud, "right here in this chair."

He glanced involuntarily at the Beretta on the table, then at the urn, instantly recognizing the action for all of the cinematic melodrama it held. He stood and shook his head, trying to shake the fog away. Maybe it was that sour beer, or the heavy odor of disinfectant in the house that was making him feel so strange.

Joe unlocked the front door and stood barefoot on the porch. A light frost the color of the moon sparkled on the grass. He filled his lungs with needles of icy air and felt better. His head began to clear. He stood on the porch and breathed until he started to shiver from the cold, then went back inside. He was beginning to re-move his clothing and crawl back into the sleeping bag when he thought of something. Pulling on his boots and grabbing his flashlight from his day-pack and the Beretta from the table, Joe went through the utility room and unbolted the back door and stepped out into the tiny backyard. The umbrella-like canopy of cottonwoods closed off the sky. He snapped on his flashlight and panned it across the grass until the beam stopped at the cluster of footprints in the frost beneath his bedroom window and the indents made by boots, widely spaced, where the man he had startled by falling out of bed had run away.

PART THREE

You stare through the plastic at the red smear of meat in the supermarket. What's this it says there? *Mighty Good? Tastee? Quality, Premium,* and *Government Inspected?* Soon enough, the blood is on your hands. It's inescapable.

THOMAS McGUANE,
AN OUTSIDE CHANCE

We cannot pity the boy who has never fired a gun; he is no more humane, while his education has been sadly neglected . . . if I were to live in a wilderness, I should become . . . a fisher and hunter in earnest.

HENRY DAVID THOREAU,
WALDEN

16

THE TOWN OF JACKSON WAS DARK AND STILL IN THE predawn of Sunday morning. Joe was groggy. He had been unable to sleep after being woken up and falling out of bed, and had spent the rest of the early morning hours going through Will's boxes, searching in vain for the missing notebook or anything else that would give him a better idea of what happened. He dressed, showered, and drove downtown, his thoughts sluggish and opaque. As his head cleared slightly, he realized he was hungry. He found a restaurant called The Sportsman's Café that would open at 5:30 A.M., according to the sign on the door, so for the next half hour he walked around the town square, his boots clumping on the frosted wooden sidewalks, his breath condensating in translucent white puffs. He studied the elk antler arches at the corners of the square, the antlers themselves turning white with age.

The stores facing the square were designer clothes shops, specialty outlets, art galleries, fly-fishing stores, The Million Dollar Cowboy Bar, which boasted saddles instead of bar stools, and restaurants that would explode his state per diem like a charge of C-4. He stopped briefly at Wildwater Photography, the business Birdy owned, and looked at the displays in the window. There were photos of happily screaming families bound up in life vests, smashing through rolls of whitewater, and another display of action shots of individual skiers. All of the subjects, Joe thought, looked like they were having the time of their lives.

He wished he were. He could not account for the slight residue of fog that still hung in his brain and hoped it was simply a combination of lack of sleep, hunger, and simple disorientation. Somehow, though, it felt like more than that. He tried not to let it alarm him. There hadn't been enough time to adjust, and he couldn't wallow in his loneliness. A game warden was dead, and Trey had given him an assignment. But first what he really needed was a big breakfast.

HE ENTERED THE RESTAURANT as soon as the proprietor unlocked the door and opened it. The man stood to the side to let Joe in and said, "Usual table, Will?"

"I'm not Will," Joe said.

The proprietor was short and thick with a bristly salt-and-pepper beard, a potato-shaped nose, and a toothpick in his mouth. He wore a stained apron over a Henley shirt and held a coffee mug. He looked dumbfounded.

"Of course you aren't," the man said after a long moment, his face flushing. "I don't know you at all."

"Joe Pickett. I'm the new guy."

"Ed," the man said, putting his coffee on an empty table so he could shake Joe's hand. "I own this place, at least for now."

Joe shook Ed's hand and chose a table by a steamed-over window near the batwing kitchen door. "I'm really hungry, Ed."

"Then you'll want the Sportsman's Special," he said. "Country fried steak with gravy, three eggs, hash browns, toast. How do you like your meat and eggs?"

"Medium rare and over-easy," Joe said. "And coffee."

"Of course."

Joe sat and unbuttoned his green Game and Fish jacket, sipped ice water and coffee, and listened as Ed cooked and filled the silence with the angry sound of sizzling food. A radio in the kitchen played scratchy country music. The Sportsman's Café seemed out of place among the art galleries and specialty shops Joe had looked into earlier. The inside was steamy and dark, with the wall nearest the restrooms covered with flyers for local horse sales and team penning events. A feed store calendar was tacked up behind the counter. The heads of elk, deer, antelope, and a pre–Endangered Species Act grizzly bear stared out from the walls. The menu, printed on a single laminated page, consisted of traditional American big breakfast fare—eggs, pancakes, waffles, patty sausages.

Joe looked up from the menu as Ed came by to refill his coffee. "You won't find any blintzes on it," the older man said, "or anything with sprouts. There's nothing on that menu with hollandaise or béarnaise sauce either. The only sauce I make is God's own sauce—gravy."

"Gotcha." Joe smiled in solidarity.

After Joe had downed a cup and a half of strong coffee, Ed brought out the platter. Joe ate with barely controlled aggression, and sat back only after swiping the plate clean with toast. There was nothing special about the food, except that it was perfect, Joe thought.

"I'm sorry about earlier," Ed said as he brought the coffeepot and the bill to the table. "Will Jensen used to be the first guy in the door about three days a week. I saw the cowboy hat and the jacket, and, well . . ."

Joe smiled. "I understand."

Ed arched his eyebrows. "You even chose his table."

At first, that disturbed Joe. Then he thought about it, and it made sense. The table he'd chosen was nearest the kitchen, so he would know who was behind him and also be able to see who entered the restaurant. Through the window, he could note the license plates of the vehicles that arrived in the sliver of a parking lot, and would be able to check vehicles that were likely hunting rigs. That Joe had chosen the table without thinking about it seemed natural, as it probably had for Will. Still, though . . .

"Will was a big fan of the Sportsman's Special," Ed said, beaming. "He even took his eggs and meat the same way."

"I'll be darned," Joe said, with a pang of disquietude.

"There will be quite a few hunters in here any minute," Ed said. "We're the only place open this early."

Joe looked at the bill. Breakfast cost more than it would have in Saddlestring, but it wasn't as expensive as he'd feared.

"You said something about owning this place for now," Joe asked. "What did you mean by that?"

Ed made change from a bulging pocket on his apron. "The lot is worth five times what the business is worth because I'm close to the square and I've been here a long time. I'm proud to say we've fed thousands of hunters and fishermen over the years—men who want big breakfasts. But the offers have been coming for the last ten years, the price is right. Some guy from Seattle wants to open up an Indonesian restaurant in Jackson, and he likes the location."

"Indonesian?" Joe asked. "Where's a guy going to get breakfast?"

Ed shrugged. "Don't know. Besides, this place doesn't fit anymore, and neither do I."

WHEN JOE STEPPED OUT OF the Sportsman's Café, he saw Smoke Van Horn coming up the wooden sidewalk with three other men. It was obvious to Joe from the look of them—heavy winter coats, crisp jeans, massive high-tech boots, an odd assortment of headgear—that they were Smoke's hunting clients.

"It's the FNG!" Smoke boomed, forging ahead of his customers and extending his bear-like hand to Joe. "How're you doing this great morning?"

"Fine, Smoke."

One of Smoke's clients, a tall man with a thin mustache and a three-day growth of beard he must have started before he left home, asked, "FNG?"

Joe knew what was coming.

"Fucking new guy." Smoke laughed. "Meet my *compadres*, Joe. Every body's from Georgia."

Smoke introduced the three men to Joe and they all took turns crushing his hand.

"Go on inside and grab a table," Smoke told them. "I'll be right behind you after I talk to the game warden. In fact, I brung you something."

Smoke dug into his coat and handed Joe a copy of the book he had written, *How the Pricks Deny Me a Living*.

"It's signed," Smoke said.

Joe flipped to the title page. Smoke had inscribed "Don't be a prick" in childish longhand, followed by his signature. Joe had to smile. Then he looked up at the hunters, asking, "Everybody's got licenses and wildlife stamps, right?"

The men looked guiltily at one another for an instant.

"Of course they do," Smoke said.

"Let's make sure," Joe said, keeping his tone light. He stood by until all of the hunters had dug into their wallets and showed Joe their licenses and stamps while Smoke glowered. Joe knew that the hunters would likely spend $5,000 to $6,000 each with Smoke, maybe more for the opportunity to get a trophy elk with the famous outfitter. There would be dozens of other clients arriving throughout the season.

"Thanks, gentlemen," Joe said. "The Sportsman's Special comes recommended."

After the three hunters had gone inside, Smoke turned to Joe. "What kind of outfit do you think I'm running?"

"From what I've heard, you run the most efficient hunting operation in terms of success ratio in this valley," Joe said.

"So why are you checking my clients' licenses like I'm some kind of peckerwood?"

Joe buttoned up his jacket against the cold, which had dropped the temperature a few degrees as dawn broke. "So they know I can," Joe said, "and so you know I will."

Smoke shook his head. "We're not going to have trouble working together, are we?"

"I hope not," Joe said. "But I'd be lying if I didn't tell you that there are quite a few notes in Will Jensen's records about you. He thought you might be salting to bring in all of those big elk for your shooters."

Smoke's face darkened. He stepped close to Joe, towering over him.

"Will never proved a goddamned thing and you know it," he said, his voice low. "D'you think salting is what accounts for my success?"

"I didn't say that."

"Do you have any fucking idea what you're saying?" Smoke growled. "You just got here."

"Yup," Joe said, "but I didn't just fall off the cattle truck. We'll get along fine as long as you operate as clean and legal as you say you do." He glanced down, saw that Smoke's fists were balled.

"In that case, mister," Smoke said, "you've got nothing to worry about."

"That's good," Joe said, reaching out, waiting for Smoke to unclench his fist and shake his hand, which he did, although with more force than was necessary.

"I'll be seeing you around," Joe said pleasantly. "Thank you for the book."

"Read it, you'll learn something," Smoke said. "So when are you headed up?" meaning into the backcountry, where his camp was located.

"Don't know," Joe said. "I've got a lot of business to attend to here first."

I like that answer, Smoke seemed to say with his eyes. His face softened. "Let me know if there's anything I can do to help you get oriented to this country. Nobody, and I mean nobody, knows it better than I do. I've been over every inch of these mountains, and been in the middle of everything. I know where the bodies are buried, if you know what I mean."

Joe nodded, smiled.

"Don't be fooled by all the rich bastards who live here now," Smoke said. "This is still the wildest fucking place in the Lower Forty-eight."

"That's what everyone keeps telling me," Joe said.

"For once, everybody's right."

"Have a good breakfast, Smoke," Joe said as he tipped his hat and walked away.

AT HIS PICKUP, JOE THOUGHT about what Smoke had asked him. They had just played out a bout of "*Where*

Will the Game Warden Be?" Joe had been sincere regarding his plans. But now that Smoke had tipped his hand, questioning him about when he'd go into the backcountry, seeming pleased to hear it wouldn't be soon, Joe made up his mind to get himself into the mountains and the elk camps as quickly as he could.

BEFORE GOING TO THE OFFICE, Joe stopped by his temporary home. He skirted through the bushes at the side of the house, found an old gate, and went into the backyard. The early morning sun had melted the frost, and even the grass, which he hoped would still be trampled, had recovered. There was no longer any hard evidence that someone had stood outside his window at three in the morning, or had run away.

He checked his watch. At home, the girls would be scrambling to finish their breakfast before church. He wondered if Marybeth had made them pancakes like he normally did on Sundays. He wished he were there with them.

JOE SPENT THE AFTERNOON DRIVING around his new district with a map on his lap, learning where the main roads were and noting landmarks. He received no calls. As it darkened, he returned to his house with a bag of hamburgers and a six-pack of beer. He called home and was transferred immediately to voice mail. He guessed that either Sheridan or Lucy was online, probably doing homework. He left a message that he was okay, and that he would call tomorrow.

17

MARY SEELS WAS SETTLING INTO HER RECEPTION DESK with a cup of coffee when Joe arrived at the office building Monday morning.

"You got some messages over the weekend," she said, handing him five pink slips. He glanced through them. Don Ennis, Pete Illoway, Marybeth, Don Ennis, Don Ennis.

"Who is Pete Illoway?" Joe asked.

"You've not heard of him?"

"No."

"I've heard him referred to as the Guru of Good Meat," Mary said, her face revealing nothing. "He's some kind of eating consultant."

"Eating consultant?"

Mary sighed. "We've got pet psychologists. So an eating consultant shouldn't be that surprising."

"I guess not," Joe said. Then: "I didn't see you at the funeral."

Mary began to answer, then stopped and simply looked at him.

"I'm sorry . . ." he said.

She waved him off. "I should have been there. I put in for the time off. I just couldn't make myself go."

Joe didn't understand. He felt she wanted to say more.

Before continuing, Mary looked around the room and up the stairs to make sure no one could overhear her. "I guess I want to remember Will the way he was, not what he turned into."

"Do you mean in the last six months? Susan told me about that."

Mary lowered her voice. "Will Jensen was such a *good* man. He was great to work for, and I thought a lot of him personally. But I really resented covering for him when he didn't show up, or when he missed meetings, or when he didn't respond to calls. It was like he became a different man in the end, one I didn't like." She looked around again and turned back to Joe. "I shouldn't have said that. I shouldn't have said that at all."

"It's okay."

"You remind me of Will, the way he was."

Joe flushed. "I take that as a compliment."

"It is a compliment."

"This is going to sound odd, but did Will ever mention any trouble he was having with people trespassing at his place?"

Mary said quizzically, "Why do you ask?"

Joe told her about waking up in the night and the footprints he found.

"In the last few months, Will said a lot of things, usually in grumbles," she said. "He said he was having trouble sleeping, and he showed up—when he showed up—looking like something the cat drug in. I remember him saying once that he couldn't sleep because somebody was thumping on the wall, but he thought it was teenagers or maybe somebody he arrested who wanted to harass him, you know?"

"Mary," Joe said, "you've obviously thought quite a bit about what happened. If you were to name what—or who—drove him over the edge, what would it be?"

Her eyes flashed. "I think I've said too much already."

"You've got a theory, though?"

She angrily shook her head, as if tossing the conversation aside, sat down at her desk, said, "I've got work to do here."

As Joe climbed the stairs, he looked down at Mary at her reception desk. She was furiously arranging her things in front of her.

You know something you're not telling me, Joe thought.

AT HIS DESK, JOE LOOKED at his watch, then dialed home. Marybeth picked up on the second ring.

"At last," Joe said.

"Not really," she said, strain in her voice. "The school just called. The bus driver didn't show up for work, so I need to take the girls to school. Then I've got to get to Barrett's right after that to defend their books against some IRS auditor who showed up without any warning."

"This has been difficult," he said, wanting to tell her about the funeral, the urn, the strange feeling in his head that was finally dissipating, the man outside his window the night before. Wanting to hear about Sheridan's injured eye, the silent 720 call.

"Can't you call tonight? The girls would love to talk to you," she said.

"Okay. What about you?"

"Oh, Joe, of course I want to talk with you. That is, if you're sober and the line isn't cutting in and out."

He winced at that. "That was a little strong, don't you think?"

"Yes, I'm sorry. But the girls are waiting in the car and I've really got to go now," she said. "Call tonight."

"I will." He hung up, a dark mood forming.

PETE ILLOWAY WASN'T IN when Joe returned the call. The message said:

"Hi, you've reached the desk of Pete Illoway of the Good Meat Foundation. I'm either on the other line or away from my desk, helping people connect with their natural environment for the good of all the species on the planet. Please leave a message. . . . "

"Sheesh," Joe said, and hung up.

DON ENNIS WAS IN, and answered the phone with the brusqueness of a man who had important things to do quickly, Joe thought.

"I called you three times yesterday," Ennis said.

"I was out," Joe said, trying not to sound defensive.

"Jensen was out a lot too. You're not like he was, are you?"

"I'm not sure what you mean."

"Never mind," Ennis said. "I'm sure by now you've run across Will Jensen's file on Beargrass Village, right?"

Joe turned and opened the file drawer, thumbing through the tabs. "I'm looking," he said.

Ennis sighed impatiently. "It's probably a thick one. When you find it you should read it over. I'm sure there are some errors of judgment you'll want to correct."

Joe saw *Beargrass* written in Will's cribbed hand on the tab of a folder. He withdrew it from the drawer and placed it on the desk blotter.

"Okay, Mr. Ennis," Joe said, "I found the file. Can you tell me what this is about?"

Another sigh. "I'm a developer, you know that because you've got my card from the other night, right?"

"Yes," Joe said. "Thank you for the—"

"A developer develops," Ennis said, cutting Joe off. "That's what I do, Mr. Pickett. I've invested millions of dollars of my own money and have millions more lined up to develop Beargrass Village here in Jackson Hole. It's a planned community unlike anything anyone out here has ever done or seen. The concept is brilliant. Forty percent of the home sites have already been committed, and we're ready to start building."

"Yes," Joe said, now understanding why Ennis had been so anxious to get in touch with him.

"Look, I believe in doing things on the up-and-up. I don't like games. I didn't become who I am by fucking around with people. Let me ask you something straight out, Mr. Pickett: Are you one of those people who is against any development?"

"No, I'm not," Joe answered truthfully.

"You're not one of those limp-wristed greenies who oppose anything new?"

"No."

"Okay, then. We can talk."

"You start," Joe said.

"The ground can't be broken until all of the permits are in place and all the state and federal bureaucrats sign off on it. Everybody has at this point, except for one."

"Let me guess," Joe said.

"That's right," Ennis said, his voice rising. "Will Jensen was *concerned* about bear and moose habitat. He was *concerned* that Beargrass Village would be built in the middle of a free-ranging wildlife corridor." Ennis said the word *concerned* with dripping sarcasm, Joe thought. "I

tried to explain to him that this project was *about* wildlife, *about* animals, and if anything, it would enhance the
habitat for the moose and the bears. I tried to *show* him,
personally, but he stood me up for two meetings and
when he finally did show up he was belligerent. He physically attacked me. I had to call the sheriff and have him
arrested."

So you're the one, Joe thought.

"I'm sorry to hear that happened," he said. "No rep-
resentative of our department should have done that."

Ennis paused, then: "Well, I guess I'm glad you're
sorry. But it doesn't change the fact that I'm nearly a year
behind in construction. Some of the delays were the fault
of the Forest Service, but this last one was because of a
single drunken, incompetent *game warden* who personally cost me a lot of money and inconvenienced more
than a few very important people.

"This is a big deal," Ennis said bluntly, "do you understand that? I've gone to the top and I want this re-
solved yesterday."

The top meant the governor, Joe thought.

"The vice president of the United States will be in my
house for a reception in two weeks. He's considering
building a house in Beargrass after he's out of office. Do
you want me to tell him he can't because the local game
warden won't sign off on it?"

Oh, Joe thought, *that* top. "So what do you want
from me?"

"I need to know how soon you can get out here,"
Ennis said. "I'll call my experts and have them assembled. They can answer any questions you've got, and
show you how we plan to address the situation with the
bears and the moose. We'll show you our strategic plan
to create the first planned Good Meat community in the
country. I think you'll leave here impressed as hell, and

you'll give the go-ahead to the project so we can get started. Finally."

"Did you say 'Good Meat community'?"

"That's what I said."

Joe recalled what Trey had told him about the practice, as well as Pi Stevenson's condemnation of it.

"Well?" Ennis asked.

"Well, what?"

"How soon can you get out here for a tour?"

Joe did a quick calculation. His intention, as of that morning, had been to get into the backcountry to check on the outfitter camps as quickly as possible. He also wanted to visit the medical examiner who had been on the scene of Will Jensen's suicide. Given the urgency of Don Ennis's request, Joe also wanted to try to address it as soon as possible. Despite Ennis's manner, it seemed to Joe that Ennis had a legitimate complaint.

"How about this afternoon?" Joe said.

"Hot damn," Ennis cried, "finally somebody I can work with."

Maybe, Joe thought.

18

TO MEET WITH DON ENNIS AND THE PRINCIPALS OF
Beargrass Village, Joe used the map provided in a glossy
four-color brochure entitled *The World's First Sustainable
Good Meat Community* he had found in the file. He
drove his pickup on the highway toward Teton Pass, past
the old-fashioned haystacks that existed purely for scenic
effect in the land-trust meadows, past the gated commu-
nities with scores of million-dollar homes almost hidden
in the timber that were referred to as "starter castles" by
the locals. He thought about what he had read in the file
that Will Jensen had assembled.

The concept of Beargrass Village had been launched
with a complicated land swap between Ennis and his
partners with the U.S. Forest Service: 7,500 acres of tim-
berland across the border in Idaho for 7,500 acres in the
county. The file contained schematics and land plats, letters of support from federal agencies including the Forest Service and U.S. Fish and Wildlife Service. The letters
showed the tremendous political clout Ennis had behind
him. There were opinions written by staff people within

his own office: biologists, fisheries experts, and the liaison for the interagency grizzly bear management team. Joe read enough to know that the staff letters pointed out potential problems with Beargrass Village, but didn't propose outright opposition to the plan. Only the grizzly expert admitted grave concerns, but the letter was written in a kind of bureaucratic "cover your ass" language that would exempt the expert from blame no matter what happened in the end. In the margin of the bear report, Will had scribbled, *This is a big problem.*

What it boiled down to, Joe saw, was just as Ennis had said on the telephone: The final approval of the project from a wildlife management standpoint would depend on the opinion of the local game warden. Will, for whatever reasons, had withheld his final written opinion and impeded the process. Now it was up to Joe.

No wonder Will drank too much, Joe thought, smiling bitterly.

THE HEADQUARTERS FOR BEARGRASS VILLAGE was a dark, modern, low-slung building built of unpeeled logs and native stone. It was set into the side of a wooded rise so naturally that it would be possible for someone not aware of its existence to drive right past the building, which Joe almost did. Fortunately, he noticed a wink of sunlight off the windshield of a black Lexus SUV in a wood-shrouded parking lot, and turned his pickup toward it. Three other late-model SUVs were in the lot. He knew he had found the right place when he saw Don Ennis emerge through a sliding glass door and wave.

"Welcome to Beargrass," Ennis boomed. Joe waved back.

Carrying the file, Joe entered and heard the door slide shut behind him. Several men sat at an enormous table in the room. A PowerPoint projector was on a stand, fan humming. Easels were positioned in each corner of the room, as well as a huge diorama of the planned development.

"Funny thing is," Joe said, surveying the room and meeting the eyes of the men at the table, "there is no beargrass in Wyoming. There's beargrass in Montana, in the northwest corner. But I guess you like the name."

Ennis blinked uncomfortably, then glared at Joe.

"That's trivial," he said in a way intended to end the discussion.

"Probably is," Joe agreed.

The three men at the table all stood to shake Joe's hand and introduce themselves. Jim Johnson was the contractor, a bearish man with a full beard, a barrel chest, and callused hands. Shane Suhn was younger, stylish and fit, and said he was Don Ennis's chief of staff.

Joe asked, "Chief of staff?"

Suhn's face hardened and paled. "Personal secretary, then," he said.

"Pete Illoway," the third man said in a melodious tone. "Pleased to meet you."

"I've heard of you," Joe said, seeing that his comment made Illoway smile with the glow of recognition. Illoway had sunburned, chiseled movie-star features and longish blond hair that curled over the collar of his Patagonia fishing shirt. He exuded health, contentment, and well-being, Joe thought. Illoway carried himself in a way that suggested he was used to being stared at and admired.

"So you know of the Good Meat Movement," Illoway said. "That's a good start."

"I know a little," Joe said, "not much."

"Have a seat, gentlemen," Ennis said, charging toward the table in the head-down way he charged toward everything. "Let's show Mr. Pickett our plan and have some lunch."

Shane Suhn dimmed the lights and handed the projector remote to Ennis. Ennis waited until Joe was seated, then stood directly behind him, pointed the remote at the projector, and triggered the first image. Ennis stood so close that Joe could smell his cologne and feel his body heat.

THE PRESENTATION TOOK TWENTY MINUTES and was dazzling in its professionalism, Joe thought. The logo for Beargrass Village, the stylized lettering set against stalks of tawny beargrass, appeared in the lower left corner of every slide and burned into his subconscious.

The concept was for 120 homes, each with ten to twenty private acres. The homes would be situated concentrically throughout the property, built with native materials within a restored landscape, much like the headquarters itself. There would be no telltale signs of construction, reseeding, commercial landscaping; it would look as if the homes emerged from the earth itself with no assistance from human beings. No home could be seen from another home. Beyond the private acres the land was common to all.

"The commons will be just as wild as it is now," Ennis said, forwarding through photos of bears, deer, moose, and grouse, "and available to all. Beargrass residents can hike on it, camp on it, hunt on it if they want to."

That got Joe's attention.

"Don't worry," Ennis said impatiently, as if he had been anticipating Joe's reaction, "everything will be by the book, in accordance with state law. Hunting licenses, all of that crap. But here's the kicker," he said, advancing the presentation quickly through drawings of barns, corrals, and a pasture so green it burned Joe's eyes.

"This is where the stock is born, raised, and eventually slaughtered. Each resident will contract for a number of animals—pigs, chickens, goats, sheep, cattle—to be cared for by the staff. The stock animals will receive the best of care and will be rotated on our pastures. They'll be raised holistically, organically, with no growth hormones, chemicals, or processed feed. If the residents want to get involved, they can. I suspect most of them will want to be a part of that."

On cue, Pete Illoway stood up and Ennis handed him the remote in a well-practiced way.

"Time for lunch," Illoway said.

The lights came up and a double door opened behind the screen. Joe could see a white-clad waiter and waitress, both Hispanic, push serving carts through the gloom. A platter filled with sizzling meats and colorful vegetables was placed in front of him.

Joe said, "Wow."

"Make sure to sample everything," Illoway said, sitting down to his own platter and rattling his silverware.

Joe cut off slices of each kind of meat. The beef was tougher than he expected, but it exploded with flavor. The pork burst with sharp juices. The chicken tasted slightly wild, with a tang of pine nuts.

"What do you think?" Illoway asked, knowing the answer.

"Everything is fantastic," Joe said.

"Have you ever had beef or chicken that tasted like that?"

"Beef, yes," Joe said, explaining that his family purchased beef in quarters or halves direct from Bill Stafford's ranch outside Saddlestring when they could afford to do so. "Chicken, no."

Illoway nodded. "Not many people have the experience you have with beef, so they're blown away by this. And very few contemporary Americans know what a chicken can taste like that's been raised naturally, with a free-range lifestyle with no hormones or chemicals introduced."

"Here we go with the lecture," Ennis sighed. Joe smiled at that.

Illoway cut another piece of beef and stabbed it with his fork, then pointed the fork toward Joe. "Modern Americans have almost totally lost touch with the natural world," he said. "They don't know where their food comes from. They think their meat comes from a Styrofoam package wrapped with plastic or from the kitchen of a restaurant. This has been one of the most fundamental and harmful shifts that has ever taken place in our culture. The connection between our food source and ourselves has been lost, and we're not the better for it.

"Think about it, Joe," Illoway continued. "For centuries, human beings have interacted with their source of food. We herded animals, cared for them, bred them to be stronger and better suited for the world. Or we hunted them in their own environment, and therefore had to learn about them and appreciate them. In turn, we learned from our animals that there is a circle of life, interconnectivity with nature and our environment. This was hard-wired into our souls, this synchronicity of coexistence. We depended on our animals to provide us with nourishment and health; they depended on us for shelter and protection.

"Enlightened people are becoming aware of how unethical, how *soulless,* our farms and ranches have become—if you can even call them farms and ranches." Illoway paused dramatically. "They're really just meat factories, where animals are packed together, force-fed and filled with growth hormones, then killed without ever living a natural life. Chickens have their beaks snipped off so they can't hurt each other. Cattle are crammed into stalls and fattened. Modern hog farms are worse than any concentration camp ever even conceived by man." To illustrate his point, Illoway advanced through a series of grotesque black-and-white photos of hogs festering with sores, beakless chickens, rivers of black blood coursing through troughs at a cattle slaughterhouse. At last, Joe thought, the photos ran out and the screen was filled with pure blue.

Illoway jabbed the piece of meat into his mouth and reached into a folder in front of him, producing the *World's First Sustainable Good Meat Community* brochure Joe had seen earlier. He slid it across the table. Joe nearly missed it, thinking how odd it was that Illoway was capable of eating after showing those pictures.

"This explains the philosophy of Beargrass Village in detail," Illoway said. "I really urge you to read it. I've also got two books and a website."

Joe put the brochure in his file.

"The idea here," Illoway said, "is to create an environment where families can regain their connection to the natural world, to the food they eat. They'll be able to participate in the birthing of the animals, the care of the animals, even the eventual slaughter of the animals. We'll have our own organic slaughterhouse on-site with viewing windows."

Joe winced.

"I know it sounds crazy," Ennis said, noting Joe's reaction, "but these people do this. I saw it in upstate New York a few years ago. Some friends of mine—wealthy Manhattanites who had gone the vegan route for a while until they were too lethargic to stand, then did all kinds of stupid diets and eating programs—took me to a farm in Connecticut. They called it a 'pure meat farm.' You know, all of the animals were raised in a pasture, eating natural stuff, even the goddamned chickens were running around. It was like something out of the eighteen eighties up there. And these friends of mine were just ecstatic. They named the cows they were going to have slaughtered, and got all emotional when they were killed and butchered, but they told me that for the first time in their lives they were connected to the real world. So I looked into it, and met Pete here, who started the whole idea. This was about the time of the first mad cow scare in the U.S. So I hired him as my consultant and brought him out here to help us plan the village."

"I do seminars in California and New York," Illoway said. "Hundreds of people pay eight hundred dollars each to come hear about Good Meat and come with me to visit our farms."

"And now you have a place for them to live," Joe said.

"Right!" Ennis cried. "We've created the first of its kind. Now I want to *build* it. All that stands in my way is you, frankly. So I hope to hell you're friendly, and not like that goddamned Will Jensen."

Several moments passed. Joe felt the eyes of Illoway, Ennis, and Suhn on him, waiting for his reaction.

"I looked at Will's file," Joe said. "The problem he seemed to have with the development has to do with the fact that by fencing it off you would shut down the traditional migration routes of grizzlies and moose."

Ennis snorted. "That's ridiculous. I already told you that. We want bears and moose in our village."

"But what about the fences?" Joe asked. "It seems to me, looking at your map, that you'd force the wildlife to cross the highway to get to winter ground."

Don Ennis glared at Joe, his eyes bulging.

"The fence does two things," Illoway interjected in his reasonable way. "One, it obviously protects the privacy of the residents. Two, it assures us that our population of stock and wildlife remains pure from disease and poaching. You should care that the wildlife and stock here is as genetically pure as possible."

Joe said, "I'm well aware of the problem with brucellosis in the elk." It was a fact that most of the wild elk coming down from Yellowstone had the disease. Brucellosis was suspected of being passed from wildlife to domestic cattle and causing the cows to abort their fetuses. "But what you're talking about sounds to me like a game farm, and those are illegal in Wyoming."

"It's *not* a game farm," Illoway said, while Ennis moaned. "It's a Good Meat community."

"Let me study the file," Joe said, "and read all of the comments."

"Here we go again," Ennis hissed.

Joe wanted to reassure Ennis, but demurred. Like the name of Beargrass Village itself, there was a falseness to the whole concept, a structure being built on a poor foundation. He didn't *want* to think that. Joe admired many of Illoway's beliefs. He felt an urge to sign off on Beargrass and get it behind him. But he couldn't.

"Sometimes," Illoway intoned, "we need to look past inane regulations toward the greater philosophical good. We need to step outside petty rules and see things for what they really are."

"Yup." Joe nodded. "I'm willing to do that. And I've got to say that I agree with things that bring people closer to the real world. But we're also talking about homes being built in a natural wildlife migration route."

"Jesus Christ!" Ennis said, slamming the table with the flat of his hand. "I thought you said you weren't against development."

"I'm *not*," Joe said. "I just want to make sure I make a decision I can live with later. So I want to study the file, go over all the materials carefully, and maybe ask some questions."

Illoway seemed to relax slightly, but Ennis did not.

"How much money do you make?" Ennis asked bluntly.

"Not much," Joe said, feeling his cheeks burn.

"I didn't think so," he said. "I've done some checking."

Was he going to offer him a bribe? Joe wondered.

Ennis said firmly, "I will *not* let my project go under because of some state flunky who makes thirty-six thousand a year. That's just not going to happen."

"Now, Don," Illoway cautioned, "I think Mr. Pickett here will be fair and reasonable."

I can see why Will punched you, Joe thought, narrowing his eyes at Don Ennis.

"Let's hope that's the case," Ennis said. Then, to Joe: "How soon can you make your decision?"

"Give me a couple of weeks."

Ennis clenched his jaw and looked away. "Two weeks? Two fucking weeks?"

"Two weeks won't kill us," Jim Johnson, the contractor, said from across the table, speaking for the first time since the meeting started. "We've waited this long already."

Ennis shot Johnson a look that made the contractor blanch. Illoway chose not to say anything.

"I've got a lot to read here," Joe said, patting the file. "I'll want to talk with some of the experts who wrote opinions, and probably ride some of the perimeter of the property where those migration routes supposedly are."

"Two weeks—no longer than that," Ennis said, turning to Joe in barely controlled fury. "And if you decide against us . . ."

"*Don,*" a woman's voice came clearly from the other side of the room. Joe turned his head to see Stella Ennis, who had apparently entered a few minutes before. Her tone was cautionary, not harsh.

Then Joe looked back and saw something pass over Don Ennis's face as Ennis looked up and saw his wife—a shadow that washed over him as quickly as it came. It was a look of pure, naked, contemptuous hatred.

19

"I APOLOGIZE FOR DON," STELLA TOLD JOE AS SHE walked him across the parking lot toward his pickup after the meeting had ended and he left Don, Illoway, Suhn, and Johnson at the table. "He gets so forceful at times he doesn't realize how he's coming across to people who don't know him."

"No need to apologize," Joe said, still a little stunned by his glimpse into Don's soul. He wondered if Stella had seen it, if she was used to her husband looking at her like that. He searched for something to say, feeling a bit flustered by Stella's presence.

"Thank you again for your help the other night," Joe said.

"You already thanked me."

She was wearing an oxblood turtleneck sweater and black slacks. The color of the sweater made her lips look even more striking than he remembered, like overripe fruit. She walked with a dancer's grace, as if her shoes didn't really touch the ground.

"Don's just not happy when he's not doing something

really big," Stella explained, a little sadly. "I thought we were moving out here to retire, to ride horses and go rafting. I love to go whitewater rafting."

"This is a good place for it," Joe said, trying to make conversation, knowing how lame his response sounded.

"Please don't patronize me."

"Sorry." Joe felt his ears begin to burn.

Stella smiled slightly, and a little sadly. "The deal was that when Don sold his companies in New York and Pennsylvania, we would buy out here and really *live*. It was a choice between going to Aspen, Steamboat Springs, Sun Valley, Santa Fe, or here. We both liked the Tetons, so Wyoming was the winner. Your governor was one of the first people Don met, and we are among his biggest contributors. Don probably told you that."

"He left that part out," Joe said.

"I'm surprised. He usually leads with it."

"He told me about the vice president, though."

"Ah," she said. "I don't know why I'm telling you all of this. It's odd; it seems comfortable to talk to you. It's like I've known you."

Joe stopped at his pickup. The easy familiarity of their conversation had him flummoxed, and slightly alarmed. He felt comfortable with her, as if they had history together.

"Don's just frustrated," she said.

"Yup, I understand that."

Stella's black Lincoln Navigator was parked on the other side of Joe's pickup.

Joe said, "What I'm not sure I understand is the way he looked at you when you spoke up." He couldn't believe he said it, and felt immediately that he shouldn't have.

Stella paused, looked at Joe quizzically. "I don't know what you mean."

"For a second there," Joe said, treading into water he wasn't sure he belonged in, "he looked like some kind of *reptile*."

She smiled at Joe, a dazzle of white teeth framed by those lips. Her smile triggered something in him, and he knew he reacted to it.

"What?" she asked.

"It's kind of ridiculous," he said. "I just thought of something I hadn't thought of in a long time. In college there was this song I really liked called 'Stella's Smile.'"

"It was about me," she said.

"Really?"

"What, do you think I've spent my life married to Don Ennis? I'm just his most recent. I had a life, you know. I was in the music business in LA. Everybody in my crowd was in the business when I was in high school. I met the lead singer and he wrote that song."

"Really?"

"Yes, *really*," she said, a little exasperated. "Some people went to college, some of us went on the road. Some of us grew up real fast, Joe."

He stared at her.

"The lead singer originally called it 'Stella's Lips,' but luckily his manager talked him out of that, thank God."

"I've never met anyone who had a song written about them," Joe said.

"Now you have," she said dismissively. But he thought she was pleased that he knew. "I have a question for you. You said Don looked like a reptile. Do you use animal metaphors often when describing people?" She looked straight at him, with boldness, as she had in the restaurant when he first saw her.

"I've never really thought about it," Joe said, "but I guess I do."

"Someone else I knew did that," she said, and her recollection brought out an almost imperceptible flinch in her eyes. "I think it's kind of charming."

Joe grunted, wondering but not asking if she was referring to Will.

"What kind of animal would Pete Illoway be?"

Joe thought about it for a moment. "A wolf."

She laughed, apparently delighted. "Jim Johnson?"

"Bear."

Joe knew what was coming next.

"What animal would you say would describe *me*?"

He felt his face flush. "Can I get back to you on that?" he asked.

She smiled at him knowingly. "But will you?"

He hesitated. He liked being with her, liked watching her talk. She was an exotic species, charming and attractive, yet dangerous somehow. He was drawn to her, despite himself. He said, "I'm bound to see you again. This isn't that big a place."

"I've found it's as big or as small as you want it to be," she said. "Jackson is unique that way."

Joe reshuffled the files in his hands.

"You don't need to do that," she said. "I saw your ring last night. You saw mine. Is your wife here with you?"

"No, she's not," Joe said, "but she might as well be."

"Good answer," she said. Stella Ennis lowered her eyes and her lips tugged into a mischievous smile. It was as if she didn't quite know where to put them, Joe thought. "Stella's Lips."

"I had better be going."

"Yes, you had better be going," she said, agreeing with him.

Joe swung into the cab of his pickup, and when he looked back she was still there, beside his truck, looking like she wanted to say something else. He rolled the window down.

"Have you found the file on me in Will Jensen's desk?" she asked.

"File?"

"I assume there's a file." She nodded. "I had to sign a release form with the Wyoming Game and Fish Department in order to go on ride-alongs. You know, agreeing not to sue the state in case a horse bucked me off or a bear bit my leg."

"You went out with Will?" Joe asked, his tone more urgent than he wanted it to be.

"Not my choice of words exactly," she said. "I accompanied him on a few elk trend counts, and once to check an outfitter camp. I absolutely loved it."

If possible, Joe felt even more flushed than he had a moment before.

"I loved the realness of it," she said. "The rawness and the danger. I'm a junkie for authenticity, if there is such a term."

Joe swallowed, looked at her. "I saw you at the funeral."

She nodded.

"You knew Will pretty well, then? Were you and Will . . ."

"Yes, Joe," she said. "We were."

He tried to picture Will and Stella together. He could only picture Stella. He felt a surprising rush of jealousy.

She crossed her arms defensively. "I admired him. He was *real*. I thought he had a quiet honesty and dignity about him, unlike most of the species. He was straightforward and unpretentious. People mistook his earnestness for lack of intelligence, which was a tragedy. I respected him very much. You remind me of him."

Joe wasn't sure he bought it, but she seemed sincere. "Even though your husband didn't respect him?" he asked, deliberately not addressing the last part of her statement.

"Believe it or not, we don't think alike," she said, "much to Don's chagrin. Actually, he prefers it if I don't think at all, except to think about how much I admire him."

Joe was on thin ice and tried to think of a way off it.

"Do you have any idea why Will chose to kill himself?"

She stared at Joe for a long time, pursing her lips. He found himself staring at them, again.

"Maybe he didn't like what he'd become," she said vaguely.

"Meaning what?"

"Meaning," she said, "that I'll need to decide what I should share with you and what I shouldn't."

"I'd like to know," Joe said.

"You had better be going," she said again, and displayed a little wave.

Joe fumbled in his breast pocket for a business card and handed one to her. She took it and slipped it into the pocket of her slacks in one quick movement, as if she didn't want anyone to see. Joe glanced toward the building. Don was standing at the sliding glass door watching them.

Joe looked back at Stella, wondered if she'd seen Don watching them, if she cared.

"You felt it too?" she said. "When we met."

He knew exactly what she meant, but feigned confusion. She smiled. "I thought so."

HE DROVE OUT OF THE LOT into the sun-dappled trees. At the moment before the road curled into the timber, he chanced a look in his rearview mirror. She was at her car, opening the door, but looking back at him.

*   *   *

"MARYBETH!" HE HEARD HIMSELF SHOUT into his cell phone.

"Joe, why are you calling now?" She sounded annoyed, her voice a loud whisper. "I'm in the middle of the audit at Barrett's I told you about. So unless this is an emergency, I can't talk."

Was it? he asked himself. *Yes!* "No, no emergency."

"Then call tonight, like we agreed."

"Okay."

"Joe, are you all right?"

"Dandy," he said, feeling as if he were telling a lie.

20

BUD BARNUM WAS STARTING TO GET IMPATIENT. IT HAD been a week since Randan Bello had come into the Stockman's, and Barnum was starting to wonder if Bello was consciously avoiding him. He knew the tall man hadn't moved on. Tubby Reeves, who managed the rifle range for the county, told Barnum that he had watched Bello put over a hundred rounds through each of his rifles the day before, and said they were nice rifles too. Bello shot long distance, peppering target after target with tight patterns at four hundred yards, the most distant standard available at the range. Reeves said Bello had three handguns as well: a heavy-caliber revolver, a mid-range semiautomatic with a fourteen-shot clip, and a little .25 caliber he wore in an ankle holster.

"More coffee?" Timberman asked, walking the length of the bar with the pot.

"Nearly changeover time," Barnum said, putting his hand over the top of his cup.

"Changeover time is getting earlier every day, it seems," Timberman mumbled.

Barnum said, "Thanks for sharing your opinion on that."

BELLO HAD CHECKED INTO THE Holiday Inn at the edge of town and not moved since. The receptionist, a blocky woman named Sharon, had once let Barnum bed her, and she still had feelings for the retired sheriff. She was willing to tell Barnum what he wanted to know. According to Sharon, Bello was out of his room early every day and didn't return until dark. He was a good guest, she said, an "easy keeper." Meaning he was quiet, didn't use many towels, kept his room neat, and put two dollars on the dresser for the maid, which was Sharon most days. He had paid cash a week in advance but told her he may be staying up to three weeks. When he left in the morning he took his rifle cases, as well as a briefcase and a heavy duffel bag. The only things he left in his room were his clothes and a few books on falconry.

Barnum had a good idea where Randan Bello went when he wasn't at the range practicing. Bello was scouting, like the hunter he was.

Earlier, during coffee with the morning men, Barnum had almost said something. The mayor had been droning on about the possible annexation of some land near the river, Guy Allen was saying that the temperature in Yuma was in the nineties, a rancher was bitching about how cattle prices had dropped because another mad cow had been found in Alberta. The conversation was the same as the day before, and the day before that. Barnum had felt the urge to lean forward, get their attention, and say, "*There's going to be a killing.*" But he restrained himself, thinking that instead of announcing it now, he would tell them later, after it had happened, that he had suspected it all along. Telling the story slowly would have more impact, he thought. He'd explain how he'd pieced it together but was powerless to stop it because the citizens of Twelve Sleep County, in their infinite wisdom, had voted him out of office and replaced him with a preening nitwit.

21

MARY SEELS LOOKED UP FROM HER RECEPTION DESK
Tuesday morning as Joe entered the lobby carrying his
briefcase and the Good Meat files. She said sternly, "You
should be parking in the back, in Will's old spot. There's
no need to use visitor parking. You're not a visitor."

"Okay," he said sheepishly, mounting the stairs to his
office. At the top of the landing he stopped and looked
down at her. She was hunched over paperwork, bent forward as if struggling under the weight of armor. He
wanted to ask her about what she'd started to tell him
the day before.

"Mary . . ."

"Not *now*," she growled.

He sat at his desk and looked around the office. He
felt much better today. He had finally talked to Marybeth. He had slept through the night for the first time in
three nights—except for that dream involving Stella Ennis that excited and shamed him when he replayed it in
his mind.

Will's notebooks were still stacked on the desktop,

and he rifled through them, not sure what he was looking for. There was unopened mail in the inbox. The huge topo map dominated the wall, seemed to lean on him, the outfitter camp pushpins looking like an unclasped beaded necklace. *I need to get up there,* he told himself. But there were other matters at hand. He rubbed his face and eyes, thought, *Where in the hell do I start?*

But all he could think of, as he stared at the notebooks, the files, the map on the wall, was Stella Ennis and that dream. He could see why someone would write a song about her. He was attracted to her, no doubt. *Entranced* would be a better word. A dark shroud of guilt, like a thunderhead, had begun to nose over the mountains.

He needed to divert his thoughts and concentrate on something that was appropriate to the situation.

Thankfully, there *was* something else that rankled him. Something Sheriff Tassell had said, a throwaway line at the time that had struck Joe as slightly off. He'd forgotten about it, but it resurfaced after he had talked through the situation with Marybeth the night before.

He called the sheriff's office and got Tassell.

"Who was the medical examiner called to Will Jensen's house?"

He heard Tassell sigh. "I'm in the middle of another meeting with the Secret Service right now. Can I call you back later?"

"No," Joe said abruptly. "All I want is the name. It's a real simple question."

"Your tone is inappropriate," Tassell said.

"It probably is," Joe said. "But all I need is the name."

"What is the problem?" Tassell asked.

"There may not be one at all," Joe said. Then: "I thought you were in a meeting. That you didn't have time for this?"

"I don't have time," Tassell said. "But—"

"Sheriff, it's public information. I just wanted to save some time instead of looking it up."

Tassell sighed again. "Shane Graves. Dr. Shane Graves. He lives between here and Pinedale. We share him with Sublette County on account of neither of us needs him much."

"Thank you."

"Joe," Tassell said, "keep me informed if you find anything."

"I will," Joe said, thinking, *Was that so damned hard?*

DR. GRAVES WAS AT HIS RANCH, and told Joe that the files and photographs were there also. Graves sounded refined, cultured, aristocratic, and not at all what Joe had expected.

"If I drive down, can I look at the report?" Joe asked.

Graves hesitated. "I'm busy all day, and I was kind of planning on spending the evening with my companion tonight. Is this an urgent request?"

"Yes," Joe said, figuring that anything that would take his mind off Stella Ennis and back to Will's suicide was urgent. "I've got to get up into the backcountry as soon as possible, and I'd like to wrap up as much as I can here before I go."

"Okay, then," Graves said unenthusiastically. "You can come tonight around six. I'll give you directions."

Joe wrote them down.

"I'll see you tonight, then," Joe said.

"You didn't say anything. I'm surprised," Graves said coyly.

"About what?"

"About my name. Graves. Most people comment on the fact that I'm the medical examiner and my name is Graves."

"I'm not that clever," Joe said. He was glad he hadn't said anything—he had assumed Graves was talking about his use of the word *companion*.

JOE SPENT THE AFTERNOON IN the corrals, learning the personalities of Will Jensen's packhorses. There were two he really liked, a black gelding and a buckskin mare who reminded him of a horse he used to have. Both seemed calm and tough, and neither balked when he saddled them or put on the boxy saddle panniers that, when filled, would carry his gear. The horses looked well fed and in good shape. They would have to be, he thought, for where he would be taking them.

THERE WERE FREQUENT DELAYS ALONG the highway south of Jackson, as Joe drove his pickup and followed a school bus dropping off children at the mouths of rural lanes. While stopped, he surveyed the homes splayed out across the floodplain valley below him, and was struck by the overall neatness. He was reminded that because Jackson was bordered on all sides by mountainous federal land, the valley itself was like a glittering island in a sea of ten-thousand-foot waves.

The bus made the turn at Hoback Canyon toward Pinedale, and Joe sighed and looked at his wristwatch. He would be late to Dr. Graves's.

Hoback Canyon, in the high copper wattage of dusk, pulsed with such color and raw physicality that it almost hurt to look at it. The road paralleled the curving Hoback River.

At a straightaway, Joe looked in his rearview mirror. The school bus was holding up a long procession of vehicles. He noted that most of the drivers were talking on cell phones or drumming their fingers impatiently on the steering wheels of their SUVs.

As the children from the bus trudged down their roads wearing backpacks and hemp necklaces and bracelets, he thought of Sheridan and Lucy, and of Marybeth. Would Sheridan, with her teenage angst and strong opinions, fare well here? He couldn't imagine it, just as he had trouble imagining them all staying in Saddlestring. Would Marybeth like it? he wondered.

Joe mulled over the possibility of Marybeth and Stella Ennis in the same town. Jackson, he thought with a sharp stab of guilt, wasn't big enough for both of them.

22

MARYBETH PICKETT WAS BOILING WATER AND MEASUR-
ing uncooked strands of spaghetti for three when there
was a heavy knock on the front door.

"Would you get that?" she asked Sheridan, who was
working at the kitchen table.

"I'm doing my homework," her daughter said.

"Sheridan . . ."

"Okay, okay," Sheridan said with a put-upon sigh,
pushing back her chair.

During hunting season, it wasn't unusual for people
to come to their house at odd hours. Normally, if Joe
wasn't there to take care of the problem, he could be
reached by cell phone or radio and would come home.
In the eight days he had been gone, Marybeth had felt
blessed that things had been quiet. Since Joe had left she
had known it wouldn't last. To top it off, there had been
a message on the phone earlier from Phil Kiner in Laramie, who was being sent north to oversee Joe's district
temporarily, saying he was delayed because he had to testify in court and wasn't sure when he'd make it.

Sheridan came back into the kitchen. "There's a man at the door who says he's here to turn himself in to the game warden."

"Oh, great," Marybeth said, setting the pasta on the counter and reducing the heat under the water.

"I think he's drunk," Sheridan whispered.

"Wonderful."

Marybeth gathered herself for a moment, then strode through the kitchen, Sheridan on her heels.

"I've got your back, Mom," Sheridan said in a low voice.

A large man wearing bloody camouflage clothing filled the doorway of the mudroom. His face was perfectly round, with flushed cherubic cheeks and glassy eyes.

"Joe isn't in," Marybeth said. "What can I help you with?"

"As I told the little lady, I'm here to turn myself in," he slurred.

Marybeth could smell whiskey on him from a few feet away.

"I was shooting at a buck but I hit a fawn somehow," the man said, choosing each word deliberately and over-enunciating. "I brung down the fawn to hand it over and to accept my citation."

"You brought it here?"

"Yes."

"What am I supposed to do with it?"

"I don't know," the man said, his eyes glistening. "Whatever you do with dead fawns."

Marybeth looked to Sheridan, who shrugged.

"I'm afraid I can't take it," Marybeth said. "My husband is . . . not back until later." She almost said Joe was out of town, but they'd agreed before he left not to give out that information.

"Oh." The hunter seemed perplexed, and angry. "I didn't have to do this, you know. I coulda just left it up there and not said a damned word."

"I realize that," Marybeth said. "You did the right thing. I just don't have any way of helping you."

"That's a hell of a note. A man tries to do the right thing and he gets turned away."

Marybeth thought she recognized in the hunter the potential for him to quickly escalate from drunk and maudlin to drunk and enraged. She didn't want that to happen, and didn't want him in her house. She was grateful when Maxine padded in from the kitchen. Sheridan reached down and grasped the dog's collar.

"If you left your number, I could have Joe get in touch with you," Marybeth said. She figured she'd give the information to him that night when he called to pass along to dispatch. Now, though, she wanted the man out of her house. The hunter was so drunk, Marybeth doubted he'd remember any of what she told him.

The hunter's eyes were now hard and dark. He glared at her and she involuntarily stepped back into Sheridan. Maxine growled and strained on her collar. The inherent danger of the situation weighed on her, and she thought of her safety and the safety of her children. If he took a step forward, she vowed, she would instruct Sheridan to let Maxine go and dial 911 while she went for the can of pepper spray in her purse.

But the man mumbled something, turned clumsily, and went out the door.

Marybeth and Sheridan stood still for a moment, watching the screen door wheeze shut.

"Whew," Sheridan said.

They heard a thump in the front lawn, then a truck start up and roar away toward Saddlestring.

Marybeth turned on the porch light and looked outside. There was a large bundle of some kind on the grass. Retrieving a flashlight from Joe's office, she went outside and found the dead fawn. It had been gut shot, and its tiny speckled body was splayed out in unnatural angles.

"That's sick," Sheridan said, joining her in the yard. "That poor little thing. You should have at least gotten his license plate number. That's what Dad would have done."

"I really don't need your help after the fact," Marybeth snapped back, still on edge.

"Fine," Sheridan said, spinning angrily on her heel and going into the house.

Marybeth called after her, "Sheridan, make sure to keep Lucy in the house."

Her daughter stopped in the doorway. "I'll be sure to send her right out."

"Sheridan . . ."

BACK IN THE KITCHEN, SHERIDAN watched her mom use the wall phone to place two calls. One, she assumed, was to the house her dad was staying in. There was clearly no answer.

"Try his cell," Sheridan said from the table.

"I did. He's either got it turned off or he's out of range."

"Call dispatch."

Her mom shot her a look, then turned back to the phone. "I'm calling Nate."

"Are we going to eat dinner at some point?" Sheridan asked, not looking up from her homework. She knew her mother would call Nate. She'd known it for a year.

NATE ROMANOWSKI ARRIVED AT 9:00, tossed the fawn into the back seat of his Jeep, and came to the door.

"I can't let him see me like this!" Sheridan said, running from the family room in her pajamas. Marybeth was amused.

"Thank you so much, Nate," she said at the door.

"Not a problem. I'm good with dead bodies."

"I hope you're making a joke."

Nate shrugged. "Sort of."

"Have you eaten? We have some spaghetti left."

His silence told her he was hungry, and she invited him in.

"Mind if I wash up first?" he asked.

"Bathroom's down the hall," she said, walking to the kitchen to retrieve the covered bowl of spaghetti out of the refrigerator and put it in the microwave to heat. She set about making him garlic bread as well.

From down the hall she heard Nate say, "Hi, Sheridan," followed by Sheridan's "*Eeek!*" and the slamming of her bedroom door.

Nate was still smiling from the exchange when he came to the table. "I appreciate this," he said. "I'm getting pretty sick and tired of my own cooking. I used to have some imagination in the kitchen, but now I seem stuck in a broiled meat rut. Oooh, and garlic bread too."

She sat at the other end of the table and tried not to watch him eat. It still struck her how interesting he was to look at, with his sharp angles and fluid movements. Despite his size and ranginess, he looked coiled up, like he could strike out quickly at any time. There was something about him that reminded her of a large cat.

"Did you get the name of the guy who left the deer?" Nate asked between mouthfuls.

"No, and I didn't get his license plate either."

"I could track him down if you want me to."

"How would you go about doing that?" she asked.

He flashed his sly grin. "You said he was a fat guy. He

probably hasn't washed the blood out of his truck. I would guess he's an out-of-stater or you'd know him. Saddlestring only has a few places to stay."

"Mmmmm."

"So do you want me to find him?"

"No," she said. "I'm just glad he's gone."

He nodded and ate.

"No one's ever liked my spaghetti so much."

"Sorry, am I eating like a pig?"

"No. I'm glad you like it."

He cleaned out the bowl, then wiped his plate with the last piece of garlic bread. "So, how's Joe doing over in Jackson?"

Marybeth sighed. "He seems harried. We've had trouble communicating."

Nate looked up sharply.

She felt her neck get red. "I mean he calls when I can't talk, or I call and the connection is bad. That's what I mean."

AT THE FRONT DOOR, NATE thanked Marybeth again for the meal.

"It's the least I could do," she said, "since I'm such a lousy game warden."

He smiled uncomfortably, she thought.

"Where are you taking the deer? Are you going to bury it?"

Nate shook his head. "Some of it's going to feed my birds," he said. "The rest I'll dispose of in a place I found out in the breaklands."

"Way out there?"

He hesitated for a moment, as if deciding whether to let her in on a secret. Then: "It's a nasty thermal spring. I found it last winter. There's natural sulfuric acid in the water. I tossed a road-killed antelope in it and the meat was gone within a week and the bones were dissolved in a month."

"Does Joe know about it?" she asked.

Nate nodded. "I showed it to him. He tried to figure out where it came from, to see if it was somehow connected to the underground thermal activity by Thermopolis or in Yellowstone Park."

"Sounds like Joe."

Nate grinned. "Tell him I said hello."

"I will," she said, "if I ever talk with him."

Nate looked at her, puzzled, then turned and went to his Jeep. Marybeth closed the door and leaned back against it, glad that Sheridan hadn't heard the exchange, and ashamed for thinking that.

AN HOUR LATER, MARYBETH answered the telephone on the first ring.

"Joe?"

"No, it's your mother," Missy said. "We're back from our honeymoon. Sorry to disappoint you."

"No, it's not that—"

"Italy was just so wonderful. The people are warm, the food is out of this world."

"We had spaghetti tonight," Marybeth said morosely, and immediately regretted saying it.

"Not like the spaghetti in Italy," her mother said. "Oh, you'll need to bring the girls over. We've gifts for everyone. Even Joe."

Marybeth told her mother that Joe was in Jackson, and had been gone for over a week.

"My third husband and I used to have a condo there," Missy said. "I lost use of it after the divorce."

"I remember," Marybeth said, not seeing the point,

other than to instinctively top anything her daughter said.

"I bet you're getting lonely," Missy said. "I know what it's like to be abandoned. You always need to know, Marybeth, that you can bring the children and stay here with them if you want to. There's room for everybody and you're always welcome. Keep in mind that this is my ranch now too."

After she hung up, Marybeth saw she had missed a call. For a moment her heart leaped. But when she listened to the message, there was only breathing. Caller ID said it came from area code 720.

SHE FELT VAGUELY UNSETTLED as she cleaned up the kitchen after her daughters were in bed. Why hadn't Joe called? Anger at him was overshadowing her concern. This was getting to be a habit.

Then, as if there were a breach in her mental dam, several unpleasant thoughts began to trickle forth, followed by a steady stream of them, then a torrent. She was *really* angry with Joe. Sure, she'd encouraged him to take the opportunity, but while she was back home struggling with Sheridan's attitude and dealing with a dead deer in the front yard, he was at a resort community. She could imagine him eating out, seeing new things, meeting new and interesting people. His days were so rich and full that he couldn't make the time or arrangements to call her. And here she was, in their crappy little house outside their crappy little town. He had left her stuck in the life that was about him, not her, not *them*. He had left her to balance her business, the family, his responsibilities, and the checkbook. She had once been a promising pre-law student. Now, she was Joe Pickett's facilitator, his unpaid assistant. She was stuck in a particular time and place while the world, like a ship on the horizon, moved on without her. Soon, she thought, it would be too far away to ever meet up with again.

Talking with her mother hadn't helped. Not a bit.

Maybe she should just follow the example of her mother, she thought, who discarded men and traded up. Look where her mother was now. *There's room for everybody,* she had said. *Keep in mind that this is my ranch now too.* And what did Marybeth have? Besides her daughters, of course? She looked around. Even her own house was owned by the state of Wyoming.

Marybeth found herself staring at her reflection in the microwave oven door. Her expression was angry, and desperate. And guilty.

Joe was doing his best. He always did his best. But she couldn't help wondering when Nate would come back and have dinner again.

23

DR. SHANE GRAVES'S PLACE WAS HUGE AND RAMBLING, built into the side of a sagebrush-covered hill three miles from the highway. In the night, it looked like a ship at sea with all lights blazing. Joe could see no other lights in any direction. He drove up a crushed stone driveway and stopped adjacent to the front door.

Graves, tall and thin with a shock of white hair and hollowed, pockmarked cheeks, opened the door before Joe knocked. Graves wore a long velour robe, socks, and beaded moccasins. He introduced himself and offered his hand. Joe suppressed a flinch at the touch of Graves's cool, long, smooth fingers. "My office is down this hallway," Graves said, leading Joe inside. "The Jensen file is on the desk as well as a box of evidence. Please don't remove any of the items from the Ziploc bags without asking my permission."

Joe followed the ME down the dark hallway, but not before stealing a glance into a well-appointed great room where soft music swelled and low-wattage lamps created a warm, subdued glow. A man about Graves's age sat on a couch in the great room. He looked to be a working cowboy—worn Wranglers, scuffed boots, long-sleeved canvas shirt, long-brimmed hat grasped in his hands—but he didn't acknowledge Joe. The cowboy sat with a forward-leaning posture with his eyes fixed on something high on the wall that suggested to Joe that the man thought that if he remained still he couldn't be seen. The cowboy, Joe guessed, was Graves's companion for the evening.

Once in his office, Graves snapped on a bank of harsh lights and gestured toward the desk. "Maybe if you told me specifically what you're looking for I could save you some time." The office was in stark contrast to the dimly lit great room in its clinical whiteness.

"I'm not exactly sure what I'm looking for yet," Joe said, hedging, his eyes still adjusting to the brightness of the room. "I'd like to read over the reports first and then see if I have any questions. Is that all right?"

"You told me on the phone it was urgent," Graves said impatiently.

Caught, Joe felt himself flush. "Sorry. It's something Sheriff Tassell told me the other night. He said that when Will shot himself, the kick of the gun drove the front sight into the top of his mouth."

Graves nodded. "Yes, it knocked out the victim's front two teeth as well. A handgun of that caliber has an enormous kick to it when it's fired."

"Is the weapon Will used in there?" Joe asked, pointing to the box.

Graves crossed in front of Joe and pulled out a large plastic bag and handed it to Joe. The .44 Magnum was huge and heavy, with a ten-inch barrel. Graves fingered the sharp front sight through the plastic with his long, white fingers. "You can see how it could happen," he said. Joe noticed that the blade of the front sight was rust-colored with dried blood.

"Yes," Joe said, hesitating. "Do you mind if I look through the files?"

"I'm not sure what your intention is here, and I hope you're not just fishing," Graves sighed. "Please don't take all night, Mr. Pickett. As you can see, I have a guest."

Joe nodded.

"There are some photos in the file that might be disturbing to you," Graves said. "I want to warn you—they're very graphic."

"I understand."

"Everybody always says that," Graves said, his smile revealing crooked beige teeth, "until they actually look at them."

JOE HEARD GRAVES PAD BACK down the hallway, and heard the music increase in volume. Graves didn't want conversation from the great room to be overheard, Joe guessed. He opened the file and read the report. It was as Tassell had described. The only item that Joe wondered about were the notes saying that no toxicology report or autopsy was recommended.

Even though he thought he was prepared, the photos shocked Joe, just as Graves had warned. Will was slumped back in the hardback chair, his long legs splayed out underneath the table. His neck was white and exposed, his bloodied chin tilted up. Both arms hung straight down. The .44 Magnum was on the floor near his right hand. In the background, the entire kitchen wall and what could be seen of the ceiling were spattered with blood, brains, bits of white bone, and hair. Joe felt an urge to get sick, and looked around the office for water to drink. He found a paper cup near the sink and filled it, noticing that his hand was trembling.

Taking a deep breath he retuned to the desk and

forced himself to look at the other photos. Will's body had been photographed from all angles. A particularly disturbing photograph was taken from behind Will, where the back of his skull was shot away. In another, a close-up of Will's mouth clearly showed the wound in the palate caused by the front sight, the two front teeth hanging from the upper gum by thin strings.

"God help me get through this," Joe whispered to himself.

HE WAITED UNTIL HE WAS SURE he wouldn't get sick before he went to find the medical examiner. He purposely clumped his boots on the tile louder than necessary as he walked down the dark hallway to the great room, making sure he could be heard.

Graves was turned toward the cowboy on the couch, large crystal goblets of red wine on the table in front of them. Again, the cowboy wouldn't look at Joe.

"Dr. Graves, may I ask you a few questions?"

Graves looked annoyed. Then he sighed, stood, and followed Joe back into the office.

"WHY WASN'T THERE A TOXICOLOGY report or an autopsy?" Joe asked.

Graves cinched his robe tight before answering. "There simply wasn't any reason for it," he said. "It was obvious that the cause of death was a self-inflicted gunshot to the head. We don't do autopsies as a matter of course unless we have a reason. We know he didn't die of a heart attack, Mr. Pickett. We're like any other medical examiner's office in the country in that respect."

"So we don't know if Will was drunk, or sick?"

Graves shook his head. "No."

"Is there any way to find that out now?"

The ME looked at Joe quizzically. "I'm sure there isn't, since the body was cremated. What are you driving at?"

"I want to know why he did it," Joe said.

Graves sighed. "Look, I'm sympathetic. But my job isn't to try to determine *why* a victim takes his life. My job is to determine *how* it happened, and give my professional opinion as to cause of death. You seem to be looking for something I just can't help you with."

Joe rubbed his jaw and thought about it. He had watched Graves carefully as he spoke, looking for a false note, but hadn't seen or heard one.

"Now, if you've looked at everything you wanted to look at . . ." Graves said, not needing to finish his sentence.

"Right," Joe said, getting his jacket.

Graves was standing at the office door waiting to show Joe out into the hallway when Joe suddenly stopped and picked up the gun in the bag.

"You can't take that," Graves said.

"I don't want it," Joe said, smiling. "I couldn't hit anything with it, anyway. But a question just occurred to me."

Graves arched his eyebrows.

Joe sat back down in the chair and grasped the handgrip through the plastic. He extended his arm, pointed the revolver at the wall, then bent his elbow and wrist and turned the gun back toward himself so the muzzle of the revolver was a few inches from his face.

"Mr. Pickett, what are you doing?" Graves cautioned, stepping back into the hallway and peering around the doorjamb. "That gun is still loaded."

Joe said, "Look how long the barrel is on this gun. I can barely reach my mouth with it like this, the barrel is so long. This is also a heavy weapon, and it's real uncomfortable to hold it this way. When you go to fire a gun of this caliber, you really need to brace yourself and lock your arms when you fire, or it'll kick right out of your hand. From this position, if I pulled the trigger the bullet would go through the base of my skull straight into the wall behind me and the gun would probably flip out of my hand across the room."

"Yes . . . but the bullet was lodged in the ceiling."

"Right," Joe said. "That's what puzzles me."

Graves said nothing.

"But if I turn it like this"—Joe brought his arm down against his chest and turned the gun upside down and aimed upward—"it would be much easier." He bent his head forward as if to sip from a straw, and the muzzle touched his lips through the thin sheet of plastic. "See what I mean?"

"Yes, I see your point," Graves said. "But I'd be more comfortable if you put the gun down on the desk."

Joe ignored the ME's request. "If I pulled the trigger with the gun in this position, the bullet would go straight up through my brain into the ceiling. It's braced well enough against me that my body would absorb the kick, and the gun would probably drop away to the floor."

"Yes."

"But as you can see, the front sight is pointed down in this position, toward my lower lip, not my upper palate."

Graves nodded.

Joe looked up. "So how is it that Will killed himself with this gun using such an awkward, uncomfortable position like I showed you a minute ago? Or that the bullet was lodged in the ceiling, not the wall? And why is it that the gun fired with such force that it cut his mouth and knocked his teeth out, but then fell to the floor beside him and wasn't thrown clear across the table?"

He put the gun down and Dr. Graves stepped back into the room.

"I don't think I can answer those questions," the ME said.

"Neither can I," Joe admitted.

"So what are you driving at?"

"Was the gun dusted for prints?"

"Yes. You can see there is still some powder residue on it. Will's fingerprints, and only his fingerprints, were all over the barrel and the cylinder."

Joe examined the gun and saw the powder gathered in folds of the plastic. "What about the handgrip and the trigger?"

Graves cleared his throat. "We found no fingerprints on either."

"At all?"

The ME nodded.

"So the gun had been wiped clean?"

"I didn't say that," Graves said. "The surface of the trigger itself is grooved, so it wouldn't hold a print. The handgrip is checkered wood, which isn't a good surface for lifting latents."

"But it *could* have been wiped clean?"

"It's possible," Graves said. "But there's no way to prove it. I wouldn't testify that the gun had been wiped clean."

Joe sat back. "Are these questions enough to reclassify this case as a possible homicide?"

The doctor set his jaw. "No, no. I think I need more than that. But let me give it some thought."

24

JOE WAS AT HIS DESK EARLY WEDNESDAY MORNING AF-
ter breakfast at the Sportsman's Café, and again there was
something wrong with his head. He had not slept
through the night because when he closed his eyes the
ceiling spun and random images hurtled down at him:
the crime-scene photos, the bear's eyes as they locked on
him and he froze, Stella Ennis with parted lips and a flash
of teeth. Now, he couldn't seem to concentrate on the
paperwork in front of him. Lines on the topo map
blurred into one another, and the list of outfitter names,
camps, and locations bled together into a blob. Not even
four cups of coffee could cut through the fog.

It was an hour before the office opened. He had arrived well before, when it was still dark out, because he
couldn't sleep. After looking at his face in the mirror in
the office bathroom—he swore there was something
wrong with his eyes—he watched the sun paint the Tetons
electric pink. It was otherworldly, and matched his mood.

Joe had torn the office apart looking everywhere for
the missing notebook. There was nothing behind the file

cabinets, and nothing had slipped between the hanging files. He had removed the desk drawers and looked inside the desk, finding only a gum wrapper. It was clean beneath the desk blotter, and there was nothing taped up behind the map or bulletin board.

When he had arrived that morning there was an envelope on his desk with his name on it in elegant script. Since there was no stamp or postmark, it had apparently been hand-delivered. He pulled out a large card and reread it. It was an invitation to a reception on Saturday night for the vice president of the United States, at the home of Don and Stella Ennis in Beargrass Village. *Jeez,* Joe thought, *the vice president!*

On the bottom of the invitation, beneath the RSVP, was written: *If you wear your red uniform shirt I'll know you want to talk. If you don't, I'll leave you alone. But you ARE coming.* It was signed "S."

Stella.

Joe imagined Marybeth's reaction when he told her about the party. It would be hard to convince her he wasn't having the time of his life without her.

LATER, HE CHECKED HIS WRISTWATCH, trying to anticipate when Marybeth might wake up at home. He hadn't called the night before because when he returned from Dr. Graves's it was after midnight. Dead tired, his dinner was a can of spaghetti and a bourbon and water. He wanted to tell her what he had learned about the crime scene and find out her impressions. She often thought of angles he hadn't considered.

Then he wanted to talk to Mary, maybe get her to tell him something about Will Jensen before taking the horses north to the trailhead to begin a four- or five-day pack trip into the wilderness to check the outfitter camps.

He had not forgotten about Smoke Van Horn, who seemed to have a professional interest in when Joe would hit the backcountry. Joe had not announced his intentions to anyone, and would tell only Mary and Marybeth, and go.

If there was anything that might clear his head, it was several days alone in the mountains. He intended to use the days not only to do his duty at the camps, but to think through what he had learned about Will Jensen's death since arriving in Jackson.

Because I sure can't focus on anything here, he thought. He considered seeing a doctor, but didn't know one in Jackson and wasn't sure how much his insurance would cover. If he continued to have nights like the one he had just had, he vowed, he would get a checkup when he got back.

AS JOE REACHED FOR THE PHONE to call his wife, it rang. Sheriff Tassell sounded angry and told Joe that he was calling from his car and hadn't even made it into the office yet. Joe was annoyed as well, having another call to Marybeth aborted before it had begun.

"Graves said you think somebody might have killed Will Jensen," Tassell said.

"I was speculating—"

"Damnit, this is exactly what I was warned about you," Tassell said. "You agreed to keep me informed."

"I didn't get in last night until after midnight," Joe said. "Did you want me to call you then?"

"Why not?" Tassell asked. "Graves sure as hell did."

"What did he tell you?"

"He said we ought to consider hiring a big-name forensics expert to look at the photos."

"So he thinks there's something there?" Joe asked, a

little surprised. He had assumed, incorrectly, that Graves was as anxious to put the death behind him as Tassell seemed to be.

"He's not sure," Tassell said. "But he made that suggestion. Dumped it in my lap, actually. Of course, the cost for that kind of expert wouldn't come out of *his* budget."

Joe grinned sourly. "So that's what this is about, huh? Maybe the state DCI would—"

"I don't want the state involved, coming in here after the fact," Tassell said impatiently. "Not based on a couple of photos and the fact that you thought the gun was uncomfortable to hold in a certain position. Jesus, why would a guy so strung out that he wanted to commit suicide even care if he was *uncomfortable* at the last second of his life?"

"It just doesn't fit," Joe said.

"Is that a reason to raise the issue? Unless we've got more than that, I can't spend our money for a high-priced outside expert."

"Don't you want to be sure?" Joe asked.

Tassell said, "Don't put that on me, Joe. You're as bad as Graves."

"You're the sheriff," Joe said. "It's your decision."

Tassell moaned and cursed. "Okay, I'll give it some thought. Those photos aren't going anywhere. Maybe once we get the VP out of town and I know where our budget is—"

"Why wait?" Joe asked.

"Because," Tassell shouted before hanging up, "that's what I do."

HE HAD JUST ROLLED THE MAPS into tubes for his trip and cleared his inbox when Mary Seels appeared at his office door and said, "Joe, your truck is on fire."

*   *   *

THE ONLY THINGS HE WAS able to save were the panniers he had packed in the back of his truck the night before. The cab and engine were engulfed in flames, loud, crackling, angry flames so loud he almost didn't hear the two biologists screaming at him from second-story windows in the building, *"GET AWAY FROM THAT BEFORE IT EXPLODES!"*

Which he did and it did, with a ground-shaking *WHUMP,* as he stood near the corrals with the scorched panniers at his feet. A huge black roll of smoke mushroomed from his pickup and hung in the air at roof level. The morning smelled of burning gasoline, oil, plastic, and melting rubber. His truck was a hot black shell by the time the fire department arrived. When the firemen turned their hoses on it the metal steamed and sizzled and the wet clouds of condensation rolled across the parking lot and made him gag as he attempted to duck beneath them.

AS JOE CIRCLED THE TRUCK, marveling that the only thing that looked intact was the gear shift knob, Assistant Director Randy Pope showed up.

"How did this happen?" Pope asked, touching the metal of the window frame and snapping his hand back from the heat.

"I have no idea," Joe said. "I drove it to work this morning, parked it, and it caught on fire."

"Were you in it at the time?"

Joe shook his head. "I was at my desk."

No one had seen the truck catch fire. The few employees who were in the office had been in the lounge area, celebrating the birthday of one of the biologists.

No one had been in the parking lot, and the lot couldn't be seen from the street in front.

"Did you smell anything burning when you drove it last?" Pope asked. "Did the gauges tell you anything? Were you overheating? Brand-new twenty-nine-thousand-dollar vehicles just don't catch on fire."

"No," Joe said, "nothing." But he thought how disoriented he had felt that morning, how dizzy he had been. Maybe some wiring was bad and he hadn't noticed it?

Pope stopped and shook his head. "Let's see," he asked rhetorically, "isn't this your *third* department vehicle that's a total loss?"

"I didn't do anything," Joe said, aware of how weak that sounded. "It just caught on fire somehow and burned up."

"When was the last time it was in for maintenance?"

Joe tried to remember. "When I got the bodywork done on it after I damaged the frame." He added, "I think. The maintenance log got burned up too."

Pope looked at Joe with condescension. "Three vehicles in five years is some kind of record, I believe."

Joe tried to remain calm. "Maybe someone torched it."

"Think so?" Pope asked. "Who have you made angry enough to do that? You haven't even been here a week."

Joe thought, Pi Stevenson, Smoke Van Horn, the society woman who killed the deer, Don Ennis . . . maybe even Sheriff Tassell. But he said, "I don't know."

FROM HIS OFFICE WINDOW, JOE watched the tow truck hook up his burned vehicle and take it away. He felt profoundly unhappy, verging on pathetic, he thought. He didn't have his family, his house, his horses, his dog. Now he'd lost his truck, along with his cell phone, weapons, and records. Plus, he still felt strange.

"How are you doing, Joe?"

He turned. Mary Seels stood at his door.

"Come in," he said. "I'm just waiting for them to bust in and take my clothes and my manhood."

She didn't laugh, but held up a key ring. "These are spare keys to Will Jensen's vehicle," she said. "There's no reason why you shouldn't use his old truck. It's perfectly fine, as far as I know."

Joe grimaced. The irony was inescapable. "I have a dead man's job, a dead man's house, the dead man's problems, and I've been mistaken for a dead man," he told her. "And now I have a dead man's pickup truck." He left out that he also had the dead man's ashes in an urn in the panniers he had saved.

She didn't respond.

He took the keys and thanked her, but she didn't leave, just lingered near the door. This time, he decided not to push her. After a few beats, she stepped back into his office and eased the door shut behind her.

"Joe, about a week before he died, Will said something to me."

Joe sat down.

"He was in pretty bad shape when he came into the office that morning," she said. "I thought he was hungover, and frankly, I wasn't very kind to him. Now, when I look back on it, I think he was sick, or really depressed.

"I gave him kind of a hard look, I guess, when I gave him his messages. He just stood there. He looked so lonely, but at the time I didn't feel sorry for him."

Mary stopped and took a breath, kneading her hands together, looking around the room as if she suspected someone might be listening. "Will said he thought they were out to get him, and they were closing in. He said he thought there was only one person he could trust in this valley. I thought at the moment he said it he meant me."

"He didn't?" Joe asked.

"No," she said, "he said someone else. That really hurt me, Joe. I know it's emotional, and irrational, but it really hurt me. I'd been covering for him for so long . . ."

"So who was it?" Joe asked.

Mary's face hardened. "He said the only person he trusted was Stella Ennis."

IT WAS LATE AFTERNOON BEFORE Joe set off for the trailhead in Will Jensen's pickup, the horse trailer hooked up behind. The interior of the truck was so similar to his own that when he realized he had not called Marybeth, he reached for the cell phone that wasn't there.

He cursed. He *had* to reach her before he rode north, into country where he would be inaccessible. He stopped at a pay phone on the side of the highway, but it was out of order. Finally, he called the dispatcher over his radio and asked her to patch him through to his home number. He hoped Marybeth would be there, and maybe he could speak to Sheridan and Lucy since school was over. God, he missed them.

His wife answered, and the sound of her voice lifted his spirits.

"Marybeth, I'm glad I caught you."

"It's about time, Joe. I was starting to think you'd run off on me."

"Honey," he said, wondering how many game wardens, dispatchers, brand inspectors, and citizens with scanners were listening to every word, "I've been patched through on the radio. So this isn't a private call."

"Oh," she said, obviously disappointed. "Why didn't you call me on the cell? Or from your office?"

"My cell phone burned up. In fact, my whole truck burned up."

Silence.

"I know it sounds ridiculous, but my truck caught on fire this morning in the parking lot. I'm calling from Will's old pickup."

"Are you okay?" she asked.

"Fine. Don't worry about anything. Look, I'm going to be out of touch for three or four days. I wanted to check in with you before I go."

Her hesitation told him everything he needed to know.

"Three or four days?"

"At least," he said. "I'm sorry."

He was in a bind, he thought. He didn't want to tell her where he was going in case someone who knew Smoke Van Horn, or Smoke himself, was monitoring the radio traffic. He wished he could explain himself fully to her to alleviate her concern and lessen her anger.

When she finally replied, she sounded cold, business-like: "Joe, when you get back and to a phone, we need to talk."

"I know. I'm looking forward to it."

"That's nice, I guess."

"Marybeth—"

"A man threw a dead fawn on our lawn last night. Oh, and we keep getting those calls."

His heart sank. He had hoped to hear that things were going surprisingly well. "I hope you called Nate," Joe said.

"Yes. He helped us out with the fawn."

"Good—"

"But there are still the calls. And Joe, we need to talk again about one of our daughters."

"Sheridan?"

"I thought you said this wasn't a private call," Marybeth snapped.

"It isn't, I'm sorry. Is she okay?"

"She's fine, but we're having some difficulties."

"Marybeth—"

"Joe, this isn't working. This call, I mean. I don't like talking with you this way. So just make sure to call me the minute you can, okay? If you can spare the time."

He heard the phone slam down and felt needles of ice shoot into his heart.

AT THE SAME TIME, NOT FAR from the Twelve Sleep River, Nate Romanowski released his red-tailed hawk and peregrine falcon to the sky. He stood back and watched them search until they found a thermal current, then climbed into the sky in wide circles. It was a clear, cloudless fall afternoon. As the birds rose, he walked away from his home into the field of sagebrush.

He walked noisily, tromping through the brush and occasionally crushing it under his boots. His noise and activity would alarm any hidden prey in the field, and startle them into flight. Nate functioned as a human bird dog for his falcons.

The peregrine released first, and dropped through the cobalt sky like a rock being dropped. He could hear it slice through the air, wings tucked, talons balled into fists. Nate hadn't seen the cottontail rabbit, but no matter. His bird had. The collision on the ground was a muted thunderclap amid a puff of dust and rabbit fur.

The red tail continued to circle, surveying the ground, while Nate walked. He passed the peregrine, who was cracking the bones of the rabbit and eating it whole. Ten minutes later, there was a flurry in the sagebrush a few feet in front of him, and a full-sized jackrabbit launched into the open and ran toward the far ridge in the direction of the road. He watched it go, marveling, as always, at the long lopey stride of the creature that produced the optical illusion of being three times larger than it actually was. He felt as much as saw the red tail target the jackrabbit and start its stoop. Nate stopped, watched the rabbit streak toward the ridge and go over it out of sight while the hawk shot downward in a perfectly murderous nexus.

Suddenly, the red tail flared, halting its descent, and altered its path. The bird clumsily flapped its wings, climbing again. Had the rabbit escaped? No, Nate decided. Jackrabbits didn't hide in holes, and it couldn't have simply disappeared. Something, he thought, had spooked the red tail. Something on the other side of the ridge.

Or somebody on the other side of the ridge.

25

FOR EX-SHERIFF BUD BARNUM, THE MORNING STARTED
out on a bad note when Stovepipe, the man behind the
counter at the city/county building, asked him to walk
through the metal detector.

"You've got to be shitting me," Barnum growled.

"I ain't," Stovepipe said. "In order to enter the sheriff's office you've got to go through the machine and get
a pass. The sheriff says no exceptions."

"Does it even work?" Barnum asked, knowing that the
metal detector was often broken when he was the sheriff.

"It does now."

"This is bullshit."

Stovepipe shrugged in response.

"I *hired* you, Stovepipe."

"And I appreciate that, Bud, I truly do."

Barnum glared. Stovepipe had always called him
"sheriff," not "Bud." As he stepped through the machine, the alarm sounded. Shaking his head, Stovepipe
motioned for him to step back.

Barnum angrily did so, then emptied his pockets,

took off his belt, and dropped his gold pen into a plastic bowl. This time, he made it through.

"I'll need to keep this stuff until you come back," Stovepipe said, handing Barnum a yellow pass.

"You're kidding."

"Nope."

"My pants . . ." Barnum said, feeling his neck get hot.

Stovepipe said, "I got string, if you need it." Barnum recognized the lengths of twine—they were what they gave prisoners in their cells so they couldn't hang themselves with their belts.

Stovepipe looked into the plastic bowl. "Hey, I remember chipping in on this pen for you. That's a nice one, all right. Looks like they ran outa room for the words though, the way they spelled 'service.'"

"Keep your fucking hands off it," Barnum said, turning toward the hallway and gripping the top of his pants so they wouldn't fall down around his ankles.

HE EXPECTED TO SEE WENDY at the reception desk. Instead, a matronly, dark-haired woman looked up.

"May I help you?"

"Where's Wendy?"

"She's been reassigned. May I help you?"

"Reassigned where? Who are *you*?" He was surprised he hadn't heard of the move, and hurt that McLanahan hadn't bothered to consult him about it.

The receptionist cocked her head in annoyance. "Back to dispatch, I believe. Now, should I know you?"

Deputy Reed had apparently heard the exchange because he poked his head over the top of his cubicle and said, "Donna, this is Sheriff Barnum."

"*Oh*," she said. Barnum caught the shadow of revulsion that passed over her face, and he was shocked by it.

"I'm here to see McLanahan," Barnum said, unable to bring himself to say *Sheriff* McLanahan.

Donna quickly looked down at a sheet in front of her for his name.

"I don't have an appointment," Barnum said, adding, "I shouldn't need one." He looked to Reed, expecting to see him smiling or nodding, but Reed had sunk back down behind his cubicle.

Donna picked up her phone, pushed the intercom button, and announced to McLanahan that "Mr. Bud Barnum" was here to see him.

"No," Donna said into the phone, avoiding Barnum's eyes and lowering her voice, "he just came in."

"Fuck it," Barnum spat, and strode through the batwing doors at the side of the reception desk. As he passed Reed he looked over, but Reed pretended not to see him. A new deputy—Barnum couldn't recall his name—watched him cross the office with contempt on his face. Barnum entered his old office and closed the door hard behind him.

McLanahan looked up and gestured toward a chair on the other side of his desk. *My* old desk, Barnum thought.

"So, what brings you here, Bud?"

Barnum sat down, grateful to be able to let loose his grip on the top of his pants.

"I was thinking about reporting something to you," Barnum said in his most gravel-filled voice, "but after the way I've been treated since I walked into this building, I'm starting to wonder why I'm wasting my time."

McLanahan smiled coldly, his eyes on his old boss. "We take security a lot more seriously than we used to around here, Bud. We don't have a choice about that."

"That son of a bitch Stovepipe took my *belt*."

"Sorry, but I told him no exceptions."

"Even for me?"

McLanahan raised his palms in a "what can I say?" gesture.

"Why'd you replace Wendy?" Barnum asked. "I promoted her to that desk job."

"Things change, Bud," McLanahan said, running his fingers through his thick hair. "As sheriff, I need to make hard decisions."

"Was it a hard decision to get your hair permed?"

McLanahan sat forward and narrowed his eyes. "Bud, I'm trying to be civil here . . ."

"What's that cost, anyway? Thirty bucks? Forty? You could just get your head wet and go stand in the wind for the same effect."

McLanahan looked away. "I'm kind of busy right now. Is there a point to any of this?"

Barnum sat silently, seething. The more he thought about it, the angrier he got.

"I groomed you for this job," Barnum said. "I overlooked your fuck-ups and taught you everything you know. Now that you've got the job, you've forgotten who got you here. What about some respect? A little acknowledgment?"

McLanahan finally turned his head back around and met his eyes. "Your exit wasn't exactly pretty. A lot of stuff came out. You're lucky I didn't pursue it after I got elected."

Barnum felt something inside him pop.

"What do you mean, *pursue it*?" he shouted.

"Bud, lower your voice or I'll have you thrown out of here," McLanahan cautioned.

"You'll have me . . . *what*?" Barnum hissed, scrambling to his feet. "I can't believe your disloyalty, you little prick."

The sheriff glared back, his face tight with anger. Barnum decided to try a different approach. "Look, McLanahan—"

"That's Sheriff McLanahan. Now get out."

Barnum's rage returned to a boil. He looked down to see that his hands were trembling. How easy it would be to dive over the desk and sink his fingers into McLanahan's windpipe, he thought.

"I'm leaving," Barnum said, his voice a whisper. "I came here to do something good, to tip you off about something. But it seems you know it all now. You don't need *my* help."

"If you came in to report a crime, sit down out there with Deputy Reed and give him the information. You know how the procedure works," McLanahan said evenly.

Barnum turned and walked out, feeling the eyes of Reed, the new deputy, and Donna on him.

Just let it happen, he thought. *Just let the killing take place. Let McLanahan and his department of clowns try to figure it out. Maybe next time they'll show me a little more respect.*

BACK ON HIS STOOL AT the Stockman's, Barnum was still shaking. His anger had turned into self-pity. When Timberman walked down the length of the bar with a carafe of coffee, Barnum gestured toward a bottle of Jim Beam on the back bar and said, "Double shot, Beam and water."

When Timberman stopped and looked at his wristwatch, Barnum said, "And don't screw around. This isn't the only bar in town."

PART FOUR

In many places, human hunters have taken over the
predator's ecological role.

MICHAEL POLLAN,
"THE UNNATURAL IDEA OF ANIMAL RIGHTS,"
THE NEW YORK TIMES MAGAZINE,
NOVEMBER 10, 2002

Grub first, then ethics.

BERTOLT BRECHT, 1898–1956

26

THE SUN WAS SETTING AND THE MOON WAS RISING AND both anchored opposite ends of the cloudless sky when Joe turned his saddle horse and packhorse from the spine of the Continental Divide onto what was unmistakably Two Ocean Pass. It was still and cold as he rode into the meadow, the only sounds the muffled footfalls of his animals in the thick, matted grass.

He reined to a stop and simply looked around. It was as Susan Jensen had described it, he thought, only more so. He could see why Will had chosen this place. Two Ocean Creek flowed narrow and clean through the meadow and split at a lone spruce. One channel flowed east, toward the Atlantic, the other west, toward the Pacific. Over the lip of the pass was the vast Yellowstone drainage and the Thorofare, the wildest and most remote wilderness in the Lower 48. The vastness was stunning: a rough carpet of dark trees and startling blue mountains as far as he could see in every direction. Surrounding him were landmarks he identified from his map: Box Creek, Mount Randolph, Mount Leidy, Terrace Mountain, Jackson Peak. Joy Peak was called that because it looked like a nipple. To the south, the crystal blades of the Tetons sliced up at the sky.

It had taken an entire day of steady riding to get there, and the light was fading. He had ridden through two snow squalls, a half dozen streams, and a surprise encounter with a skinny black bear who had not heard him ride up because she was so intent on extracting every last grub from a rotten log. The bear had thankfully run away, crashing loudly through the timber. Joe was pleased that his horses showed no fear and were, in fact, calmer than he was when it happened. The sight of the bear had reminded him to load his shotgun with slugs. The butt of the shotgun was now within quick reach in the saddle scabbard. Will may have preferred his .44 Magnum, but Joe felt much more comfortable with the shotgun. His bear spray was clipped on a lanyard that hung from his neck.

He embraced the wilderness around him as he would his daughters and welcomed the real danger and beauty it presented. He felt alive, and alert, in contrast to how he'd felt since his arrival in Jackson. He could not completely remove himself from that world, but he tried to put it on a back burner to be dealt with later. But it refused to go away.

There was Beargrass Village, and Don Ennis. Joe had no doubt, having reread Will Jensen's files and notations, that Will had planned to eventually turn down the project. Joe's own conclusions were the same, unless some new information came to light or Ennis agreed to radically alter his plans. Ennis must have known how Will was leaning, just as he must know how Joe would interpret the same data. Beargrass Village was not an inevitability carved out of the mountains by the sheer will of Don Ennis and his investors. It had major problems, and both Will and Joe recognized them. Whether Don Ennis would accept Joe's analysis remained to be seen. Joe doubted it, based on his meeting with the developer. A battle loomed. How far would Don Ennis go to win it?

And then there was Stella. At the thought of her, Joe felt himself slump a bit in the saddle. Stella was an enigma, although she showed no waffling in regard to what she said she was after. While she said she was looking for authenticity, she had chosen the life of pretense—married to a man who possibly hated her and living with him in the resort town of Jackson Hole. He wondered what kept her there and why she had chosen Will. Had it been merely an attraction for a man in uniform? Joe didn't think so. It was more, much more. Almost as if she had passively accepted being categorized by others because of her beauty and circumstances (whatever they had been) and was only now realizing she could change them. When Will died, she found his replacement in Joe Pickett, or so it seemed.

Why did she stay in his thoughts? Was the danger she offered as attractive to him as her manner and beauty? Susan Jensen had called her a predator. Maybe she was, Joe thought. So why didn't he mind being prey?

He couldn't answer the questions, and wasn't sure he wanted to. Instead, he shook his head, trying to clear the thoughts away. Concentrating on the terrain and the sky, he breathed the cool mountain air as deeply as he could. He listened to the breath of wind in the treetops and the footfalls of his horses and the warm squeak of leather on leather from his saddle.

AFTER PICKETING THE HORSES IN the meadow and setting up camp for the night, Joe dug the funeral urn out of a pannier and carried it down the slope to the creek.

He'd been thinking about how to do this, and hadn't come to a decision. Should the ashes be scattered on the ground, in the water, or in the wind? He chose the wind, shaking the ashes out gently, watching as the last shaft of sun lit up the gray-white powder before it settled in the grass.

"Rest in peace, Will. I mean that."

He couldn't think of anything else to say.

BY MID-MORNING THE NEXT DAY, Joe had visited four outfitter camps and was working his way north toward the state cabin. Before riding into the camps, he had followed Trey's advice and straightened up the diamond hitches on his packhorse. The camps were clean and the outfitters pleasant and professional. There was a guide for every two hunters, licenses and permits were valid, and food was hung up away from the camps, as per regulations. The outfitters seemed pleased to meet him, and offered him meals and coffee. They were free with information about where they thought the elk were, the locations of other camps, and the quirks of other outfitters. Like most taciturn outdoorsmen, who barely spoke in town, the outfitters couldn't stop talking. All agreed that snow was needed to get the herds moving south toward them.

"Have you run across Smoke yet?" was the most common question. It was asked with combinations of amusement, condemnation, and awe.

AS JOE RODE OUT OF HIS SIXTH CAMP of the day, he noticed how much his head had cleared from the day before. Whether it was the air, the elevation, or the isolation, he didn't know. But he felt normal again, without the fog that seemed to have moved into his brain since his arrival in Jackson. Maybe he'd just needed to get into the mountains, be alone, do good work.

The possibility that Will's death hadn't been a suicide never really left him, though. Neither did his feeling of being disconnected from Marybeth and his family. He thought how Marybeth and the girls, especially Sheridan, would love this, and he wished somehow they could be with him.

AT THE RATE HE WAS GOING, he thought he could make it to the state cabin by late afternoon. His plan was to stay at the cabin for at least two nights and check out the rest of the outfitter camps in the Yellowstone drainage from there. When the trail split, he absentmindedly neck-reined his horse to take the right fork, and was two miles from the main trail when he realized his mistake. The path had faded into a narrow game trail as it switchbacked up through the trees. The timber was too thick to turn his horses around—especially the wide load of the packhorse—so he continued to climb in search of a clearing. The incline got worse as he climbed, the horses laboring with the pitch. He leaned forward in the saddle, waiting for a break in the dark timber to signal that he'd reached the top.

When the trees finally thinned and the sky broke through, he stopped the horses on a small grassy shelf to let them rest. While they did, he took his map and walked to the top of the rise to figure out where he was. He noted the mountain landmarks he'd identified earlier. With his fingertip, he traced his location to the state cabin and found he had inadvertently taken a shortcut. If he continued down the other side of the mountain he could ride up Clear Creek drainage and approach the cabin from the side, shaving off at least eight miles and making up for the time he'd wasted on the wrong trail. The route would be rugged, as there wasn't an established horse trail, but his horses had shown they were more than up to the task.

Climbing back into the saddle, he flinched with familiar pain in his knees caused by riding for a day and a half, and headed northwest.

It was above the drainage, while he was still hidden in the timber, when he looked down and saw a man doing something he shouldn't be doing.

AT FIRST, JOE COULDN'T FIGURE OUT what he was seeing. He had dismounted and tied up his horses out of sight in a thick stand of aspen, and was watching the man in the meadow through his binoculars. His digital camera with the zoom lens was at the foot of the boulder he peered over.

The man was over five hundred yards away, moving around in a pocket clearing on the other side of Clear Creek. He was walking around in a circle, stopping at intervals to kick at the ground. There was something long and thin on his shoulder—a rifle, maybe. No, Joe saw as he focused in, it was a shovel. The man was big and lumbering, but he moved gracefully. His back was to Joe and he had yet to turn and show his face. As the man continued his circle and moved into shadow, Joe swung his binoculars toward the trees on the side of the clearing. Three sorrel horses stood motionless by the trunks of pine trees. One horse was saddled, the other two carried panniers that appeared to be empty. Joe surmised that the man had packed something up the drainage in the panniers and buried his cargo in the clearing.

Then the man stepped from the shadows into the sun,

removed his hat and wiped his brow with his sleeve. Joe focused his binoculars on the face of Smoke Van Horn.

Smoke was wearing a flannel shirt, a fleece vest, jeans, and a gun belt with a long-barreled revolver. He looked up and down the drainage, then swung his eyes to the trees where Joe was hiding. Joe slunk down behind the boulder so Smoke wouldn't see the glint of his lenses and unpacked his camera. He wondered if Smoke felt he was being watched, knowing how prescient that feeling could be.

Rising again, Joe took five quick shots of Smoke as he took a last look at the sky, turned with his shovel, and lumbered back toward his horses. Joe gave Smoke twenty minutes to ride away before he emerged from behind the rock.

THE CLEARING WAS TRAMPLED DOWN not only by Smoke's boots, but by what looked like hundreds of elk tracks. Elk pellets as fresh as the night before stood in clumps throughout the grass.

Joe photographed the clearing, the tracks, and the nine fresh mounds of dirt in a sloppy circle in the clearing. He knew what he would find when he kicked the dirt clear on the mounds, and he found it: fifty-pound salt blocks. Violators had learned in the past few years not to place the salt aboveground, where it was obvious from a distance. If they buried it out of view with a thin cover of loose dirt, the elk would find it easily but the blocks would be almost impossible to spot without literally being on top of them.

The toughest thing about arresting an outfitter who was baiting elk with salt was catching him doing it. The outfitter could always claim that it wasn't he who placed the blocks out. Even if the outfitter was caught with salt blocks in his panniers, he could claim they were for his horses. No, in order to arrest someone for illegal salting, or what the regulations called "hunting near an attractant," he would literally have to be caught in the act of putting the salt down. Just to be sure he'd gotten it all, Joe reviewed the photos on the screen display on the back of his camera. They were long shots, several not in sharp focus. But there was no doubt that the man with the shovel was Smoke, and what he was burying were salt blocks. Although Joe had blundered into the situation by taking a wrong trail, Smoke had been caught red-handed.

Will Jensen had suspected Smoke of salting for four years, but could never nail him for it.

"Now you can *really* rest in peace," Joe said aloud.

He looked at his wristwatch, then at the sky. There were three hours of daylight left, and he figured it would take two to get to the state cabin. Smoke's arrest in his elk camp would need to wait until tomorrow.

THE STATE CABIN WAS OLDER, smaller, and more beat-up than Joe had imagined it would be. The setting was nice, though, and the cabin had a small front porch that looked out over a meadow and a small lake that had been named, without much imagination, State Lake.

In the last half hour of dusk, he corralled the horses, dragged the panniers into the one-room cabin, unshuttered the two cracked windows, and got a fire going in the ancient woodstove. He worked quickly, his goal to enjoy a light bourbon on the front porch as the sun set. He was delayed when he had to sweep mouse excrement off the floor and counter, and clear a bird's nest from the top of the chimney pipe. By the time he poured warm bourbon from his flask into his metal camp cup, the sun had sunk into State Lake.

While steak sizzled and potatoes fried in cast-iron skillets, Joe sipped and took measure of the cabin. The logs it had been built with were grayed and cracking with age, and they needed re-chinking. Rusted spikes driven into the logs served as coat and equipment hangers. A calendar from 1963 had never been replaced. The bed was an old metal-framed single, with a thin mattress, gray with age and dirt. He flipped through a puckered journal that listed the cabin's visitors and occupants for the last twenty years. He recognized the names of game wardens and biologists, and saw where Trey Crump had signed in fifteen years before. The last page and a half of entries were all by Will Jensen. Joe was surprised to see that the last entry by Will was made just three weeks before.

Somehow, in the sequence of events that led to Will's death, he had missed the fact that the ex–game warden had used the state cabin. In fact, he had been up there for the week preceding his death.

Joe looked at the last signature. Although it looked like Will's writing—Joe had seen so much of Will's cribbed style that he felt he was an expert on it—the name was written in a shaky, uncertain hand. There were loops in the letters where there normally weren't loops, and the pen had crossed over the lines. And something else, something so tiny that Joe had to lift the journal to the propane lamp to see it. At first, he thought that Will, for some reason, had jotted a period after his name, as if making some kind of statement. But it wasn't a punctuation mark, it was a single, tiny letter: "S." He recognized the scrawl from the invitation he had held in his hand two days before.

Joe lowered the journal. *Stella had come up here with him?* How dare she? How dare he? Despite himself, he looked over his shoulder at the bed and imagined her in it. He was jealous of Will, and ashamed of himself.

Then something occurred to him, and he quickly walked across the cabin and flipped up the old mattress. There it was: Will's last notebook.

And something else. A nicker of a horse outside the cabin, followed by a deep, throat-clearing cough.

"Hey, FNG! Something smells mighty good in there! And I brung along a bottle!"

Joe's stomach clutched and his mouth went dry as he recognized Smoke's voice. He tossed the notebook back under the mattress and turned toward the door, noting that his shotgun was within quick reach in the corner. He wondered if Smoke had seen him coming down from Clear Creek and was there now to make sure Joe wouldn't be able to ever tell anyone.

27

SHERIDAN HAD OVERHEARD THE PLAN HER MOTHER and Nate made regarding the 720 phone calls to their house. Despite the fact that it seemed like a good plan, she wasn't very happy about it. In fact, she wasn't very happy about anything at the moment.

For the third time that week, Nate was eating dinner with them. Sheridan noticed the first night that her mother had used the nice plates from the pantry, the ones they usually used only on holidays or when they had special company. The playful way her mother and Nate talked with each other, adult-to-adult, bothered her. And she noticed—boy did she notice—how attentive her mother was when it came to Nate, asking questions and saying things like: "Would you like some more? I seem to have made too much," and, "I've never seen anyone enjoy my cooking so much."

Maybe, Sheridan thought, if her mom cooked like that when her dad was home, and used the nice plates, her dad would enjoy it as much. When she had told her mother that earlier, before Nate arrived, she received a withering look.

Sheridan had first noticed the friendship between Nate and her mother the year before and at the time couldn't process what bothered her about it so much. Now she knew. Her mother was mildly flirting, and Nate didn't mind. Because of her feelings for them both, and for her father, Sheridan's only way of dealing with it at the time, and now, was to be angry with her mother, to create disorder. This was becoming easier to do all the time.

"Nate is here to help us," her mother had said. "The least we can do is give him dinner."

"He hasn't had time for a falconry lesson for two weeks," Sheridan countered, "but he sure has time to come over here."

Sheridan couldn't believe what she felt—jealous of her own mother. But there was more to it than that. What about her dad?

Lucy was oblivious to it all, which also angered Sheridan. Her sister made things worse by asking, "Is Nate coming over tonight?"

After dinner, Nate and her mother waited for a call from 720, and Sheridan thought it was a pretense. Nate didn't *need* to sit in the living room after dinner drinking coffee for his plan to work.

NATE HAD FOUND OUT THAT area code 720 was from Denver. When her mother said they didn't know anyone in Denver, Nate replied that he didn't think the calls were coming from there.

"I'm pretty sure it's the number from a calling card," Nate said. "The company that distributes it is based in Aurora, Colorado, which is a suburb of Denver. I think the calls are being made locally by someone disguising his identity by using a third-party number. I have an idea where the calls might be coming from, but I can't prove anything unless I catch him in the act."

"What do you want me to do?" her mother had asked.

"Next time he calls, keep him on the line. Don't hang up on him. Talk to him instead, ask him questions. I think that's what he wants, to get you upset. But while you've got him on the line, call me immediately on your cell phone so I know we've got him live and I'll know if he hangs up or not. That way, I can check out my theory."

"Where do you think he's calling from?"

Nate shrugged. "Didn't you say you can hear some background noises sometimes? People talking, even some music?"

"Yes."

"There are only a few public places open that late at night," Nate said. "So I'm thinking it's a bar or a restaurant."

"I see. Who do you think it is?"

"It's just a guess," Nate said. "I don't want to say anything until I confirm it."

"Just make him stop," her mom said. "Every time the phone rings I think it's Joe. And I don't want to miss Joe's call because this idiot is on the line."

Nate nodded, and sipped his coffee.

"Don't hurt him, Nate."

"Never," Nate said, in a tone meant to be disbelieved.

WHEN THE PHONE RANG AN hour later and her mother said, "Seven-two-oh," to Nate, he was out the door and in his Jeep before she picked up the receiver.

Sheridan watched as her mother opened her cell

phone and speed-dialed Nate's number while asking, "Why do you keep calling me? Is there something you want? Why won't you talk to me?"

TEN MINUTES LATER, BUD BARNUM looked up in time to see the old-fashioned accordion doors crash in and a huge pair of hands reach into the phone booth and grab his collar.

"Hey!"

Nate Romanowski jerked the receiver from his hand and asked, "Marybeth?"

When he heard an answer, Romanowski let the phone drop and was on Barnum like an animal.

"Help me!" Barnum cried out to the patrons seated at stools at the Stockman's Bar, but no one stepped forward. Even Timberman, who had a sawed-off shotgun and a tape-wrapped pool cue under the bar, froze where he stood.

Romanowski pulled the ex-sheriff close and spoke quietly from an inch away: "From now on, you will leave that family the fuck alone."

Barnum tried to reply but found himself being violently pulled along, Romanowski's hands still on his collar, aimed for the bar. A few drinkers had the presence of mind to grab their mugs and step away, but most didn't, and when Romanowski launched him onto the bar face-first and pulled him down the length of it, beer splashed into his mouth and whiskey stung his eyes.

Romanowski didn't let go until he had wiped the bar clean with Barnum and sent him hurtling off the other end, where he crashed in a heap with a sound like wet laundry being thrown on the floor.

Barnum lay there, trying to get his breath back, wiping at the sting in his eyes, when he felt more than saw Romanowski lean over him, again inches away. He felt his lips pried open by thick, callused fingers, and he cried out sharply when pain shot through his mouth and his cupped tongue filled with hot blood.

He sagged sideways, not moving, and opened his eyes to see Romanowski toss cash on the bar and announce he was buying the house a round.

Romanowski pointed a finger at Timberman: "If you ever see Barnum head for the telephone booth again, warn him off. He likes to intimidate families. He uses a calling card so they can't tell who's harassing them."

With that, Romanowski gave Barnum a look of icy contempt and walked out of the Stockman's.

After they were sure he was gone, several of Barnum's old friends helped him to his feet. They hadn't helped when he needed it, he thought. They had frozen and watched. He tried to say, "*Get your hands off me, you fuckers*," but his voice slurred and blood spattered from his mouth.

"Bud, you've got to get that thing out," one of the men said, reaching toward Barnum's mouth.

The ex-sheriff turned angrily away and reached up, feeling drops of blood spatter hot on his hand.

Tears filled his eyes as he pried the calling card out from between his front teeth, where Romanowski had shoved it up well into his gum. Removing the plastic card resulted in a fresh torrent of blood. His friends stepped away, even as Timberman approached with a bar rag.

"*Stay away from me!*" Barnum roared, spattering them all. He was well aware of how quickly this story would travel through Twelve Sleep County.

SHERIDAN COULD TELL from the way her mom's face went white that she could hear what was happening on the other end of the line.

"What did you expect?" Sheridan asked.

"I said not to hurt him," her mother said. "It sounded like Sheriff Barnum."

Sheridan weighed that and nodded. "He hates us, all right."

Her mother slowly hung up the phone. "I can't believe I live in a place where people hate us."

"It's because of what Dad does," Sheridan said.

"Then maybe he should do something else!" her mother said angrily.

Sheridan turned her back on her mother and went into her bedroom and slammed the door. She was still awake when she heard the sound of Nate's Jeep pull up outside.

If she filled her backpack with clothes and started walking, she wondered, how far could she get before the sun came up?

BARNUM KNOCKED HEAVILY on the door. With the other hand, he held a bar rag soaked with blood to his mouth. The front of his shirt was covered with it. Even the underside of his hat brim was flecked.

He saw a band of light appear beneath the door and the peephole darken for a moment, then heard the bolt being thrown.

Randan Bello stood wrapped in a towel, his eyes in slits. "What in the hell happened to you?" he asked.

"Never mind that," Barnum croaked. "I know what you're doing in Saddlestring, and I'm here to help."

Bello stepped back away from the door and examined Barnum from his bloodstained boots to his hat.

"Come in, Sheriff," Bello said.

*   *   *

OUTSIDE THE MOTEL, Nate Romanowski cruised through the parking lot in his Jeep with his headlights off. His .454 Casull lay unholstered on the passenger seat.

Hunters, mainly. Plates from Colorado, Michigan, Pennsylvania. Hunting states. Except for the SUV Barnum had parked next to, the one with the Virginia plates. Interesting.

Nate slowed to a crawl but didn't tap his brakes so his brake lights wouldn't flare. He leaned across the passenger seat and looked up at the windows that were lit. He saw a man with a profile that looked familiar—someone from a long time ago—approach the window and reach out with both hands for fistfuls of curtain. But before the man pulled the curtains closed, Nate saw the silhouette of Bud Barnum's crushed cowboy hat over his shoulder.

Nate thought of his red tail flaring two days before.

Instinctively, he rubbed the hand grip of his weapon with his thumb.

28

SMOKE VAN HORN WAS A HUGE MAN WHO SEEMED TO fill up the cabin when he entered the room, accompanied by the smell of wood smoke, grease, horses, and leather that hung in his oversized sheepskin coat. His face was massive and naturally thrust forward, like a fist.

"Nice night out there," Smoke said to Joe. "We need some snow, though, to get the elk moving."

He let his coat slide off his shoulders, then tossed it on the bed across the room as if he'd done it a hundred times before. Perhaps he had, Joe thought. Under the coat, Smoke wore the same clothes Joe had seen him in that afternoon in the meadow, as well as the holster and .44 Magnum.

"I was just scouting the territory when I saw the light from your cabin," Smoke said in a too-loud voice, "so I thought I better check it out. I've thrown more than a few backpacker types out of your place before, you know. A couple of years ago some hunters moved in before Will got up here, and I sent them packing too. I figure this place is paid for by my tax money and license fees, so I don't want nobody trashing it."

"I appreciate that," Joe said, as he dished steak and potatoes onto his plate. "Can I offer you some?"

"I filled my belly with pemmican while I was riding," Smoke said, shaking his head, "but that sure smells good."

Joe filled a second plate and sat it on the table in front of the outfitter. He tried not to turn his back on Smoke at any point, but to stay in front of him. The outfitter exuded an aura of pure physicality and danger, even though he had not yet said or done anything that could be considered threatening. Joe watched as Smoke withdrew a collapsible camp cup from a shirt pocket, shook it out, and filled half of it with Wild Turkey from a bottle he had brought in with him.

"Want some?" Smoke asked, already pouring it into Joe's tin cup.

"Thanks," Joe said, adding water from a canteen.

"That's ruining two good drinks," Smoke said, raising his cup, a wide smile cracking the fist. "Here's to fall in Wyoming and two good men."

While they ate, Smoke noticed Joe looking at the .44 Magnum.

"Something wrong?" Smoke asked through a mouthful.

"Do you ever take that off?"

"Nope."

"Have you ever considered carrying bear spray?"

"Nope."

"Have you ever had to use it?"

"Yup," Smoke said. "This steak needs something. You got any ketchup or hot sauce?"

*   *   *

SMOKE SURPRISED JOE BY GATHERING up the dishes and dumping them in an old plastic tub that he'd filled with hot water from a pot on the stove. Joe said, "You don't have to do that."

"Camp law," Smoke said, not turning his head. "You cooked, so I clean. Have another snort. And give me a re-ride on mine, will you?"

Joe picked up the bottle and began to pour it into his cup, then thought better of it. He refilled Smoke, and put the bottle back down with a thump so Smoke would think Joe had taken some. Instead, Joe added more water to his cup.

"I've got to admit," Smoke said, washing a plate with his back still to Joe, "you are more wily than I gave you credit for when I met you outside of the Sportsman's. You must have known at the time you'd be coming up here into the backcountry, but you didn't give it away."

Joe didn't respond.

"That was an old trick of Will's too. He liked to keep everyone guessing. Shit, if I was the game warden, I'd probably do the same damn thing. This is a lot of country for just one man, ain't it?"

"Yes, it is."

"You ever seen anything like this before?"

"My district is in the Bighorns," Joe said. "We've got some rough country."

"Nothing like this," Smoke said, turning and taking a long drink, "nothing like this."

He banged the empty cup down. "How 'bout another re-ride?"

"It's your whiskey," Joe said, pouring again.

Smoke cleaned the last of the plates and suspended the skillet over the soapy water. "Do you wash your cast iron, or keep it seasoned?"

"Seasoned, I guess," Joe said.

"Good man," Smoke said, wiping out the skillet hard with paper towels. "Not many folks know anymore how much good taste and character you lose in your food when you wash the damn skillet every night with soap. Cast iron is meant to be seasoned."

Smoke sat down at the table when he was through, the drying towel still draped over his arm. "I suppose I ought to think about getting back to my hunters pretty soon," he said. "They'll be wondering if a bear got me."

Joe felt a tightening in his chest. It didn't feel right to let Smoke go back happily to his camp, only to arrest him in the morning.

"Something wrong?" Smoke asked, studying Joe's face.

"Let's have a nightcap," Joe said, putting off his decision.

"Nightcap, hell," Smoke said, pouring generously again, "let's tie one on."

"THIS IS MY THIRTY-SECOND YEAR up here," Smoke said wistfully. "I love it as much as my first."

Joe nodded.

"Things have changed, though. I see it in Jackson all the time. But I never thought I'd see it up here, and it pisses me off."

Smoke shifted and leaned across the table, his face thrust at Joe. Joe stanched an impulse to jump back.

"I'm a third-generation outfitter," Smoke said. "I got the same camp my dad and my grandpa used. A couple of years ago I sat down during a blizzard when we couldn't hunt and I figured out that we've probably brought twenty-five hundred dead elk through that camp over the years. That's a hell of a lot of meat. I also figured out that over the years we've probably contributed over a half a million in license fees, and we've spent about four million in the county to keep our business running. I'm the best there is at what I do, so I feel pretty damned good about it, overall. I get to show these out-of-staters there is still some wildness left in this world, and that they'd better show some goddamned respect for it. I've been known to send a whiner or two home, even at a financial loss to me, if that son of a bitch don't respect what we've got up here."

"Twenty-five hundred elk is a lot of elk," Joe said.

Smoke weighed Joe's comment for a minute, his eyes narrowing, then decided it was neutral, not critical.

"It is," Smoke continued, "but in the big scheme of things, it's not enough. Because of federal policies, we've got too goddamn many elk up here to sustain a healthy herd. There's no good reason to have ten thousand elk come down to be fed on the refuge, like pets. They're weak as a herd, and they spread diseases among themselves. The herd needs to be culled. It's a goddamned meat farm, except that shooting them for meat is looked down on."

Joe smiled. "You sound a little like Pi Stevenson."

"Damnit!" Smoke shouted, thumping the table with his hand and making the cups jump. "Don't get me started on *her.* Her stupid solution is to let the herds grow until they all starve to death in front of our eyes. Then listen to her bitch."

"I can imagine," Joe said.

Suddenly, Smoke broke out into a grin. "I used to have these kinds of discussions with Will Jensen all the time, right at this table. You're a lot like him."

"You're not the first to say that."

"It's a compliment," Smoke said. "I liked the hell out of old Will, even though he wanted to arrest me and throw my big wide butt in jail. He would have, you know. But I respected him, he was a man of his word. Too bad he went nuts in the end."

"Were there people who hated him enough to kill him?" Joe asked abruptly.

The question didn't faze Smoke. "A few, I suppose. Your friend Pi Stevenson supposedly made some threats. I probably did too, when I was drinking. He made me pretty mad a couple of times."

"But in the end you got along?"

"In the end he was crazy," Smoke said. "Taking up with that Ennis woman the way he did. He even brought her up here one time, which told me he was forgetting who he was and where he was at. I consider this a cathedral, and he violated it. It got worse with the fights he got into, and then getting arrested himself . . ."

Joe watched Smoke closely.

"Before all of that, though, we coexisted pretty damned well, I'd say. We gave each other a wide berth. I think he even admired me, in a way, although he never actually said it. I'm one of the few who doesn't mind the bear population increasing or the wolves the Feds released on us," Smoke said. "They're a part of all of this. We need 'em to get the herd sizes down to a level that makes some kind of sense. But I have arguments with the way those animals are portrayed by some folks, like they're on a higher plane than us humans. It's pretty damned simple, really. The Feds—and people like Pi Stevenson—don't love the wolves and bears as much as they hate people. They're winning the game, it seems to me. That pisses me off too."

Joe found himself warming to Smoke, enjoying his company and his passion. Smoke was like a lot of the people he knew in Twelve Sleep County. He wondered, though, at what point Smoke's rage turned into violence. Joe admonished himself not to become complacent with this man.

"You know about that meat town they're trying to build outside of Jackson?" Smoke asked, his face wide with incredulity.

"Beargrass Village," Joe said. "I know about it."

"Not only is there no beargrass in Wyoming," Smoke said, his face flushing red, "but the whole fucking idea is to create an artificial environment for raising pure meat for millionaires! Jesus! They think that's real, somehow. It ain't real. This"—Smoke sat back, pointed toward the window—"*this* is real. It's just messy, and it's complicated, but it's real. Why'n the *hell* don't they experience this?"

Joe shrugged. Smoke was getting more animated as he talked, and louder. Joe saw the flashes of eloquent rage Smoke was known for, the rhetoric he used at public meetings to dominate discussions and make himself the scourge of agency officials.

"I'd like to bring a couple of those Beargrass jokers up here and let 'em shoot an elk, gut it, and hang it up in the trees. 'This is how we get meat,' I'd say."

Joe conspicuously looked at his watch, trying to signal an end to the evening. It was late and he was tired. Smoke ignored him.

"When I tell people what I'm telling you, they laugh at me," Smoke said. "They didn't used to, but they do now. They act like I'm something out of another century, some kind of throwback. I am, I guess."

Smoke drained his cup and poured another before Joe could object.

"I'm a goddamned arachnidism," Smoke said.

"You're a *spider*?" Joe asked, knowing Smoke meant *anachronism.*

"I don't mind being feared or hated," Smoke said, lowering his head, "but I *hate* to be fuckin' laughed at."

Smoke's silence was striking after all of his loud talk.

"I'm sorry," Joe said.

"About what?" Smoke finally asked, his voice soft for the first time since he had arrived at the cabin.

"For the spider joke," Joe said. "I knew what you meant."

Smoke almost imperceptibly nodded his woolly head.

"You know I saw you today, putting those salt blocks down," Joe said.

Joe thought he sensed a sudden, cold calmness in Smoke's demeanor. Maybe it was the way he was gripping his cup.

"I thought somebody was watching me," Smoke said.

"I've got pictures of it."

"So what are you going to do about it?"

Joe glanced quickly at the shotgun in the corner. Two steps, and he could grab it.

"I was thinking of riding into your camp and arresting you tomorrow," Joe said. "But I don't think either one of us wants me to do that in front of your hunters and guides."

Smoke sighed heavily, his shoulders slumping. "No, I wouldn't want that."

"We could do it tonight," Joe said. "It's not like I was planning to drag you in chains into Jackson. I'll write you up, give you the citation, and we'd go to court eventually."

Smoke shook his head. "That'd mean my outfitter's license and my reputation, Joe. You might as well shoot me on the spot."

Joe couldn't argue with the first part. "Smoke, you knew what you were doing."

"Yes," the outfitter said, a spark in his eyes, "I knew it. But I bet you didn't know who else used salt in that same meadow for years."

"I'm confused."

"You sure as hell are," Smoke said, again leaning forward, the color returning to his cheeks. "Your own Game and Fish Department. For twenty years, they put salt blocks out to lure the elk out of Yellowstone so they could be shot. For years before that, the Forest Service did it. At the time, it was considered good management."

"Really?"

"Really. It wasn't until a few years ago, when some crusaders like Pi Stevenson decided it was unfair, did salting become a crime."

Joe said nothing.

"You want me to take you out tomorrow on horseback and show you all the salt sets in this wilderness? Not only the ones put there by outfitters, but natural salt licks in the ground? Elk need salt. It's good for them. Salt blocks don't attract any game that isn't already there. All salt does is help group them up in one place, so a dude can get a clean shot and cut down the odds of wounding an elk and losing track of it in the timber. Besides, what if a hunter shoots an elk that just showed up at a natural salt lick? What about that?"

"That's different," Joe said. "Putting salt blocks out isn't natural."

Smoke's cup exploded with a pop from his tightened grip. Joe felt drops of Wild Turkey hit his face. Smoke's voice rose as he talked. "Neither is feeding hay to ten thousand goddamned elk so tourists can look at 'em on the elk refuge, Joe! Neither is letting the herd explode in numbers in Yellowstone because there are no natural predators left, or introducing a species of gray wolf in the state that never actually lived here. Neither is building a goddamned private village so rich people can raise their own 'pure' food that's the result of hundreds of years of genetic engineering!"

Joe pushed his chair back and stood up. The shotgun

was within reach. "I'll make a deal with you, Smoke. If you destroy the salt sets and give me your word you'll never do it again, we'll pretend this conversation never happened."

Tracing his finger through the spilled whiskey on the table, Smoke said, "I can't do that, Joe."

"Why not?"

"Because I don't think what I did is wrong. It's all a big game, just like everything these days. It's a big game set up to get rid of people like me."

"Then I need to write out the citation," Joe said, his voice wavering.

"I ain't going to quit my way of life, Joe," Smoke said, looking up. "Not because of a set of rules that don't make biological or scientific sense. I won't let you take my life away from me."

"I gave you a choice I shouldn't have given you," Joe said.

"And I appreciate that," Smoke said. "Don't think I don't. It shows you're the fair man I thought you were, just like Will. But my decision is made."

Joe felt his heartbeat in his ears as he pulled his citation book out of his panniers and wrote out a ticket. In his peripheral vision, he was aware of both Smoke's position at the table—slumping back, both hands on the table where he could see them—and the shotgun propped up in the corner.

"I'll trust your word if you say you'll get rid of that salt set."

"I know that, Joe. I appreciate your trust. But it ain't going to happen."

Shaking his head, Joe tore out the ticket and handed it to Smoke. Smoke took it, slowly wadded it up into a ball, and dropped it on the table into the pool of whiskey.

"That won't change anything," Joe said, feeling sudden malevolence emanate from Smoke's person the way the odor of horses and wood smoke had earlier.

"I ain't going to let you do this," Smoke said, rising almost sadly from the table. "I got no place to go."

Joe said, "It doesn't have to be this way, Smoke."

"Yeah, it does."

Joe stood with the back of his hand brushing against the barrel of the shotgun while Smoke retrieved his coat, gathered the bottle, and lumbered out the door without another word.

HE BREWED COFFEE TO HELP him stay awake and read through the pages of the last spiral notebook. The door was bolted shut, and a heavy gun case was pushed against it. The shutters were closed so no one outside could look in and see him. The horses had been moved closer and picketed at the front and back of the cabin so Joe could hear if they sensed someone approaching. The shotgun, still loaded with slugs, was on the table where he read. He could not recall ever being as scared. When a squirrel suddenly chattered from a tree outside, Joe was up with the shotgun pointed at the door, his heart thumping.

Even the things he read in the notebook, as terrifying and revealing as they were, could not make him tear his mind away from the threat of Smoke outside. Will's notebook was a journal of the madness that had engulfed him. The ex–game warden's writing changed from cribbed, guarded comments to large block letters, with sections underlined so violently that the paper had ripped. Then the handwriting changed again, to outright loopy. The content changed from reports and observations to Will's innermost thoughts and fears. What scared Joe was imagining Will, a man as guarded and reserved as anyone he had known, turn into something else. The last entry was from three weeks before:

> They're getting to me somehow. They're inside my head and inside my body. They know where I'm going and they track my movements. I know it sounds crazy, and it IS crazy. Maybe it's just me, but I don't think so. They figured out a way to screw me up.

And there was more.

29

A HALF HOUR BEFORE THE SUN BROKE OVER THE EAST-
ern mountains, while the mist still hung tight to State
Lake, Joe heard the black gelding snort in alarm. From
somewhere in the shadowed trees where the trail tun-
neled through, an approaching horse called back. Joe's
eyes shot open in his sleeping bag, and despite the cold,
it was as if an electric current had jolted him awake.

He had bedded down on a ground cloth in the tall
grass behind a gnarled stand of ancient pine trees. Somewhere around three in the morning, after rereading the
spiral notebook and coming to surprising conclusions,
he felt he could no longer stay in the cabin and wait. He
felt trapped in there, with no way of knowing if Smoke
was coming back for him and, if so, from which direction. So he had stoked up the stove so that smoke would
curl out of the chimney pipe as if the cabin were occupied, and dragged his sleeping bag and the ground cloth
out into the night. He slept in his clothing with the shotgun parallel to his legs.

Sitting up, he could see the front door of the cabin

through the tree trunks. The black gelding, his ears straight up, looked down the trail in the direction where the approaching horse had responded. It was colder than he had anticipated as he unzipped his sleeping bag, the cold numbing his hands and face. He rolled out of the bag, hearing the frozen grass crunch beneath him. He rose to his knees and stayed hidden behind brush while peering down the trail in the same direction the gelding was looking.

Smoke, who had obviously dismounted, appeared out of the shadows on foot. His big blocky form was unmistakable. Clouds of condensation billowed around his head, then snapped away into the air. Joe thought it was remarkable that a man so large could walk so quietly.

It took ten minutes for Smoke to position himself in front of the door of the cabin. The outfitter had approached as if he were hunting—taking a few slow steps, stopping to look around, sniff the air, and listen. Joe was frozen on his knees, the icy metal of the shotgun stinging his hands.

Smoke held his big revolver in one hand and the bottle of Wild Turkey in the other. Joe could see less than a half-inch of the liquid sloshing in the bottle as the man moved. There was a clumsiness about him, his movements slow and deliberate. Joe tried to remember how much whiskey had been left the night before—a half-bottle at least.

"Joe Pickett, you in there?" Smoke hollered at the door. "Come out, sir. Let's settle this." To Joe, it sounded like "*Lesh settle thish.*" Smoke was blind drunk.

Joe rose to his feet, hoping his knees wouldn't pop from the cold and alert Smoke. He shouldered the shotgun and stepped quietly through the brush and trees until he was less than twenty feet behind the outfitter.

He racked the pump of the shotgun. "Drop your weapon and turn around, Smoke." Joe's voice sounded stronger than he thought it would. He fought a trembling in his chest muscles that wasn't from the cold.

Smoke snorted as if amused, and his shoulders listed as he turned his big head slightly. "Didn't expect you to be there," he slurred. "I expected you'd be all nice and warm in your cabin."

"Drop the gun, Smoke."

Smoke turned a little more. The gun remained at his side. "Didn't I hear that somebody took a gun off of you once? An outfitter?"

Joe was thinking the same thing, but he didn't answer. That had happened five years before, but would always stay with him.

"Drop it and we'll talk. My offer still stands."

"Oh, the offer," Smoke said. "I'm not taking it. I tole you that."

Clumsily, Smoke turned and the quick movement seemed to make him swoon. He staggered, regained his balance, set his feet, and looked through bloodshot eyes at Joe.

"That was a good trick, hiding in the grass."

"I expected you to come back," Joe said. "I didn't want things to get western."

Smoke nodded slowly, as if Joe had delivered a complicated theory and it took him a moment to digest it.

"But they will," Smoke said.

"They don't have to."

"This is the way I go out," Smoke said, as much to himself as to Joe. "In a blaze of glory. What do you think I could do if my license was taken away from me? If I lost my grandpa's elk camp?"

"There are plenty of things to do," Joe said.

"Then why aren't *you* doin' 'em?" he asked, and smiled. "Instead, you're sleeping in the cold with a damned shotgun."

"Smoke—"

"It ends here," Smoke said, squinting. "I just got to figure out which one of you to shoot." The muzzle of the revolver started to rise, and Joe could see its gaping mouth.

"Don't do that," Joe said. "Come on . . ."

The pistol fell back. Smoke grinned. "What, can't you shoot a fella who's looking you in the eye?"

Joe thought about the bear, how he had frozen. How Trey had fired because Joe couldn't. This was different, though, he thought. Smoke wasn't really going to go through with this. *Hell,* Joe thought, *I like Smoke.*

"There you are," Smoke growled. "I got a fix on you now."

Casually, Smoke raised the gun again and fired. The explosion was ear-shattering, and despite the sudden red-hot roar of pain in his side and the ringing echoing in his head, Joe could hear dry pine needles rain down on the grass.

"Got you," Smoke said, letting the gun down slowly from where it had kicked over his head until it settled again at eye level. His watery eyes were swimming. "Why ain't you fallin'?"

Joe peered down the barrel of his shotgun and shot Smoke square in the middle of his chest. He racked in another slug as Smoke stumbled back a few feet, a confused look on his face. He could see a wisp of smoke rising from a hole the size of a quarter in the outfitter's sheepskin coat.

Joe watched the gun, which had dropped back to Smoke's side, start to rise again.

"Don't make me . . ." Joe said.

The gun rose unsteadily but purposefully, and Joe shot him again in the chest. This time, the outfitter dropped straight down as if he were a puppet with his strings clipped. His gun fell to the ground on one side, the whiskey bottle on the other.

"Oh my God," Joe said, running to Smoke and falling to his knees. The outfitter was breathing shallowly in quick breaths, his eyes fluttering, his face horribly contorted.

Smoke said, "It really hurts, it really hurts, it really hurts . . ."

Beneath him, a pool of dark blood flooded through the grass, steaming in the cold with a sharp metallic smell.

"It really hurts, it really hurts, it really hurts . . ."

Setting his shotgun aside, Joe found one of Smoke's big callused hands and squeezed it. There was no pressure back. The outfitter coughed a wet, hacking cough and a dollop of blood shot out through one of the holes in his coat, spattering Joe's sleeve.

"Smoke?"

"It really hurts, it really hurts, it really hurts . . ."

Joe looked up toward the cabin, wondering stupidly if there was a first-aid kit inside. But the outfitter had taken two twelve-gauge slugs in his chest. There was no way anyone could fix him now, or save him.

"Smoke, can you hear me?"

It really hurts, it really hurts, it really hurts . . .

With a rattle that sounded exactly like a playing card in a bicycle spoke, Smoke seized up and his hand clenched back and his last blood-smelling copper breath wheezed out of his chest like a bellows.

JOE STAYED MOTIONLESS, his eyes closed tight, until the sun broke over the mountains moments later and he felt the sudden warmth on his back. Letting Smoke's hand drop, he stood and his head reeled, and he nearly fell on top of the body. His side screamed at him, and his right arm was shaking uncontrollably. For the first time, he looked down. Blood had soaked through his three layers of clothing and glinted darkly in the morning sun. He took a sharp breath through gritted teeth, hoping the pain would stop searing him, but it didn't. He needed something to put the fire out.

Blindly lurching through the trees, almost tripping over his sleeping bag, he made it to the rocky edge of the lake and pitched forward into the icy water.

As the water numbed him and pink curlicues of blood swirled to the surface from where the bullet had creased his ribs and inner arm, he thought, *I've shot and killed a man, and it was awful.*

30

LEADING TWO HORSES, JOE PICKETT RODE SOUTH OUT of the Thorofare, on the trail to Turpin Meadows, in what became a kind of trek of lamentation. Smoke's body was wrapped in the ground cloth Joe had slept on the previous night, and it was roped over the back of the outfitter's own sorrel, the third horse in the string. Joe led his procession through camp after camp along the trail, too injured and tired to fully engage the guides and hunters who wanted to hear the whole story. The only men whom he told were the hunters from Georgia in Smoke's camp, with their hired guides looking on. The guides stared at the canvas bundle on the back of their boss's horse.

"We wondered where he went this morning," Smoke's lead guide had said, shaking his head sadly. "I always knew that hot head of his was bound to get him into trouble."

There was no anger, no accusations aimed at Joe from Smoke's men, which surprised him. What he saw was stoic sadness. And overt selfishness: "We can still hunt, can't we?" one of the hunters asked.

"I don't see why not," the guide said, with just a hint of disgust.

"I'm sorry and all," the hunter said, looking to the other hunters for support, "but some of us paid real good money for this."

"I know," the guide said, eyeing his clients and spitting a long brown stream of tobacco juice between his boots. Then, to Joe: "Sometimes I wish I'da never gone into the service industry."

BEFORE SETTING OUT THAT MORNING, Joe had patched himself up. The crease from Smoke's bullet had split the skin on his side and sliced a three-inch gash on the inside of his right arm. The bleeding from his side was profuse. He had lost more blood than he realized, which made him light-headed. He grimaced while he pinched the wound together, catching a glimpse of a white rib, which had also been nicked. There was a roll of gauze in the cabin but no medical tape to hold it to his side, so he used silver duct tape instead. He was a fan of duct tape, once telling Marybeth that it was one of the five greatest inventions of modern history. Painfully, he pulled on a fresh shirt over the dressing and tossed the heavy, wet one into the cookstove to burn.

THE NEWS PRECEDED HIM AS he rode. Outfitters communicated with one another in a combination of ways— face-to-face meetings, radio calls, and satellite phones, known as the "outfitter telephone line." Normally, the "line" was used to pass along word that the elk were moving, or that a guide had been bucked off his horse and was injured, or that a hunter was sick or disillusioned and needed a ride back to the trailhead. In this case, the

news was that the new game warden had shot and killed
the most infamous among them, Smoke Van Horn, the
Lion of the Tetons, in a gunfight.

As Joe rode south, they anticipated him in each camp.
In one of the camps he had checked on the day before,
both the guides and their clients stood silently on the
side of the trail with their cameras, and Joe heard the
whispery clicks of shutters as he rode by.

A hunter dressed in head-to-toe camo gear said, "It's
like something out of the Old West!"

JOE WAS SLUMPING IN HIS SADDLE, fighting shock and
the exhaustion that came from it, when he reached the
edge of Turpin Meadows at dusk. The Tetons were backlit by the setting sun, their profiles sharp and black
against a bruise-purple sky.

As he led the horses toward the campground, he saw
emergency vehicles, ambulances, and sheriff's department SUVs in the lot, and people milling around. Apparently, Joe thought, one of the outfitters had been able to
get the news to Jackson.

When they spotted him coming, he watched the small
crowd stop what they were doing and turn toward him
as one, some raising binoculars. One of the sheriff's men
unnecessarily whooped his siren for a moment, to signal
Joe to come in.

"YOU'LL NEED TO TURN OVER all of your weapons,"
Sheriff Tassell told Joe as he helped him down from his
horse. "We'll get you to the hospital and then I'll need a
statement from you."

Joe nodded grimly and dismounted. He could feel the
scab of the wound in his side crack open under the dressing.

"How bad are you hurt?" Tassell asked.

"Not too bad," Joe said. "I need some stitches, I think. Lost some blood."

"You need the ambulance to take you in?" Tassell asked.

"No."

Tassell turned to his deputies and gestured toward the third horse. "Untie the body and put it in the ambulance," he told them. "Tell the driver to go straight to Dr. Graves's."

Joe walked slowly toward his pickup.

"You're not driving yourself," the sheriff called after him, exasperated. "What in the hell are you thinking?"

Randy Pope stepped out from the small crowd. He wore crisp jeans, new boots, a snap-button shirt, and a denim jacket.

"I talked to Trey Crump," Pope said. "He said to tell you you're on administrative leave until the investigation of the shooting is concluded. As you know, it's routine procedure."

Joe nodded. "I figured that would happen." Looking Pope over, he said, "Looks like you've been to the western-wear store."

He ignored Joe's comment. "He said to tell you to give him a call as soon as you could."

"I planned to," Joe said.

Pope stepped in close. "So was it a gunfight, like they say?"

"It was more like assisted suicide," Joe said glumly. "Smoke fired first."

"Then you shot him?"

Joe nodded, too tired to speak.

Pope sighed and looked toward the darkening sky. Stars were beginning to poke through like needle pricks in dark fabric. "I need to work overtime just to keep up with the paperwork you generate," he complained.

*   *   *

TASSELL TURNED HIS SUV OVER to a deputy and drove Joe's pickup, while Joe slouched in the passenger seat.

They were on the blacktop when the sheriff said, "This is Will Jensen's truck, isn't it?"

Joe nodded. "Mine burned up."

The sheriff shook his head. "I heard about that. Things tend to happen around you, don't they? Just like Barnum said they would."

Joe didn't respond.

"Will tried for years to build a case on Smoke, and in the three days you're up there you *kill* the guy."

"It wasn't like that," Joe said, but didn't want to explain. He was thinking about the contents of the last spiral notebook. How it was all coming together. How ugly it had been for Will at the end.

THEY DROVE IN SILENCE UNTIL Joe could see the lights of Jackson in the distance. It seemed as if he had lived there forever, not just a few days. The ambulance was stopped on the highway in front of them so that a long column of tourists on horseback could cross the highway en route to their guest ranch for the night. Tassell stopped directly behind it, the headlights of the pickup shining into the ambulance and illuminating the body wrapped in the ground tarp.

"There goes my budget for medical examinations for the fiscal year," Tassell sighed.

AFTER AN EXAMINATION, a blood test, twenty stitches in his side and eight in his arm, Joe was remanded to the hospital for a night of observation. He was given sedatives by a doctor whose name tag identified him as "Dr. Thompson," who also wore a Day-Glo button that read "ski bum." The sedative was starting to dull the pain and bring him down. Before he went to sleep, he reached for the telephone at the side of his bed.

"Marybeth," Joe said, thrilled at hearing the sound of her voice, "I just killed the only man in Jackson Hole I really understood."

31

AS HE DRESSED THE NEXT MORNING, JOE TRIED TO RE-
call the conversation he'd had the night before with Marybeth, and snippets came floating back. It had been difficult
to concentrate with the drugs kicking in, and the only thing
that kept him awake during the conversation was the tone
of her voice, which was urgent and somehow melancholy at
the same time, as if she wanted to be angry with him but the
circumstances prevented it. At the time, it was important for
him to hear her voice, to touch base, to reestablish something. He needed her to be his anchor, to reel him back
home from where he was. But she had other concerns.
Sheridan was being difficult, having attitude problems, and
life between Marybeth and her oldest daughter was getting
tougher. "It's a mother and daughter deal," Marybeth said,
as if Joe would understand that. In response, he offered to
talk with Sheridan—they had a special rapport, he thought—
but Marybeth said their daughter was already in bed.

He vividly remembered her telling him that Barnum
was the 720 caller, the "720" being from a calling card,
and that Nate had caught the ex-sheriff in the act in the

Stockman's Bar. The news of Barnum's humiliation had swept through town, she said, and the old ex-sheriff was lying low, nowhere to be found. Joe cautioned his wife to watch out for Barnum.

"He blames me for his bad luck," Joe said.

"Don't worry," she said, "Nate is around."

"That's good."

"Yes," she said, after a long pause, which led him to wonder. Then: "It is good, isn't it?"

It seemed there was something else she wanted to say but didn't.

She had offered to leave the girls with her mother and come to Jackson right away to see him, but he told her not to.

"I'm more tired than hurt," he said, fixing his eyes on a blank television screen to keep them from closing, "and there's a lot I need to do in the next couple of days. Remember that missing notebook I told you about?"

He could not remember how their conversation had concluded. What had he told her? Had he outlined his suspicions? If he had, he couldn't remember her response. The details weren't there, but what stayed with him as he dressed was a recollection of vague misconnection, as if they had been talking past each other, telling each other different stories, each with a point that the other didn't, or couldn't, grasp.

"SO YOU'VE DECIDED YOU'RE FINE and you'll release yourself from the hospital?" Dr. Thompson said. "Usually a doctor does that. Namely me."

Joe was standing with his back to the door, cinching up his belt. He turned to see Dr. Thompson holding a clipboard chart and leaning against the doorjamb. "I needed a good night's sleep more than anything," Joe said.

"I don't disagree with your prognosis, given your, um, condition."

Joe was confused.

"Let me look at your wound and get it redressed," Thompson said. "Then we should probably have a little talk. You need to start taking better care of yourself, Mr. Pickett."

"I'm not sure what you're talking about," Joe said. "Am I sick?" He thought of how he had felt since arriving in Jackson, the foggy mental state, the sleeplessness, his lack of ability to concentrate. He steeled himself for bad news.

Thompson looked at Joe with amusement in his eyes, as if signaling him they could drop the pretense.

"Look, I'm a doctor, not a cop," Thompson said. "The blood test we took last night is confidential information. No one can find out what's on it. But you seem like a nice enough guy, and you have law enforcement responsibilities, and you carry lots of guns around with you. So you need to be aware of the side effects of your, um, indulgences."

"My *what*?"

"First, take off your shirt and let me look at that wound."

STELLA ENNIS WAS WAITING FOR him in the hospital lobby, and the sight of her stopped him cold. She looked up at him over the top of a Jackson Hole newspaper.

"How are you feeling?" she asked.

"Not as good as I thought, apparently." His voice was shaky from the discussion he'd had with Dr. Thompson.

"You look pretty good," she said, smiling.

"You do too."

She laughed, throwing her head back. "You should have seen me ten years and fifteen pounds ago. I would have blown you away."

She wore a black turtleneck sweater with silver and

gold threads running through the fabric, and gray slacks. Her thick auburn hair brushed her shoulders. She shook the newspaper with exaggerated force.

"Did you know you're a celebrity?" she asked.

"No."

"How about I buy you breakfast?"

"Okay."

"We need to talk."

"Yes," Joe said, "we do."

THE MORNING WAS CRISP AND BRIGHT, the sun not yet well enough established to have burned the frost off windshields and lawns. They walked along a slick wooden sidewalk to a restaurant near the hospital that was crowded. The place specialized in baked goods and had a sign out front that read GET YOUR BUNS IN HERE.

"I used to love this place," Stella said, taking him by the hand and leading him past it, "but I'm a little too familiar in there and it isn't as good as it used to be. Let's go to the Sportsman's Café."

"That's my favorite," Joe said.

"I know," she said, rolling her eyes. "It was Will's favorite too."

ED SEATED THEM IN THE BACK BOOTH near the kitchen door, and Joe ordered the Sportsman's Special. Stella smiled knowingly at the order.

"I know," Joe said. "Will's choice too."

"It's spooky," she said, ordering coffee and a bagel.

Joe looked at her across the table, and she looked straight back. Her name had come up so many times since he'd met her. He'd thought about her, even dreamed about her. The fact that he hadn't told Marybeth about her said more than he cared to think about. When Stella looked back at him he had the impression he'd been on her mind as well, but he wasn't sure in what context. It was as if they'd been circling each other for days, each looking for an opening.

"You start," she said.

He sipped his coffee, burning his tongue. "It's been a long time since I've had breakfast with a woman other than my wife," he said.

She smiled. "I believe that. Do you want to leave?"

It took him a moment to respond. "No."

"I don't want you to leave either."

He took another sip, looking at her over the top of his cup, trying to convince himself that what he was doing was part of his investigation.

"You've never met a woman like me," she said softly. He watched her lips, saw a flash of white teeth when she spoke.

"You're right."

"Don't worry," she said, cutting the words off, as if she'd planned to say more.

"I found Will's last notebook," he said.

"In the state cabin?"

He nodded.

"I looked for it afterward," she said wistfully, breaking their gaze. "I'd hoped he brought it down with him. Where was it—under the mattress?"

"Yes. I saw your initial in the guest book. I recognized it from the invitation you sent."

She smiled, and her eyes filmed over, as if remembering something that touched her. It wasn't guilt, he thought.

"I wanted to leave some kind of record," she said. "In case something happened to me. Or to both of us. You know that outfitter Smoke Van Horn? The one you shot? He saw us together up there. He didn't approve."

"I know."

"He was the least of our worries, though. He didn't realize I was trying to save Will."

"Were you?"

"Obviously I didn't do a very good job of it."

Joe started to speak when Ed slid a big platter in front of him and handed Stella her bagel on a plate.

"These are on the house," Ed said. "Enjoy!"

Joe looked up. "What's the occasion?"

"This is my last day of business here," Ed said, his eyes betraying his beaming mouth-only smile. "Jackson has plumb outgrown me."

"Damn," Joe said.

"I'd have done the same for Smoke," Ed said. "He was a good customer too.

"See that up there on the shelf?" Ed gestured to a garishly painted ceramic lion's head. "That was in honor of Smoke, the Lion of the Tetons. Some of his hunters presented it to him at breakfast once, and he forgot it when he left. I put it up there and it's been there ever since. He always said he wanted it back, but he never took it with him."

Joe could feel Stella's eyes on him, watching his reaction.

"It's a shame," Ed said.

"You mean Smoke? Or your last day of business?" Joe asked.

Ed turned back toward the kitchen. "Both, I guess," he said over his shoulder.

JOE AND STELLA TALKED LONG after the dishes were cleared. He had drunk so much coffee he felt jittery. She asked him about what had happened at the cabin, and he recounted it all. She seemed fascinated by the story, but focused in on what he was thinking at the time, and how he felt after, not the details of the shooting. He was again taken by how comfortable he was with her, how easy she was to talk with. He wondered if Will had felt the same way. Then he answered his own question: of course he did. He'd said as much in his notebook.

"I DON'T KNOW WHAT TO SAY," Joe said. "I'm talked out."

"I think you do," she said. "You're just scared of the words."

He looked up at her.

"Just because you love someone doesn't mean you can't care for another just as much. It's about context. It doesn't have to be an either/or situation. You can have both."

Joe felt his eyes grow wide, and squinted them back. He felt the *ZING*.

"I don't know," he stammered.

"I'm safe," she said, leaning across the table toward him. "You will never meet a woman as safe as I am. I have no agenda, and I don't want either of us to get hurt. But I want to be with you, Joe, if only for a little while. As long as it's real, and as honest as we can make it."

"What about Don?" Joe asked, not even believing he had asked.

"Don't ruin the mood," she said abruptly. "Don thinks of me as part of *him*. And since Don is obsessed with the very idea and concept of Don Ennis, well . . ."

Ed appeared with the pot of coffee. Joe didn't know whether to embrace him or send him away.

"WHAT IS IT YOU'RE TRYING to find out here?" he asked, looking out the window.

She was quiet for a few moments. Then: "I told you.

I'm looking for authenticity. Genteel authenticity. All my life I've been surrounded by people who pose, who play a role. For the first twenty-five years of my life, I didn't know the difference between actors and the real people they based their performances on. I'm sick of the inter-pretation. I want to go to the source."

"And you think you'll find it here?"

She laughed, tossed her head back. "Not in Jackson, no. But yes, I think I'll find it out here. I think I'm get-ting real close right now."

Joe felt his face get hot. He wondered what kind of authenticity Stella thought she could find in a married man. How could it be authentic if lying was integral to the relationship? But he couldn't say it.

"We're the last people left in here," Joe said, looking around. "I should get going."

"And do *what*?"

He thought about it. "I've got some things I need to check out."

She narrowed her eyes, trying to read him.

"Look," he said, "I'm not sure why I trust you, but I do. Maybe it's because Will did. You've got to answer a question."

He saw a flash of fear in her dark eyes. What did she think he was going to ask?

"When you went up to the state cabin with Will, did he seem to get better? His mental state, I mean?"

"At first, yes," she said. Was that relief he noticed in her face? "The first day up there he said he felt like him-self again. He loved Two Ocean Pass, and said he wouldn't mind spending the rest of his days there."

"He is," Joe said, "but go on."

She hesitated a moment before continuing. "By the second day, though, he was in bad shape again. He'd have terrible headaches, and he couldn't eat. His hands shook.

I tried to help him, you know, keep him distracted. But he was too far gone. He was really depressed when we rode back down. That was a week before, you know . . ."

Joe nodded, thinking.

"What?" she asked.

"This morning Dr. Thompson gave me a little lecture about taking care of myself. He said I had drugs in my system."

Stella looked at Joe, puzzled.

"He said it was barbiturates. He said even though I'd taken the stuff days before, there were still traces in my blood. He asked me about Valium and Xanax, and warned me that both have some serious side effects."

She listened intently, watching him, something going on behind her eyes.

"Stella, I've never taken drugs in my life. Somehow, they were introduced. It must have happened before I went up into the Thorofare. I haven't really felt normal since I got here, so now I'm guessing this has been going on for a while."

"I don't understand," she said.

"I think the same thing happened to Will. Maybe somebody got to him, figured out a way to drug him. He was under a lot of pressure, and if he didn't know he was being drugged it would have made it worse for him, made him think he was going crazy. It was just a matter of time before he did something horrible."

She looked stricken, her face drained of color. She knew something, but he didn't know what.

"You're coming to our party tonight, aren't you?" she asked suddenly.

Joe sat back. "I hadn't thought of it. I forgot about it, to be honest with you. I never RSVP'd."

"You need to come," she said, reaching across the table and grasping his hand.

"Why? It doesn't seem like the kind of thing I'm good at."

"It's important to me that you come," she said, her eyes burning into his. "It's *essential*. I'll make sure you're on the guest list. The Secret Service wants a guest list by noon."

"Stella . . ."

"What you just told me opens everything up," she said. "It's like a light just went on. But I need to think about it, and make sure I'm on the right track."

"What are you talking about?" he asked.

"Come tonight," she said, grabbing her jacket and sliding out of the booth. "Everything will come together tonight. We'll have everybody we need in one room."

He didn't know what to make of that. He wanted to believe she was on his side, on Will's side. That she was going to help solve the puzzle of Will's death, but in her own way.

She seemed to confirm it when she strode around the table and bent down and kissed him full on the mouth. Her lips were warm and soft, and he could still taste them as she walked out of the Sportsman's Café without looking back.

It took a moment for Joe to get his wits back and stand up. When he did, he saw Ed looking at him over the top of the batwing doors.

"Don't say it," Joe said. Dark thunderheads of guilt had already begun rolling across his sky.

"Just like Will," Ed said anyway.

32

"AT LEAST ONCE A DAY HE TAKES HIS BIRDS OUT," BELLO said, while driving. "He lets them fly around and he puts food out for them or holds it in his hand. The birds drop out of the sky to eat it."

"He's training the birds to hunt with him," Barnum said. "It's called stooping."

"I don't care what it's called," Bello said testily. "I just care that he does it once a day, usually in the afternoon."

The ex-sheriff felt a rise of anger but said nothing. Bello shouldn't talk like that to him, he thought. He was getting sick of the lack of respect people showed him, Bello included.

"Like I told you," Bello said, swinging his SUV off the state highway onto the two-track that led to the stone house and the river, "before we actually get to his place the road goes up over a rise. It's about three hundred yards from the house. He can't see a vehicle approaching until it comes over the top. When I was scouting him, that's where I put the sandbags, up there on that rise behind some sagebrush. He never looked in my direction. The sandbags are about a hundred yards apart, so we'll have sight lines from two angles."

"What if he hears us coming?" Barnum asked. "The noise of a car carries a long way out here."

"That's why we walk the last mile to the rise," Bello said tersely. "I'm guessing your old legs can handle that."

"Fuck you, Bello," Barnum said, not fighting his anger this time.

Bello laughed dryly. "That's the spirit, Sheriff."

Their rifles were between them on the seats, muzzles down. Bello's .300 Winchester Mag had a satin finish and an oversized Leupold scope. Barnum's old .270 looked like a hillbilly gun beside it, Bello said when he saw it.

"Forty elk and a drunken Mexican with a shovel would disagree," Barnum shot back.

BELLO HAD TOLD HIM THE STORY almost casually the night before, as they sat on opposite sides of Bello's room at the Holiday Inn. Both had cocktails in hand that Barnum had mixed.

Nate Romanowski had been known by a code name, the Falcon, and was one of the best the agency had, Bello said. He was out of the country for years at a time. But like others who were too tightly wound and too independent, Romanowski had started to choose which orders to follow and which ones to disregard. When he was called back to headquarters, it took three months for him to show up, and he clashed immediately with the new director. The Falcon quit loudly, in agency terms, intimating he would talk if they tried to stop him. "You've never seen paranoia like the paranoia we had in our outfit," Bello said, showing his teeth.

Two operatives, one a friend of Randan Bello and the other his son-in-law, were sent to find the Falcon and

assure themselves, and the agency, that he had no intention of talking after all. The operatives took annual leave
to do it, so the agency couldn't be accused of official covert activity within the country. Their last dispatch was
from northern Montana, via e-mail, reporting that they
had heard about a loner who fit the profile of the Falcon.
The suspect was a falconer who drove an old Jeep and
packed a .454 Casull from Freedom Arms in Wyoming.
The next day, the bodies of the operatives were discovered by a passing motorist, who reported the accident to
the Montana State Patrol.

"Romanowski killed them both?" Barnum asked.
"Why didn't we hear anything about it?"

Bello drained his glass of scotch and held it out for a
refill.

"The inquiry concluded that the engine on their vehicle quit on a switchback road and they lost control and
rolled eight times. Both were crushed."

Barnum looked over his shoulder as he poured.
"You're pretty sure he did it though." It was a statement,
not a question.

"Sure enough that the day after I retired I headed out
here to Wyoming," Bello said. "My daughter has never
remarried."

"Kids?"

"Nope. I've got no grandkids."

Barnum thought of his own grandchildren, teenage
dark-skinned delinquents on the reservation he had
never even met. No great loss, he thought.

"Why are you telling me all of this?" Barnum asked,
finally.

"Because you asked," Bello said, drinking and looking
out the window. "And you offered to help."

*   *   *

BARNUM HADN'T BELIEVED HIM at the time—Bello's explanation just hadn't sounded right. Nevertheless, he had gone along, because he had reasons of his own.

Bello pulled off the two-track more than a mile from the rise and turned off the engine. Climbing out, he pocketed the keys, slung the .300 over his shoulder, and buckled on a large fanny pack. Barnum followed suit, sliding his .270 out of the truck. He loaded it with 150 grain shells and worked the bolt.

"Are you ready?" Bello asked in a low voice.

Barnum nodded, and they shut the car doors softly. There was a slight breeze coming from the direction of the river, which was good because it made it even more unlikely that their car had been heard.

Bello walked around the SUV and handed Barnum a small Motorola Talkabout set to channel four.

"Keep the volume all the way down," Bello said. "If you need to talk to me about something, hit the chirp key and then turn the volume up a quarter of the way. But I hope we don't need to talk."

Barnum clipped the radio to his shirt pocket.

"Remember the plan?" Bello asked.

"No, I forgot it," Barnum said gruffly, being sarcastic.

Bello's eyes bored into the ex-sheriff. "Strange time for jokes."

"When we have a visual," Barnum said, using the same words Bello had used earlier, "we signal each other by waving our hands, palms out. Then we both sight him in and when you give the signal, a double chirp from the radio, we fire at the same time so we increase our chances of knocking him down for good."

"Aim for his chest," Bello said, interrupting, "with the crosshairs on the middle of the widest part of him. Forget about taking a head shot at this distance."

"When he's down," Barnum continued, stepping on

Bello's words, "we wait an hour, keeping the body in the scope and checking for movement. If we don't see any, you'll go down and drag him into the river. I'll stay back and keep watch down the road."

Bello listened intently, his eyes on Barnum, making sure the ex-sheriff had everything correct. Barnum didn't like being looked at that way, and didn't make a secret of it in his rehearsed delivery.

"Okay, then," Bello said, turning and walking down the middle of the two-track. Barnum followed.

There were problems with Bello's plan, Barnum thought. He'd reviewed it the night before, turning it over again and again, and finally figured out what was wrong with it: He was being set up. When Bello double chirped and Barnum fired, Bello would deliberately miss, so the only slug to be found in Romanowski's body would be the .270 round. Everyone knew Barnum hunted with a .270, and a ballistics check would tie the slug to the rifle.

Barnum was well known as a drinker and a talker, and the whole town was aware of his humiliation at the Stockman's. If Romanowski's body was found, and it would no doubt wash up somewhere downriver, Barnum would be a suspect.

By then, Bello would be long gone.

Of course, Barnum would implicate Bello. But, Barnum had realized, what did he really know about the man from Virginia? Was his name even Randan Bello? Barnum had never seen an ID. Was he even from Virginia, or were those stolen or counterfeit plates on his car? The man had been meticulous since arriving about leaving no records by paying for everything with cash. He had spilled everything out to Barnum so easily about the agency, and his son-in-law, and his intentions. Bello didn't seem like the kind of man to expose himself that way. The only reason he had done so, Barnum concluded, was because he saw in the ex-sheriff a way to pin the murder on someone else.

But that wasn't going to happen, Barnum said to himself while he walked. When that double chirp came, the ex-sheriff was going to swing his rifle around and shoot Bello in the head.

That would give the morning men at the Burg-O-Pardner something to talk about.

"I went to the sheriff with my concerns," Barnum would say, widening his hound-dog eyes, looking at each community leader in turn, "but he practically threw me out of his office. So I had to take care of things myself."

"Sounds like we need a new sheriff," someone would say, *should* say, perhaps the mayor. And they would all look to him.

"I don't know, fellows," Barnum would say humbly. "I was just getting used to being retired."

BELLO STOPPED AND GESTURED at the sky. Barnum squinted, seeing the black speck of a falcon streaking across a pillowy cumulous cloud.

"His birds are out, which means he's in the open," Bello whispered over his shoulder, his back to Barnum. "This will work perfectly."

"Yup," the ex-sheriff said absently, seeing something in his peripheral vision. He turned, and learned he could actually see a bullet coming when it was aimed straight at his head from a quarter of a mile away, even before he could hear the shot.

PART FIVE

A thing is right when it tends to preserve the integrity, stability, and beauty of the biotic community. It is wrong when it tends to do otherwise.

ALDO LEOPOLD,
A SAND COUNTY ALMANAC

33

THEY'RE GETTING TO ME SOMEHOW, WILL JENSEN WROTE ON the last page of his notebook. *They're inside my head and inside my body. They know where I'm going and they track my movements. I know it sounds crazy, and it IS crazy. Maybe it's just me, but I don't think so. They figured out a way to screw me up.*

Joe sat at the table in the statehouse and reread the last few pages of the notebook again. He wished Will had been more specific.

Who were "they"? What did he mean "they" were inside his head? If Will was right, how could "they" track his movements, as he claimed?

Then he read the next passage, the one that had chilled him in the cabin:

There is something so wrong with me. I'm not alone anymore. There is somebody inside my head. I've lost everything and my mind is next to go. Maybe it already has. I do things as if someone else were doing them. I watch myself say and do things, I know it's my body, but it isn't me. Dear God, will you help me? Will anyone? Nobody else will except Stella.

JOE'S EYES LEFT THE PAGE and settled on an envelope on the table, the invitation to Don and Stella Ennis's party. Stella was the only person Will trusted. She was the connection. Was she close enough to Will in the end to report his movements? And how, exactly, could she facilitate "them" getting into his head, as he wrote?

Joe couldn't make himself believe it was Stella, not after the way she had looked at him across the table. No one, he thought, could fake that kind of concern in her eyes, act *that* well. She had been on Will's side in his struggle; he had trusted her. But during breakfast, when Joe had mentioned the traces of drugs the doctor said were in his system, she reacted unpredictably. The information clearly triggered something in her mind. But he knew one thing—he had to make a decision about Stella that had nothing to do with Will. And he had to do it tonight.

Joe rubbed his eyes. His head was full of questions about Will, but as of yet, he had no answers. He felt tired and frustrated and mainly just wished he had a beer. Forgetting about his stitches, he pushed back from the table and felt a sharp stab of pain. As the day wore on, his wound hurt more. Dr. Thompson had given him a prescription for Tylenol 3 to dull the pain, and he decided to take one.

As he filled a glass from the tap on the refrigerator, he looked absently out the window at Will Jensen's old pickup in the driveway. Along the sidewalk, a neighbor wearing a tam was walking his dog, glancing furtively toward the house the way nosy neighbors do.

Suddenly, Joe froze, the tablet on his tongue, the water glass an inch from his lips, several thoughts hitting him at once.

Traces of drugs.

Will's pickup.

The intruder in his yard that night, clunking against the house.

He knew how they had done it.

And they were doing it to *him*.

He lowered the glass, spit out the tablet, and opened the front door. The neighbor looked up, his eyes widening for a moment, then his face broke out into a relieved smile.

The neighbor said, "Goodness, for a second there I thought you were—"

"I *know*," Joe said.

Puzzled, the man continued down the sidewalk.

Joe threw open the pickup door and shone a flashlight into the entrails of colored wires under the dashboard. It took a moment before he found what he was looking for. Even as he touched it with the tips of his fingers, he was chilled how they had pulled it off.

He climbed out of the truck shaking his head.

"Hey, can I talk to you for a minute?" Joe yelled to the neighbor, who was halfway down the block.

"Me?" the neighbor asked, pulling on his dog to turn it.

Joe waited until the man came back. "You've lived here for a long time, right? You knew Will Jensen?"

"Yes," the man said cautiously.

"Do you walk your dog every night?" Joe asked.

The man nodded. "As long as the weather doesn't keep us in."

Joe's mind was spinning. "Were you walking your dog the night Will Jensen died?"

34

THERE WERE SECRET SERVICE AGENTS IN ADDITION TO armed security guards checking invitations at the front gate of the Ennis home. Joe waited behind a black Lexus SUV until it was cleared to proceed, wishing he'd washed the pickup before coming.

A security guard shone a flashlight into Joe's face and asked him to remove his driver's license from his wallet.

"I know you," the guard said, seeing his name. "You're the guy who shot Smoke Van Horn."

Joe nodded and looked away. A Secret Service agent stepped from behind the guard and walked around the front of the truck to the passenger side and opened the door. The agent was lean and young, with an earpiece and cord that snaked down into his jacket. "Are there weapons in this truck?" he asked, looking around inside.

"Standard issue," Joe said, pointing out the carbine under the seat, the shotgun in the gunrack, the cracker shell pistol in the glove box. He was glad he'd left his holster and weapon in the statehouse.

"This is a problem," the agent said, stepping back and speaking into a microphone in his sleeve.

Joe waited, and several cars pulled up behind him.

Finally, the agent climbed into the cab with Joe and shut the door. "Sorry for the inconvenience, but the vice president will be here soon. We'll need to park you away from the premises," he said. "I'll walk you to the front door, and I'll need your keys while you're inside. When you're ready to go tonight, just tell one of my colleagues and I'll meet you at the front door and walk you back to your truck."

THE ENNIS HOME WAS SPACIOUS, with high ceilings, marble floors, and walls of windows that framed views of the Tetons. The furniture was made of stripped and varnished lodgepole pine, the style favored locally, and a massive elk antler chandelier with hundreds of small lights hung from a faux–logging chain. The home was crowded with guests bunched around portable bars, waiting for bartenders in tuxedos to pour their drinks. Joe scanned the crowd in the front room for anyone he might know, and saw no one familiar. Everyone, he noticed, looked exceedingly healthy and fit. The men wore open collars and jackets with expensive jeans or khakis, and the women wore cocktail dresses or ultra-hip outdoor casual clothes. He felt out of place, as he normally did. The feeling was made worse when guests gestured toward him and nodded to one another and he realized he was, in fact, being talked about.

A tall man with silver hair and a dark tan—Pete Illoway, the Good Meat guru—broke out of one of the knots of people and strode across the floor with his hand held out to Joe in a showy way. Cautiously, Joe took his hand, wondering what he wanted, while Illoway leaned into him.

"Good work up in those mountains, Mr. Pickett," Illoway said, pumping Joe's hand. "Smoke Van Horn will *not* be missed. He was an anachronism, and the valley had passed him by."

Joe said nothing, not accepting the praise nor refuting it, thinking about when Smoke had called himself an "arachnidism."

"May I buy you a drink, sir?" Illoway asked.

"That's okay, I can get it myself," Joe said.

Illoway smiled paternalistically, then signaled a bartender and pointed to Joe.

"Bourbon and water, please," he said.

Don Ennis strode purposefully into the room, parting the crowd, saw Joe, and stopped as if he'd hit an invisible wall. Ennis looked at Joe coolly for a moment, then broke into a stage grin and walked over just as Joe's drink arrived.

"Glad you could make it, Mr. Pickett," Ennis said. "I know Stella will be pleased."

Joe wondered what he meant by that.

"Everyone's talking about the incident up in the Thorofare," Ennis said. "You've become quite the celebrity."

"Was it really a gunfight like in the movies?" Illoway asked eagerly.

Joe shook his head. "Not really. It was pretty bad," he said, the image coming back of Smoke's vacant eyes, the way he chanted, *It really hurts, it really hurts, it really hurts.*

"Well done," Ennis said smartly.

"I said it was bad," Joe snapped back. "It isn't something I'm proud of or something you two should be so damned pleased about."

"But it couldn't have happened to a better guy," Illoway said, raising his glass as if he hadn't heard a word Joe said. "He was an absolute asshole, if you'll pardon my

French. Totally against Beargrass Village, and very vocal about it in public meetings. He was Old World, not New World, if you know what I mean."

"Speaking of," Ennis interrupted. "Have you come to a decision on your recommendation? I know we've still got a few days, but . . ."

Joe had been waiting for this. What he wasn't expecting was to find out Illoway and Ennis thought Joe had done them a huge favor by shooting Smoke.

"I still haven't filed my recommendation," Joe said evenly, "but I'm going to recommend that the concept not go forward unless you install some gates or bridges so the wildlife can migrate. We can't have a situation where the game is forced to cross the highway to get to lower ground. That would be dangerous to drivers and to the herds."

Something dark and cold passed over Ennis's face, as if Joe had double-crossed him. It was the same expression Joe had briefly seen when Stella entered the meeting room the week before.

"You're fucking kidding me," Ennis said in a tight whisper. "You're kidding me, right?"

"Nope," Joe said. "It's the same recommendation Will Jensen was going to make, as you know. I found his last notebook where he came to that conclusion."

Illoway reached for Ennis's arm, but Ennis pulled away, his eyes narrowing into slits.

"Don . . ." Illoway cautioned Ennis. "Now is not the time." Turning to Joe, Illoway said, "You know, if native species are allowed into the village they could infect our pure meat stock through interaction. I'm sure you're aware of that."

Joe shrugged. "Sure, it's possible. But I don't think you can have a perfectly controlled environment in the middle of wild country. A wise man once told me that real nature is complicated and messy." He enjoyed saying that, but tried not to smile.

"Who was that?" Illoway asked; he looked offended by the thought.

"Smoke Van Horn," Joe said, "the night before I shot him."

"I thought you were smarter than Jensen," Ennis spat. "He was nothing but a philandering drug addict. He was an insect compared to the size and scope of this project."

Joe looked at Ennis and took a sip of his drink. "How do you know he took drugs?"

Ennis looked like he was about to explode. Joe wanted to see it happen, see what the man said and did when he was enraged. Only the entrance of the vice president and his wife averted the concussion. Ennis turned away to greet the man, but before he did he looked over his shoulder and said, "We're not through here."

"No, we're not," Joe said evenly. "You and I have a lot to discuss."

Illoway looked at Joe and shook his head sadly. "What are you trying to do here? And what did you mean when you said we knew what Will Jensen's decision was going to be?"

"Oh," Joe said, his voice calmer and more measured than he felt. "I think you know the answer to that."

HE FOUND STELLA IN THE LIVING ROOM, with her back to the bar, sipping from a tall glass. She was well dressed in a crisp white billowy shirt, a short black skirt, and knee-high black boots. For some reason, he assumed her toenails were painted red. She seemed amused by the sight of him, amused by the evening in general. He noticed that she giggled out loud when one of the trophy wives, who was straining for a look at the vice president in the other room, accidentally dropped a cracker covered with some kind of soft white cheese on the leg of her cream-colored pantsuit.

"I'm glad you came," she said when he joined her.

"Your husband isn't," Joe said.

"What was going on in there? It looked like you were trying to bait him."

"I was," Joe said.

"Are you sure you know what you're doing?"

Joe smiled. "I never do. I just bump around sometimes until I hit something."

She finished her drink and handed the glass to the bartender. "Another gin and tonic, please. And what would you like?"

"I have a drink."

"Then have another." She turned around. "Ed, will you please get my friend a bourbon and water?"

Ed looked up. He was taller than Joe, his broad face impassive, his eyes challenging. Joe had obviously broken up a story Ed was telling Stella before the pantsuit incident, and he resented it.

"Ed once skied down the face of the Grand," she told Joe, her eyes widening. "Only twelve people have ever done it."

"Eleven," Ed corrected.

"Ed makes a dozen," she said, and Joe realized she was poking fun at the bartender, but Ed didn't get it. Instead, he puffed out his chest while he poured, straining the buttons on his shirt.

"That's pretty impressive," Joe said, but his mind was still on Don and Pete Illoway, how close he'd come to getting Ennis to blurt something.

She added, "He's got pictures he'll show you. He showed them to me within five minutes of meeting him."

Now you're pushing it, Joe thought. But Ed was easily

flattered. He made the drink and handed it to her. "Here you go, Mrs. Ennis."

"And don't forget the bourbon and water for Joe here," she said.

"Yeah," Ed grunted.

Joe and Stella exchanged glances. She was repressing a smile. Gesturing toward the sliding glass doors, she asked, "Have you ever seen the sun set on the Tetons?"

"Oh," Joe mused, "about a dozen times so far."

"Hmpf."

"But I need some air. Thanks for the drink, Ed," Joe said, leading Stella toward the sliding glass doors.

"Make sure he didn't spit in it," she laughed. "Ed's sweet on me."

"Aren't we all?"

"It's my gift to boys," she said, smiling, flirting, but shooting a look at Joe that had just a little bit of fear in it.

THE DECK WAS CLEAR OF GUESTS because they were all in the great room meeting the vice president. Joe and Stella walked to the corner of the deck, out of the light. Joe followed the trail of her scent through the thin outdoor sweet smell of sage and pine.

"It's a little cold," she said, putting her drink on the railing and hugging herself with her arms. "Don't you want to meet the vice president?"

"Maybe later," Joe said.

"We're going whitewater rafting tomorrow," Stella said. "It will probably be the last time we're able to do it this year before the snow starts flying. The original plan was to take the VP as our guest so Don could sell him on the idea of buying a place in Beargrass, but the Secret Service saw the stretch of river this afternoon and all of the places somebody could shoot at him—not to mention the class four rapids—and put a kibosh on the whole idea. Would you like to come with us instead?"

"That's a nice offer," Joe said, "but I'll pass."

"You should come along anyway. It's the last trip of the year. And maybe the last time for me for a long time," she said ominously.

"What do you mean?"

He could see her eyes glisten in the light of the stars. "Don's about to replace me for a newer model," she said. "I can just tell. The other day he looked at me across the table and said, 'Did you know you have some gray hairs?' He said it in the same tone he uses when he looks at the odometer and says, 'Ninety thousand miles.' That means we'll have a new car within the week.

"He doesn't have her in the wings yet," she said, "but it won't take him long. Don always wants the best, and, well, I'm getting up there in years. His trophy isn't so shiny anymore. I always knew it would happen. That's why he had the prenup, after all. I knew it would be a short ride. But I was determined that it would be a short, *fun* ride. With lots of white-water rafting."

Joe looked away, into the darkness of the trees beyond the deck. He could see very little, but he felt something inside him, a kind of warm surge. "Why are you telling me this?" he asked.

"Who else can I tell?" she asked. "Ed? Pete Illoway? One of the trophy wives in there? My mother would just say, 'I warned you about him.'"

"But you never left him," Joe said. "Instead, you had a fling with Will Jensen. I think maybe you like all of this"—he gestured to the house—"a little more than you want to admit."

"That's cruel, Joe," she said in a flat voice.

"Yeah," he said, "it is. But I'm not in a very charitable mood right now. I'm missing my wife and my family more than I can tell you. I can't wait to get back to them. Marybeth is my best friend. When I'm with you, I feel like I'm cheating on her. And I hate feeling that way. I'm no substitute for Will, Stella. That's just one of the things I've figured out tonight."

Joe stood in silence, not wanting to look at her. He knew she was crying, and it bothered him. But he couldn't embrace her, not yet.

"Stella?"

She roughly wiped away the tears on her cheeks and looked up at him.

"Why did you murder Will Jensen?"

"Oh, God," she said, as if he'd slapped her. Her eyes were wide now. She looked scared.

"I know it was you," he said. "I knew it was someone, by the way the gun was fired. Then tonight, before I came out here, I figured out that Will had been drugged, and how it was done. I didn't know it was you who killed him until I talked to some old guy walking his dog. He said he saw you enter Will's house that night after he talked to Will. The neighbor didn't hear the shot, but when he looked out on the street after midnight, your car was gone."

She hugged herself tighter and rocked a little. The surge he had felt inside earlier got hotter. His arms and chest were tingling, and he was finding it difficult to concentrate. Something was happening to him.

"Don't hate me, Joe," she said finally. "I loved that man. I loved the fact that he was real, that he was ordinary. He was a good man, like you."

Joe's legs were getting weak. He leaned against the railing so he wouldn't sway.

"I didn't know they were drugging him. I didn't know until this morning, when you told me at breakfast that the doctor found traces of drugs in you. Then I did some checking with my doctor. He said that drugs like Valium and Xanax can make someone who is already depressed turn suicidal, especially if the victim doesn't know he's being drugged. The doctor told me someone else had been asking about the effects of these drugs earlier in the year—my husband. Don wanted to know what they would do to a person. Don told the doctor he suspected an employee, but obviously he had another purpose in mind. All I knew was that Will was getting worse, and acting out. He was humiliating himself. People were starting to make fun of him. He lost his family and he was about to lose his job, and it broke my heart. He was such a good man.

"When we were up at the state cabin," she said, "he was normal again for a day. He felt guilty being there with me, but he was normal. I thought I had broken through to him. Then he started to shake and get sick. I now know he was suffering withdrawal from the drugs, but he didn't know that and neither did I."

Joe felt hot fingers reach up through his neck, pictured his brain being gripped like a softball. He tried to focus on Stella's words, but they kept slipping out of his grasp.

"When I found him that night he was in terrible shape," she said, sniffing back tears. "His gun was on the table and he couldn't even move. He had thrown up on himself. I guess he thought if he ate all that meat he would flush something out of his system, but it didn't work. My heart was aching for him. He told me I was the only person he loved, but he couldn't take it anymore. I begged him to let me take him to the hospital, but he wouldn't go. He was pathetic, this fine, decent man. This man so unlike the men I had always known."

Joe grabbed the railing with both hands to steady himself, looking out into the darkness. His eyes burned, Stella's words suddenly loud, pounding against his head.

"Twice, he tried to put the gun in his mouth, but he was too far gone. I was crying hysterically, but I got the gun from him and I told him I loved him and I did it for him," she said, the words coming out in a rush. "If I'd known the reason he was in that condition was because my husband . . . that Don was shoving Will out of his way and getting back at me at the same time . . ."

She looked away from Joe and gasped. Groggily, Joe turned to see what she saw. He now knew that he had been drugged, that Ed, or the bartender before Ed, or Pete Illoway, had slipped something into his drinks. There was a roaring in his ears, and he couldn't focus on what Stella was saying or on the figures who now stood at the sliding glass door. He heard Don Ennis say, "Stella!" very sharply and saw the vice president, who was next to Ennis, look from Don to Stella to Joe, his reticence causing the Secret Service agents surrounding him to shoulder their way through the door onto the deck.

Joe launched himself forward, nearly falling, and hit Don Ennis square in the nose with a looping round-house right, snapping the developer's head back against the sliding door, which shattered, cascading glass onto the carpet inside and the deck outside. Just as quickly, Joe was tackled and overwhelmed. The last thing he saw was the redwood of the deck, winking with shards of glass, rushing up to meet him.

TWO HUNDRED AND FIFTY MILES away, under the same stars and slice of moon, an SUV with Virginia plates was aimed at the lip of a remote canyon called Savage Run. The driver, who had coaxed it up there over some of the roughest country he had ever seen, eased the gearshift into drive and stepped out as the vehicle rolled forward, picked up speed, and vanished over the edge. It took four full seconds for the sound of the crash to reach the top.

35

A HARSH SHAFT OF SUN FROM A SKYLIGHT BURNED RED
through his eyelids, and Joe awoke covered in sweat with
a screaming headache on a metal-framed cot in the Teton
County jail. He turned his head to the side, away from
the light, and the movement created a wash of nausea
that rose in him. He staggered to the metal toilet in the
corner of the cell, threw up, and leaned against the cold
cinderblock wall, breathing deeply. His mouth tasted like
he'd been sucking on pennies.

"Morning, sunshine," a Secret Service agent said,
standing outside his cell. Joe recognized him as the one
he had first seen in the sheriff's office.

Joe looked at his wrist, but saw a pale oval of skin
where his watch should have been.

"What time is it?" he croaked, noticing they had also
taken his belt, boots, and everything in his pockets.

"Noon."

"Man," Joe said, "my head is killing me."

"You took a few lumps," the agent said. "By the way,

you popped your stitches last night so the doctor sewed you up again."

Joe raised his arm and saw the dried bloodstains on his clothes, then raised his shirt and looked at the new bandages. There was no mirror in the cell, but when he rubbed his unshaven face he felt several cuts and bruises, and his bottom lip was swollen and sore. *Boy,* he thought, *if Marybeth could see me now, she'd be so proud.*

"I'm Agent Cameron," the man said, "and you, my friend, are in a shitload of trouble."

Joe looked over at Cameron, the the words setting him back.

"What do you have against the vice president?" Cameron asked bluntly.

"Jeez . . ." Joe moaned, "I've got nothing against him."

"Then why'd you go after him that way?"

"I didn't go after him," Joe said. "I went after Don Ennis."

Cameron shifted, peering at Joe through the bars.

"Yeah," Cameron said, "that's what we thought. But Mr. Ennis tried to make the case that you were attacking the VP and he stepped in front of him to protect him from you."

Joe said, "You were there, weren't you? You know it didn't happen that way."

"We wouldn't have let it happen that way," Cameron said. "But maybe you were swinging for the VP and hit the wrong guy?"

"I hit who I was trying to hit," Joe said.

Cameron showed a slight smile. "Yeah, it was obvious you were after him and not the VP. I was just testing you. But Mr. Ennis seems to call a lot of the shots around here, and I think he would like you to stay in this jail cell a lot longer."

Joe reached up with both hands and smoothed his hair back. There were lumps on his scalp too, and he winced. "Have I been charged with something? Can I talk with the sheriff?" Joe asked.

"I don't think the sheriff is back yet," Cameron said. "He had to leave early this morning because there was some kind of accident on the river. Apparently, someone drowned in the whitewater."

Joe almost didn't make the connection, but when he did he said, "Oh, God."

"They're looking for her body downriver, I guess," Cameron said.

Joe closed his eyes tight and slid to the floor.

"Was she worth punching her husband and landing in jail?" Cameron asked.

Yes, Joe thought, *yes she was.*

JOE SAT AT A CONFERENCE TABLE in the sheriff's office with Randy Pope, Trey Crump, and Tassell. His hands were handcuffed and on the table in front of him. The skin on his knuckles, where he had hit Don Ennis, was peeled back and scabbed over.

Trey was seated next to Joe. "I came over as soon as I heard. Mr. Pope called me last night."

"Does Marybeth know?" Joe asked. "I haven't been allowed to make a call."

Trey raised his eyebrows sympathetically. "I called her this morning."

Joe looked down. He could not imagine what Marybeth must be thinking. "How did she take it?"

"Not well," Trey said, "but I told her we'd figure a way out of this."

He leaned into Joe. "I heard about what happened with Smoke Van Horn. I know you're not pleased about what you had to do, but I'm damned proud of you, Joe. After that bear, you had me worried."

"Me too," Joe confessed.

Tassell cleared his throat. He looked wrung out and angry. "I'd like to remind everyone here that Mr. Pickett is under arrest for assault, so I'd appreciate you not having side conversations. Letting him out of the cell to talk with you is a courtesy."

"Thank you," Joe told Tassell. He looked at Trey, said, "Thanks for telling Marybeth that, but I *did* hit the guy. My only regret is that I didn't shoot him—"

"Joe," Trey cautioned, interrupting, "watch what you say here."

Joe was struck by the wisdom of that and went silent.

"We might have a way to get you out of this," Pope said.

Joe turned to him. Pope sat on the other side of the table with Tassell.

"I talked with Don Ennis an hour ago at the hospital," Pope said. "He was very distraught, as you can guess. The poor guy lost his wife this morning. But he did say he'd consider dropping the charges if we would transfer you out of here."

"Was he in the boat when it happened?" Joe asked.

Pope looked back, confused. "What difference does that make? Didn't you hear me? He said he'd consider dropping the charges."

"Who was in the boat?"

Pope angrily slapped the table and addressed Joe's supervisor. "Trey, we have a terrible situation here, as you know. We could have one of our game wardens charged with aggravated assault—the second employee in this same district to get arrested. If that happens, it will look like the governor has completely lost control of this agency. I risk my reputation to get this guy out of it, and he doesn't seem to care!"

Trey sighed heavily and leaned toward Joe. "Joe, what's going on? We could both lose our jobs over this."

"His wife drowns but he has the presence of mind to negotiate my transfer?" Joe asked. "Does that sound like a grieving widower to you?"

"Shock affects people in different ways," Pope said weakly, again talking to Trey as if he couldn't deal with Joe. "Don Ennis has a direct line to the governor, Trey. He's not somebody we can fuck around with anymore. We let you give Will Jensen a long leash, and then Joe here. Things couldn't have gone worse under your watch. Now we've got to think of *our* survival, and I'm talking about the whole agency."

"What did you offer him?" Joe asked Pope. "Did you tell him we'd approve Beargrass Village?"

Pope flushed red but didn't answer.

"You did," Joe said.

"I'm trying to keep you out of jail!" Pope shouted. "Why can't you get that?"

Joe stood up, and he noticed that both Trey and Tassell pushed back from the table in case they needed to restrain him.

"Don Ennis caused Will Jensen to break," Joe said. "He started to do the same to me. He probably killed his wife this morning. And you"—he pointed awkwardly across the table with his handcuffs at Pope—"just gave him what he wanted all along."

The room was silent, until Pope asked, "Can you prove a single thing you're saying?"

Joe hesitated. "Some of it," he said. "But you'll need to give me the rest of the day to nail it all down."

Trey looked from Pope to Tassell. "Let's give Joe a chance here. Is that all right with you, Sheriff?"

"I don't think I like where this is headed," Sheriff Tassell said, shaking his head. "I don't think I like it at all."

* * *

ON THE WAY TO THE STATEHOUSE in Tassell's Cherokee, the sheriff kept shaking his head. "We lose a couple of people every year on the river," he said. "Unlike homicides, it isn't that unusual." He had told Joe, Pope, and Trey that while going through the rapids, Stella apparently lost her grip on the rope and was thrown from the boat. Don Ennis said she must have been tugged underneath his raft because they didn't see her again. Teams were searching for the body, but they hadn't found it yet.

"We've had situations where the body isn't found for weeks," Tassell said, "sometimes even longer. If it gets pinned under the water against rocks, we just have to wait. One guy wasn't found for over a year. His body washed all the way down to Palisades Reservoir and an ice fisherman found him when he was drilling a hole in the ice."

"Who else was in the boat?" Joe asked again.

"Don, of course," Tassell said, "Pete Illoway, and some guy named Shane Suhn, who works for Ennis. They all corroborated the story."

"How do we know she was in the boat?"

"Some other rafters saw her when they launched," Tassell said.

"Where did it happen?" Joe asked. "Where on the river?"

"At the start of the worst stretch of whitewater," Tassell said. "That's where most of the drownings take place. People get used to nice easy rapids, and then they hit the hard stuff and they aren't prepared for it."

Tassell leaned across the table to look at Joe. "You've seen all those Snake River rafting pictures around town? That's where they're taken, because the rollers are so big."

Joe thought about the photos he had seen in the window of Wildwater Photography.

"She wasn't inexperienced," Joe said. "She'd been on that stretch of the river many times."

"But why would Don kill his wife?" Tassell asked.

"She discovered something about him," Joe said. "And he was planning to dump her."

Trey turned in his seat, hanging an arm over the back of it, narrowing his eyes at Joe. "How well did you know her, anyway?"

"Well enough," Joe said.

"I thought you were going to say 'not well enough.'" Pope grinned.

Joe glared at him, and Pope looked away.

AT THE STATEHOUSE, JOE SHOWED them how the piece of siding on the back of the house could be removed. They watched as he took it off and peeled back a layer of pink insulation, revealing a line of copper tubing and a metal screw-top fitting that had been soldered onto the tube.

"This line connects directly from the well in the basement to the drinking water outlet on the refrigerator inside," Joe said. "It was the surest way they could drug Will. They couldn't put it in his food, because he ate out a lot and rarely cooked, except for that last night. But if they could connect it to his drinking water"—Joe fingered the valve where a bottle of liquefied narcotic could be connected by a fitting with a dispensing valve on it—"they knew it would get him." He showed them how the valve could be adjusted to dispense a quantity of the drug into the line. It was still set at one-quarter open, enough to affect Joe but not disable him.

"Christ," Tassell said, looking over the mechanism.

"The first night I was in the house I heard somebody out here," Joe said. "I heard a clunking sound, probably after they hooked up the bottle and fumbled with putting the siding back up. But I didn't figure this out until yesterday. Once I knew it was drugs, things started to make sense."

"So they didn't actually murder him," Trey said. "They created a scenario where he would either get fired, get arrested, or do himself in."

"Right," Joe said. "He was under a lot of strain after his wife left, and that's when they installed it. And they also knew that after she left he'd be in worse shape, and more vulnerable. Ennis knew Will was going to veto Beargrass Village, and the only way the project could go forward was if Will was gone and discredited. Will couldn't figure out what was happening to him—you can read it in his journals. The drugs just made things worse to the point that he couldn't see another way out of it." Joe had made the decision not to tell them what he knew about Stella's part in it. He didn't see the point, now that she was gone and Will's death had been ruled a suicide.

"But we don't know who rigged this up," Pope said. "You're speculating here."

"I am," Joe said. "But who besides Don Ennis had the means to do something like this? Who gained from Will going off the deep end?"

"You've got a point," Trey said.

"Another thing," Joe said. "Susan Jensen told me that Will's cremation was paid for by some anonymous person. She thought it was someone who liked Will, or the family. I'll bet if we check the crematorium we'll find out the check came from Ennis, or Beargrass Village, or one of his other companies."

"Why would he do that?" Pope asked.

"In case someone wanted to dig up the body and do

an autopsy later," Joe said. "To prevent the discovery of drugs in Will's system."

Tassell rubbed his face with his hands and moaned.

"Let me show you something else," Joe said, leading them around the house to the driveway.

JOE EXPLAINED THAT HE HAD located the transmitter in Will's pickup the previous afternoon, before he went to the party at the Ennises'. After searching the wheel wells, bumpers, and motor, he found it mounted under the dashboard within a spider's web of wiring. Will's line about *They know where I'm going and they track my movements* made him think of the truck.

"They knew were he went, what he said, what he told people over his radio," Joe said. "Since game wardens spend more time in their vehicles than they do anywhere else, it was like tapping his office."

Trey nodded, leaning into the cab to look under the dashboard. "If we check the frequency on that transmitter and match it to a receiver, we've found who was listening in."

"I'd guess the receiver is in a room at Beargrass," Joe said. "That's how they knew what decision he was going to make on Beargrass Village. They listened to him talk to biologists and others about the migration problems a fence would cause."

"So that's why they torched your truck," Tassell said, still with a pained expression on his face. It was as if Joe's discoveries were causing him escalating physical pain. "It was easier to do that than run the risk of getting caught putting another transmitter in *your* vehicle. They knew you'd just take Will's truck instead, and you did."

Joe stood back and let the men hash out theories and make connections. Trey bought what Joe had shown them; Pope was intrigued but wary because if Joe was right he would look foolish for his agreement with Ennis, and Tassell was pained by the prospect of confronting one of the most powerful and willful men in Teton County. While Joe listened, he saw the neighbor in the tam come out of his house with his dog. He had kept Stella out of it so far, figuring it was the least he could do. Even though he knew she was dead, the fact hadn't really sunk in yet.

"Let's go back to the station," Joe said, interrupting. "I've got an idea how we might be able to get Ennis to admit he murdered his wife."

Pope and Tassell looked at Joe with incredulity.

They were in the Cherokee before the neighbor made it down the block, for which Joe was grateful. That man, he had learned the day before, was a talker.

36

PI STEVENSON WAS IN THE PROCESS OF FLIPPING THE OPEN sign to CLOSED in the window of Wildwater Photography when Joe rapped on the door. She started to point to the sign, then recognized him and unlocked the bolt.

"What happened to *you*?" she asked, recoiling from the bruises and lumps on his face.

"Is Birdy here?" Joe asked, not wanting to take the time to explain.

"He's in the back," she said. "Would you like to come in?"

"I've got some colleagues with me," Joe said. He saw her look over his shoulder at the sheriff's SUV, which was parked against the curb.

"Am I in trouble again?" she asked.

"Not that I know of," Joe said, stepping inside and signaling Tassell and Trey to follow. The studio was small, the walls filled with action shots of skiers and rafters and a few obligatory Tetons at daybreak. A long front counter divided the public area from a small office and a curtained darkroom. A red light was on above the darkroom entrance, and Joe assumed that's where Birdy was.

"What do you want?" she asked. "We were just about to close up for the day."

Joe looked straight at her. "How would you like to contribute to a real bad day for Don Ennis and Beargrass Village?"

Her eyes lit up, and she beamed. Then, with determination, she turned and shouted over her shoulder, "Birdy!"

"YOU'VE GOT TO BE REAL careful here," Joe told Pi and Birdy. "You can't lie, and you can't insinuate anything at all, even if he presses you, or wants to negotiate over the phone. Do you understand me?"

Pi nodded, trying to contain her enthusiasm. She was both giddy and nervous at the same time. For his part, Birdy seemed pleased to have Pi so happy with him for agreeing to go along with Joe's idea.

"I'll be on the phone in the office," Tassell warned, looking from Pi and Birdy to Joe. "If anything you say comes across as even a hint of extortion or entrapment, I'm pulling the plug on this. We'll have the call recorded, and it has got to be clean enough to stand up in court if we need it."

The store's office was crowded. One of Tassell's deputies had brought in the owner of the local Radio Shack, who was opening up boxes containing a tape recorder and an 8mm video camera. Randy Pope was at the Game and Fish building, calling the agency director and the governor to let them know what was happening. Joe wondered why Pope had been so anxious to leave, but was pleased the man wasn't there.

"What if he acts like he doesn't know what we're talking about?" Birdy asked.

"That's fine," Joe said. "That means he's either inno-
cent or he's buying time to deal with you later. My guess,
though, is he'll want to take care of things right away. He
won't really believe you have anything, but he's too im-
pulsive not to make sure. He's a man of action. If that's
the case, we want him to come here. We don't want a
meeting set up anywhere else. You've got to be careful
not to tip him off in some way. If that happens, we've lost
our opportunity."

Over his shoulder, Tassell asked his deputy if the telephone tap was working, and the deputy said it was. The
owner of Radio Shack looked excited to be able to play a
part in the operation, Joe thought.

"What about the video camera? Where are we going
to put that?" Tassell asked.

The man from Radio Shack and the deputy looked
around the room theatrically for a good location.

"How about on the shelf behind the counter with all
the other cameras? We can put a piece of tape over the red
light so they won't know it's on," Trey said, pointing over
Tassell's head. Birdy had a display of old and new cameras
that he used for photographing skiers and rafters.

"That makes sense," Tassell said, rolling his eyes at the
obviousness of it.

"Give us a minute," the Radio Shack owner said. "I
want to test everything."

While they waited, Joe went over things again with Pi
and Birdy.

"And to think this was all about meat," Pi said triumphantly. "Flesh-eaters lose their moral bearings when
confronted with the possibility of not getting what they
want, which is more flesh. Or in this case, better flesh."

Joe was confused for a moment, and could feel Tassell
staring at him. He motioned Joe into the office and shut
the door.

"She's a loose cannon," Tassell said. "She'll screw this up and we'll get hung out to dry for entrapment."

"Can you think of another way?" Joe asked.

Tassell hesitated. "No."

Joe opened the door and went back to the counter, Pi and Birdy looking at him expectantly.

"Are we still on?" Birdy asked.

"We're on," Joe said.

"Let's get this son of a bitch," Pi said, her eyes dancing.

Joe sat down, filled with sudden doubt. It had taken him over an hour to convince Tassell to try this, and the sheriff had reluctantly agreed, but only after talking with the county attorney. Tassell was concerned that Pi and Birdy's animal rights agenda was so vehement that they would do or say *anything* to implicate their target. Every word that was said, every inference, would be recorded on audio- and videotape to be scrutinized by lawyers and judges in what could be a hostile court. Looking at the glee in Pi's face, Joe wasn't so sure the sheriff wasn't right.

JOE SAT AT THE COUNTER across from Pi and Birdy while Pi arranged the speaker phone in front of them. His assignment was to coach them through the phone call if necessary, and to warn them if they got into dangerous territory. Joe handed her the business card he had received a couple of weeks before, the one that read: "Welcome to town. I worked with Will. I'll be in touch."

As she punched the buttons, Joe turned to Tassell, his deputy, the Radio Shack owner, and Trey, and placed his finger to his lips. They all nodded back.

After three rings, a receptionist answered, "Beargrass Village."

"May I speak to Don Ennis, please?" Pi said.

"Who may I ask is calling?"

"Pi Stevenson and Birdy Richards," she said, looking up at Joe and smiling. "It's extremely important."

"Hold, please." There was a click and the silence was filled with soft classical music.

Joe turned and raised his eyebrows at the Radio Shack owner and the deputy, who both wore headphones. Both men turned thumbs up. The recording equipment was working.

"Come on the line, you bastard," Pi said, curling her lip. Joe shushed her.

"He's an asshole," she said. "What if he doesn't take our call?"

Joe shrugged and gestured toward the phone. He didn't want to get into a discussion with her that could be overheard if the receptionist suddenly came back on the line.

"He's probably sitting in his lounge chair eating raw flesh," Pi said, and Birdy giggled.

Joe looked at them both with exasperation.

But when the receptionist picked up, Pi was all business.

"Mr. Ennis suffered a traumatic event today and he's resting," the receptionist said. "May I please take your name, number, and a message so he can call you back?"

Joe saw a spark in Pi's eyes as she said, "I suggest you wake him up. This call concerns the traumatic event. Again, it's extremely important that we talk to him."

Uh-oh, Joe thought, trying to catch her eye. *Don't go any further with it.*

The receptionist hesitated. Joe could almost see her trying to figure out what to do.

"This is something Mr. Ennis will want to hear himself," Pi said. When she finally looked up, Joe motioned to her to back off. She smiled and dismissed Joe with a "don't worry" look.

"Please hold," the receptionist said, and the music came back.

Tassell had crossed the room and was hovering be-hind Joe.

"I know," Joe whispered to him. His stomach was knotting up, and Pi said frivolously, "I think we've got the hook in the bastard's mouth. Now he'll know what fish feel like."

"Pi—" Joe started to say, when the music stopped suddenly.

"This is Don Ennis." His voice was a harsh, no-nonsense baritone. "This is not a good time to call. What's so goddamned important?"

Pi mimed the act of reeling in a fish while she spoke: "Mr. Ennis, this is Pi Stevenson—"

"Is there somebody there with you?" Ennis inter-rupted. "I thought I heard another voice."

Joe thought, *Shit.*

"Yes, there is," Pi said smoothly, and Joe felt his scalp crawl. "I'm here with Birdy Richards. He's the owner of Wildwater Photography, and I work for him."

Joe let out a long, silent sigh.

"I thought you were that animal-rights kook."

"One and the same, Mr. Ennis, but that's not why I called."

"What is it, then? I told you this was a bad time."

"Well, we thought you would want to know," she said.

"Know what?"

Birdy leaned forward toward the phone. "Mr. Ennis, this is Birdy Richards. Do you know what we do here at Wildwater Photography?"

"No, and I really don't care."

Birdy glanced at Joe, hurt. Joe gestured for him to go on.

"We've got cameras placed on the banks of the Snake River," Birdy said. "Where the rapids are. We take pictures of the rafters when they come through the whitewater. The rafters usually don't even know it, because they're having too much fun or they're too scared to look for the cameras. Then, at the take-out spots, we pass out flyers saying the rafters can buy photos of themselves shooting the rapids if they come into town to my shop. We have proof sheets ready by the time they get here that they can look at, and I sell the shots either as prints or I can put them on a disk. About five to seven percent of the rafters decide they want pictures made of their Snake River experience."

As Birdy talked, Joe began to relax. Birdy had made his sales pitch often enough that he sounded comfortable. Joe could imagine Ennis's mind racing with the possibilities of what he was being told.

"Of course," Pi interjected, "that means ninety-five percent of the photos aren't sold to anyone. Sometimes, they turn out to be the most interesting shots taken."

Stop there, Joe gestured to her.

"What the fuck?" Ennis said. "What are you telling me exactly?"

"Just that we get a lot of pictures we don't quite know what to do with," Birdy said.

Pi leaned forward, and Joe mouthed, *No!* She sat back, pouting.

"So," Ennis said, his voice hushed, "are you telling me your cameras shot all of the rafters on the river today?"

Birdy looked at Joe, fear in his eyes. He obviously didn't know how to answer the question, how to parse his words so he wasn't lying. The fact was, Birdy's cameras shot only rafts for companies that enrolled in his program and agreed to tape photocells on their rafts that would signal the remote cameras to work. All the other rafts, including the Ennis raft, would have passed by unnoticed.

"Mr. Ennis," Pi said, while Joe cringed in anticipation, "what we're saying is that we got a lot of pictures we just hate to see go to waste. Some real prize-winners."

Okay, Joe thought, signaling her. That was vague enough.

"Jesus Fucking Christ," Ennis growled.

"We thought you'd find that interesting," Pi said, beaming at Joe and yanking an imaginary hangman's noose above her head.

"Would you consider possibly selling the photos you took today?" Ennis asked.

"Sell them?" Pi said innocently.

"You know what I'm talking about," Ennis said. "Quit fucking around. I want to look at them, and maybe I could buy some of them. I want you to bring them to me."

Tassell's deputy sneezed in the back of the room.

Ennis went silent.

Joe covered his face with his hands.

"Who was that?" Ennis asked.

Birdy looked stricken. His wide forehead was beaded with sweat. Pi, for the first time, looked scared.

Then Joe mouthed, *The dog.*

"Just the dog," Pi said to the phone.

"The dog?"

"Pi feeds the dog a vegan diet," Birdy said, running with it. "He doesn't get enough protein so he catches a lot of colds. I keep telling her that dogs need to eat meat, even if people don't."

"Dogs can survive perfectly well without meat," Pi said heatedly, meaning it. "They can get their protein from soy and other natural products."

"Jesus, you people," Ennis said disgustedly.

Again, Joe relaxed.

"Mr. Ennis," Birdy said, "we can't bring the pictures there. They're here on the computer. But if you want to, you can come look at them at the shop."

Again, silence. Joe guessed Ennis was deliberating what to do.

"Has anyone else seen the photos?" Ennis asked.

"No, sir."

"Does anyone else know about the photos?"

"Not yet, sir," Birdy said, hanging the *yet* out there.

"Sit tight. What's the address?" Ennis barked. "I'll be there in thirty minutes."

WHEN THE CALL WAS CONCLUDED, Birdy flopped forward into his arms as if completely spent, and Pi pumped her fist in the air and screamed, "Yes!"

Joe turned and looked at the sneezing deputy, who was beet red. Then to Pi and Birdy: "Great job."

37

RANDY POPE ARRIVED AT THE PHOTOGRAPHY SHOP AS the sheriff and his deputy were hiding their vehicles on adjacent streets. Pi and Birdy stood around nervously near the counter, waiting for Don Ennis to arrive. Joe and Trey Crump were behind the curtain in the darkroom, and Trey motioned to Pope to join them so he couldn't be seen if Ennis drove by and looked through the front window.

"The director doesn't like it," Pope said, as Joe slid the curtain closed behind him. "He's ordering you to pull the plug on this before we all wind up in court for entrapment."

Joe was thankful for the darkness because the look he gave Pope could have resulted in a charge of insubordination.

"We're too far along for that," Trey said in defense. "We can't stop anything now. Ennis is on his way."

"Didn't you hear me?" Pope asked. "I said the director doesn't want us involved with this. He thinks the governor may have already heard from Ennis about Joe assaulting him. It looks like a vendetta by the agency against one of the governor's biggest supporters."

"It's *my* vendetta," Joe said, "against a guy who caused the death of a game warden as well as his own wife."

Pope turned on Joe, prodding him in the chest. "You shouldn't even be here. You're officially suspended for the shooting. You're so far over the line I can't even see you. And you can forget about taking over this district."

"Touch me again with that finger," Joe said, "and I'll break it off."

Trey shouldered his way between them, and Joe stepped back, trying to calm down. Despite the darkness of the room, he saw orange spangles flash in his vision and knew he was seconds away from lashing out at Pope.

"Randy," Trey said in a calming voice, "Ennis all but admitted he killed her. He's coming here to try to buy the pictures so he can't be implicated. Everything is on tape, and even Tassell thinks it's clean and legal."

"But there aren't any pictures," Pope said. "The poor guy probably thinks he's being framed by those nuts out there, and he doesn't know what to do."

Beyond the curtain, Joe heard Tassell, his deputy, and the owner of Radio Shack enter the shop and assemble behind the closed office door. The stage was now set for Ennis.

"You weren't here," Trey said. "They never told Ennis they had pictures of him murdering his wife. Ennis just assumed they did, and he's coming here. Once he's in the shop, he'll say something that incriminates him. Then the sheriff will arrest him. If he doesn't incriminate himself, he walks away."

"I don't like it," Pope said. "And the director *ordered* us to back off."

"He can order whatever he likes," Trey said with an

edge Joe had rarely heard. "He's out in two months, and we'll have a new governor. Maybe we'll even get someone who cares more about arresting a murderer than kissing up to his contributors."

Joe heard Pope spin away and start for the curtain to leave.

"Stay here," Trey said, and Joe could see the faint outline of Trey reaching up and grabbing the assistant director by the arm. Pope stopped.

"When this is over," Pope hissed, "and Don Ennis walks out of here, I'm going to suspend your asses."

"I'm already suspended," Joe whispered. "Are you going to double suspend me?"

Pope started to talk when a bell tinkled out in the shop and someone pushed the door open with enough force that it banged against the wall.

Joe leaned toward the curtain and cocked his head so he could hear what was going on. He hoped the video camera on the shelf was working, and that Tassell was watching on the monitor.

Joe heard the shuffling of several sets of feet, thinking Don had brought support. The bell tinkled again as the door shut, and there was the sound of the lock being thrown.

"You're Pi Stevenson?" It was Ennis.

"Yes, I am." She didn't sound as nervous as Joe felt.

"What was your name again?"

"Birdy Richards."

"What the hell kind of name is 'Birdy'? Jesus, you people."

"Don, let's just get what we came for." Joe recognized the voice of Pete Illoway.

Ennis: "Right. First, have any copies been made?"

Birdy: "No. No copies."

Ennis: "Is anything still in the cameras on the river?"

Birdy: "No. They've all been downloaded to the computer."

Ennis: "Then I'll pay you for the computer. Shane, grab that thing and we can go."

Shane Suhn, Joe recalled, Ennis's chief of staff.

Suhn: "That's just the monitor, Don. That won't help us. You don't know anything about computers."

Ennis: "Then take whatever the fuck it is that has the pictures on it, Shane."

Birdy: "Hold it. I never said you could have my computer. I need to make a living."

Pi: "Damn right. And what are you going to pay us? We aren't just going to give you Birdy's equipment and you go home. Maybe we should just call the sheriff after all."

Ennis: "You shut the fuck up, lady. You're playing in the big leagues, and you don't even know it."

Illoway: "Don . . ."

Pi: "You don't have any intention of paying us, do you? You're going to do something to us so we don't talk."

Ennis: "Tell me what you saw in the photos."

Pi: "Not until you tell us what you're planning to do."

Ennis: "Shane, remember what we discussed on the drive over?"

Suhn: "You want me to do it here? Now? If somebody looked in the window they could see us."

Ennis: "I don't give a shit. She won't shut up."

Illoway: "Look, how much do you want for the computer? Give us a number."

Ennis: "You're spending my money, Illoway."

Illoway: "Give us a number."

Suhn: "Maybe we ought to see the pictures first. Maybe there's nothing on them. Maybe it's just a bunch of us having a fun time on the river, and somebody falls in. That won't prove anything."

There was a long silence. Joe was tempted to inch the curtain back to see what was taking place.

Illoway: "Shane's right, Don. The photos may not prove a thing."

Ennis: "Fire up that computer and let's have a look at them."

Birdy said, "It's on," and Joe could feel the terror in his voice.

When would Tassell decide he had heard enough, Joe wondered, and come out? How far would Tassell let Pi and Birdy go, searching for photos that didn't exist on the computer?

Ennis: "Where are the photos?"

Birdy: "Give me a minute. The computer was sleeping and it'll take a second to boot up."

Ennis: "What's that?"

Birdy: "It's asking for my password."

Ennis: "Hurry up, goddamnit."

Then Pi spoke. Her voice was strong, challenging. "What are you guys thinking?" she asked. "Are you thinking that you can't see when Don here cuts the straps of her life vest? Or that you can't see it when he shoves her out of the boat just as you enter the whitewater? Or that you can't see when he hits her with his oar to keep her from crawling back in the boat?"

Ennis: "I never hit her with my fucking oar!"

Now, Joe thought. *Tassell needs to come out now.*

Pi: "Maybe it was Pete Illoway, the eating consultant, who was whacking at her with his oar. I'm not sure."

Illoway: "We're fucked, Don."

Suhn: "Okay, you two, step away from the counter."

"There's no need for *guns* here," Pi said frantically, shouting out the word *guns*. "We can work something out. Really, we can."

Ennis: "It's too fucking late for that, girlie."

Joe was about to rip the curtain aside and hurl himself into the shop when he heard the office door open and Tassell say, "*HANDS ON THE COUNTER! All of you! NOW!*"

Joe didn't have a weapon, so he stepped aside so Trey could push through the curtain with his Beretta drawn. Joe saw Ennis look up, his face pinched and white. Illoway was looking at the door. Shane Suhn had a semiautomatic pistol pointed at Pi.

"Drop that," Tassell hollered at Suhn, who quickly lowered the weapon and dropped it with a clunk on the floor.

"I thought you were never going to come out," Pi said angrily.

"Keep your hands in view on top of the counter," Tassell said.

"Including us?" Birdy asked.

"Step away from them," Tassell said, and Birdy and Pi scrambled out of the way.

"You set us up, you bastard," Ennis said finally, glaring at Tassell. Ennis had two black eyes and white tape across his nose. Joe had done more damage the night before than he realized. When Ennis saw Joe, the developer's eyes narrowed further.

"You," was all he said.

Tassell announced that all three were under arrest for the murder of Stella Ennis.

"Don't forget Will Jensen," Trey said.

"That comes later," Tassell said.

Illoway, Joe thought, looked like he was about to cry. Instead, he screwed up his face, glanced for a moment at Ennis, and said, "Don did it."

Ennis turned on Illoway. "You fuck—"

"We didn't even know he planned to throw her out of the boat until he did it," Illoway said. "Maybe Shane did, but I didn't."

Suhn acted like he'd been slapped. "I didn't know about Stella," he said. "But I can tell you all you want to know about the game warden."

Joe felt a release inside, and exchanged glances with Trey.

Ennis was livid. "Jesus, you guys. Just shut up! Where's your loyalty?"

"My loyalty is to the Good Meat Movement," Illoway said. "That's more important than one developer."

"I'll get us out of this," Ennis said. *"Just shut up!"*

"Get yourself out of it," Suhn said. "You don't pay me enough to go to prison for you."

Ennis was red and trembling with rage. He fixed on Pi, who didn't even try to contain her glee. "Those fucking pictures," he said.

"What pictures?" Pi grinned.

38

JOE WAITED FOR MARY TO CONCLUDE A TELEPHONE conversation while he stood at the front counter holding a box with his possessions in it. When she hung up and looked up at him, he extended his hand.

"Thank you for everything, Mary," he said. "You made me feel welcome here."

She blushed as she briefly shook his hand, then looked away.

"I just got off the phone with Susan Jensen," Joe said. "I was a little surprised by her reaction."

"How much did you tell her?" Mary asked.

Joe thought about his answer. "I told her that Don Ennis had been drugging her husband, which led to his death. And I told her I scattered Will's ashes on Two Ocean Pass. She didn't seem as relieved as I thought she'd be."

"Nothing about Stella?" she asked. Joe wondered about Mary's exact meaning for a second, then decided Mary didn't know about Will's last seconds.

Joe shook his head. "That didn't seem necessary.

Stella didn't enter the picture until after Susan had left with the boys anyway."

Mary arched her eyebrows in a way that told Joe he was wrong about that. But she didn't pursue it.

"You probably heard that Don Ennis hired Marcus Hand as his defense lawyer," Mary said. Hand was a flamboyant attorney who lived in Jackson and was nationally famous for freeing guilty clients.

"I heard."

"Hand's already claiming it was entrapment," Mary said. "And that Pete Illoway and Shane Suhn are lying to keep themselves out of jail. If they don't find Stella's body soon, he'll claim Ennis didn't even murder her."

Joe nodded. He could only imagine how the recorded words and images from the studio would be twisted and reinterpreted for a jury. He tried not to think of what Stella's body would look like when it was finally found. The image made him shiver. The condition of her body would likely be beyond any possibility of providing evidence that she had been injured before drowning, and Hand would no doubt make an issue of that.

Tassell's men had found a receiver in Shane Suhn's office at Beargrass Village that was tuned to the transmitter in Will's truck, as well as cassette tapes of Jensen's radio communications. They also brought back the developer's telephone log, which Joe got a look at. The most interesting thing on the log was a call to Ennis immediately following Pi and Birdy's call. It was from Randy Pope, urging Ennis to contact him immediately. Luckily, Ennis had already left for Wildwater Photography and hadn't been warned off.

"Don Ennis will be out on the street within a year, is my prediction," Mary said.

Joe shrugged in a "what can you do?" gesture.

"But it looks like there won't be any Beargrass Village," she said, her expression of relief revealing, for the first time, what she thought of the project. "Not with Pete Illoway pulling out of it. Without his blessing, it would be just another million-dollar housing development, and Jackson has enough of those."

Joe wasn't sure what to say next. He picked up his box. "I rented a car until they replace my pickup," he said. "The county attorney will need Will's truck for evidence at the trial."

She looked up. "Will you be coming back?"

"Do you mean for the trial, or for good?"

"For good."

He looked away. "I don't know where I'll be," he said, thinking of Pope's threats, knowing his career probably hinged on who was elected governor. "I'm still suspended."

"I hope you come back," Mary said, a softness around her eyes Joe found touching. "I think you're a good man."

Not as good as you think, Joe thought but didn't say.

"Right now, I need to get home," he said, and carried his box out the door.

IT FELT STRANGE TO BE in a compact rental car instead of a high-profile pickup, he thought, as the National Elk Refuge passed by his window. It felt like he was sitting on the pavement as he drove, and when he looked in his rearview mirror he saw the grilles and headlights of vehicles behind him, not the drivers.

While he drove, Joe reviewed what had taken place in Jackson. He had been instrumental in bringing down a multimillionaire and stopping a Good Meat development, and in the process had partially avenged a game warden's reputation. He had also killed a man he had no ill feelings toward. Now, Joe was returning to Saddlestring under suspension, with a cloud of guilt still hovering over him in regard to his feelings for Stella, in a compact car with a motor already struggling with the ascent into the mountains. But he couldn't wait to get home. It felt like he'd been gone a year.

The sight of the gleaming white Tetons in his rearview mirror did nothing for him. Neither did the thought of Don Ennis skirting the charges due to the machinations of a celebrity lawyer.

When Joe first met Sheriff Tassell following Will Jensen's funeral, the sheriff had said, "There are people here who don't think they need to play by the rules." Later, Smoke Van Horn had called it all a big game. Both, Joe thought, were right.

He pictured Marybeth, Sheridan, and Lucy. How little he had thought of them recently, how his life and struggles had been his alone. How he had almost strayed. He pulled over to let the little engine cool down and put his head in his hands.

Joe couldn't remember ever having felt so small.

39

IT WAS MID-AFTERNOON WHEN JOE TURNED OFF BIG-horn Road. The sight of his home filled him with joy and trepidation, Lucy's bike in the yard, Toby nickering to him from the corral, dried leaves in the grass that needed raking. Unfortunately, his mother-in-law's SUV was in the driveway next to Marybeth's van.

He climbed out of the rental car and stretched, not used to being cramped up like that for hours. Maxine didn't recognize him until he got out—she was looking for his pickup—and came bounding outside through the screen door.

"Dad!" Lucy yelled from her window. It was one of the best things he had ever heard. Marybeth appeared smiling at the front door, looking blond, fit, and beautiful. They embraced just inside the front gate, Lucy now running out to see him.

"Joe," Marybeth said, "why didn't you call ahead?"

"My cell phone burned up in the fire," he said.

"Your face," she said, running her palms over his features, "it's bruised. You need to tell me everything that's happened."

Joe looked up, saw Missy in the doorway. He thought her smile was not genuine.

"Later," he said.

"We have steaks in the freezer I can thaw," Marybeth said. "I want to cook you a big dinner."

Joe smiled.

MISSY STAYED FOR DINNER, much to Joe's chagrin. She told him about Italy, about the food and the style of clothes they wore there, about the service in first class. Joe wanted to burst, there was so much to tell Marybeth. And so much he wanted to hear.

Sheridan sat sullenly at the table, and Joe felt the tension between her and Marybeth, even if neither said anything.

At one point, while Missy was describing Venice, Sheridan looked up and said, "I'm glad you're home, Dad."

"I am too," he said.

She made an "it's been rough" eye roll, then bent her head back to her plate. Joe saw that Marybeth had watched the exchange carefully, and he wondered what was to come later, after Missy left.

There was something about Marybeth, he thought. She seemed extremely pleased to see him, but overconciliatory and a little guarded. If she wasn't angry with him, he decided, it was something else. Something had come between them, and he couldn't guess what. His suspension, the fact that he had killed a man? His arrest? All of the above? Or maybe, he thought, it had been their distance. In fifteen years of marriage, they had never been apart for so long. Again, the cloud of guilt that was Stella washed over him. He decided not to tell her. Now was not the time. He didn't know if there ever would be a time. And he wouldn't ask her what was wrong, what it was that made her seem different, defensive, even guilty. He would eat steak and keep his mouth shut.

AFTER THEY CLEARED THE DINNER dishes off the table, Joe went down the hallway toward the bathroom and glanced into Sheridan's room. It was different, and it took him a moment to figure out what had changed.

"Where are your falconry posters?" he asked her. Over the past three years, Sheridan had filled a wall with depictions of falcons and hawks of North America, as well as *National Geographic* wildlife shots of falcons in flight and going for a kill. They had been replaced by photos of rodeo cowboys and rock musicians cut out of magazines. He looked at her bookshelf and saw that the books on falconry that Nate had given her were gone.

Sheridan looked up from her homework. "I guess I've got new interests."

"That came about pretty quickly," he said.

"Dad," Sheridan said, "Nate is gone. Didn't Mom tell you that?"

"No."

"I guess I'm not all that surprised," Sheridan said.

Joe continued down the hallway, puzzled.

MARYBETH AND MISSY WERE HAVING coffee at the table when Joe came into the dining room.

"What's this about Nate?" he asked, interrupting Missy, who was talking about Venetian glass.

The look on Marybeth's face struck Joe. There was some fear in it, as well as caution. "He's been gone for three days," she said.

"That's not so unusual," Joe said, thinking of Nate's long absences.

"This time, his phone is disconnected," Marybeth said.

Joe still didn't understand the gravity behind Marybeth's meaning.

"Joe," she said, "he seems to have vanished the same night Sheriff Barnum disappeared."

"And good riddance to that man," Missy chimed in.

Now, Joe got it.

IT WAS LATE IN THE EVENING when he returned to the house. Missy was finally gone, and Marybeth had fallen asleep on the couch with the television on. Joe hung up his jacket in the mudroom and gently woke her.

"Did you find him?" she asked, rubbing her eyes and stretching. Stretching provocatively, Joe thought.

He shook his head. "The bison's gone," Joe said. "His mews is empty, and the house is locked down tight. His Jeep is gone too."

"Joe, do you think—"

"No," he said, sitting down beside her. "He's somewhere. But it sure seems strange that he wouldn't let you know he was going since he agreed to watch over things here."

Something passed over her face that he couldn't read, something he wasn't sure he wanted to find out more about.

They sat in silence for a moment, and she said, "I'm so glad you're home."

He nodded. "Me too."

"What are we going to do, Joe?" she asked.

"That's a big question. You mean with my job?"

"That," she said, and didn't finish her thought.

"It depends on who gets elected governor," Joe said. "Trey thinks a lot depends on the election, and who is appointed director of the agency."

"I've heard Randy Pope's name mentioned."

Joe sighed. "Me too."

She seemed to want to tell him something, he thought, but she remained silent.

THEY OPENED A BOTTLE OF WINE left over from Missy's wedding and took it to bed with them. They made love voraciously the first time, tenderly the second. What struck him was how different she felt at the outset, and familiar she became.

He watched her wash her face at the sink beneath the mirror, and studied her as she climbed back into bed with him.

"Don't ever leave for so long again, Joe," she said, snuggling up to him.

"I won't," he said. Then: "We've got to work on some things, don't we?"

He felt her tense up, then gradually relax. "Yes, we do."

THE NEXT WEEK, JOE SAID, "Remember when you told me about that fawn in the yard?" Marybeth was next to him on the couch, and he reached over and brushed her hair behind her ear.

"Yes."

"You said Nate picked up the body and took it away." She nodded.

"To that sulfuric mineral springs he showed me, right?"

"Yes."

"I went there today," Joe said. "I had a hell of a time

getting there in that stupid little car, but I got close enough I could walk in."

Her eyes grew wide as she listened.

"I saw the remains of the fawn," he said. "Only part of the skull was left, and a few thigh bones. The rest will dissolve within a few weeks. But those weren't the only bones in the spring."

"Oh, no," she said, covering her mouth with her hand.

"The bodies of two men were in there too," he said. "Most of their flesh had been eaten away, but I could tell they were men by the size. There were two skulls, each with big holes in the forehead."

She brought up her other hand and peered at him over her fingertips.

"And I found this near the spring," Joe said, fishing in his breast pocket. He handed it to her. It was a pen, the gold nearly eaten off. But the words TO SHERIFF BAR-NUM FOR 28 YEARS OF SVC could still be seen on the barrel.

Marybeth looked at Joe hard. "What are you going to do?"

"I'm going to report it," Joe said, fully aware of the implications of that. "But I'm going to do it anonymously."

THREE DAYS LATER, AFTER RECEIVING the call from Trey Crump telling him that the shooting of Smoke had been investigated and Joe was cleared, he finally went into his home office. Joe had been consciously avoiding it since glancing at his desk the first day home and confirming his fear about mounds of paperwork. Now, he sat in his chair, looked at the pile of envelopes and parcels, and didn't know where to begin. He sorted through the mail, putting it roughly into piles relating to the agency, letters from hunters and fishers, and general mail. There was one small envelope he didn't know how to classify. It was addressed to J. Pickett and had no return address. The postage mark on it said LAGUARDIA AIRPORT—NEW YORK CITY. It was postmarked two days before.

Nate? he thought.

He slit open the envelope, pulled out a single card. It read:

Good work, my hero. I'm glad I'm such a good swimmer.

While I'm pretty certain I'd at last found what I've been looking for, you are home now. And since I'd never dream of interfering, at least not uninvited, my search must continue, though at least now I have a solid reference.

I respect family very much. I bet you didn't know that.

Someday, though, I may change my mind. And you might change yours.

It was signed with that single, familiar "S."

ACKNOWLEDGMENTS

I WOULD LIKE TO ACKNOWLEDGE THE PEOPLE AND sources who helped me research and write this book, starting with Bill Long, Wyoming game warden, of Jackson, who let me "ride along." Readers who would like to contribute to a very worthy cause can send contributions to Bill Long's Trumpeter Swan Fund: The Wyoming Wetland Society/TSF, P.O. Box 3216, Jackson, WY 83001, a 501c(3) organization, tax ID 74-2487790.

D. P. Lyle, M.D., author of *Murder and Mayhem*, provided expertise on pharmacology and forensics; Tom Reed and his *Great Wyoming Bear Stories* provided background on trapping and managing Wyoming's grizzly bears; and detail on the Thorofare is from *Hawks Rest— A Season in the Remote Heart of Yellowstone*, by Gary Ferguson.

Special thanks to my agent, Ann Rittenberg, who read the early drafts and offered support, encouragement, and her sharp pencil; my wonderful editor, Martha Bushko, who makes every book better; and Michael Barson and Dan Harvey for their professional support.

Ken Siman deserves special credit for the idea in the first place, as well as resource material on the pure meat/good meat movement.

Sources used and quoted within this book include all sides of the issues, including Michael Pollan, "The Unnatural Idea of Animal Rights," *The New York Times Magazine*, November 10, 2002; Gary Snyder, *The Practice of the Wild: Essays*, North Point Press, 1990; Peter Singer, *Animal Liberation*, second edition, A New York Review Book distributed by Random House, 1975, 1990; Matthew Scully, *Dominion: The Power of Man, the Suffering of Animals, and the Call to Mercy*, St. Martin's Press, 2002; Jim Harrison, *The Raw and the Cooked*, Grove Press, 2001; Richard K. Nelson, Ann S. Causey, Bruce Woods, *A Hunter's Heart*, Henry Holt and Company, Inc., 1996; Henry David Thoreau, *Walden*; Thomas McGuane, *An Outside Chance*, Houghton Mifflin, 1992; Stephen E. Ambrose, *Undaunted Courage, Meriwether Lewis, Thomas Jefferson, and the Opening of the American West*, Simon & Schuster, 1996; James Swan, *In Defense of Hunting*, HarperSanFrancisco, 1994; and Aldo Leopold, *A Sand County Almanac*, Ballantine Books, reissue edition, 1990.

TURN THE PAGE FOR AN EXCERPT

Ranch owner and matriarch Opal Scarlett has vanished under suspicious circumstances during a bitter struggle between her sons for control of her million-dollar empire. Joe Pickett is convinced one of them must have done her in. But when he becomes the victim of a series of wicked and increasingly violent pranks, Joe wonders if what's happening has less to do with Opal's disappearance than with the darkest chapters of his own past. Whoever is after him has a vicious debt to collect, and wants Joe to pay...and pay dearly.

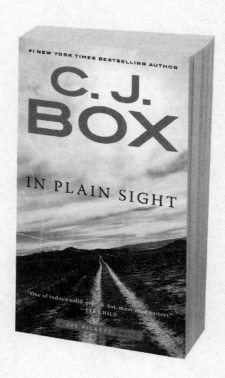

#1 NEW YORK TIMES BESTSELLING AUTHOR

C. J. BOX

IN PLAIN SIGHT

"One of today's solid-gold, A-list, must-read writers."
LEE CHILD

A JOE PICKETT NOVEL

1 *Twelve Sleep County, Wyoming*

WHEN RANCH OWNER OPAL SCARLETT VANISHED, NO one mourned except her three grown sons, Arlen, Hank, and Wyatt, who expressed their loss by getting into a fight with shovels.

Wyoming game warden Joe Pickett almost didn't hear the call over his radio when it came over the mutual-aid channel. He was driving west on Bighorn Road, having picked up his fourteen-year-old daughter, Sheridan, and her best friend, Julie, after track practice to take them home. Sheridan and Julie were talking a mile a minute, gesticulating, making his dog, Maxine, flinch with their flying arms as they talked. Julie lived on the Thunderhead Ranch, which was much farther out of town than the Picketts' home.

Joe caught snippets of their conversation while he drove, his attention on his radio and the wounded hum of the engine and the dancing gauges on the dash. Joe didn't yet trust the truck, a vehicle recently assigned to him. The check-engine light would flash on and off, and occasionally there was a knocking sound under the hood that sounded like popcorn popping. The truck had been issued to him as revenge by his cost-conscious superiors, after his last vehicle had burned up in a fire in Jackson Hole. Even though the suspension was shot, the truck did have a CD player, a rarity in state vehicles, and the sound track for the ride home had been a CD Sheridan had made for him. It was titled "Get with it, Dad" in a black felt marker. She'd given it to him two days before, after breakfast, saying, "You need to listen to this new music so you don't seem so clueless. It may help." Things were changing in his family. His girls were getting older. Joe was not only under the thumb of his superiors but was apparently becoming clueless too. His red uniform shirt with the pronghorn antelope Game and Fish patch on the shoulder and his green Filson vest were caked with mud from changing a tire on the mountain earlier in the day.

"I think Jarrod Haynes likes you," Julie said to Sheridan.

"Get out! Why do you say that? You're crazy."

"Didn't you see him watching us practice?" Julie asked. "He stayed after the boys were done and watched us run."

"I saw him," Sheridan said. "But why do you think he likes *me*?"

" 'Cause he didn't take his eyes off of you the whole time, that's why. Even when he got a call on his cell, he stood there and watched you while he talked. He's hot for you, Sherry."

"I wish *I* had a cell phone," Sheridan said.

Joe tuned out. He didn't want to hear about a boy targeting his daughter. It made him uncomfortable. And the cell-phone conversation made him tired. He and Marybeth had said Sheridan wouldn't get one until she was sixteen, but that didn't stop his daughter from coming up with reasons why she needed one now.

In the particularly intense way of teenage girls, Sheridan and Julie were inseparable. Julie was tall, lithe, tanned, blond, blue-eyed, and budding. Sheridan was a shorter version of Julie, but with her mother's startling green eyes. The two had ridden the school bus together for years and Sheridan had hated Julie, said she was bossy and arrogant and acted like royalty. Then something happened, and the two girls could barely be apart from each other. Three-hour phone calls between them weren't unusual at night.

"I just don't know what to think about that," Sheridan said.

"You'll be the envy of everyone if you go with him," Julie said.

"He doesn't seem very smart."

Julie laughed and rolled her eyes. "Who cares?" she said. "He's fricking awesome."

Joe cringed, wishing he had missed that.

He had spent the morning patrolling the brushy foothills where the spring wild turkey season was still open, although there appeared to be no turkey hunters about. It was his first foray into the timbered southwestern saddle slopes since winter. The snow was receding up the mountain, leaving hard-packed grainy drifts in arroyos and cuts. The retreating snow also revealed the aftermath of small battles and tragedies no one had witnessed that had taken place over the winter—six mule deer that had died of starvation in a wooded hollow; a cow and calf elk that had broken through the ice on a pond and frozen in place; pronghorn antelope caught in the barbed wire of a fence, their emaciated bodies draping over the wire like rugs hanging to dry. But there were signs of renewal as well, as thick light-green shoots bristled through dead matted grass near stream sides, and fat, pregnant does stared at his passing pickup from shadowed groves.

April was the slowest month of the year in the field for a game warden, especially in a place with a fleeting spring. It was the fifth year of a drought. The hottest issue he had to contend with was what to do with the four elk that had shown up in the town of Saddlestring and seemed to have no plans to leave. While mule deer were common in the parks and gardens, elk were not. Joe had chased the four animals—two bulls, a cow, and a calf— from the city park several times by firing .22 blanks into the air several times. But they kept coming back. The animals had become such a fixture in the park they were now referred to as the "Town Elk," and locals were feeding them, which kept them hanging around while providing empty nourishment that would eventually make them sick and kill them. Joe was loath to destroy the elk, but thought he may not have a choice if they stuck around.

The changes in his agency had begun with the election of a new governor. On the day after the election, Joe had received a four-word message from his supervisor, Trey Crump, that read: "Hell has frozen over," meaning a Democrat had been elected. His name was Spencer Rulon. Within a week, the agency director resigned before being fired, and a bitter campaign was waged for a replacement. Joe, and most of the game wardens, actively supported an "Anybody but Randy Pope" ticket, since Pope had risen to prominence within the agency from the administrative side (rather than the law-enforcement or biology side) and made no bones about wanting to rid the state of personnel he felt were too independent, who had "gone native," or were considered uncontrollable cowboys—men like Joe Pickett. Joe's clash with Pope the year before in Jackson had resulted in a simmering feud that was heating up, as Joe's report of Pope's betrayal made the rounds within the agency, despite Pope's efforts to stop it.

Governor Rulon was a big man with a big face and a big gut, an unruly shock of silver-flecked brown hair, a quick sloppy smile, and endlessly darting eyes. In the previous year's election, Rulon had beaten the Republican challenger by twenty points, despite the fact that his opponent had been handpicked by term-limited Governor Budd. This in a state that was 70 percent Republican. Rulon grew up on a ranch near Casper, the grandson of a U.S. senator. He played linebacker for the Wyoming Cowboys, got a law degree, made a fortune in private practice suing federal agencies, then was elected county prosecutor. Loud and profane, Rulon campaigned for governor by crisscrossing the state endlessly in his own pickup and buying rounds for the house in every bar from Yoder to Wright, and challenging anyone who didn't plan to vote for him to an arm-wrestling, sports-trivia, or shooting contest. The word most used to describe the new governor seemed to be "energetic." He could turn from a good old boy pounding beers and slapping backs into an orator capable of delivering the twelve-minute closing argument by Spencer Tracy in *Inherit the Wind* from memory. His favorite breakfast was reportedly biscuits and sausage gravy and a glass of Pinot Noir. Like Wyoming itself, Joe thought, Rulon didn't mind leading with his rough exterior and later surprising—and mildly troubling—the onlooker with a kind of eccentric depth.

He was also, according to more and more state employees who had to deal with their new boss, crazy as a tick.

But he was profoundly popular with the voters. Unlike his predecessor, Rulon reassigned his bodyguards to the Highway Patrol, fired his driver, and insisted that his name and phone number be listed in the telephone book. He eliminated the gatekeepers who had been employed to restrict access to his office and put up a sign that said GOV RULON'S OFFICE—BARGE RIGHT IN, which was heeded by an endless stream of visitors.

One of Rulon's first decisions was to choose a new Game and Fish director. The Board of Commissioners lined up a slate of three candidates—Pope included. The governor's first choice was a longtime game warden from Medicine Bow, who died of a heart attack within a week of the announcement. The second candidate withdrew his name from consideration when news of an old sexual harassment suit hit the press. Which left Randy Pope, who gladly assumed the role, even declaring to a reporter that "fate and destiny both stepped forward" to enable his promotion. That had been two months ago.

Trey Crump, Joe's district supervisor, said he saw the writing on the wall and took early retirement rather than submit to Pope's new directives for supervisors. Without Trey, who had also been Joe's champion within the state bureaucracy, Joe now had been ordered to report directly to Pope. Instead of weekly reports, Pope wanted *daily* dispatches. It was Pope who had nixed Joe's request for a new pickup and instead had sent one with 150,000 miles on it, bald tires, and a motor that was unreliable.

Joe had been around long enough to know exactly what was happening. Pope could not appear to have a public vendetta against Joe, especially because Joe's star had risen over the past few years in certain quarters.

But Pope was a master of the bureaucratic Death of a Thousand Cuts, the slow, steady, petty, and maddening procedure—misplaced requests, unreturned phone calls, lost insurance and reimbursement claims, blizzards of busywork—designed to drive an employee out of a state or federal agency. And with Pope, Joe knew it was personal.

"DAD!"

Joe realized Sheridan was talking to him. "What?"

"How can he tune out like that?" Julie asked Sheridan, as if Joe weren't in the cab.

"I don't know. It's amazing, isn't it?" Then: "Dad, are we going to stop and feed Nate's birds? I want to show Julie the falcons."

"I already fed them today," he said.

"Darn."

Joe slowed and turned onto a dirt road from the highway beneath a massive elk-antler arch with a sign hanging from chains that read:

THUNDERHEAD RANCHES, EST. 1883.

THE SCARLETTS

OPAL

ARLEN

HANK

WYATT

Julie said, "My grandma says someday my name is going to be on that sign."

"Cool," Sheridan replied.

Joe had heard Julie say that before.

EVEN THOUGH JOE HAD SEEN the Thunderhead Ranch in bits and pieces over the years, he was still amazed by its magnificence. There were those, he knew, who would drive the scores of old two-tracks on the ranch and look around and see miles and miles of short grass, sagebrush, and rolling hills and compare the place poorly with much more spectacular alpine country. Sure, the river bottom was lush and the foothills rose in a steady march toward the Bighorns and were dotted with trees, but the place wouldn't pop visually for some because it was just so open, so big, so sprawling. But that was the thing. Because of the river, because of the confluence of at least five significant creeks that coursed through the property and poured into the Twelve Sleep River, because of the optimum diversification of landscape within a thousand square miles, and the vast meadows of thick, nutrient-enriched grass, the Thunderhead was the perfect cattle ranch. Joe had once heard a longtime rancher and resident of the county, Herbert Klein, say that if aliens landed and demanded to see a dog he would show them a Labrador, and if they demanded to see a ranch, he would skip his own and show them the Thunderhead.

It was also an ideal ranch for wildlife, which posed an opportunity for Hank, who ran an exclusive hunting business, and a problem for Joe Pickett.

"Look," Sheridan said, sitting up.

A herd of pronghorn antelope, a liquid flow of brown and white, streamed over a knoll ahead of them and to the right, raising dust and heading for a collision with the pickup.

"They don't see us yet," Joe said, marveling, as always, at the graceful but raw speed of the antelope, the second-fastest mammal on earth.

When the lead animals noticed the green Wyoming Game and Fish pickup, they didn't stop or panic but simply turned ninety degrees, not breaking stride, their stream bending away from the road. Joe noted how Sheridan sucked in her breath in absolute awe as the herd drew parallel with the pickup—the bucks, does, and fawns glancing over at her—and then the entire herd accelerated and veered back toward the knoll they had appeared from.

"Wow," she said.

" 'Wow' is right," Joe agreed.

"Antelope bore me," Julie said. "There are so many of them."

For a moment he had been concerned that the lead antelope was going to barrel into the passenger door, something that occasionally happened when a pronghorn wasn't paying attention to where he was going. That was all he needed, Joe thought sourly, another damaged pickup Pope could carp about.

That's when the call came over the mutual-aid channel.

Joe said, "Would you two please be quiet for a minute?"

While the entire county was sheriff's department jurisdiction, game wardens and highway patrolmen were called on for backup for rural emergencies.

Sheridan hushed. Julie did too, but with attitude, crossing her arms in front of her chest and clamping her mouth tight. Joe turned up the volume on the radio. Wendy, the dispatcher, had not turned off her microphone. In the background, there was an anxious voice.

"Excuse me, where are you calling from?" Wendy asked the caller.

"I'm on a cell phone. I'm sitting in my car on the side of the highway. You won't believe it."

"Can you describe the situation, sir?"

The cell-phone signal ebbed with static, but Joe could clearly hear the caller say, "There are three men in cowboy hats swinging at each other with shovels in the middle of the prairie. I can see them hitting each other out there. It's a bloody mess."

Wendy said, "Can you give me your location, sir?"

The caller read off a mile marker on State Highway 130. Joe frowned. The Bighorn Road they had just driven on was also Highway 130. The mile marker was just two miles from where they had turned onto the ranch.

"That would be Thunderhead Ranch then, sir?" Wendy asked the caller.

"I guess."

Joe shot a look toward Julie. She had heard and her face was frozen, her eyes wide.

"That's just over the hill," she said.

Joe had a decision to make. He could drive the remaining five miles to the ranch headquarters, where Julie lived, or take a fork in the road that would deliver him, as well as Sheridan and Julie, to the likely location of an assault in progress.

"I'm taking you home," Joe said, accelerating.

"No!" Julie cried. "What if it's someone I know? We've got to stop them."

Joe slowed, his mind racing. He felt it necessary to respond, but did not want to put the girls in danger. "You sure?"

"Yes! What if it's my dad? Or one of my uncles?"

He nodded, did a three-point turn, and took the fork. He snatched the mic from its cradle. "This is GF forty-three. I'm about five to ten minutes from the scene."

Wendy said, "You're literally there on the ranch?"

"Affirmative."

There was a beat of silence. "I don't know whether Sheriff McLanahan is going to like that."

Joe and the sheriff did not get along.

Joe snorted. "Ask him if he wants me to stand down."

"You ask him," Wendy said, completely breaking protocol.

AS THEY POWERED UP THE two-track, Joe could see that Sheridan and Julie had huddled together.

"Can you keep a secret?" Julie whispered, loud enough for Joe to hear.

"Of course I can," Sheridan said. "You know that. We're best friends."

Julie nodded seriously, as if making up her mind.

"You can't tell your parents," Julie said, nodding at Joe. Sheridan hesitated before answering. "I swear."

"Swear to God?" Julie asked.

"Come on, Julie. I said I promise."

"Tighten your seat belts, girls," Joe cautioned. "This is going to be bumpy."

The scene before them, as they topped the hill, silenced Julie and whatever she was going to tell Sheridan. Below them, on the flat, there were three pickups, each parked haphazardly in the sagebrush, doors wide open. Inside the ring of trucks, three men circled each other warily, raising puffs of dust, an occasional wide swing with a shovel flashing the late afternoon sun.

Out on the highway, two sheriff's department SUVs and a highway patrolman turned from the highway onto an access road, their lights flashing. One of the SUVs burped on his siren.

"Jesus Christ," McLanahan said over the radio, as the vehicles converged on the fight. "It's a rodeo out here. There's blood pourin' outta 'em . . ."

"Yee-haw," the highway patrolman said sardonically.

Joe thought the scene in front of him was epic in implication, and ridiculous at the same time. Three adults, two of them practically legends in their own right, so blinded by their fight that they didn't seem to know that a short string of law-enforcement vehicles was approaching.

And not just any adults, but Arlen, Hank, and Wyatt Scarlett, the scions of the most prominent ranch family in the Twelve Sleep Valley. It was as if the figures on Mount Rushmore were head-butting one another.

It was darkly fascinating seeing the three of them out there, Joe thought. He was reminded that, in a situation like this, he would always be an outsider looking in. Despite his time in Twelve Sleep County, he would never feel quite a part of this scenario, which was rooted so deeply in the valley. The tendrils of the Scarlett family ranch and of the Scarletts themselves reached too deeply, intertwined with too many other people and families, to ever completely sort out. Their interaction with the people and history of the area was multilayered, nuanced, too complicated to ever fully understand. The Scarletts were colorful, ruthless, independent, and eccentric. If newcomers to the area displayed even half of the strange behavior of the Scarletts, Joe was sure they'd have been run out of the state—or shunned to the point of cruelty. But the Scarletts were local, they were founders, they were benefactors and philanthropists—despite their eccentricities. It was almost as if longtime residents of the area had declared, in unison, "Yes, they're crazy. But they're *our* lunatics, and we won't have anyone insulting them or judging them harshly who hasn't lived here long enough to understand."

Arlen was the oldest brother, and the best liked. He was tall with broad shoulders and a mane of silver-white wavy hair that made him look like the state senate majority floor leader he was. He had a heavy, thrusting jaw and the bulbous, spiderwebbed nose of a drinker. His clear blue eyes looked out from under bushy eyebrows that were black as smears of grease, and he had a soothing, sonorous voice that turned the reading of a diner menu into a performance. Arlen had the gift of remembering names and offspring, and could instantly continue a conversation with a constituent that had been cut off months before.

Hank, the middle brother, was smaller than Arlen. He

was thin and wiry with a sharp-featured bladelike face, and wore a sweat-stained gray Stetson clamped tight on his head. Joe had never seen Hank without the hat, and had no idea if he had hair underneath it. He remembered Vern Dunnegan, the former game warden in the district, warning Joe to stay away from Hank unless he absolutely had the goods on him. "Hank Scarlett is the toughest man I've ever met," Vern had said, "the scariest too."

Hank had a way of looking coiled up when he stood still, the way a Brahma bull was calm just before the chute gate opened. Hank was an extremely successful big-game guide and outfitter, with operations in Wyoming, Alaska, and Kenya. His clients were millionaires, and he was suspected of using less-than-ethical means to assure kills of trophy animals. Hank had been on Joe's radar screen even before Joe was assigned the Saddlestring District, and Hank knew it. All the game wardens knew of Hank. But Joe had never found hard evidence of any wrongdoing. Hank's legend was burnished by rumors and stories, such as when Hank single-handedly packed a two-hundred-pound mountain sheep twelve miles across the Wind River Mountains in a blinding snowstorm. Or Hank crash-landing a bush plane with mechanical problems into the middle of a frozen Alaskan lake, rescuing two clients, amputating the leg of one of them while they waited for rescue. And Hank dropping from a tree onto the back of a record bull moose and riding it a quarter of a mile before reaching forward and slitting its throat.

Wyatt was the biggest but the youngest. His face was cherubic, without the sharp angles his brothers' had. Everything about Wyatt was soft and round, his cheeks, his nose, the extra flesh around his soft brown eyes. He was in his early thirties. When people within the community talked about the historic Scarlett Ranch, or the battling Scarlett brothers, it was understood they were referring to Arlen and Hank. It was as if Wyatt didn't exist, as if he was as much an embarrassment to the community as he was, no doubt, to the family itself. Joe knew very little about Wyatt, and what he had heard wasn't good. When Wyatt Scarlett was brought up, it was often in hushed tones.

Joe was close enough now that he could see Arlen clearly. Arlen was bleeding from a cut on the side of his head, and he shot a glance over his shoulder at the approaching vehicles. Which gave an opening to Hank, the middle brother, to swing and hit the back of Arlen's head with the flat of his shovel like a pumpkin on a post.

Julie screamed and covered her face with her hands.

Joe realized what he was thrusting her into and slammed on his brakes. "Julie, I'm going to take you home . . ."

"No!" she sobbed. "Just make them stop! Make them stop before my dad and my uncles kill each other."

Joe and Sheridan exchanged glances. Sheridan had turned white. She shook her head, not knowing what to say.

Joe blew out a breath and continued on.

ARLEN WENT DOWN FROM THE blow as the convoy fanned out in the sagebrush and surrounded the brothers. Joe hit his brakes and opened his door, keeping it between him and the Scarletts. As he dug his shotgun out and racked the pump, he heard McLanahan whoop a blast from his siren and say, in his new cowboy-slang cadence, "DROP THE SHOVELS, MEN, AND STEP BACK FROM EACH OTHER WITH YOUR HANDS ON

YOUR HEAD. EXCEPT YOU, ARLEN. YOU STAY DOWN."

The officers spilled out of their vehicles, brandishing weapons. The warning seemed to have no effect on Hank, who was standing over Arlen and raising his shovel above his head with two hands as if about to strike it down on his brother the way a gardener beheads a snake.

Joe thought Arlen was a dead man, but Wyatt suddenly drove his shoulder into Hank and sent him sprawling, the shovel flying end-over-end through the air.

"Go!" McLanahan shouted at his men. "Go round 'em up now!"

"Stay here," Joe said to Julie and Sheridan. His daughter cradled Julie in her arms. Julie sobbed, her head down.

Joe, holding his shotgun pointed above the fray, stepped around his truck and saw three deputies including Deputy Mike Reed rush the three prone Scarlett Brothers. Reed was the only deputy Joe considered sane and professional. The others were recent hires by McLanahan and were, to a man, large, mulish, quick with their fists, and just as quick to look away if an altercation involved someone who was a friend of the Sheriff's Department—or, more specifically, McLanahan himself.

Arlen simply rolled to his stomach and put his hands behind his back to be cuffed, saying, "Take it easy, boys, take it easy, I'm cooperating . . ."

Wyatt, after watching Arlen, did the same, although he looked confused.

It took all three deputies to subdue Hank, who continued to curse and kick and swing at them, one blow connecting solidly with Deputy Reed's mouth, which instantly bloomed with bright-red blood. Finally, after a pepper spray blast to his eyes, Hank curled up in the dirt and the deputies managed to cuff his hands behind him and bind his cowboy boots together with Flex-Cuffs.

AFTER TWO YEARS AS COUNTY sheriff, McLanahan still seemed to be somewhat unfinished, which is why he had apparently decided in recent months to assume a new role, that of "local character." After trying on and discarding several personas—squinty-eyed gunfighter, law-enforcement technocrat, glad-handing politician—McLanahan had decided to aspire to the mantle of "good old boy," a stereotype that had served his predecessor Bud Barnum well for twenty-four years. In the past six months, McLanahan had begun to slow his speech pattern and pepper his pronouncements and observations with arcane westernisms. He'd even managed to make his face go slack. His sheriff's crisp gray Stetson had been replaced by a floppy black cowboy hat and his khaki department jacket for a bulky Carhartt ranch coat. Rather than drive the newest sheriff's department vehicle, McLanahan opted for an old county pickup with rust spots on the panels. He bought a Blue Heeler puppy to occupy the passenger seat, and had begun to refer to his seven-acre parcel of land outside the city limits as his "ranch."

McLanahan squatted down in the middle of the triangle of handcuffed brothers and asked, "Can one of you tell me just what in the hell this is all about?"

Joe listened.

"Mama's gone," Hank said, his voice hard. "And that son-of-a-bitch there"—he nodded toward Arlen—"thinks he's going to get the ranch."

McLanahan said, "What do you mean she's gone? Like she's on a vacation or something?"

Hank didn't take his eyes off of Arlen. "Like that son-of-a-bitch killed her and hid the body," he said.

"*What?*" McLanahan said.

There was a high, unearthly wail, an airy squeal that seemed to come down from the mountains. The sound made the hairs on Joe's neck stand up. It was Wyatt. The big man was crying.

Joe looked over his shoulder at his pickup truck, to see if Julie had heard. Luckily, the windows were up and she was still being held by Sheridan.

"Mind if I stand up now?" Arlen asked the sheriff.

McLanahan thought it over, nodded his assent, and told Deputy Reed to help Arlen up but to keep him away from Hank.

Joe squatted down a few feet from Wyatt.

"Are you okay?" Joe asked. "Are you hurt?"

Wyatt just continued to sob, his head between his knees, his back heaving, tears spattering the ground between his boots. Joe asked again. Wyatt reached up with his cuffed hands and smeared his tears across his dirty face.

"Where's my mom?" Wyatt asked, his words mushy. Joe noticed Wyatt had missing teeth. "Where did she go?"

"I don't know," Joe said. "She can't be far."

"But Hank says she's gone."

Joe said, "I'm sure we'll find her."

Wyatt's eyes flared, and for a second Joe thought the man would strike out at him.

"*Where's my mom?*" Wyatt howled.

"Pickett!" McLanahan yelled, "What are you doing over there?"

Joe stood uneasily, searching Wyatt's upturned, tragic face for a clue to his behavior. "Making sure Wyatt's okay," Joe said.

"He's not," McLanahan said, and one of the deputies laughed. "Trust me on that one."

Joe looked at Arlen, and Hank. Both brothers were turned toward Wyatt, but neither said anything. They simply stared at their younger brother as if they were observing an embarrassing stranger.

Joe walked over to Deputy Reed, who was holding a bandanna to his split lip.

"What do you think the deal is with Opal?" Joe asked, out of earshot of the Scarlett brothers.

"Don't know," Reed said. "But I do know that old woman's just too goddamned mean to die."

WHILE SHERIFF MCLANAHAN INTERVIEWED EACH of the brothers quietly and individually, Joe concluded that he was no longer needed and, by inadvertently bringing Julie, he had done more harm than good.

"I've got Julie Scarlett, Arlen's daughter, in my truck," Joe told Reed. "I don't want her to see any more. I think I need to get her home to her mother." Joe gestured toward Arlen.

"You mean Hank?" Reed asked.

"No," Joe said. "I mean her dad, Arlen."

Reed squinted. "Arlen isn't her dad."

Joe wasn't sure what to say. He had dropped Julie off before at the big ranch house where she lived with Arlen, her mother, and Opal. As far as Joe knew, Hank lived alone in a hunting lodge on the other side of the ranch.

"What do you mean?" Joe asked.

Reed shrugged. "When it comes to the Scarletts, nothing is as it seems. Julie and her mother moved out of Hank's place years ago, but from what I understand, Hank is her dad."

Joe wondered if Sheridan knew this, if Julie had told her. Or if Reed was mistaken.

"Either way," Joe said, "I think I should get her home."

Reed nodded. "If you see Opal, give us a call."

"I will. Do you really think she's missing?"

Reed scoffed. "Do you really think those men would be out here beating each other with shovels if she was back home baking cookies? The whole damned county has been scared of the day when Opal passed on and those three would start fighting for the ranch. Now it looks like that day has come."

As Joe turned toward his truck, he heard McLanahan shout at him. "Where do you think you're going?"

"To the ranch," Joe said over his shoulder. "It looks like you've got things handled here."

"It's okay," Reed told his boss. "He's got Hank's little girl with him."

"I'll need your statement," McLanahan said. "It sounds like you were one of the last people to see Opal alive."

Joe turned, surprised. He had talked to Opal the day before about charging fishermen access fees. One of the brothers must have told McLanahan that.

"When do you need the statement?"

"Tonight."

Joe thought of Marybeth's last words to him that morning. She asked him to be home on time because she was cooking dinner and wanted to have the whole family there for a change. With her business thriving, that was a rarity. He had promised he would be home.

"Can it be tomorrow morning?" Joe asked.

The sheriff's face darkened. "No, it can't. We've got to jump all over this one, and what you've got to tell us may help."

Joe looked up. He saw that Julie's head was up, her eyes on her uncles and father. He wanted to get her away from there, and quickly.

"Tonight," McLanahan called after him.

"Tonight," Joe said, walking away.

He opened the door to his truck and said, "I'm so sorry you saw this, Julie."

She cried, "Please, just take me home."

C. J. Box is the author of twenty-four Joe Pickett novels, eight stand-alone novels, and a story collection. He has won the Edgar, Anthony, Macavity, Gumshoe, and two Barry awards, as well as the French Prix Calibre .38, the Western Heritage Award for Literature, and two Spur Awards. An avid outdoorsman, Box has hunted, fished, hiked, ridden, and skied throughout Wyoming and the Mountain West. He has been executive producer on shows based on his books, including ABC TV's *Big Sky* and *Joe Pickett* on Paramount+.

VISIT C. J. BOX ONLINE

CJBox.net

 AuthorCJBox

 CJBoxAuthor

C. J. BOX

"One of today's solid-gold, A-list, must-read writers."

—Lee Child

For a complete list of titles and to sign up for our newsletter, please visit prh.com/CJBox